PHOENIX SUB ZERO

PHOENIX SUB ZERO

by **MICHAEL DIMERCURIO**

DONALD I. FINE, INC.
NEW YORK

Library of Congress Catalogue Card Number: 93-74477
ISBN: 1-55611-392-7

Manufactured in the United States of America

10 9 8 7 6 5 4 3 2 1

Designed by Irving Perkins Associates, Inc.

To every man who has gone down into the darkness, heard the creak of a steel hull popping from the depths, felt hunger for sleep and real air and a hot shower and clean sheets, and faced death—if not from the torpedoes and depth charges of the enemy, then from the sea herself. To every man who is or has been or will be a submariner, this book is for you.

. . . Take heed in your manner of speaking
That the language ye use may be sound,
In the list of the words of your choosing
'Impossible' may not be found . . .

—ADM. R.A. HOPWOOD, RN
"THE LAWS OF THE NAVY"

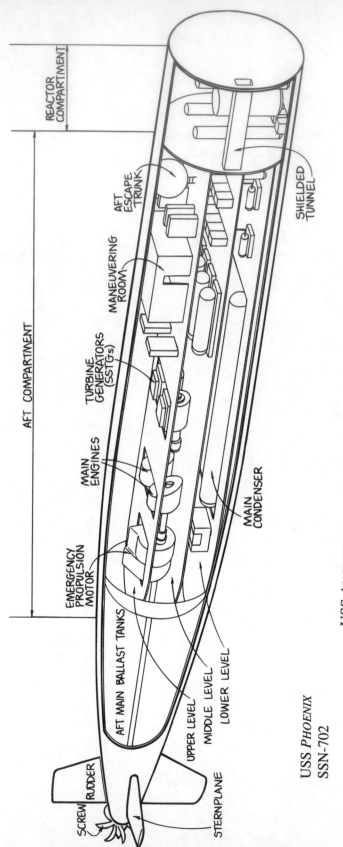

REACTOR COMPARTMENT

AFT COMPARTMENT

SHIELDED TUNNEL

AFT ESCAPE TRUNK

MANEUVERING ROOM

TURBINE GENERATORS (SSTGs)

MAIN ENGINES

MAIN CONDENSER

EMERGENCY PROPULSION MOTOR

AFT MAIN BALLAST TANKS

UPPER LEVEL

MIDDLE LEVEL

LOWER LEVEL

SCREW

RUDDER

STERNPLANE

USS *PHOENIX*
SSN-702

USS *AUGUSTA*
SSN-763

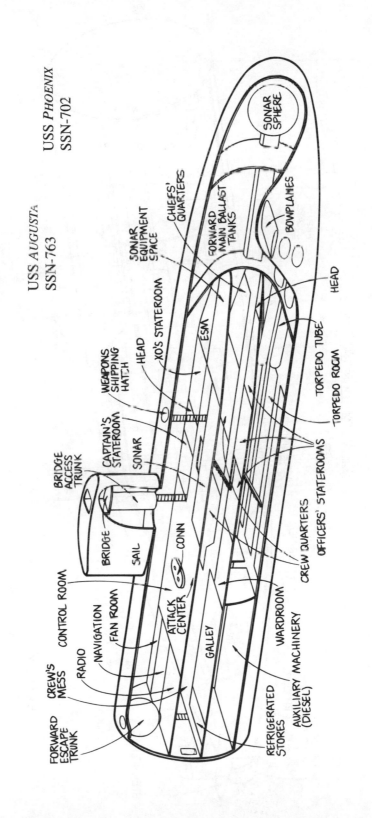

USS *AUGUSTA*
SSN-763

USS *PHOENIX*
SSN-702

FORWARD ESCAPE TRUNK
CREW'S MESS
CONTROL ROOM
RADIO
NAVIGATION
FAN ROOM
BRIDGE ACCESS TRUNK
CAPTAIN'S STATEROOM
WEAPONS SHIPPING HATCH
HEAD
BRIDGE
SAIL
CONN
ATTACK CENTER
SONAR
XO'S STATEROOM
ESM
SONAR EQUIPMENT SPACE
CHIEFS' QUARTERS
FORWARD MAIN BALLAST TANKS
SONAR SPHERE
BOWPLANES
HEAD
TORPEDO TUBE
TORPEDO ROOM
OFFICERS' STATEROOMS
CREW QUARTERS
WARDROOM
AUXILIARY MACHINERY (DIESEL)
REFRIGERATED STORES
GALLEY

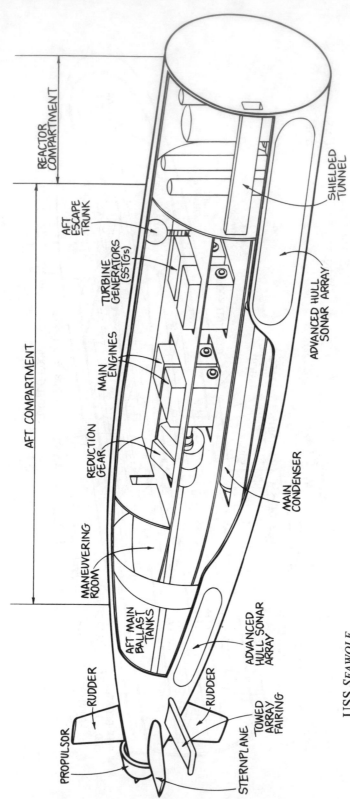

REACTOR COMPARTMENT

SHIELDED TUNNEL

AFT ESCAPE TRUNK

TURBINE GENERATORS (SSTGs)

MAIN ENGINES

ADVANCED HULL SONAR ARRAY

REDUCTION GEAR

AFT COMPARTMENT

MAIN CONDENSER

MANEUVERING ROOM

AFT MAIN BALLAST TANKS

ADVANCED HULL SONAR ARRAY

RUDDER

RUDDER

PROPULSOR

STERNPLANE

TOWED ARRAY FAIRING

USS *SEAWOLF*
SSN-21 (AFT SECTION)

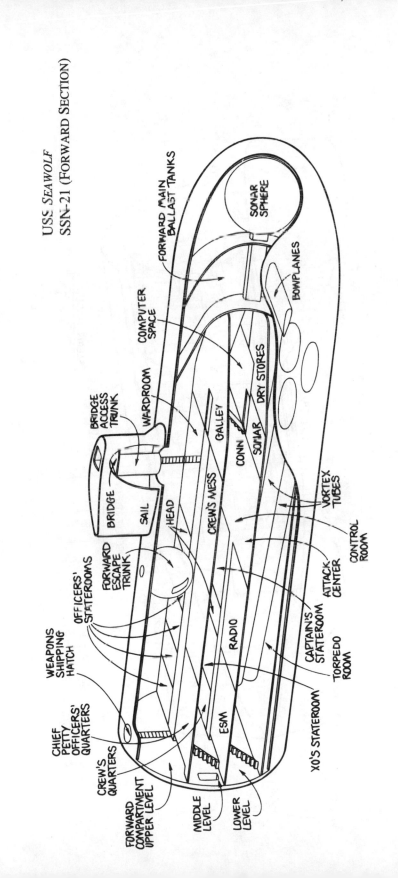

USS *SEAWOLF*
SSN-21 (FORWARD SECTION)

FORWARD MAIN BALLAST TANKS

SONAR SPHERE

BOWPLANES

COMPUTER SPACE

DRY STORES

SONAR

WARDROOM

GALLEY

CONN

VORTEX TUBES

BRIDGE ACCESS TRUNK

BRIDGE

SAIL

HEAD

CREW'S MESS

CONTROL ROOM

FORWARD ESCAPE TRUNK

ATTACK CENTER

OFFICERS' STATEROOMS

RADIO

CAPTAIN'S STATEROOM

TORPEDO ROOM

WEAPONS SHIPPING HATCH

ESM

XO'S STATEROOM

CHIEF PETTY OFFICERS' QUARTERS

CREW'S QUARTERS

FORWARD COMPARTMENT UPPER LEVEL

MIDDLE LEVEL

LOWER LEVEL

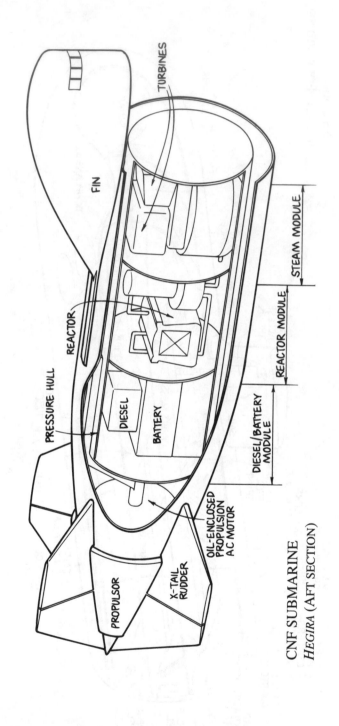

CNF SUBMARINE
HEGIRA (AFT SECTION)

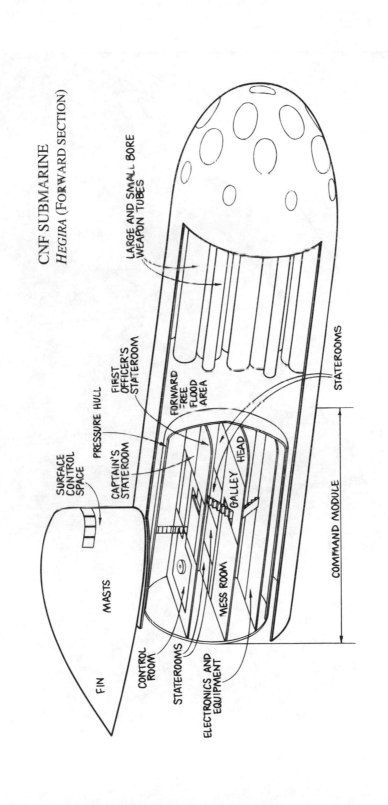

CNF SUBMARINE
HEGIRA (FORWARD SECTION)

LARGE AND SMALL BORE
WEAPON TUBES

SURFACE
CONTROL
SPACE

PRESSURE HULL

FIRST
OFFICER'S
STATEROOM

CAPTAIN'S
STATEROOM

FORWARD
FREE
FLOOD
AREA

STATEROOMS

MASTS

GALLEY

HEAD

MESS ROOM

COMMAND MODULE

FIN

CONTROL
ROOM

STATEROOMS

ELECTRONICS AND
EQUIPMENT

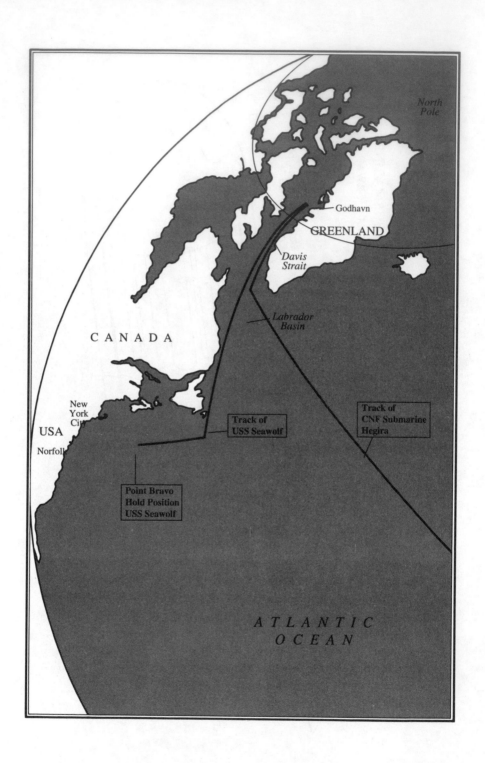

EUROPE

CYPRUS

Kassab

Track of
CNF Submarine
Hegira

West
European
Basin

ITALY

*Strait
of
Sicily*

SICILY

SPAIN

Mediterranean

USS Augusta
Barrier
Search

*Strait
of
Gibraltar*

USS Phoenix
Barrier
Search

AFRICA

(United
Islamic
Front)

PROLOGUE

WEDNESDAY, CHRISTMAS DAY

The Hiroshima missile dived for the desert floor and armed the final detonator train of the Scorpion warhead. After a descent through the low clouds, the missile broke out into the clear over the abandoned town of Bajram-Ali, Turkmenistan. A few hundred meters east of the town center and mosque, the missile's high explosive detonated.

The explosion, in its first millisecond, ruptured a bag of vinyl acetate monomer mixed with a dozen other chemical components; in the next it ruptured a high-pressure bottle of ethylene gas, the chemicals mixing and reacting in the high temperatures and pressures of the fireball; finally the pressure pulse reached a bag of finely ground iron filings. The explosion scattered the filings as it spread, 1,000 meters above Bajram-Ali. The iron filings drifted to the town below. As they did, the reacting chemicals from the missile formed a thin milky atomized liquid that rained down and wetted the buildings and streets. Ten minutes later, the milky chemicals had dried into a sticky glue. The iron filings, mixed in with the glue, were stuck to the surfaces of the streets and roofs and walls of the decaying structures. Within 1,000 meters of the Hiroshima missile detonation, iron filings were glued to every horizontal and vertical surface.

An hour later a small army of technicians took the town apart, digging samples from the road, cutting bricks out of building walls, running metal detectors along pavement, deploying fire hoses to try to wash off the glue and its iron filings. The glue resisted all attempts to rinse it away.

Late that evening, an urgent encrypted radio message was transmitted to the United Islamic Front of God headquarters stating that the weapon test had been a great success, promising that when the iron filings of the Scorpion test warhead were replaced by highly radioactive and poisonous plutonium, doped with cobalt–60, the target town would be so contaminated that it would have to be abandoned for 20,000 years, and that every soul within two kilometers of ground zero would die a slow, painful and ugly death of radiation poisoning, all accomplished with only a fraction of the plutonium needed to build the smallest nuclear weapon.

The message concluded that when the Scorpion warhead was employed against the target American city—Washington, D.C., at the moment—the course of the world war would be turned, and victory would soon be forthcoming.

On the other side of the world, on the fourth deck of the Pentagon's E-ring, the chief of naval operations, Adm. Richard Donchez, picked up the six-month-old memo he'd written to the president and read it with mixed emotions, part amusement that he had been dead right, part regret that its recommendations had been ignored. Its four dry pages of thick Pentagonese had advocated assassinating Gen. Mohammed al-Sihoud, dictator and leader of a thirty-nation coalition called the United Islamic Front of God, spanning all of North Africa, most of the Arabian peninsula, and half of Asia. At the time, Sihoud had just begun the invasion of India after already swallowing Chad and Ethiopia in a month-long blitz.

Had the memo's decapitation assault been implemented when it was proposed, the war would never have gotten out of hand. But it had, and finally, after India had appealed to the United Nations, America and the major nations of Europe had formed the Western Coalition and declared war on Sihoud's United Islamic Front. After endless preparations for the invasions, the war had turned into a bloody three-front meatgrinder of a ground war, as Donchez had predicted. And now, a half-year late, President Dawson had ordered Donchez to propose the Navy's "most innovative recommendations" to win the war quickly. Donchez had considered giving him the old assassination memo back, the central ideas still viable, but had not out of tact. Finally, Monday, the president had given his approval to take out General Sihoud. Donchez had proposed that Operation *Early Retirement* commence immediately, Christmas Day, but the president had balked at killing the general on a holy day. Donchez relented, ordering the operation to commence on the day after Christmas, two minutes after midnight local time, making it late afternoon of Christmas Day eastern standard time.

Donchez propped his feet up on the huge desk, put his hands behind his bald head and looked out the windows at the snowy landscape of the Potomac River below, the familiar Washington skyline, the vista lonely on Christmas, the town's workers and lawyers and politicians home with their families. In another half hour, the operation would commence, starting with the liftoff of a cargo jet full of Navy Sea/Air/Land commandos and the firing of sea-launched Javelin cruise missiles at Sihoud in his headquarters bunker. By early afternoon Thursday, Donchez expected to hold a press conference reporting the death of General-and-Khalib Mohammed al-Sihoud, and with him, the end of a war that had the potential to kill millions of Americans.

Donchez stared out the window for some moments, deciding to wade through his urgent paperwork during the time he must wait before the decapitation assault against Sihoud kicked off. He took his feet off the desk and rifled through a file marked VORTEX MISSILE TEST—EXERCISE BONECRUSHER—AUTEC SUBMARINE VS. SUBMARINE LIVE FIRE. After he read it, he put it back on the desk, ran his hand across his bald scalp, his face an annoyed frown, and picked up the phone.

Michael Pacino sat back in the deep recliner in front of the fireplace, the Virginia Beach weather finally cool enough to justify lighting the fire. For the last hour he had dozed, waiting for Christmas dinner, falling into a deep sleep. His face twitched and beaded with sweat as he dreamt, his sleeping visions obviously troubled.

When the phone jangled he sat up, his eyes wide, the room slowly coming into focus, Janice's low Southern accent distant as she answered the call. By the time she asked him to pick up the phone, his heart rate had slowed to its normal rhythm. He climbed out of the easy chair and walked to the phone, wondering what his duty officer wanted on a slow holiday afternoon. His submarine, the USS *Seawolf*, sat inert and helpless in a shipyard drydock, a gaping hull-cut opened in her flank, her torpedo room brutalized by the shipyard workers and the overgrown Vortex missile tubes being jammed in. It seemed a crime that in the middle of a hot war on the other side of the world, the most advanced submarine in the U.S. Navy rested on the drydock blocks, useless.

"Captain Pacino," he said curtly into the phone, expecting a young lieutenant to report another problem. But it wasn't the ship calling.

"Mikey," Admiral Donchez's voice boomed in Pacino's ear. "Merry Christmas."

Hillary Janice Pacino, a slim attractive woman with golden hair curling halfway down her back, lit a cigarette and listened to the phone conversation in the background, her expression growing steadily unhappy as it became obvious that Pacino would be leaving. Thirty seconds after the conversation ended, right on cue, he appeared in the kitchen.

"Where to this time?" she asked, her voice surprisingly calm.

"Autec. Bahamas test range. Donchez's Vortex missile test. He wants me to watch. His jet is picking me up in two hours."

"On Christmas Day?"

"The missile test goes down tomorrow."

"What's the big rush? It's not like you're going to war. If there was one Christmas I thought you'd make, it was this year. Your ship is in the dock and you're being relieved in two months. Why are you going now? Because the chief of naval operations asks and you jump?"

"No. Because Dick Donchez asks and I jump. We still have time for dinner."

"How long?"

"Two days, maybe three."

Pacino watched as his wife clammed up and began moving around the room, banging pots and plates. He climbed the stairs and packed a bag, wondering himself why a weapon test was so important that he had to drop everything on Christmas Day to see it.

Ten minutes later he stood in front of the television, the news channel reporting on the Coalition invasion of southern Iran. Pacino bit his lip in frustration, wondering for the hundredth time why *Seawolf* had to sit out the war. If he had to be away on Christmas, he thought, it could at least be to take the ship on a mission. He thought about his old captain, Rocket Ron Daminski, who was now on patrol in the Mediterranean aboard the *Augusta,* there since Thanksgiving, probably spending the holiday watching old movies in the wardroom and complaining bitterly about being at sea, driving his crew crazy.

Too bad, Pacino thought, there was nothing for a sub to do during the ground war except poke holes in the ocean. Or so it seemed.

Book I

ROCKET RON

1

THURSDAY, 26 DECEMBER

Eastern Mediterranean
Ten Nautical Miles East of Cape Greco, Cyprus
Operation *Early Retirement*
USS *Augusta*

The Javelin cruise missile blew out of the dark water of the Mediterranean, momentarily frozen in space above an angry cloud of spray until the weapon's rocket motor ignited in a violent fireball, hurling the missile skyward with an agonizingly bright flame trail.

The crosshairs of the periscope view framed the fiery parabola of the submarine-launched missile's trajectory as it flew to its peak, 1,500 feet into the clear starlit sky, then arced downward on its way to its ground-hugging approach to its target. Commander Ron Daminski trained the periscope view downward until the missile rocket motor cut out, and the flying automaton vanished into the night. Daminski removed his eye from the periscope optic module for a moment, just long enough to look at the battle-stations crew surrounding him in the cramped rigged-for-black control room of the Improved Los Angeles-class attack submarine USS *Augusta*. Satisfied, he returned to his periscope and trained it in a slow circle, a surface search, while the crew prepared to launch the second Javelin warshot missile from the forward vertical launch system.

"Missile two on internal power, Captain. Target is locked in and readbacks are nominal," the executive officer, Danny Kristman, reported, as emotionlessly as if he were commenting on the weather. "Ready for launch in three zero seconds."

"Open the muzzle door," Daminski ordered, training his periscope view forward to see the second launch.

"Door open, WRT tank pressurized . . . Five seconds, sir. Three, two, one, mark."

"Shoot," Daminski commanded.

"*Fire!*" Kristman barked, the roar of the missile tube the punctuation to the order.

Daminski watched as the second Javelin cleared the water and lifted off toward the east. When it too had disappeared, he lowered the periscope and turned to executive officer Kristman.

"XO, you have the conn. Secure battle stations, take her deep and continue orbiting at the hold point."

"Aye, sir."

The deck took on a down angle as Kristman made the orders, the hull groaning and popping loudly from the sea pressure as the *Augusta* descended into the depths. From the periscope stand Lieutenant Commander Dan Kristman glanced across at Daminski as the captain yawned, stretched, and tried to fight the sleep he'd evaded for the last three nights.

"Rocket Ron" Daminski, so named for his intensity and white-hot temper, had just turned fifty, unusually old for the job of commanding the submarine *Augusta*. He was stocky and short, his hair beginning to recede from his lined forehead, yet he still carried himself like the athlete he had once been, in spite of bad knees and several dozen old football injuries. He spoke with a thick Brooklyn accent and frequently referred to himself as an "ignorant New York Polack," but he dismissed the fact that he had been a brilliant engineer at Rensselaer Polytechnic Institute. Still, he was a troubled officer, always passed over for promotion, and had no illusions that his career would have any further surprises.

Daminski had been aboard *Augusta* four months, ever since the previous captain had run aground and been relieved for cause. The investigation had shown that the ship had become sloppy and poorly trained, and the admiral in command of the Atlantic's submarine forces had sent out the ultimate sub-fixer, some would say ass-kicker, Rocket Ron Daminski, a ten-year veteran of straightening out ill-performing submarines.

At first, the crew had dreaded Daminski's arrival, with good reason. Once aboard, the man was a hurricane, sweeping through every department, finding fault with every division, every officer, every chief, and most enlisted men. Each flaw, regardless of significance, was treated by Rocket as a treasonous personal affront. Every excruciating day had brought several dozen of his demeaning emotional outbursts, but over weeks, the boat had responded. Even the men who professed to hate Rocket Ron began to give him the credit as the ship began to function smoothly, going from the squadron dog to the squadron's best, until they were certain to win any exercise. Daminski's tantrums became less frequent, his inspiring speeches more frequent, until over the last month he had become almost jovial in his praise for the men and officers. The ship was ordered to the Mediterranean to support the war against the United Islamic Front, a cause for celebration, the notice that *Augusta* had arrived.

Through the entire ordeal of putting *Augusta* back on track, Rocket Ron Daminski had never revealed much of his personal life to the crew. It was known that he was married to his second wife, a pretty and voluptuous younger woman named Myra; the two of them had three small children. Daminski had filled his stateroom with pictures of his family, nearly wallpapering an entire bulkhead with their photos. Kristman had noticed that not one photograph included Daminski himself. He had on a recent occasion noticed Daminski mooning over a letter from his wife, so deeply in thought that it had taken Kristman three tries to get the captain's attention. Daminski carried the letter with him everywhere—not in his shirt or pants pockets, but against the skin of his chest. In one recent emergency drill, Daminski had rushed to the control room in his boxers and T-shirt—which in an emergency was considered normal—and the letter from Myra had been stuck in the waistband of the boxers beneath Daminski's T-shirt. Kristman could now see the slight rectangular bulge in Daminski's submarine coveralls where the letter was stowed as Daminski yawned again and ran his huge misshapen football-injured fingers though his hair.

As the ship pulled out of the dive, the deck again became flat. Daminski stepped off the raised periscope stand aft to the twin chart tables, a cigarette appearing between his lips as he bent over the chart. Across the landmass to the east, the thin orange pencil lines traced the serpentine tracks of the Javelin missiles. The lines terminated at a city just north of the Iranian border, the capital city of the United Islamic Front of God, Ashkhabad, in a country called Turkmenistan. A country that five years before was barely on the map, a two-bit ex-Soviet republic, but was now the center of a thirty-nation confederation of Muslim states. The uniting of the Islamic states had taken almost five years, yet in that time the Western intelligence agencies seemed caught by surprise that it had happened, believing until it was too late that the Muslims still hated each other even more than the West. In this, the spooks had been as wrong as they had in the months before the fall of the Shah's Iran.

And as history proved once more, there was no limit to what a single determined man could do. The twentieth century had seen one dictator after another take the reins of power and threaten the world, but most paled next to Mohammed al-Sihoud, the dictator of the United Islamic Front of God. Sihoud had made Turkmenistan his hub territory, the UIF's capital the city of Ashkhabad, where the Combined Intelligence Agency, now paying very close attention, indicated he had been for the last two days.

There in a concrete reinforced bunker on the northern city limits of Ashkhabad, General-and-Khalib Mohammed al-Sihoud was about to get a very nasty surprise. The operation's name, "Early Retirement," was appropriate. Never before in the century had a world war against a dictatorship been conducted by a concerted attempt to assassinate the dictator. This war was to be different.

Executive officer Kristman joined Daminski at the chart. Both men studied the tracks of the Javelin cruise missiles for several quiet moments. Kristman spoke first.

"Think this is going to work, Skipper?"

"I don't know, Danny. Probably depends on the SEAL team commandos. We're just insurance."

"At least we got to shoot *something* at that bastard."

Daminski nodded, knowing what Kristman meant. In the last ten months of the war, the work had been done by ground troops of the Army and the Marines while the glory had gone to the Navy and Air Force fighter pilots. Meanwhile the surface and submarine navies had paced the seas restlessly, effectively useless against the massive and deadly combined land forces of the United Islamic Front.

"I'm going to grab some rack," Daminski said. "Get the section's officer of the deck on the conn and station yourself as command duty officer. Call me if anything comes in on the ELF circuit."

"Yessir."

Daminski walked forward to the tiny cubbyhole of his stateroom, shut the door, and sank into the narrow bed. He had been awake going on forty hours, since the flash message announcing the kickoff of the operation had come in on the sub broadcast. Daminski was exhausted, but he knew he was much too wired from shooting the cruise missile warshots to fall asleep.

He pulled the letter from Myra from inside his shirt and read it again, the dogeared stationery proclaiming in her loopy handwriting that she loved him but was leaving him anyway. *You are just too intense to live with . . . I can't watch you run this house like you run one of your submarines. The children cry when you come home and laugh when you leave, and I*

can't bear to see that anymore. Please get yourself some help, and when you are at peace, come back to us. But until then, don't come home . . .
Daminski put the letter back in his shirt and stared at the dimly lit overhead for a moment, but finally closed his eyes and tried to imagine the Javelins, what they were doing that very instant, gliding through the night at 650 miles per hour, a mere twenty feet above the ground, following the contour of the land, screaming in over the terrain of Turkmenistan en route to General Sihoud's hidden bunker.

Turkmenian Plain
Seventy-Five Miles West-Northwest of Ashkhabad

Commander Jack Morris missed his beard. It had been a ZZ-Top hairy thing, extending down his chest almost to his belly button. He missed his long hair as well, feeling odd every time he turned his head and didn't feel the old ponytail dragging across his back. His shooters, the men of SEAL Team Seven, until just months before, had been a ragged-looking band of bikers, the Navy's finest counterterrorist unit. The start of the land war against the UIF had changed all that, forcing the Sea/Air/Land commandos, the SEALS, back into regulation Navy uniforms and grooming standards. Jack Morris didn't like that—it interfered with unit integrity. The SEALS needed to feel different; there was something healthy about coming onto base looking like a truck driver and getting away with it—it was a concrete sign that SEAL Team Seven was different than the rest of the Navy, and therefore better. One last time Morris ran his hands through his weirdly short hair and looked around the cargo compartment of the Air Force KC–10H/A transport jet, the plane illuminated only by a few dim hooded red lights.

Unloaded, the KC–10's interior was cavernous, but tonight it held two dozen tons of combat equipment and three augmented platoons of Team Seven, each platoon manned by thirty-three of the meanest sons of bitches in all of the U.S. armed forces. Or any armed force. Morris looked around him at the men—almost without exception, they were all sleeping. In a way, that would be expected, since they'd been flying for what seemed like days, and it was well after midnight local time. But it was also odd, for these men were only hours from the biggest and hottest combat operation the team had seen since the bloody liberation of the USS *Tampa* two years before. Many of the men were not expected to return from the mission, and some who would return would leave parts of their bodies behind. Still, Morris thought, they would be in better shape than the UIF people in General Sihoud's bunker complex.

One of the aircrew from the flight deck came back into the cargo cabin and waved ten fingers at Morris—ten minutes till they were over the drop zone. Morris heard the jet engines suddenly throttle up, their noise rattling his skull. The plane cabin tilted upward dramatically as the aircraft climbed. Morris unlatched his seat harness and stood, his muscles sore from the long jet ride. He stepped forward, leaning into the incline of the deck, tapping awake his sleeping executive officer, Lieutenant Commander "Black Bart" Bartholomay. As Bart's eyes opened, Morris shouted "ten minutes" in his face. Bart stood and got the men into action while Morris headed forward. He entered a short narrow corridor at the forward end of the cargo bay, the doors on either wall leading to crew quarters, galley, and the head. At the end of the passageway Morris pushed open the door to the flight deck and squeezed in. The flight crew barely noticed him, the navigator/flight engineer knowing his purpose.

"You sure we're in the right place?" Morris asked. He'd been disappointed before by the Air Force, once having been dropped fifty miles south of the planned jump point, landing his platoon several miles offshore instead of on the beach.

"We got here somewhat roundabout, Commander—we had a few radar detects. This good enough for you?" The flightsuited crewman pointed out the navigation satellite readout and offered a chart up to Morris's face. After a moment Morris grunted.

"We're doing the pop-up now, Commander. About time to get ready with your guys."

"Any sign of activity?" Morris asked, ignoring the officer's warning. The Air Force "zoomies" knew what he meant, Morris thought—*is anyone getting ready to shoot us out of the sky?*

"Nothing now. We're clear."

Morris turned and left without a word and hurried aft.

Within two minutes all three platoons of Team Seven were on their feet preparing their gear. The deck of the cargo jet remained inclined as it continued its rapid climb to 45,000 feet. While at altitude they would be vulnerable, Morris thought, checking his watch, wishing he were already in free fall instead of another piece of cargo in a damned Air Force jet.

Morris pulled on his full face oxygen mask and checked the seal. When the men were ready, he nodded to the airman who opened a panel and depressurized the cabin. Almost immediately the compartment became frigid. Morris shivered and lied to himself that it was from the cold and not from fear. Morris checked his connection to his cargo crate—he and every SEAL would be tethered to a heavy equipment case during free fall and parachute descent. After an endless five minutes the loading ramp was unlatched and rolled slowly open. Only a few stars in the blackness showed through the gaping hole. Morris connected his

InterSat scrambled VHF secure voice tactical radio to the boom microphone in his oxygen mask and spoke to his troops.

"Listen up, assholes," he said into his mike, "we've got damned little time in the drop zone. I want the DPV's assembled in four minutes tops and we're on the way. Don't forget we're doing this for one thing and only one thing—to bring back the head of one Mohammed al-Sihoud on a stick. Everybody got that? Let's get off this bus and go."

Morris stepped to the edge of the ramp first and let his toes hang out over seven miles above the desert floor. Black Bart's voice crackled in his earpiece.

"Fifteen seconds."

Morris spent the time going over the mission in his mind, trying to visualize the main bunker compound in ruins, the security forces running in helpless circles, Sihoud in confusion, maybe trying to escape in a truck, the barrel of a SEAL MAC–10 automatic pistol in his nose.

"Five seconds . . . two, one, go."

Morris jumped into the blackness.

Ashkhabad, Turkmenistan
Main Bunker Complex
Headquarters of the Combined Armed Forces of the United Islamic Front

From the outside the Main Bunker appeared to be a large mosque, no different than hundreds spread across the Islamic nations of the Arabian peninsula, Asia, and North Africa. Four high walls shaped the structure, a tall minaret tower rising out of the eastern wall, presiding over a square central courtyard. The western wall, toward the direction of Mecca, contained the sanctuary. Five times during the broiling hot spring day, the faithful of the Main Bunker would emerge into the courtyard in response to the calls to worship from the minaret, perform the ritual prayers, bowing down deeply in the direction of Mecca. Ritual cries of *Allahu Akbar* rang out over the courtyard, the combined voices directed heavenward proclaiming the greatness of Allah.

Ten meters beneath the courtyard, below three meters of high-strength prestressed reinforced concrete and twenty centimeters of lead shielding, the upper level of the bunker began. The first sublevel contained the quarters for the lower ranking soldiers of the United Islamic Front of God's Combined Armed Force. The next two levels were the junior and senior officers' quarters. The third level housed the plush quarters of General-and-Khalib Mohammed al-Sihoud, although General Sihoud spent little time there, instead commanding his armies from field command posts. The final level, thirty-five meters beneath the rocky terrain of southern Turkmenistan, was the headquarters area with its maps, computers, and communications consoles linked to the antennae arrays hidden in the minaret forty meters above.

In the hushed and dimly lit headquarters deck, the Combined Air Force supreme commander and chief of staff to General Sihoud, Col. Rakish Ahmed, walked to the communications console set against the east wall of the bunker's fourth sublevel's tactical control room. Several junior men manning the console jerked to attention in their seats as Ahmed drew close and leaned over to see the displays. Ahmed scanned the computer screens in search of good news, and finding none, turned toward the Khalib—the Sword of Islam—Mohammed al-Sihoud, who stood in the center of the room with a displeased look on his face, his swirling white silk *shesh* robe flowing to the computer floor tiles of the command center, a colorful belt holding a remarkable long knife in an ornate scabbard on his hip. Ahmed saw Sihoud's knowing glance, and wondered whether Sihoud had already guessed what was to be said. Ahmed had worked as Sihoud's chief of staff for over a year, and the two men had learned each other's minds well.

General Sihoud was a striking leader, incredibly tall for one of Bedouin ancestry, with the expected dark skin stretched across startlingly unexpected Western features, his brilliant violet-colored eyes shining commandingly from his aristocratic face. Ahmed considered the bluish purple eyes for a moment, knowing that Sihoud was almost ashamed of them—they gave away the fact that his Bedouin roots were mixed with the blood of a White Russian. Sihoud's paternal grandfather, though Russian, had been born in what was then the Turkmen Soviet Socialist Republic, rising to the rank of general in the Red Army. General Tallinn had married a young Muslim girl named Raja Sihoud, had taken a post in Moscow, then returned ten years later with a young son. The general had been killed on the march to Hitler's Berlin, leaving the son to grow up an anti-Soviet Islamic revolutionary. Named Yuri Tallinn, he changed his name to Ali Abba Sihoud, and had only lived to see his thirty-seventh year before being executed for crimes against the Soviet state. Mohammed al-Sihoud had been only seven years old when he watched the kangaroo court sentence his father to death. Now, thirty years after the Soviet bullet had passed through his father's brain, Mohammed al-Sihoud found his eyes a liability, a reminder of what had been Russian, but to Ahmed the deep purple eyes made the leader that much more marked by the hand of destiny.

Not that destiny was helping them now: it was beginning to look as if the tide of the war was turning, the offensive brown streaks staining the computer-generated maps on the oversize consoles on the west wall of the headquarters level, the brown symbolizing the armored forces of the Western Coalition, the West's three recent invasions into UIF soil. Their

white-faced soldiers might soon march deeper into the heart of the
United Islamic Front. There was only one way out of this, one way to
stop the bleeding of the Islamic armies in the deserts, and that was to
implement Ahmed's plan, to use his plutonium polymer dispersion
weapon, the Scorpion, and bring this war home to the leaders of the
Coalition, the Americans. Ahmed wondered if Sihoud would welcome
the missile or object to it. Although it would seem odd that the Khalib
would spurn such a superweapon, General Sihoud continued to cling to
a belief that the Islamic soldiers engaged in their holy *jihad* could still
defeat the overfed soldiers of the Coalition without the marvels of high
technology. But in this belief, Sihoud was mistaken. Perhaps it was he,
Rakish Ahmed, who had let down the United Islamic Front in his failure
to make Sihoud understand. Perhaps now was the time to bring Sihoud
to the realization that a head-to-head battle with the Coalition could not
be won.

And there was the other matter on Ahmed's mind, the reports coming
in of a Coalition plot to kill Sihoud. Sihoud's stubborn refusal to command from the bunker made him play into any Western plot to assassinate him—Sihoud's own bravado might be the factor that got him killed.

"General-and-Khalib, I'm worried about the Coalition invasions,"
Ahmed said. "I've had a computer simulation run to project the near
term outcome. I've been optimistic in my assumptions of our troop
losses, fuel usage, and supply distribution. I've also projected that the
Coalition's supplies are held up and that their troops are poorly deployed. And the computer still shows the Coalition marching into Ashkhabad within the year."

Sihoud reached into his scabbard for his knife. He pulled the instrument out, a long shining blade below a beautiful pearl handle with at
least a dozen precious gems shining even in the dim light of the command center. Sihoud, as he always did when deep in thought, ran his
finger slowly along the edge, and there were times when Ahmed was
amazed that Sihoud never cut himself.

"A computer simulation," Sihoud said. "As if an adding machine
could capture the fighting spirit of our men. Rakish, you are too much
the flying-machine technician, too little the field-soldier warrior."

Ahmed gestured toward the oversized monitor repeater above the
computer console, the map on it showing North Africa, the Middle East,
and western Asia, the territories of the United Islamic Front of God,
now under attack from the invading forces of the American and European armies. The Coalition had invaded the western shores of Morocco
in North Africa. A central invasion force had obtained a foothold on the
Sinai Peninsula and within weeks would target Cairo. A third force had
come ashore in the southeast on the southern coast of Iran, the preinva-
sion bombing so violent that much of southern Iran's civilian population

was wiped out, including Rakish Ahmed's own town of Chah Bahar. Rakish Ahmed knew of this war crime personally—he had been in the town to see to defenses along the coast, and at the Khalib's invitation had stopped at his home to see his wife and young son. An hour after his arrival, the Coalition bombers had arrived, bombing the town into dust, killing Ahmed's family, nearly killing him too. The episode had shaken him severely, his sleep filled with nightmares, his days spent fighting off memories.

The Coalition forces would come, Ahmed thought. Their objective was to drive toward Ashkhabad. Toward Sihoud.

"Khalib, we do not have the force for a three-front counterattack. We have material problems. The Japanese tanks and trucks and self-propelled artillery are excellent weapons—if they have fuel. The Firestar fighter jets have engine problems, they throw turbine blades—and what good are the most sophisticated electronics in the air if the airplanes are unable to fly? We have severe supply problems—supplies of every nature are short. We will barely be able to keep the men in the field fed. Our battle deaths cannot be replaced by young recruits. The Coalition is starting to bomb the refineries. The sky is growing black with oil fires. In six months our tanks and planes will begin to run out of fuel."

Sihoud ran his finger slowly along the knife's edge.

"So you believe our *jihad*—now just begun—is hopeless," he finally said in his melodious voice. For a moment Ahmed considered not the words but the voice itself, the voice that had mesmerized the leaders and peoples of the nations of the Islamic world, had in spite of their animosities forged them together into a solid formidable confederation. A confederation that had nearly united central Asia, North Africa, and all of Arabia; the consolidation had continued with the invasion and occupation of Chad and Ethiopia, both campaigns taking less than four weeks. But Sihoud's expansion had stumbled badly in the invasion of India. Chad and Ethiopia had taken the world by surprise, the media confused by propaganda from both nations that the sizable Muslim populations of the two countries had invited Sihoud in. The same illusion could not be maintained for the crossing into India. The Indians had fought bravely and appealed loudly to the West, and the West had finally decided to take a stand. The Indian adventure, rather than expanding the UIF, had instead united the Western Coalition and brought American, British, and German weapons to bear against Sihoud, and there was no way that Sihoud, even with his unique charisma, could stand up against that. It took Ahmed a moment to realize that General-and-Khalib Mohammed al-Sihoud was looking at him intently, waiting impatiently for an answer.

"I am sorry, I was thinking. What was your question?"

"Rakish, you tell me of the problems of the world and you expect me perhaps to wave this knife and make them all go away." Sihoud fixed his violet eyes on Ahmed's for a moment, the dark swirling irises drilling into Ahmed's, as if looking for a character flaw. "You are a pilot, a scientist who deals with numbers and pieces of metal. I am a foot soldier and I deal with the hearts and souls of men, fighting men. We are here to defend our claim to the continent, not to fret about oil reserves and turbine blades."

"General, it is never easy to acknowledge that a battle or a war might be lost." Rakish chose his words carefully, knowing that to anger Sihoud could mean demotion, perhaps even removal from a war he wanted to fight and needed to fight. "But I have a plan involving the use of a new weapon developed in our Mashhad weapon test lab, a weapon I designed but did not tell you about out of fear that it might fail." Sihoud's eyes, always so calm, came up to Ahmed's, his expression naked, malevolent. Ahmed continued. "Imagine for a moment the power of a weapon that would humble a nuclear bomb. A weapon that would not even need to be *used* to stop the Coalition. A bomb so terrifying that if we just threaten to use it, would cause Washington to withdraw Coalition forces from UIF soil. But I suggest we do not just threaten to use it. I recommend we deploy it as soon as—"

"You told me we did not have the plutonium for a nuclear weapon, in spite of my orders, Colonel Ahmed. Now suddenly there is a super weapon?"

"We started with the airframe of the Mitsubishi Hiroshima missile, the high-altitude supersonic cruise missile we worked so hard to buy from our Japanese advisors."

Sihoud glared at Ahmed, but seemed to be paying close attention.

"We filled the warhead space with what we call the Scorpion warhead. Its core is a lightweight high explosive. The HX is surrounded by three layers—a vinyl acetate monomer liquid bladder, a high-pressure bottle of ethylene gas, and a bag of finely ground plutonium particles." Ahmed checked Sihoud, knowing the general hated overly technical briefings, but there was no other way to explain the system without the details. "The cruise missile flies at supersonic speed toward its target at an altitude of eighteen kilometers, slowing and diving at the last moments to about a thousand meters above ground zero. The high explosive detonates, blowing the monomer and plutonium dust into the ethylene bottle which then ruptures, and the heat and pressure of the explosion create a sort of reactor system. The monomer and ethylene react to form a liquid polymer emulsion—glue, if you will, sir—which suspends the plutonium in a matrix that floats down to the ground below. The glue cements the plutonium onto every surface it contacts—no wind or rain or decontamination procedure can dislodge the plutonium, and the radioactivity of the plutonium is enough to kill the entire target population within about two kilometers of ground zero, and the deaths are not merciful ones.

Radiation poisoning causes a slow and painful death, exactly what the enemy deserve. The target is so contaminated that it must be abandoned forever."

Sihoud looked at Ahmed and replaced the knife in its scabbard, his face filled with something that had not been there moments before, a look that Ahmed imagined to be some evidence of a newly found hope.

"How many can we make?"

"Three, perhaps four."

"This weapon, the Scorpion. You put it in the Hiroshima cruise missile . . . but the Hiroshima only has a range of 3,500 kilometers. That's not far."

"We can target Europe from UIF territories but—"

"But that isn't good enough. We need to target their seat of power."

"Washington . . . I have a plan to deliver the warhead there, but it will take some time," Ahmed gestured at the electronic map showing the advancing armies of the Coalition, "and we must hurry."

"What is the plan?"

Ahmed glanced at the electronic chart, wondering if this was the time to tell General Sihoud the rest of the bad news, perhaps the worst news of all. He saw Sihoud's penetrating eyes and decided that Sihoud needed the facts, whether or not he elected to believe them.

"Before I go into the Scorpion deployment plan, I need to tell you about something else, something of an immediate nature—"

"Another assassination plot, Colonel?"

"In a way, sir. I have been seeing intelligence that Coalition forces may plan a decapitation operation. They may try to take you out and we need to respond to that quickly."

"There will be no *decapitation*, Rakish. These are the same people who fought Hitler, Ho Chi Minh, Hussein. Not one of them were ever assassinated, Colonel."

"Exactly, sir. That's why we worry that you will be the first."

"Your paranoia begins to reflect on you, Rakish. A warrior does not worry about assassination plots. But go ahead. What's the proof?"

"A large airliner took off from Volgograd several hours ago on the way to Alma-Ata and disappeared over the Aral Sea. It never landed, yet it is not on our radars. It makes me very suspicious. This plane could be bringing paratroopers."

"An airplane," Sihoud said skeptically, beginning to lose interest. "An airplane lost on a radar screen. This is not something even worth a discussion, Colonel."

"Yes, sir, I'm sure you're right, still . . . At about the same time the mystery jet took off, our geosynch satellite detected three sudden heat blooms in the Arabian Sea off Karachi and two more in the Mediterranean east of Cyprus."

"Heat blooms . . . ?"

"Infrared scanned heat sources, sudden and very hot."

"Perhaps gun tests or flare launches. Disposal of defective ordnance, maybe."

"Or maybe the Coalition is targeting us with cruise missiles. The heat blooms could have been their rocket motor first stages."

"That's it?"

"We can't track cruise missiles from the ground, sir. We don't know if they are coming. And the aircraft approach is perplexing. As I said, it could hold paratroopers."

"Enough of this," Sihoud said. "Two weeks ago you were certain a commando force had landed outside Ashkhabad and was coming for me. We never heard from them. I will not fight this war from the rear, Colonel. We must return to the field."

Ahmed nodded, feeling equal parts frustration that Sihoud was not hearing him and hope that Sihoud was right.

Seven Miles South of Kizyl-Arvat, Turkmenistan

Augusta's first-fired Javelin cruise missile hugged the ground, barely twenty feet above the brushland of the Turkmenian plains, flying at 650 miles per hour. As it did every six minutes, the onboard JavCalCor computer commanded a full self-check and the missile's systems reported in. Fuel was getting low at forty percent; fuel flow rate was within limits. Compressor inlet, combustor discharge, and turbine discharge temperatures were all nominal. The warhead system reported satisfactory interlocks with the detonator train disconnected and open-circuited. The guidance system reported that the rudder and elevator control surfaces were functional. The navigation system was taking continuous fixes on the terrain-following contour-radar set, and the shape of the land below matched the computer memory; the flatness of the Turkmenian Plain had caused some concern, but a backup star fix showed the terrain navigation to be within limits. The missile was about a half mile ahead of where the clock indicated it should be, and since arrival at the target at a precise moment in time was vital, the computer decided to slow the missile down by twenty feet per second. The amidships fuel flow control valve shut slightly, cutting down on the combustor fuel feed. The combustion chamber's discharge temperature dropped and the turbine whined down slightly. Nozzle thrust fell a fraction and the missile slowed.

The computer scanned the memory map of the Turkmenian terrain and the approach to the Main Bunker Complex outside of Ashkhabad.

The weapon would approach from the north at reduced altitude. At a range of one mile it would execute a pop-up maneuver, climbing almost vertically up to 2,000 feet, then arc over and dive into the bunker from directly overhead. The computer reminded itself to wait 200 milliseconds after impact before detonating the warhead's compact high explosive, to ensure the weapon had traveled all the way to the fourth sublevel before exploding—the target was almost 140 feet below the ground floor level of the mosque.

The missile's only concern was successfully flying the remaining miles to the target and detonating in the proper sequence.

Seventy Miles North of Ashkhabad, Turkmenistan

The 200-knot slipstream punched into SEAL commander Jack Morris's guts and threatened to send him tumbling in spite of his textbook-correct body position. He bounced through the turbulence, feeling the shock of the cold after the shock of the wind began to die down. He sailed in the thunderous gale winds of free fall at 115 miles per hour, terminal velocity with his flying-squirrel thermal coveralls, wondering what the wind chill was—wind of 115 miles per, starting with air at forty below zero. Whatever it was, it would be cold enough to freeze him into an iceball in another few seconds if not for his electrically heated suit. He fell toward the black desert below, trying to see the luminescent altimeter. This jump was to be a hop-and-pop, the free-fall portion less than a minute. As expected, he felt a minor jolt as the drogue chute popped out of his back, the altimeter automatically deploying the parachutes of the entire team at the same altitude. The drogue rose overhead and pulled out the silk of the mattress-shaped parasail. Jack Morris felt a hard jerk, as if the gallows trapdoor had opened and sent him dangling, but instead of choking him the harness gave him a stern kick in the crotch.

A half second later the bungee cord attached at one end to his harness and at the other to his heavy equipment crate grew taut as the box continued to fall. Taking the weight of the crate nearly deflated the parasail for a moment; Morris waited and let the chute stall out, knowing that this was the moment that killed most sky divers. A deploying canopy could tangle itself and get in the way of the reserve chute, like Bony Robbins's had before Christmas. His main chute had become a cigarette, an obscenely tangled streamer flapping uselessly in the wind above him. Bony had struggled to cut away the main, but the reserve's altimeter had kicked in and pushed out his reserve, which promptly became tangled in the main chute. Bony had hit the frozen cornfield at over 100 miles an hour. But Morris's main behaved and filled with wind while the equipment crate settled out forty feet below. Morris steered south and looked for the rest of the 100-man force. In the moonless night, he couldn't see anyone, but he could hear the canopies around him. There was no noise from the KC–10 jet. It had already dived back down to terrain-hugging altitude now that the SEALs were out, most likely streaking home as fast as the coffee-drinking, paper-pushing zoomies could fly.

The jump point had been seventy miles from the UIF main bunker. They had left the jet at 45,000 feet and opened the parachutes after a minimal fall. Morris had counted on flying the parasails twenty miles with the wind. By the time they hit the desert floor, they would still be fifty miles from Sihoud's living room. With fifteen minutes to assemble the desert patrol vehicles, that gave them an hour and a half to get to the bunker perimeter with a half hour of contingency time. So far the mission had been on-target: the jet hadn't been gunned down and, assuming the bus drivers knew where the hell they were, the jump had gone off without incident. But every mission screwed up somewhere. The only difference between a successful raid and a miserable rout was the magnitude of the unexpected foul-up. Plenty could still go wrong, he thought as he glanced at the altimeter and compass. The landing could be rough with the equipment crates, perhaps injuring some of the men. The DPVs could be damaged, and without the desert patrol vehicles they would not make the fifty-mile trip in time. They might find company waiting when they landed, or at the bunker perimeter, or anywhere in between. And even once they secured the perimeter, the goddamned Javelin cruise missiles might decide to hit the SEALs, and it would be Jimmy Carter and Iran all over again.

Morris turned up the thermostat on his suit, the fabric filled with electrical heat resistors like an electric blanket. He continued flying the parasail south, his equipment crate swaying below him while he waited for the trip to end. Finally his altimeter read 1,000 feet, and he jettisoned the cargo crate. His chute seemed to fly up for a moment as his descent eased from the lost weight. Morris strained his ears and heard the sounds of parachutes popping open on a hundred equipment crates as they were released. The digital altimeter reeled off the numerals, until Morris's toes were only a few hundred feet from the ground. He strained his senses, his eyes on where the horizon would be if it were visible, and tried to feel the ground with his mind. He'd always hated night jumps like these made on moonless nights; night-vision goggles had never worked for him on night drops, since the single combined monocular lens took away depth and caused vertigo. Somehow he had always been able to sense the approach of the ground at the last second, in time to flare out the parasail. Failure to pull its trailing edges down to stall it out meant crashing at up to forty miles per hour, enough kinetic energy to maim a man.

He held his breath and waited, finally hearing more than seeing the ground. He pulled his chute-control cables from the harness straps all the way down to his knees, and the parasail wing-shaped canopy inclined upward into the airflow, tilting up like an airliner flaring out over a runway. The aerobraking worked, slowing Morris almost to a stop, neatly collapsing the canopy just as his combat boots hit the sand at walking speed. Morris stepped away from the deflating parachute and let it flap in the wind on the sand. He released the tabs on his harness, unzipped and took off his flying squirrel suit, and dumped his oxygen mask on the pile, rolled it all up into a ball, and buried it in the sand. Surrounding him were a hundred SEALs doing the same. Morris reached into his vest and pulled out his night-vision goggles and strapped them on. The desert came to life around him, men scurrying for the equipment crates, pulling out weapons and ammunition and pieces of the desert patrol vehicles.

Morris walked the sand, watching his men opening the crates, a few men sent to find crates that had landed a few hundred feet outside the drop zone. The contents of the crates were snapped together quickly, the tightly packed crate contents becoming space frame vehicles, with aluminum tubes for the framing, collapsed tires with inflation bottles, unfolding seats made of lightweight and compact foam, the heaviest components the engines, the transmissions, and the machine guns. Not believing in keeping his hands clean, Morris bent to help one heaving group of men tilt an engine assembly up to accept the front portion of one of the DPV frames. The men worked frantically, bolting high-horse-power engines together in the dark, the clumsy night-vision goggles the only aid to sight. Morris stepped back and allowed himself a moment of pride. With a pit crew like this, any Indianapolis racer would be a winner. The moment ended too soon as Morris checked his watch. It had been eight minutes since his boots had hit the desert. Too damned long.

Morris found Black Bart Bartholomay and went over the assault plan one last time while an ensign and a chief assembled their DPV–4. Once completed, the lightweight and queer-looking vehicle resembled the bastard son of a moon buggy and a Baha race car. It held four SEALs, driver included, had oversized dune tires, two frame-mounted machine guns, and a 300 horsepower supercharged small-block Chevy. The desert burst into loud burbling noises, the drivers gunning their engines. Morris strapped on his motorcycle-style helmet, got the radio boom microphone adjusted, and loaded the clip into his MAC–10 machine gun, the weapon heavy and satisfying in his hand. Bart returned from a tour of their assembly area and reported that all DPVs were running and there had been no injuries on the insertion. The mission was still on track, if a few minutes late.

Morris checked the DPVs' geosatellite navigation system, the NAVSAT receiver no bigger than a loaf of bread, and looked at the map. Heading one seven seven led straight into the main bunker. He climbed into the DPV with Bart driving, the ensign on the rear gun, the chief next to him. He tapped Bart's thigh, and Bart cautiously accelerated, avoiding getting stuck in the sand, and the high-tech dune buggy sped off to the south, two dozen buggies following behind it in a roaring race.

Ashkhabad, Turkmenistan
Main Bunker Complex

"How will we deliver the Scorpions to Washington? And how soon can we do it?" General Sihoud stared at the electronic chart on the wall and thought about the destiny of the Islamic people, how the Westerners had only gained a foothold on UIF soil so that their eventual withdrawal from Muslim territory would be that much more significant for the UIF.

After all, fourteen centuries ago Mohammed had himself been driven from Mecca to Medina—the holy exile, the *hegira,* during which Mohammed founded Islam. The Prophet had then fought his way back to Mecca in an astonishing and triumphant battle, winning an immortal glory. By the time he was forty Mohammed and Islam had taken over the Arab world.

Now Sihoud had been given the Scorpion, just as Mohammed had received supernatural power from the archangel Gabriel, and now the war would be won. The infidels would sneak away and hide, and Mohammed al-Sihoud would triumph. Sihoud truly believed that.

2

THURSDAY, 26 DECEMBER

Ashkhabad, Turkmenistan
UIF Main Bunker Complex

Sihoud yawned. It was many hours past the time he had hoped to sleep, and there was more to do before dawn than stare at the machine's screens. He had a war to win, troops to command, armies to move, but first he must deal with his Iranian chief of staff, the worrying technocrat Rakish Ahmed. Still, he reminded himself, Ahmed was more than worth his pay—he had delivered the Scorpion weapon. For that Sihoud could stand to indulge his worldly fears; he just wished Ahmed could comprehend that they were destined to prevail. He believed that.

Colonel Ahmed frowned in low conversation with one of the officers at the tactical command console, who occasionally put one finger in the air and talked into a secure radiotelephone. Sihoud could see Ahmed's expression grow darker. Finally he turned from the console and faced Sihoud, a pained look on his face.

"Sir, we need to leave, *now*. I believe an attack is imminent on this command center." Ahmed had been trained by the Iranian Air Force to state the conclusion first, the supporting evidence last. It was a habit that irritated Sihoud, but he waited. "An antiaircraft station, the north post, reported radar contact on a large airborne blip. The radar was a height-finding unit, and reported the plane climbed up from zero to fourteen kilometers very rapidly, then dived back down again. At first we didn't believe it, but the south station just confirmed, they saw the same thing. This correlates to the lost jetliner, sir. It has to be paratroopers." Ahmed paused to grab a radio handset and barked orders into it, something about a Firestar fighter and a Kawasaki U–10 truck at the south utility tunnel exit.

Sihoud calmly shook his head. There were no paratroopers and there would be no withdrawal through the utility tunnel. Ahmed had too little faith.

The night before, Sihoud had had a dream, a dream of conquest. Angels from heaven had fought beside him, one telling him he would rule all of Asia and all of Africa, that the infidels were to be cast into the seas. No part of the dream portended any threat. Sihoud felt it down to the marrow of his bones. The only thing that mattered at the moment was deploying and firing the Scorpion plutonium missiles with their cargo of death, the wages of sin, delivered by Allah's agent on earth, General Sihoud.

Ahmed still stood there with the radio handset plugged into one ear. "We shot missiles at the aircraft, General. None of them hit—the plane was too far away. General, I have a U–10 truck waiting for us and a Firestar at the airstrip—"

"*Stop.* If the plane was so far away that our antiaircraft missiles could not reach it, it must have been very distant. How far away was it?"

"About a hundred kilometers, perhaps slightly more."

"A hundred kilometers. And these paratroopers will have a long walk ahead of them. Did your radars show any parachutes?"

"No, sir, but—"

"Colonel, come with me."

Sihoud led Ahmed to a partitioned corner of the room and snapped his fingers. An attendant brought two cups of steaming tea. Sihoud sipped the brew and stared through the steam at Ahmed, his eyes now showing some compassion. When he spoke his resonant voice was quiet, even gentle.

"Colonel Ahmed, Rakish, my friend, you are thinking about your wife and son, are you not?"

"I'll always think about them, but that has nothing to do with this bunker being threatened."

"I wonder, Rakish. I wonder whether losing your family and your home has made you think you might lose me too. I assure you that will never happen."

As Sihoud talked Ahmed's mind wandered . . . 200 meters down a utility-access tunnel there was a U–10 truck waiting for him and Sihoud,

and four kilometers further south a Firestar fighter was being pulled
from a hangar, fueled, and warmed up, all on Ahmed's orders. As chief
of staff he was also responsible for Sihoud's security, and that part of the
job was almost the toughest. Because Sihoud was fearless to the point of
foolhardiness. The man really did believe he was invulnerable—a dangerous self-deception. And if Sihoud did not want to be protected, there
was little to be done until the worst happened. Perhaps then he would
listen. Ahmed decided to keep the U–10 truck and the Firestar waiting
and ready. While Sihoud continued to talk Ahmed pulled out a machine
pistol in a leather holster and strapped it on over his fatigues. The heavy
feeling of the weapon made him feel better, and for a moment he was
able to relax. Now Sihoud was asking about the Scorpions.

"The Scorpions, Colonel. How will we deliver them and how soon?"

Ahmed had been waiting for the question. He knew Sihoud would not
like the answer but then neither did he.

"Delivery by aircraft will not be possible. The air force fighters are
fully occupied here and in any case their range is too limited to cross the
Atlantic. Commercial airliners are no good—their parts have all been
used to keep our squadrons of fighters in the air, and the mechanics are
all at the fronts. I have considered hijacking an airplane and landing it
where we could load the missiles but that would betray the operation.
The transport of the missiles must be kept absolutely secret."

Sihoud suspected that Colonel Ahmed's plan must be unconventional
indeed for Ahmed to brief him this way.

"Finally, sir, the unit's launch must not be detected, another reason
air deployment is out of the question. The American air-traffic control
system is sophisticated and an unidentified aircraft that drops a piece of
cargo that then goes supersonic would be immediately detected—"

Sihoud nodded as the colonel continued. Ahmed's American educa-
tion annoyed him, even at times like these when it would help their
purposes. Ahmed had been trained by the U.S. Air Force back in the
days of the Shah, and had studied engineering at a so-called prestigious
university in the American Northeast. Ahmed claimed to have studied
his American military counterparts and know their weaknesses. Of
course, so far that had not helped them avoid the devastation brought
about by the Coalition. Sihoud decided to hurry Ahmed along.

"Fine, Colonel. No air transport or delivery. What is your alternative?"

"The *Hegira,* Khalib. We can bring the missiles close to the U.S. coast
and fire them from the sea. The Americans will be caught by complete
surprise."

Morris watched as Lt. Buffalo Sauer sighted in on the U–10 utility
truck's front left tire, a tough shot since the truck was doing about

twenty miles per. A moment later the silently fired bullet hit the rubber and blew the tire apart. The U–10 swerved, almost lost control, then slowed and stopped. Two soldiers climbed out and shouldered their weapons while staring at the offending wheel. There was a brief argument until one nodded and walked to the rear of the vehicle for the spare. He bent over to find the tire iron and was dead before he could straighten up, Ensign Dobbs's blade having sliced his throat open. The other soldier was still looking at the tire when Chief Hansen and his knife dispatched him. Hansen carefully lowered the body to the sand. Neither man had made a sound in dying. Hansen was cleaning his knife blade with a rag from the truck when the truck's radio clicked to life, the quick syllables of Arabic blasting out of it. Hansen pulled out his MAC–10 machine gun, checked the hush-puppy silencer and fired into the radio console. The unit disintegrated, the desert was again silent.

Morris checked the horizon in each direction for signs of other security troops. The northern perimeter of the tall mosque was open and deserted. The outskirts of the city approached near the southern perimeter, the houses and streets quiet. Morris pointed at Cowpie Clites, who walked to the electrified fence, strapped on heavy rubber gloves, and tested the fence wire with a hand-held meter. It was dead, the western perimeter crew done with the work on the high-voltage transformer. Clites produced a pair of bolt cutters and cut a large hole in the fencing, then stepped back. Morris waved his men in, where they took up positions surrounding the mosque less than 200 yards away.

Morris checked his watch. He had timed their insertion to the second, and so far had been right on schedule. The teams had abandoned the DPVs two miles west of the bunker and had crept silently the final distance, going slowly to eat up the contingency time. The plan called for impact of the Javelin cruise missiles just as the men entered the fence of the compound. If the missiles came too early, survivors, perhaps Sihoud himself, could get away clean. If the Javelins took their time and arrived too late, it would leave the SEALs exposed, lying on the sand waiting for the cruise missiles to come, their discovery by UIF troops meaning immediate execution. Or worse, imprisonment and interrogation.

Morris did not trust cruise missiles. They had a nasty tendency to get lost or fall short or get shot down. Sometimes all three at once. If the operation had been Morris's to plan he would have saved the Javelins for the next war and gone in now, MAC–10s blazing. But some admiral in the Pentagon wanted to share the action with the black-shoe Navy and had ordered the firing of the missiles from hundreds of miles away at sea. Morris bit his lip, knowing that expensive toys were sexy to the brass, but the only thing that won wars was an infantryman with a rifle, the concept taken to its extreme with the SEALS, where infantryman and rifle were replaced with commando and compact-silenced machine gun.

He strained to hear, wondering if the slight whine was his blood rushing in his head or the noise of the Javelins. The whine grew louder, fuller, the sound of high-speed turbofan engines. Jet engines. He trained his night-vision monocular to the sky and thought he saw the airframe of one of the missiles climbing to the sky, starting its pop-up. Only seconds to go now, he thought.

For a moment Sihoud was stunned. But Ahmed looked calmly at him after saying that the *Hegira* would bring the missiles to the coast of America and fire them. The *Hegira!* A submarine? It was so preposterous that it almost made a twisted kind of sense.

The *Hegira* was Ahmed's predecessor's idea, and a silly idea at that. Up until now Sihoud had regretted his decision to support the acquisition, but now he wondered.

Sihoud's last chief of staff had been the head of the Egyptian navy, Admiral Al Abbad Mansur, who had insisted that they were vulnerable from the Mediterranean and the Indian Ocean. It would be ridiculous, Sihoud had insisted, for a mighty land power to fear the sea, and foolish to try to match the seagoing forces of the West with a blue-water navy. Mansur had proposed a different solution, the purchase of three of the Japanese-designed Destiny-class submarines. At first Sihoud had continued to resist, but at Mansur's persistence he had listened.

Mansur had pointed out that a small nation armed with submarines could alter the outcome of a war. He pointed to the Falklands War, in which the British submarines had bottled up the Argentine fleet, the Argentinians afraid to risk their surface ships against an unknown submerged threat; and there was the Persian Gulf War, in which unrestricted shipping by the West had allowed them to mass force on the continent. Mansur insisted that littoral warfare using submarines could be the edge that could save the union in a fight, and Sihoud finally had agreed.

The Japanese had designed the Destiny-class submarines for export sale, and in addition to the usual thorough Oriental design, the submarine was relatively inexpensive—for a submarine—only fifty-five billion yen. Three years ago that had not been a grand sum, even though it was the equivalent of an entire squadron of Firestar fighters. The submarine would allow them to patrol the Mediterranean and protect UIF soil from a Western assault from the sea, Mansur insisted, and a second unit in the Indian Ocean would keep them safe from the other side. With perhaps a third guarding them on the Atlantic, no aircraft carrier task group could threaten them. At the time, it had made sense, and while it was a considerable amount of money, it would have given the UIF a three-ocean navy with only three ships. Perhaps Mansur's vision had been correct, but the acquisition of the ships had been a failure.

The Japanese had had design problems, as the Destiny-class was brand new and would supposedly revolutionize underwater combat. Delivery had been over two years late, and by then the invasions of Chad and Ethiopia were under way. By the time the first submarine was completed, Sihoud had begun the land attack on India, and by then there had still been no threatening moves by Western navies. In the intervening year Mansur had made other equally damaging mistakes—the India invasion had been full of them—and Sihoud had felt he had no choice but to execute Mansur. It had taken six months to train the crew of the first Destiny-class submarine, and since its delivery it had been tied up uselessly in Kassab on the Mediterranean. It had spent time at sea, but mostly it had one mechanical problem after another. Colonel Ahmed had taken over for Mansur—Sihoud had wanted an air force officer, having had his fill of the navy, and needing advice about using the new aircraft. Sihoud was himself an expert on the armies, and kept his own counsel on the use and command of the ground troops—he had heard reports from Western media accounts that called him the equal of the great generals, even comparing him to such as Alexander the Great, Napoleon, even Attila the Hun. When Ahmed had taken the chief of staff position, Sihoud had sent him to Kassab to report on the Destiny-class ship, named *Hegira* by Admiral Mansur in honor of the Prophet's holy exile. Ahmed reported it to be a miraculous piece of technology, but a useless one for a land power such as the United Islamic Front of God. Sihoud still recalled Ahmed's report—*the Americans have a name for such a thing as this: they call it a White Elephant.* The air force would do all that the submarine would do, Ahmed concluded, and more. Sihoud had agreed, and the submarine had sat unused ever since.

And so it was ironic to hear the submarine mentioned in Ahmed's plan to deploy the Scorpion missile. He must have had this in mind all along. So strange for an air force officer to abandon his beloved airplanes for an odd ship like the *Hegira,* but it would offer a secret way to get the missile to its target. Except it would take much too long . . .

"How long to get to within missile range of the U.S.? Of Washington?"

"Sir, I hope you will forgive my action in this matter but I ordered the submarine loaded with the weapon components and it put to sea yesterday. It will take time to manufacture the three warshot weapons, perhaps a week or two. And these will be assembled aboard the *Hegira* while she is in transit. By the time she arrives at her firing station, the missiles will be ready. Even if we were to fly the weapons to the U.S. we would still have to wait for the units to be assembled. I apologize for the unavoidable delay, sir, but in a matter of weeks this war will be quite different."

Sihoud nodded slowly, wondering where the next weeks would lead to in this grisly land battle. The approach of the tactical watch officer intruded into his thoughts. The youngster was hollow-cheeked and ill fed to begin with, but the fear in his face made his appearance that much worse.

"Colonel, sir—"

"What is it, Massoud?"

"We've lost contact with the perimeter guards. All patrols. We had a strange static on one of the radios, like someone was about to transmit, then nothing. I've sent a platoon out to check, but—"

"Take command," Ahmed ordered. "Send out all the security troops, then seal all portals. The Khalib and I are leaving now for the field. Send for the Seventh Islamic Guard to take protective positions at the bunker until further notice."

Javelin Unit One, the first-fired missile from Daminski's *Augusta,* flew over the flat desert, getting closer by the second to the target. The terrain comparisons were matching the setpoints and the final star fix showed the unit now one point zero five miles from the target—five seconds away if the unit were to continue flying straight on. But now was the time for the pop-up. The winglets rotated while the fuel-flow valve opened wide to full throttle. The combustors' temperature soared, the turbine spooled up, the nozzle thrust escalated to the full 3,000 pounds-force of push, and the unit climbed for the sky, the desert below growing more and more distant, only the stars above in view. The pressure altimeter unwound as the missile soared over 1,000 feet, then 2,000. Finally the missile, having traded speed for altitude, slowed at the point of its pop-up arc, the winglets now demanding the missile dive.

The JavCalCor computer checked the high explosive's arming status. The detonator train was ready, waiting only for the spark from the fuse. The weapon rotated in space, beginning its dive, the radar-seeker window now seeing the horizon, then the mosque of the main bunker complex a half mile below. Still on full thrust, the unit accelerated toward the mosque below, picking up speed as the mosque grew in its vision cone until it blocked out all else. The missile passed through the sound barrier and was going Mach 1.1 when the courtyard tiles of the mosque flew up and smashed into the seeker cone.

Sihoud felt Ahmed grab his arm and drag him to the south stair tower, pausing only to take up two automatic rifles. Sihoud followed him, knowing what Ahmed was thinking, and beginning to wonder if his aide was correct in his caution, although there was still a part of him that resented this move to leave so suddenly. But then, Ahmed was right about the need to be in the field and not in an underground bunker.

The two men rushed up the stairs. Ahmed handed Sihoud a rifle. At the last landing from the door to the courtyard of the mosque above, there was a metal door to the utility tunnel. Ahmed operated the button combination lock, unbolted it, and pulled Sihoud in. They passed through an untidy storage area to another door. Ahmed unbolted it and pushed Sihoud into the utility tunnel, a cramped pipe of precast concrete, not even two full meters in diameter, filled with water pipes, electrical conduits, phone cables, sewer pipes, and ventilation ducts. There was barely enough room for a man crouching over to move through the tunnel. Sihoud hurried through it, feeling like a damn fool coward. He reconsidered about twenty meters down the tunnel and pulled on Ahmed's sleeve. Ahmed stopped and heard Sihoud tell him to stop and return to the command center. It was a terrible place to argue with the general, but that was what he had to do.

For Javelin Unit One, the next milliseconds passed quickly, the missile's mission almost complete. The radar-seeker window was crushed by the impact with the mosque courtyard floor, but behind it an armor-piercing shield of uranium protected the JavCalCor and punched through the mosque floor. The kinetic energy of the missile sliced through the lead shielding, then the reinforced concrete. By then most of the unit's speed was lost, but it kept enough momentum to blitz through the first and second sublevels, through Sihoud's quarters, and through the overhead of the tactical control center. The weapon's timer, started at the moment of impact with the courtyard above, correctly predicted the missile's arrival at the fourth sublevel, and anticipating this, had ignited the fuse ten meters higher while still smashing through the floor of the senior officers' quarters. The fuse lit off and ignited the intermediate explosive, which began the detonation of the high explosive just as the unit crashed through into the command center.

The ton of PlasticPac high explosives—a patented, secret high-density mix with over eighteen times the explosive power of an equivalent weight of TNT—released its chemical energy, the explosion reaching outward to the consoles and men in the room. The underground command center was walled with more concrete, held in place by packed sand. The confined explosion smashed the contents of the room against the reinforced walls, the explosion shock-wave a hammer, the concrete sand-braced walls an anvil. The force of it had nowhere to go but up, blowing the ceiling above it upward, rupturing the decks of the levels above.

Javelin Unit One had been the first missile to arrive in the coordinated attack. Although timed for detonation at the same time, the next four missiles arrived late—late on a scale of milliseconds—but the other four explosions added to the destruction of the first, sending the shredded contents of the bunker skyward in a black and orange mushroom cloud of debris mixed with the remains of what milliseconds before had been men.

Five seconds after the impact of Javelin Unit One against the mosque floor there was little left of the command center but airborne debris and the fires and smoke within the pit in the earth where the bunker had once been.

For over two minutes the debris fell out of the sky and rained down on the sand surrounding the smoke-blackened hole, the impacting chunks of concrete and metal making little sound as they hit the sand; or if they did make sounds they were lost in the roaring of the orange mushroom cloud rising several thousand feet over the desert floor.

Jack Morris felt more than saw the detonations of the cruise missiles. At first the ground trembled a bit as the first missile hit the mosque floor. The explosion shook him as it detonated below, the sound at first muffled by the layers of concrete below the earth, but immediately after missiles two through five hit the bunker there was the roaring noise as the force of the explosions burst out of the hole in the ground. The minaret tower seemed to disintegrate into a thousand fragments and fly slowly off into the night. A misshapen orange mushroom cloud rose several thousand feet overhead, turning the dark moonless night into a harshly lit mid-afternoon. Morris hugged the sand as the pieces from the explosion began to hit the ground around them, mostly a rain of sand and grit from what had once been concrete. When the debris shower ended, Morris looked up and whistled, his abused ears unable to hear his own exclamation of incredulity.

The admirals who had sent the Javelins had miscalculated, Morris thought. With the new explosive, the missiles had been overkill. Although difficult to see from the ridge of sand, from where Morris lay, there was nothing left of the bunker to sift through. The idea of survivors was the dream of a Pentagon bureaucrat. Morris stood and signaled the men in, the fires from the explosion calming and dying down, the smoke still billowing out of the crater of what had once been the headquarters bunker of the Combined Armed Forces of the entire goddamned UIF. Morris's radio earpiece crackled with terse reports from the other platoon commanders as the SEALs surrounded the bunker, the reports confirming Morris's analysis that there would be no survivors to take alive, no General Sihoud to interrogate. Morris got closer to the hole, peered in, nodded, and gave the orders to begin the extraction.

* * *

Ahmed had not yet mouthed his first word to tell Sihoud to continue through the tunnel when the tunnel suddenly turned upside down, the walls burst, and what had been an escape route became an airless tomb.

For the next five minutes the collapsed tunnel was filled with the booming noises of the explosions. Then all was silent.

All this way, Morris thought bitterly, just to watch a bunch of million-dollar missiles overdo the work the SEALS could have done with precision. He and his commandos left the bunker compound at the same fence holes they had cut and ran at a six-minute-mile pace to the DPVs, cranked the engines, and headed four miles farther northeast. Three of the buggies had failed—sand in the supercharger blowers, Morris figured, making a few of the DPVs heavy with added men. When Morris's satellite navigation unit blinked, he gave the order and shut down the buggies. The units were parked side by side in three rows of seven, the last man out of each DPV pulling a pin out of an assembly under the seats. The commandos ran a hundred yards to the north and hit the sand. A few seconds later the DPV destruct mechanisms kicked in and blew the buggies into smoldering ruins, the fires from their explosions guiding in the extraction aircraft.

Morris waited, frustrated, knowing that the extraction had been planned later, assuming there would be a longer action at the mosque. But he hated waiting on bus drivers, particularly Air Force bus drivers. After what felt like twenty minutes but was closer to five, Morris heard the beating of the rotors. The four V–22 tilt-rotor Ospreys flew overhead, circled, and tilted their rotors to the horizontal, descending vertically and touching down on the sand. Morris and the men climbed into the odd aircraft, half-chopper, half-transport, and buckled in. Morris's V–22 lifted off and tilted the props, the aircraft now a turboprop high-speed transport. As the plane accelerated south toward occupied southern Iran, Morris took one last look at the burning remains of the mosque. There was no way anyone could have survived the explosion. Still, Morris had hoped to load Sihoud's dead body aboard the V–22 with them, the ultimate war trophy. Well, every mission, he told himself, screwed up somehow. This mission's screwup was just an overabundance of firepower.

Morris leaned back in the seat, and although only a hundred feet over UIF territory and only minutes removed from combat, fell into a deep sleep.

3

Chah Bahar was a peaceful village on the sea. Ahmed had gone home on leave to see his wife and four-year-old-son Nadhar. The sun was warm as he walked the street with his family hours before he had to fly back to Ashkhabad. Abruptly out of the south, the sound of jet engines, too big and heavy for UIF jets. His ears were filled with the sounds of the Western Coalition Stealth bombers, the whistle of the descending cluster bombs, the oddly muffled cough from his wife as the shrapnel hit her. He felt himself running, Nadhar's body in his arms. As the first bombs hit, he and Nadhar fell to the dirt, Ahmed on top, the bombs exploding around them. His ears rang from the low pass of a black bomber. He braced himself as the fuel-air explosive canister hit the ground and detonated, the explosion smashing into him. He felt the impact of shrapnel, then the conflagration sucked the air out of the sky, leaving him gasping, certain he was moments from death, but finally the flames faded and he drank in the air. Even before he looked Ahmed sensed his son had been hit by the shrapnel. And Col. Rakish Ahmed, supreme commander of the Combined Air Forces of the United Islamic Front of God and chief of staff to General-and-Khalib Mohammed al-Sihoud was obliged to watch as his son died. The final wave of Stealth bombers flew over then, their bellies full of another round of cluster bombs. Ahmed was forced to leave Nadhar's body and run for cover. His anger and grief would coalesce into a hunger for revenge . . . his understanding that his own personal loss was shared by thousands his troops had left fatherless never really occurred to him . . .

In the broken service tunnel of the headquarters bunker, Ahmed's uniform was soaked in cold sweat. His heart was pounding, his breath wheezed. The vision of the smoking ruins of Chah Bahar vanished in a swirling storm of dots, yellow and red and blue dots.

He shook his head, slowly realizing he had been unconscious, unable to escape the Chah Bahar nightmare even when knocked out by an enemy attack on the bunker. He heard rushing noises, dripping noises . . . the noise of air as it rushed in and blew out. The sounds grew in volume. Choking, rasping, retching noises filled the dark space. He tried to move, going nowhere at first, feeling pressure from something lying on top of him. A slick feel against a harder surface. A liquid. Blood or water.

He tried again to move, trying his arm first, surprised when it followed his command. His other arm, then his legs. He tried to get up but was pinned. He tried to roll, and felt a jagged piece of steel jab into his ribs. He rolled the other way and felt pressure ease up, allowing him to breathe. There was still no light, but another sound, a spurting, sprinkling noise.

The attack on the bunker had come, as Ahmed had predicted. The tunnel, their intended escape route, had partially collapsed, its concrete upper half smashed to dust by the fist of the explosions. What had been the floor of the tunnel was littered with smashed pieces of concrete, sand, dirt, wires and cables. No sign of Sihoud.

It hit him then . . . Sihoud was dead, and with him the hopes of the thirty nations and half billion people of the Union. The United Islamic Front, in minutes, had been doomed. The attack had, as Ahmed feared, been a decapitation. Because without Mohammed al-Sihoud, everything was lost. Ahmed heard his own voice call out for the Khalib.

Soon his voice was drowned by another sound. What before had been a spritzing sound, a dim noise of rain, now became a sound of rushing force. The water pipe, which had once fed the bunker, had ruptured and was flooding the remains of the utility tunnel. The water had submerged his face, and he twisted into a violent roll. The same piece of steel jabbed into his ribs, and he decided he would rather be stabbed to death by the reinforcing steel in the chunk of concrete that held him down than be drowned by the water line. The steel cut into him, ripping open the skin at his ribs, cutting into muscle and scraping bone, coming close to puncturing the lung beneath the bone, until his chest was no longer in contact with the metal, only the smooth underside of the concrete chunk. By then the water had risen over Ahmed's prone body. He continued to twist and felt his back scrape across the concrete block. In a corner of his mind, prepared for death, he realized that he was free. He pumped his legs and pushed with his hands and was able to half-stand.

His head splashed out of the water into the damp darkness of the half-collapsed tunnel, water up to his waist. He had to find Sihoud. He had to shut off the flooding water. He had to get them out of the tunnel.

He had to get Sihoud to a place of safety. As he searched in the rising water for Sihoud, he realized it would be no good merely to get the Khalib to another command post, to a field battlefield company. What had happened would happen again and again until the enemy had achieved their goal of killing Sihoud and decapitating the Union. He had to find the one place on earth where the coalition's commandos and assassins would be unable to reach him. The water, the rising water in the tunnel, had keyed a dim memory in Ahmed's mind, but as yet he was uncertain what the connection was. And then it suddenly seemed obvious. Sihoud had to go into exile, much as the Prophet Himself had gone into exile to Medina almost fourteen centuries before. The Prophet's exile had been called the *hegira,* and so would Sihoud's. And like the Prophet Mohammed, Sihoud would return in glory, not with horses and swords but with high-altitude radar-invisible supersonic cruise missiles loaded with radioactive plutonium.

Five steps down the tunnel Ahmed tripped on something. He reached down into the water, grabbed hold, and pulled with all his strength. Sihoud had been trapped under a piece of metal, but he must have been unconscious because the metal rolled off easily. His head came out of the water. He was not breathing. Ahmed leaned Sihoud's face back and clamped his lips on the lips of the Khalib and blew.

As the water rose in the tunnel, Ahmed felt the broken concrete tunnel begin to shift, the water undermining footing in the packed sand. He continued to blow into Sihoud's mouth. The water continued to rise. How long could he try to bring life back to Sihoud before giving up and trying to save himself? But then he thought that no decision was in fact a decision. Without Sihoud there was no hope for the UIF or for Ahmed himself, and with the war lost, Sihoud and Ahmed's family dead, what was there to live for? Sihoud suddenly stiffened and expelled water.

It was well past three o'clock in the morning and something was seriously wrong. Airman Abdul Djaliz squinted at the horizon where the smoke and flames were dying out but still discernible over the dim light of the few sodium arc lights illuminating the asphalt at Ashkhabad's Sunni Air Base.

It had been perhaps forty minutes before that the call had come from the main bunker HQ to pull the most airworthy Firestar fighter from the hangar, warm it up, and load liquid helium into the electronic warfare pod's tank. That had taken only fifteen minutes. The sleek swept-winged jet sat on the pad, her turbines purring smoothly, the heat haze from the exhaust nozzles causing the strip lights to waver slightly. The canopy was up and the ladder was pulled up to the cockpit. For the fifth time in a half hour Djaliz climbed to the top of the ladder and peered in at the pilot's status console, goosing the computer through its fifth checklist.

The liquid crystal display recited the aircraft's latest statistics, flashing graphics and charts and temperature profiles, oil pressures, hydraulic system status. All of it within limits. Djaliz lowered himself back down to the ground and reexamined the electronic warfare pod slung under the pointed nose of the large jet, the one he'd filled with supercold liquid helium. The ungainly size of the pod marred the sleek streamlined beauty of the aircraft. The pod was new with the latest modification of the Firestar, this particular pod nearly fresh out of the crate from Osaka. Djaliz worried over it for a moment and climbed the ladder again and this time climbed all the way into the cockpit, putting the pilot's flight helmet aside on the engine control console. He dialed up the menu for the electronic warfare pod and ordered a self-check.

He waited a moment while the computer tested the inputs and readbacks from the pod and tested the circuits to the large transmitters housed inside. The display recited that the pod was ready for combat, ready to fry the electronics of any approaching aircraft that challenged this particular Firestar in a dogfight. Djaliz checked the time, wondering if he should radio back to headquarters that he was wasting the jet fuel, that no one had shown up for whatever mysterious mission HQ had had in mind.

The young airman stood and climbed out of the cockpit, his jaw dropping as the speeding U-10 crashed through the security gate without bothering to scan in. He dropped to the ground and unholstered his pistol, about to command the intruder to halt. The truck drew up to the jet, parking off the side of the starboard wingtip, as if the driver wanted to avoid blocking the jet's takeoff. Djaliz leveled his automatic pistol at the driver, who seemed unconcerned with him. He called out to the man, who opened his door and walked around to the front of the vehicle.

Djaliz stared down his gunsight . . . at Colonel Ahmed, supreme commander of the Combined Air Force. Djaliz quickly holstered his weapon. Ahmed ignored him in his rush to the passenger door. When he opened it, Djaliz could see the form of the Khalib himself, Mohammed al-Sihoud. He at least had enough presence of mind to snap to attention, eyes focused on the horizon, but from the corner of his eyes he could see that the Khalib was in bad shape.

"*Help* me with him, airman," Ahmed ordered.

The two men grabbed the arms of the Khalib, who seemed conscious but weak, dazed.

"Sir, what happened?"

Ahmed shook his head, hauling the general to the ladder.

"Get him in the back seat," Ahmed said when they had reached the ladder. "General, can you climb?"

"I think so." The airman helped him up the steep ladder.

Ahmed returned to the U–10, found a clipboard with a scrap of paper and scrawled on it. He looked it over, checked his watch and continued writing, finally folding the paper in two, then again. He hurried over to the jet. Djaliz had gotten Sihoud into the rear seat and was strapping him in, putting on his flight helmet and strapping on the oxygen mask. He stepped back down the ladder and faced Colonel Ahmed.

The colonel looked Djaliz over for a moment, then handed him the piece of paper.

"You know where the Quchara Communication Base is?"

"Twenty kilometers on Highway 2, north, sir."

"Take the U–10 and get to the base as fast as the truck can go. Have them transmit that immediately on the VLF set—very low frequency. Can you remember that? Very low frequency."

"But, sir, why will they do that on my say so? I'm an airman—"

Ahmed reached into his tunic and pulled a chain around his neck until it broke. He handed the bar-coded identification card to the airman.

"Give them that. If they have doubts call me on the airborne UHF frequency of the day. Have you got all that?"

Djaliz stood at attention and saluted.

Ahmed was already four steps up the ladder. Djaliz watched as the colonel strapped on the helmet, lowered the canopy and waved down at him. Djaliz ran for the wheel chocks, pulled them both out and ran clear of the jet. As he looked up Ahmed had already taken the turbines to half-thrust and was thundering down the taxiway to the end of the runway. Less than a minute later the jets roared on full afterburner as the colonel kicked the aircraft up to full power. The takeoff run took only seconds, the Firestar's nose pointed skyward, blasting off the runway, rising nearly vertically into the sky. Soon all Djaliz could see were the twin flames coming from its tailpipes, and then they vanished in the darkness.

Djaliz seemed to wake up from a dream then, the paper soaked with the sweat of his hands. He unfolded it and read the colonel's hurried scrawl.

TO CNF SUBMARINE HEGIRA: BY THE ORDERS OF THE KHALIB, SURFACE AT DAWN AT NORTH 35 DEGREES/EAST 30 DEGREES AND PREPARE TO RESCUE TWO SURVIVORS. GOD IS GREAT. COLONEL R. AHMED SENDS.

4

Thursday, 26 December

Eastern Mediterranean Basin

The predawn darkness shrouded the calm waters of the Mediterranean, the dim starlight barely able to separate the dark water from the black sky on the horizon. Three hours later the water would be a sapphire blue, shimmering and beautiful and clear, but now the water was black and forbidding. The water was filled with sound, the central and western basins always busy with commercial traffic, even now that the nations of the northern coast found themselves at war with those on the south. If anything, the war had accelerated the flow of freighters and tankers in and out of Gibraltar, the ships filling the sea for miles with the noises of their cavitating screws. The noise of the hundreds of ships competed with the marine life that inhabited the warm water. Clicking of shrimp, chattering of dolphins, moaning of whales all filled the underwater with sound waves.

There in the wash of noise, under 100 meters of water, a silent ghost passed through a school of shrimp, the startled fish clicking loudly. The shape of the intruder was sleek and long, starting with an elongated elipsoidal nose, a cigar-shaped twelve-meter-diameter cylinder following, the shape seventy-five meters long, tapering to a point. In the middle, a tall fin towered over the cigar body, the rear of the fin angled down to the cigar, the dorsal fin of an exotic fish. At the tapered end of the body was a set of tail fins; the tail planes were attached to the hull at an angle, forming an X-shape. The underwater vessel continued swimming east, gliding silently through the water.

The soundless shape was the Combined Naval Force submarine *Hegira*. Inside the envelope of smooth outer steel were twenty-one torpedo tubes, a cramped pressure hull, and a large oil-enclosed alternating current motor driving the half-hull-diameter propulsor impeller. The pressure hull was a cylinder half the length of the ship, beginning just forward of the fin and ending five meters forward of the X-tail rudder, the cylinder only thirty-eight meters long, of which only the forward thirteen meters were habitable by men, the remainder taken up by modular machinery compartments. The aft compartment was the battery and diesel module; forward were the reactor module and steam-power module. None of these aft modules could be entered when the ship was submerged. The machinery spun and churned under computer control.

The forward module, designed for the crew, was the command module, three decks high. The lower deck was mostly taken up by the electronic equipment of the Second Captain system but had a row of tight bunks on the port bulkhead. The middle level was split into four staterooms, a messroom, and a small galley and head. The upper deck was occupied by ship-control functions in a large open control room, a computer room, a radio room, and two additional rooms on the forward elliptical head of the pressure vessel. The smaller forward room was the first officer's stateroom. The second was the captain's stateroom, an L-shaped space, the corner of the room formed by the head between the captain's and first officer's staterooms.

At the head of the conference table in the captain's stateroom, a man frowned down at a large spread of ship's blueprints, the roll of drawings kept flat by plates and glasses. The man was slim, middle-aged, dark-skinned, gray-haired, with an air of authority. And at this instant, of frustration.

Commander Abbas Alai Sharef tried a bite of his food but found it tasteless as it had been all day. He pushed his plate away, crossed his arms and stared at the ship's plans. Finally he leaned on the table and stared at the elevation view of the submarine, looking for an answer until his head began to ache. The task before him seemed impossible.

He stretched and glanced around at the room, not seeing it as claustrophobically cramped but as a haven from the demands of the ship. The stateroom's L-shape was little more than five meters long. The port side was partially unusable because of the curvature of the hull. Where the hull came down in its slow incline there was a cubbyhole containing his bunk and his desk. At the end of the desk was a computer module with dual display screens and a keyboard section with function keys. The module was part of the Second Captain system, a computer that controlled and monitored all functions of the automated submarine, a system that caused Sharef a measure of ambivalence. Next to the Second Captain console a green-shaded lamp on the desk spread a warm light over the papers strewn over its large wooden surface.

The aft wall of the room was covered with a Persian rug, its pattern of an intricacy that could hold a visitor's glance. The rug had been a gift from Sharef's mother, given to him the year she died. Sharef spent a moment looking at it, searching for the intentional flaw sewn in, the flaw inserted to acknowledge that human perfection was an insult to Allah. But as usual, Sharef was unable to find the flaw. Beneath the rug, the conference table took up much of the room, the table able to seat eight men. At the end of the table on the centerline wall was a stern portrait of Mohammed al-Sihoud. Sharef barely noticed it; the frown on his dark face appeared, then vanished quickly. The forward starboard corner of the room was taken up by the walls surrounding the shared head, doors opening into it from both the captain's stateroom and the first officer's.

Sharef returned to the ship's plans, looking for an answer, returning to the nonanswer that the mission was impossible. He ran his fingers through hair so gray as to be almost silver, most traces of the jet black it had been five years before gone, the gray continuing in the color of his thick mustache. He was forty-five years old, young to be one of the highest-ranking naval officers in the Combined Naval Force. He was of medium height, although his military carriage and muscled frame gave a taller impression. His cheek and throat bore a long scar, resembling a sabre wound, from his days in the Iranian navy. The wound had opened in his face and neck when the superstructure of the Mark 5 frigate *Sahand* had exploded a moment after the American missile struck it. Sharef had met a surgeon in Japan who offered to make the scar disappear, but Sharef had declined, the mark reminding him of lost shipmates and of the innocent days when he had thought himself invincible. The sinking of the *Sahand* seemed to be a fence across his life, separating his youth from his cynical middle age, which arrived early in his thirty-sixth year.

Sharef was usually a calm man, even in crisis. This, he thought, was perhaps the major reason he had been chosen to command this flagship of the Combined Naval Force. He was a quick study, able to grasp a tactical situation immediately, although he seemed blessed with this ability only in naval matters—when it came to understanding people he felt he was often at a loss. And when it came to women, he was completely adrift. More than once he had wondered if that was the reason he had chosen the life of the sea in his youth. Not as an adventure or out of love for it, but as an escape from what custom decreed was a normal life with a wife and children.

As he paced the room he allowed his normally disciplined mind to wander back to the women he had known, the years flashing by rapidly until 1978, when he had been at Oxford, before Iran's revolution. He had felt awkward in England, knowing his dark skin and thick accent had set him apart. But there had been a woman, just a year or two from being a girl, who had made it clear she was attracted to him. So oddly forward, the Western women, *and* so exciting . . . He had felt helpless, driven by his own youth and the freedom of a foreign land, the restraints of Islam far away. But when the Ayatollah came and with him the revolution, Sharef had been forced to make a choice between the beautiful British girl—and the new world she had shown him—and his homeland and culture. He had returned home, his perceived sense of duty stronger than his love for Pamela, and although he still felt the decision had been the right thing to do he still felt the void. He had never seen or heard from her after her letter telling him she was married and moving to the United States.

For a moment Sharef lingered over the forward bulkhead with its photographs of his past ships. On the far left was the Iranian navy frigate *Alvand,* his first ship. That had been before Oxford, before Pamela, before the revolution. Next to it was the picture of the destroyer *Damavand.* For four years after the revolution he had been her navigator. Under the Ayatollah things had been so uncertain that *Damavand* rarely left port. Next there had been the Vosper Mark 5-class frigate *Sahand,* when he had been assigned as first officer at the age of thirty-two. Three years later, in April of 1988, the *Sahand* was at the bottom of the Persian Gulf, blown to pieces by Ronald Reagan's U.S. Navy attack that sank half the Iranian fleet. He saw that as an overreaction to the Iranian boarding of the merchant ships bound for the northern Persian Gulf hauling war materiel to Iraq. The episode had been forgotten by most of the world since it happened at sea far from the television cameras, but Sharef would not forget it. He still wondered if he had any business being alive after what had happened to *Sahand.*

At age thirty-five he had taken command of the Mark 5-class frigate *Alborz,* three years that he looked back on with nostalgia. After several years of shore duty on the United Islamic Front combined staff he had decided that shore duty was not for him. The UIF had acquired a Russian-built Kilo-class diesel-electric submarine, the *K–102,* its image captured in the next photograph. Sharef, a veteran of the surface fleet, had outranked the sub's captain when he reported aboard as the first officer. He had learned the submarine navy's ways quickly, and two years later was selected (ahead of *K–102*'s captain) to command the ex-Russian Victor III nuclear submarine *Tabarzin. Tabarzin*'s photograph had been shot from high over her drydock, the slim and graceful form marred by scaffolds and gangways and temporary platforms. Sharef had enjoyed that first experience with nuclear power, marveling at how well it suited underwater combat. His command tour had gone so well that he was the Combined Naval Force's first choice to go to Japan and receive the Destiny-class submarine *Hegira*.

The picture of *Hegira* had been taken as the ship ran on the surface at full speed, the bow wave smashing over the leading edge of the fin, the flag of the UIF flying from a tall mast. Sharef himself was recognizable on top of the fin in the bridge, driving his new ship from the shipyard, the sea ahead of him, the year in Japan behind him. And behind him as well the woman he had met there, the nuclear engineer named Yashiko Una, who had been in charge of the crew's propulsion plant training. And just as duty had called him away from Oxford and Pamela, it now called him away from Yashiko.

A knock came at the door. It would be Abu-i-Wafa, the weapon-test director, wanting the answer to the impossible. As Sharef stepped to the stateroom door, an idea did occur, an idea that seemed stupid and risky but *might* answer Abu's requirements. And so dangerous that it might cost the UIF the submarine.

The man standing at the door was not Abu, but Sub.-Lt. Omar al-Maari, one of the junior officers, handing Sharef a message clipboard. He read the odd message from Ahmed, Khalib Sihoud's aide. What did he mean about rescuing two survivors. Survivors of *what?*

Sharef left his stateroom and walked to the control room, shaking his head.

Arlington, Virginia
Pentagon E-Ring
U.S. Navy Flag Plot

Admiral Richard Donchez was perhaps only the second Chief of Naval Operations in navy history ever to dirty his hands with the details of combat operations. In the last five years the office of the number-one admiral in the navy had been changed from an administrative command to an operational billet. Which was fortunate for the U.S. Navy, because Dick Donchez would not have taken the post unless it allowed him to be more of a tactician than a paper pusher. It had also been beneficial to the navy and to the course of the war with the United Islamic Front. The most recent example of this was his design of Operation *Early Retirement,* the mission to assassinate Sihoud and, if successful, end the war early.

Donchez was tall, and although in his sixtieth year, he swore he was losing an inch of height each time he checked the mirror. In fact, the only discernible signs of age were his cueball baldness, the bushiness of his gray brows, and his *slightly* diminished height. But Donchez's mind was sharper than it had ever been. He was dressed now in his service dress-blue uniform, the sleeves heavy with gleaming gold, the wide band nearest the end of the sleeve, three slim bands running up almost to his elbow, the sharp pointed star presiding over the stripes. Over his left breast pocket six rows of colored ribbons climbed toward his shoulder, the gold submarine pin above them. The pin resembled an airman's wings, but on closer examination the wings were scaly fish with curving tails pointed outward, the odd heads facing an old-fashioned diesel submarine plowing through rough seas. The pin was solid gold, a gift from his old Annapolis roommate's widow, given him when he had first been promoted to flag rank.

Donchez stood before one of the plot walls of the room, the electronic plot showing the Mediterranean, the colors and lines and dots each signifying the deployment of his forces. Donchez's right hand was shoved into his coat pocket, his left fist clutching the long Havana cigar, the end glowing, the smoke rising to the overhead where the red NO SMOKING sign was bolted into the wall. Alongside Donchez were a group of senior officers, admirals in charge of the operational groups: Adm. Kenny McKeigh, the commander in chief of the Atlantic naval forces; Adm. John Traeps, commander in chief of the Mediterranean naval forces; Adm. Dee Watson, the vice CNO for operations. Also Donchez's aide, a plump and rumpled captain from naval intelligence named Fred Rummel.

Donchez puffed the Havana as Rummel continued his briefing.

". . . about an hour after the explosion of the Javelins a Firestar fighter took off from the Sunni Air Base in Ashkhabad and headed west. Vector analysis shows it heading for the Med. Of course we've seen hundreds of Firestar sorties over the last few days but this particular flight, coming so soon after the attack and leaving from Ashkhabad itself, leads us to believe that it may be connected with someone in the command structure."

"How long ago?" Donchez said.

"Twenty-five minutes."

"What are we doing about it?"

John Traeps answered for his Med forces. He gestured to the Med plot while he spoke. "Sir, the USS *Reagan* carrier task force is off of Tripoli, Libya. She scrambled two F–14s about ten minutes ago. They should be intercepting the Firestar in the next half hour, as long as we can keep tracking it. The task force commander has authorized shooting it down."

"No," Donchez said quietly, still looking at the tip of his cigar.

"Excuse me, sir?"

"Don't shoot it down. If we do we'll never know who the hell got out of Ashkhabad."

"Aye, aye, sir, but how can we—"

"Instead of intercepting, have the fighters tail the Firestar and force it down."

The briefing broke up. Donchez left the room and walked rapidly to his office suite, Rummel and vice CNO for operations Dee Watson following. Watson was, as he himself proclaimed, the ugliest and most obnoxious admiral in the fleet; although he was hard to take, someone Donchez might not have chosen for his number-two man, he was savvy and had a penetrating grasp of tactics and a detailed understanding of special warfare. A former Aegis-class cruiser commander, Watson was the only surface-warfare officer in Donchez's inner circle, the remainder predominantly aviation types or submariners. No one spoke until they were in the special-compartmented-information-facility portion of the office.

"Are you thinking what I'm thinking, sir?" Rummel asked Donchez.

Donchez nodded, stubbing out the cigar in the ash tray.

"Sihoud."

"Son of a bitch got past us," Watson said.

"We'll know in the next hour, anyway," Donchez said, pulling out a fresh Havana and flicking his lighter at its tip.

"I think I'll go on back to flag plot, see what's shakin'," Watson said in his cracker accent. "By your leave, sir."

"I'll be down as soon as we have something, Dee."

Donchez smoked in silence for a moment, then looked at Rummel.

"Think I should call General Barczynski?"

"Are you coming down with something, sir?"

Donchez chuckled. "Just testing."

"Maybe we should have shot the Firestar down after all, sir."

"Firestars aren't up to the task against F–14 Tomcats. The flyboys will bring Sihoud to us, now that the goddamned SEALs screwed up."

"Ah, hell, Admiral, maybe this Firestar is just some panicky lieutenant trying to get away from our missiles."

"We can only hope."

Eastern Mediterranean

The Firestar had flown without incident for almost an hour, cruising at twelve kilometers altitude at one and a half times the speed of sound.

During the trip Ahmed let the computer fly the aircraft, content to monitor the systems, keeping a careful eye on navigation and the electronic sensors that guarded against incoming missiles and radars. Other than the normal surface-and air-search radars at sea in the Med and in the southern shores of Greece, there had been no unusual activity. Ahmed had even begun to wonder if it were perhaps too quiet. Occasionally he selected his onboard monitor to the rear-facing camera, checking General Sihoud. The Khalib had slept most of the trip, his flight helmet against the canopy. The Firestar had skirted Israeli territories to the north and crossed over Kassab and the dark waters of the Mediterranean before Sihoud awoke.

The general tapped on the top of Ahmed's seat, trying to get his attention.

"Go ahead and speak into the oxygen mask, General. It has a voice-activated intercom."

"Where are we?" Sihoud asked, his voice rasping and weak.

"How do you feel, sir? If you're thirsty there's an insulated bottle under the right console."

Sihoud fumbled for the bottle. Ahmed watched the Khalib on his monitor, seeing how tentatively he moved. He wondered if the general would be strong enough to make it to the submarine—the only way other than a high-risk ditching to get to the sub would be to bail out at the lowest speed and altitude the jet could fly, as near the surfaced submarine as possible. And bailing out, taking a parachute's g-forces, hitting the water and swimming to a submarine were not easily done by sick men. Ahmed bit his lip.

"I think I need to see a doctor, Rakish. As soon as we land." Sihoud coughed violently.

"General, we will not be landing. This is the last flight for this aircraft. We will be abandoning it over the sea. The *Hegira* will be waiting for us."

"*What?* What are we doing?"

"Sir, for the next two weeks the war will be fought without you. I have already raised Generals Ihaffe, Ramadan, and Ben Abbas. They all reported they had explicit instructions from you on the conduct of the campaigns in North Africa, the Sinai, and southern Iran. I told them that the primary objective is not to counterattack but to hold on for the seven to ten days it will take us to assemble the Scorpion missile and deliver it to its target."

"You told them about the Scorpion on a radio circuit, Ahmed?"

"No, Khalib. I only told them to hold on and give us the time. They do not need to know about the Scorpion, not yet. The fewer who know, the less chance of compromising the surprise of this operation. I do not want the Americans waiting for us."

"The generals are smart and good fighters, but they are not coordinated without me, Rakish. I must return to the field for our defense. I need to—"

"Sir, wherever you are, the eyes of our enemies are watching, and they will continue to send their squads to kill you. If you believe that the armies are lost without you for fourteen days, imagine the war without you forever. This is how *they* think, General, and they are not stupid. The attack on the main bunker was not just a missile attack." Ahmed felt he had to say the next part, not out of pride but to convince the Khalib that the Coalition was after his head. "There were troops, dozens of them, dropped by parachute, probably from the airplane that we detected. We found their mobile vehicles in the desert. They penetrated the bunker perimeter and murdered our security troops. If the missiles didn't kill you, the assassins would. There is nowhere that you are safe, General, not until the Scorpions are on their way. Until then you will do best by going aboard the *Hegira* and waiting. And while you wait you will get your strength back and recover from your wounds."

Ahmed waited for Sihoud to digest his words, worried that the Khalib would veto the plan—for that matter, so would he had he sat in Sihoud's place.

But there was no answer from the aft seat.

Lt. Joe Galvin flipped through the tactical attack plan binder, a stenopad-sized flip chart strapped to his thigh, and searched through the alphanumeric codes, knowing that he'd just been screwed.

The letters *sierra delta foxtrot* had been transmitted by the air boss just a few seconds before, and Galvin knew the code transmission meant their mission was being changed. For the tenth time in this war, Galvin had felt like turning off the radio after his F–14 Tomcat fighter lifted off the deck of the *Reagan;* at least that way the brass would not be able to redirect his missions in flight. But as soon as the thought had formed Galvin stifled it. What good was a fighter if it couldn't be redirected in mid-flight—little better than a mindless bullet. And if fighter pilots wanted to be replaced by robotic cruise missiles, they could all keep thinking like Galvin had been before.

Finally the letters SDF stared up at him from the tactical plan page, large block letters defining the code as CLOSE ON BOGEY, ESTABLISH CONTACT, AND FORCE TO LAND. WEAPON RELEASE PROHIBITED EXCEPT IN RESPONSE TO HOSTILE FIRE.

"Well, Giraffe, looks like a small change in our rules of engagement," Galvin called.

"Let me guess," the radar intercept officer called on Galvin's headset. "Return to the ship and forget about it."

Galvin was almost able to see the sour look on his RIO's face. Eugene

Fredericks, radio handle GIRAFFE, was a sarcastic, witty soul, tall and gawky, earning him his less-than-macho moniker; it seemed even worse in contrast to Galvin's own handle, TAILBACK, taken from his days on the 1988 Army-kicking Annapolis team.

"Worse," Galvin replied. "We're ordered to close on the guy and force him to land."

"Yeah, right. I see what you mean. What keeps the SOB from shooting at us?"

"Absolute fear of the United States Navy?"

"We're dead."

"Give me an intercept vector and call it out to Vinny."

"Roger. We'll take his seven o'clock, Vinny his five."

Ahmed looked to the east, knowing dawn was coming, minutes away. The rendezvous point was less than twenty minutes ahead. He had started to think about the message to the *Hegira,* wondering if the young airman had gotten the transmission through, and if he did, if the submarine's captain received it and believed it. The alarm indicator sounded sudden and shrill in the whisper-quiet cockpit.

The central video screen dropped the images of the navigation display and flashed up a tactical view of the Firestar in screen-center with two approaching hostile aircraft astern. Four flashing screen annunciators proclaimed REAR FACING N16 MISSILES ARMED. The range to the incoming aircraft was fifty kilometers, close but in range of the N16 radar-homing antiair missiles. The computer was seconds away from firing the missiles when Ahmed overrode the command.

There were times when computers were much too simple and linear, he thought. The tactical screen had analyzed the incoming radars and shown them to be coming from F–14s, the American fighters called Tomcats. Tomcats were old, the first models designed in the 1970s. The Shah of Iran had bought several dozen for the modernization of his squadrons, and Ahmed, then a captain, had flown the jet for a year before the revolution. It was big and heavy, designed for the demanding duties of carrier landings for the U.S. Navy. As an air force jet it was at best a compromise. Against a computer-controlled Firestar, it was barely a threat—at least against a healthy well-maintained Firestar that didn't throw turbine blades in the middle of an encounter, blowing itself out of the air before an enemy missile got anywhere close.

The critical fact was that these jets were *navy* aircraft, not air force Eagles flying out of Cyprus but carrier-based fighters, and the only carrier in the Mediterranean at the moment was the *Reagan* off Libya, over 2,000 kilometers west. And that made no sense. Ahmed expected the jets to have fired their medium-range air-to-air missiles by now, and the ships of the carrier task force should have fired long-range surface-to-air

missiles long ago. Further, the F–14s should have approached from
ahead, or from the north or south. For them to come in from *behind* him
was not a missile-attack tactic but a dogfighting tactic. They had wasted
valuable time in this maneuver, time they would not have taken if they
were intent on downing the Firestar.

Ahmed overrode the computer's impulse to fire the rear-facing N16
missiles. In the moment before he reached a conclusion he felt a gnaw-
ing annoyance that the Firestar had been detected at all by the Americans. The electronic stealth systems had failed, or the Americans had
developed a countermeasure. But he was certain that there was no
countermeasure for the electronic-warfare pod slung under the
Firestar's nose.

The tactical display updated, basing its guesses on intercepted radar
signals from the F–14s. The jets were closing steadily, edging forward
cautiously instead of screaming in at him. Ahmed considered one last
time the idea of attacking the fighters, then dismissed it. More jets
would come from the carrier, as well as a score of missiles, and if the
Firestar's detection-avoidance systems had failed, the Americans could
find him and blow him out of the sky by the application of overwhelming
force and numbers—he and Sihoud were only one jet against an entire
carrier full of F–14s. And this close to the rendezvous point, he had no
time for taking on the Americans.

The F–14s were now thirty kilometers astern. Ahmed's engines were
throttled down to sixty percent power, his speed lowered from the maximum to time their arrival at the rendezvous point. He could spool up
the turbines and outrun the fighters, but that would only delay the confrontation. Delay would help if he could get to the rendezvous point
with the F–14s far behind.

But he *knew* what they were doing. They were going to try to force
him and Sihoud down to see who they were, perhaps take them into
captivity. It had to be, he saw the overwhelming logic of it. He too would
have made such a decision if he had been the American commander.
And there would be no way to abandon the Firestar with the F–14s
watching. He might make it to the water, but the *Hegira* would be seen.

So shoot them, he thought. *We're only fifteen minutes from the rendezvous point.* A competing voice, a stronger and more rational one, spoke
. . . *there are more waiting behind these. Shoot these and five more will
come, and ten more, until they have killed the Khalib or have him in
chains.* The survival of the Union was at stake. Ahmed bit his lip and
waited. When the jets were within ten kilometers, he had made a decision.

The electronic-warfare pod. The untested Japanese unit that promised so much but held such great risk. Ahmed wasted no more time and
energized the pod's circuits and waited as the liquid helium refrigeration

unit surrounding the superconducting energy storage coil cooled down to operating temperature. The computer reported the successful cool-down and asked to take command of the port jet engine. Ahmed acknowledged the computer request and allowed the machine to take one of the Firestar's engines off-line, the starboard jet throttling up to compensate. The port jet came up to full power, its turbine no longer providing the jet with thrust but spinning an auxiliary power turbine designed only to supply power to the energy-storage coil of the electronic-warfare pod. It would take several minutes to charge the pod, agonizing minutes for Ahmed, who still wanted to fire the missiles at the incoming enemies.

If the EW pod worked, the F–14s would be destroyed, their old-fashioned semiconductor chips melted into useless butter. Unfortunately, the unit might also destroy the Firestar, which would then fall into the sea a hundred kilometers short of the rendezvous point, and the Khalib would die or be taken prisoner.

The port engine roared at full throttle, all its tremendous power channeled into the EW pod's energy coil, the voltage building up to unprecedented levels. Ahmed waited, knowing the unit might not wait for his command but might unleash its energy in an unrestrained explosion, the voltage ripping out from a coil leak and blowing the Firestar apart.

The rendezvous point was now five minutes away, short in timespan when still above the sound barrier, but more than 100 kilometers over the horizon, a very long swim. And now the American F–14s drew up on the Firestar's wingtips as dawn broke over the eastern Mediterranean.

5

THURSDAY, 26 DECEMBER

Eastern Mediterranean

Commodore Sharef pressed his eye to the eyepiece of the periscope as the *Hegira* ascended toward the surface from her cruising depth of 300 meters. As the cold rubber shroud of the eyepiece contacted the skin of his eye, the surrounding control room vanished, replaced with blackness, not a coal blackness but a light twilight darkness, just a shade brighter than midnight, just light enough so that Sharef thought he could see the crosshairs of the periscope reticle against the dark view. His deep-cushioned lumbar-supported periscope control seat tilted back as the deck of the ship angled upward, climbing toward the danger of the surface. He rotated his periscope view directly upward, searching for the bottom of the waves.

"One hundred meters, Commodore. All hull arrays report surface contacts distant." The deck officer, Commander Omar Tawkidi, reported from the sensor control area of the room, the aft starboard corner. That corner's Second Captain video screens displayed the noises, directions, and frequencies detected on the large-area hull arrays—the raw data—as well as the Second Captain's analyzed guesses about the meanings of the sounds and the relationships of the sound sources to the *Hegira*. There were at that moment ten surface ships being tracked by the hull array sonars, all of them distant, the closest farther than forty-four miles to the west.

High above, the water began to grow lighter. As it did, Sharef commanded the view to rotate downward so that he peered out at a forty-five-degree angle from the vertical and began rotating the periscope control seat with a silent servomotor. Soon he could see the waves high above, the large silvery bottom flanks of them showing the calm weather above. As the waves moved closer Sharef rotated the periscope seat faster while turning his view flatter. There were no shadows from hulls not detected by the hull arrays. Sharef's view broke through the waves and cleared while the deck beneath him leveled out.

"Commodore, depth twenty-seven meters," Tawkidi announced.

"Very good, Deck Officer."

For several minutes Sharef sat at the periscope control seat, rotating it in slow circles, concentrating on the surrounding sea, still wondering what Colonel Ahmed's message meant. The sea was a deep shimmering blue, the sky streaked with wisps of clouds. The sun had just climbed over the horizon where dark Mediterranean met bleached sky. The "survivors" should be there. Tawkidi, the navigator, had pronounced them within 500 meters of the rendezvous point.

Sharef's orders were to surface, but surfacing violated every instinct. All a submarine possessed for tactical advantage was the blessed quality of being invisible. To surface meant to relinquish the cover of the depths and emerge where every surface-search radar and airborne patrol craft could see him, where satellite spy-eyes would gobble up imagery of his presence, compromising his mission—a mission he had been told was crucial to the survival of the Islamic Front. And for what? To find a boat cast adrift or a yacht whose *survivors* would be here supposedly waiting for him.

And yet the orders, orders from the Khalib himself, had been explicit. Surface at dawn. The mission, after all, was the Khalib's, and the Khalib could order this ship to do anything it was capable of. And surfacing was possible, if unwise. And the orders, if they were authentic, had not come directly from the Khalib with his usual authentication sentence but had been sent in his name by his chief of staff, an air force officer, Rakish Ahmed. And Sharef knew what Ahmed was capable of doing to win the war his way. But then, if the message had been genuine, sent in the heat of an emergency, by not surfacing Sharef might be endangering a plan vital to Islamic security, hard as that was to imagine.

For some moments Sharef's instincts did battle with his sense of duty. Duty won out. He looked again at the sea for a sign that indicated he should surface, and saw only the sea and the sky.

"Deck Officer, surface the ship. Stop the engine."

"Very good, Commodore. Ship control—"

"Surfacing now," the operator at the ship-control station called.

Sharef's view of the surface expanded as the submarine ascended. Beneath his periscope view the curving fin emerged from the sea in a wash of foam and spray, the cylindrical hull following. The ship slowed from its dead-slow-ahead crawl and rocked gently, seemingly without purpose, in the waves.

Sharef ordered the ship-control team to the surface-control space on top of the fin, handing the periscope over to the sensor-control officer, then hurried to the ladder to the surface-control space. The hatch was opened, the panels in the fin laid aside, and morning sunlight flashed against the side of the cubbyhole as Sharef climbed into the sea air. He sucked in the smell, glad in spite of the tactical stupidity of surfacing. He looked out over the gentle waves and wondered how long he should wait before abandoning this fool's errand. A chart of the area appeared in his mind, memorized, and he examined it, thinking of how to clear the area so that his departure course could not be determined by the watching satellites. Perhaps he could pretend a malfunction, begin to head back east toward port at Kassab and after a few moments resubmerge, continue heading east for a few minutes, then back in the cloak of the sea's depths, turn back to the west and run for Gibraltar. He even began to order one of the officers to get a harness and walk out on the deck as if examining or repairing something, just to look good for the satellites.

He had turned to Tawkidi to make the order when the distant rolling thunder came from the sky. Sharef raised his binoculars and tried to find the sound, but the sky looked empty. He continued to search the sky for the source of the sound. Nothing. He checked his wristwatch and wondered if the ASW forces of the Coalition would soon come to sink the sub, now that they had surrendered their only true advantage—stealth. He told himself he would give Colonel Ahmed an hour. After that he would resubmerge and continue the mission.

The skies were silent, the sea empty. If the mission ended as it started, it would truly be a failure.

Ahmed looked out his canopy at the F–14 Tomcat fighter on his port wing. In the growing light of the morning the jet's markings were clear. On the gray fuselage under the high delta wing were block letters spelling NAVY. At the nose a star was framed in a circle with horizontal stripes on either side. The twin tails were painted black with a white skull over two crossed bones, the letters VF–69 beneath the emblem. The wings were loaded with missiles. In the Tomcat's canopy the pilot in the front seat pointed over at Ahmed, then at himself, his intentions unmistakable: *follow me.* Ahmed glanced out to the starboard wing and saw an identical Tomcat. As he watched, the second jet slowed and faded back until he was a hundred meters directly behind Ahmed's Firestar. That maneuver was also understood—*one false move and the rear F–14 fires his cannons.*

The pilot on the port wing waved again, the gesture the indication that the three-jet formation was to turn. The F–14 banked over into a gentle turn to the left. Ahmed followed until the screen display showed that they were now headed to the east. Toward Cyprus. Undoubtedly to an airfield on the island, where he and Sihoud would be taken prisoner. Somewhere over the western horizon a nuclear submarine would be surfacing, the captain wondering what had happened to them. On the central status screen the words flashed ELECTRONIC WARFARE POD POWER STORAGE 85%. One last time Ahmed wondered about fighting the Tomcats, but by then the rear F–14 was too close for the N16 missile to get a hit. Ahmed began to regret his earlier impulse not to fight the American jets—if he had they would be over the *Hegira* by now. He was committed to using the electronic-warfare pod but there was a better than even chance that the pod would cripple all three jets, tumbling Ahmed and Sihoud into the sea. One thing was certain, that death would be better than capture. Ahmed waited the endless minutes while the planned rendezvous point with the *Hegira* grew distant behind them, the port jet engine still whining shrilly as it charged the EW pod's storage coil.

The escorting Tomcat on the port wing began to descend to a lower altitude. Ahmed followed, his altimeter display numerals rolling down as the Firestar dived. Sihoud, quiet up till then, woke up, startled by the closeness of the F–14s and the unexpected position of the sun. The center console flashed background colors rapidly while announcing EW POD ARMED. RELEASE COUNTDOWN SEQUENCE ESTABLISHED: SECONDS—10.

The numbers on the screen slowly counted down until they reached zero, and with scarcely a sound the EW pod detached from the Firestar's nose and plummeted to the sea below. Ahmed took one last look at the instrument console and tightened his grip on the control stick.

Joe Galvin glanced over at the Firestar fighter, a nagging feeling that this had been too easy, that the pilot of the UIF jet should be fighting back. A photograph flashed in his mind, the old *Newsweek* glossy of the Iraqis lined up by the dozens, surrendering to the U.S. Army three days into the Persian Gulf's ground war. It seemed the propaganda about the Muslims fighting to the death was often rhetoric. In any case the pilot in the Firestar was like the Iraqis, no doubt a scared second lieutenant flying a piece of machinery he could not really understand. When the Firestar landed at the Nicosia airfield, air force technicians would take it apart to the last bolt, analyze every printed circuit, every line of code written in the hard drive of the computer. The pilots would be detained and questioned, then shipped to a POW compound in Sardinia for the rest of the war. For these Muslim pilots the war was about to end—all they had to do was lower the landing gear, put out the flaps, and touch down on the Coalition airfield.

Galvin's mind was already envisioning the day of liberty in Nicosia, wondering what the women were like there.

He looked down into the cockpit to check his altitude for the approach vector to Nicosia, and so did not see the pod dropping from the nose of the Firestar.

The pod fell away from the Firestar and counted seconds. It had been fed the initial altitude by the Firestar's computer and was careful not to fall so far that it hit the surface of the ocean before doing its work. Once the Firestar above and ahead was outside the preset minimum distance, the relay contacts closed in the controller of the pod. The contacts completed a circuit that engaged the high-voltage output-breaker, an oil-enclosed heavy-duty casing with two contact hammers, each the size of a human fist. The hammers, loaded by high-tension springs, slammed into the bus bars of the high-voltage direct-current circuit, linking the dormant energy of the helium-cooled superconducting coil to the oscillators and the transmitter antennae. The current flowed from the ultrahigh-voltage coil, changed from a DC current to AC in the heavy-duty oscillators, and cascaded to the transmitters, which broadcast the resulting electromagnetic energy out into space.

The arrangement was simple, the only new element the coil and the ability to store such a huge amount of energy in so small a package, and then to release it all at once to components strong enough to accept it. The pod was no more complicated than a radio transmitter, in fact sharing many of the same submodules, and so similar in function that it could be considered a radio transmitter of a sort. The difference was in its construction—there were no electronics. The workings of the pod were either fiber optics, as in the wiring of the Firestar, or were done with pre-vacuum-tube technology using magamps, large iron cores with copper wire wrapped around primary and secondary transformer ends. There were no transistors, no semiconductors, no integrated circuits, no microprocessors, not even any magnetic-tape drives. The pod had no conventional electronics because it was designed as an electronics killer.

The transmissions emanating into the atmosphere from the overworked transmitters had been seen by people decades before, but until the Yokashiba Company in Japan had manufactured the pod, the effects could have been produced only by a nuclear warhead. The American military called the transmissions EMP for electromagnetic pulse, the sudden wave of E-M power emitted immediately after a violent nuclear explosion. EMP had long been the fear of electronics designers, and for good reason—after an EMP anything using electronics would fail to function. Defenses were considered, research done, equipment given shields said to "harden" the electronics, to protect them from EMP, but in the end nothing could defend the Pentagon's machinery against an enemy employing several dozen nuclear warheads in high-altitude air bursts. The final defense against EMP had been the Strategic Defense Initiative—Star Wars. SDI's multibillion price tag had been sold (and bought) as a civilian missile defense, but its true purpose was to guard trillions in Pentagon war machinery from EMP warheads detonated over the skies of the United States, destroying computers, radars, missiles, aircraft, communications, the vital but vulnerable network that linked and moved and protected the country, all the network's nodes and connections built with silicon electronics.

The pod's transmissions continued until the superconducting coil drained its electrical energy, the voltage dropping precipitously until exhausted. The unit shut down and fell into the sea.

The electromagnetic transmissions left the unit in a spherical wave pattern, traveling at the speed of light, taking the merest fractions of a millisecond to reach the three jets flying above.

Lt. Joe Galvin's stick trembled for a moment. He looked down at his panel and watched every light and indicator wink out, every needle fall to its powered-down position, some failing at the high peg, some at the low peg, some failing in the position at time of failure. Both jet engines flamed out at the same time. The intercom ceased working, which was why he never heard Giraffe's exclamation of anger when the radar screen winked out as well as the missile status panel.

The latest model of the F–14 was built with high-tech electronics, and there had been attempts to harden the circuitry against EMP pulses, but the designers had, in effect, shrugged, knowing hardening circuits meant adding weight. The shielding had been penetrated in the first microsecond of the Firestar's pod's transmission. As had every electronic module in the jet. Every radar, weapon-control circuit, avionic instrument, radio, and computer. All fried to a crisp after five seconds of the electromagnetic onslaught. The engines, controlled by an onboard computer, their fuel injection regulated by powerful microprocessors, no longer had fuel injection, the chips destroyed. Both spun down, leaving the jet without electrical power—the voltage controllers on the generators gone anyway —and without thrust. The designers had never approved of fly-by-wire technology—the Tomcat's control surfaces were moved by hydraulics, and the hydraulics were controlled by aircraft-grade cables linked to the hydraulic control valves. So for the first five seconds after the pod transmission, the F–14 Tomcat inhabited by Lt. Joe "Halfback" Galvin and

Lt. (jg) Eugene "Giraffe" Fredericks continued to fly, flying deaf and dumb and blind, but flying just the same.

In the sixth second after the pulse transmission, the jet—now a thirty-five-ton glider—began to oscillate in roll, pitch and yaw. The control surfaces, although actuated by the powerful man-controlled hydraulics, were computer stabilized. Without computer intervention in the control surfaces, the F–14 would crash into the sea seconds after catapult launch. True, the computer's input was minor, but crucial. Without it, Galvin's flying machine began to vibrate, even as he aimed the jet for the sea in a desperate attempt to keep air flowing over the wings now that there was no longer any power.

Galvin attempted to correct the oscillation, reversing the stick to the right as the jet banked left, then as the overcorrection registered he tried to reverse the bank to the left again. At the same time the nose kept trying to rise and Galvin fought it with steady downforce on the stick. The nose put in its request for attention, the jet swinging to the left, requiring right rudder, then swinging to the right.

Galvin was tasting a magnum dose of adrenaline; he was young, in shape, highly trained, and the recipient of millions of dollars of flight time. The simulators at Pensacola had flown a simulation of loss of all electronics, not as hairy as this, but even so it was only done so that the students could see how hopeless it would be to stay in the aircraft. Which brought up the so-called Womb Concept in the background of his mind. Just as some televisions could flash up a small box in the corner of the screen, enabling the viewer to watch two television shows at once, Galvin's mind played its own sideshow separate from the main track attempting to control the aircraft.

What the hell had happened to cause such a gross failure of the jet—some kind of missile hit? Couldn't be, the wings and control surfaces still functioned. And what kind of missile flamed out the engines and turned off the power to the avionics? What to do next? The jet had no power, and no attempt at engine restart would work, not without electrical power or electronics. Besides, an attempt to restart the engines would require Galvin to dive for the deck for maximum velocity to windmill the compressors, and that would just kill them sooner. The standard operating procedure for this casualty was to punch out. The plane was obviously uncontrollable. No recovery was possible, and to try to do a water landing with this oscillating control would be suicidal.

So what could he be waiting for? Which was when he thought of the Womb Concept, as described by an appropriately grizzled Marine Corps flight instructor who had bailed out of three jets and consequently would never be promoted above the rank of major. Boy, the major had drawled, there's gonna come a time when you're gonna know your plane's a goner, and when it comes you're gonna cling to that stick like a newborn to his mamma's tit, and do you know why? That aircraft can be falling apart all around you and you're gonna want to stay in the bitch because inside, no matter how bad it gets, you feel comfortable and safe there. You control things there. Outside, you're just a passenger, and more likely some shark's dinner. Inside you're used to being in charge, out there you're a victim. And let me tell you, son, more aviators have died because of the Womb Concept than any other reason. The goddamned fools know they've gotta punch out, the airplane's a total, but what do they do? They stay in the cockpit because it's warm and safe, the womb, and outside it's cold and hard and dangerous. More pilots die from staying in the womb than any other reason, so when your time comes, and it will, just remember: *Get the fuck out.*

The major's lecture seemed to reach something inside. It was either that or he remembered that the hydraulic-control system would be losing pressure any second. Without power to recharge the hydraulic accumulators the hydraulic pressure would eventually decay until Galvin had no control over the aircraft at all and no pushing or pulling on the stick would matter. And with no control, the aircraft would go sideways in the airstream and disintegrate faster than the space shuttle *Challenger.* As fast as he could, Galvin let go of the stick and pulled the D-ring at his crotch up to his waist and tried to count to twenty—at this level of adrenaline-induced excitement, counting to twenty might take only two seconds, maybe three, and it would take a full two seconds for the canopy to blow off and the ejection seat to kick in.

As Galvin waited he wondered whether the ejection mechanism could be knocked out by whatever had paralyzed the jet. Not that it would matter, because if the mechanism stalled or failed, the F–14 would disintegrate within another few seconds anyway. A ring of explosive bolts blew the jet's canopy off, the cockpit suddenly roaring with turbulence. A few heartbeats later Galvin's seat kicked him in the ass, pushing his seat up the rails to the airflow above. A lanyard attached to the seat bottom pulled a pin in a rocket motor, launching the seat into the slipstream. Galvin's eyes were shut tight, but if they had been open he would have seen his F–14 dive toward the sea, tumble out of control, her wings shearing off, the cloud of fuel vapor exploding in a puff, the debris from the jet raining down on the sea.

Galvin tumbled for a moment, his body parting company with the ejection seat. A few moments later his parachute bloomed overhead, the harness tightening over his crotch as the chute inflated. When he opened his eyes, he saw Giraffe's parachute open a few hundred feet below. Off toward the horizon he saw, then heard the explosion as the second F–14 lost control and crashed into the sea—from the absence of parachutes, Vinny and Sully had obviously succumbed to the Womb

Concept. And then he heard something that at first confused, then enraged him.

Jet engines. High overhead, a Firestar fighter, the same bastard they'd been escorting to Cyprus, turned and flew off to the west, as if nothing had happened.

Galvin cursed as the water came up and splashed into his nose as he landed. As he released his parachute, he began to hope he wasn't bleeding and inviting a shark attack.

Ahmed felt the pod detach; he counted off the seconds waiting for it to release its energy, one eye on his central console. For a moment he wondered if the pulse would send the Firestar in a spin to crash into the sea. At that thought the central console blinked out, the display shrinking to the size of a pencil dot, then fading altogether, the dying panel evidence of the death of the onboard computer. Ahmed waited for his aircraft to shut down but the engines purred on, their control circuits still functional. He pulled up slightly on the stick, to see if the control surfaces were still working, and the Firestar began to climb. It was only then that he noticed the Tomcats were no longer with him. He continued climbing, aware that colliding with one of the F–14s would kill him as swiftly as a missile could, and saw the jet that had been his port wingman spiral in a dive toward the sea, vibrating and oscillating as it descended. As he watched, the canopy blew off and two ejection seats flew out. The F–14 banked violently and went broadside into the airflow. The slipstream blew the wings off, broke the plane in half and ignited the fuel in an orange ball of fire that rapidly dispersed in a black cloud. Two parachutes bloomed. Ahmed leveled the jet and flew a circle, trying to find the other F–14. He searched for it, finally seeing it only as a splash and a brief explosion as it crashed into the sea. There was no sign of the pilots of the second jet.

Ahmed glanced at the sun and turned the aircraft to the west and flew on toward the rendezvous point, hoping the submarine captain had waited for them. He had lost perhaps only five minutes, but sea captains were an impatient lot, an independent lot, and sometimes resented or even ignored their orders.

The computer systems were no longer functional, now that the console screen had died—that had remained electronic, and so had perished, but the navigation backup system remained up. It was an old-fashioned set of numbers engraved on plastic wheels and rotated by the nav backup system's calculator from inputs from the geosynchronous navigation satellite over the Mediterranean. By the display readout on the console there was not much more to go to get to the rendezvous point.

Soon he could see the tall fin of the submarine *Hegira,* the ship stopped, waiting for them. Ahmed circled the ship, now at only a few hundred meters altitude, then climbed into the sky in preparation to abandon the Firestar.

"Khalib? Are you awake?"

"I am . . ." Sihoud sounded drugged, barely conscious.

Perhaps that was better, Ahmed thought. He had worried that the trauma of ejecting from the Firestar would be too much for the general, but there was nothing else to do. Ahmed climbed, uncertain of his altitude, flying the aircraft by the seat of his pants now that the computer was gone. He throttled the jet down, losing his forward speed. He had to get the aircraft to be just at stall-point before ejection to lessen the force of the slipstream.

"General, in a few moments we will be ejecting. If you can, try to keep your elbows tucked in tight to your chest and your feet on the footrest. I'll be ejecting the seat for you. All you have to do is ride the parachute down."

There was no answer. Ahmed's mouth felt coppery and his flightsuit felt wet with his sweat. He could not help thinking again that this was a bad idea . . . the ejection could easily kill the general. He needed immediate medical attention and floating for an hour in the Mediterranean was not a way to get it. Ahmed knew he was out of options—then pulled the stick steadily back while reaching for the canopy manual-release handle. He rotated the red handle to the arm position, then all the way to the release position. Thirty explosive bolts fired and the canopy vanished, the cold air of the slipstream blasting into the cockpit, threatening to knock off their oxygen masks and flight helmets. The violence of it smashed Ahmed's helmet against the headrest several times, reminding him to get on with the eject sequence before they were both beaten into comas. Ahmed throttled the engines down to idle and pulled the stick all the way back to his crotch. The jet inclined upward, the forward airspeed decaying. The stick trembled as the jet protested the lack of lift on the wings. At the moment of complete wing-stall, the jet's kinetic energy at a minimum, Ahmed lifted the protective cover off the switch marked REAR SEAT EJECT and popped the toggle switch past its detent, then inward at a right angle. Behind him Sihoud's ejection-seat rocket motor ignited, spraying Ahmed with heat and flames as the general flew out into the atmosphere. The jet then stalled completely, its nose diving for the sea. Ahmed held on long enough to get the aircraft out of the way of Sihoud's descent, then armed the switch between his legs for his own ejection seat. Just before hitting the switch he keyed the jet's turbines to full thrust and felt the acceleration for a moment, then released the stick and snapped the ejection switch.

It happened so fast that Ahmed's senses were overwhelmed. His spine shuddered as the ejection seat blasted into his posterior, the downward g-forces threatening to black him out. The airflow smashed into him, carrying away his oxygen mask and ripping his thigh pad off his flight-suit. The world tumbled around him in a vicious spiral, leaving Ahmed feeling like he was being bounced down a blue tunnel. Finally the turbulence ended, leaving only the wind of free fall. The seat parachute deployed, jerking Ahmed upward. He looked for Sihoud's parachute but couldn't find it. He floated down toward the water.

The end of the ride came, the inviting blue water soaking him. He cut away the seat and found the parcel strapped into the seat cushion and pulled it free, then released the pin. The parcel blew up into an inflated raft, big enough for two men, a small compartment of rations and water tucked into one section of it. When the raft steadied, Ahmed climbed into it and began his search for General Sihoud and the submarine.

6

THURSDAY, 26 DECEMBER

Arlington, Virginia
The Pentagon

The snow had been falling since nightfall Wednesday and was now, in the early hours of a sleepy Thursday morning, piled almost a foot deep. Adm. Richard Donchez's staff car rear door opened and the admiral burst out and took the icy steps to the VIP entrance two at a time. Captain Rummel met him just inside the door. Donchez barely acknowledged him, ignoring the VIP elevator and sprinting up the stairs to the fourth deck. As he hurried he doffed his heavy overcoat and unloaded it on Rummel, his hat next.

Donchez scanned into Flag Plot and entered the room, his first Havana firing up as he joined Admirals Dee Watson and John Traeps at a chart table littered with messages, code publications, and intelligence briefs. At the far wall an enlarged electronic chart glowed dark green, a lighter shade marking the shores of the Mediterranean. Hieroglyphics denoting ships and aircraft and bases cluttered the chart, vectors drawn from some of the symbols, others moving visibly as the chart updated every thirty seconds.

Donchez wasted no time. He stared through the cloud of cigar smoke at vice CNO Watson and commander Mediterranean forces Traeps.

"What is it?" he asked curtly.

"Firestar fighter, Admiral." Watson's jowls sagged almost all the way to his dirty collar, which was soaked with sweat despite the chill of the room. "Son of a bitch swatted away the escort F–14s like they were flies. Both crashed into the sea. We've got no idea why. One crew was recovered. The pilot reported he lost all power and thinks it was something the Firestar did. The SOB kept flying to the west. And that ain't all I show him, John."

Traeps pulled a satellite photograph off the table. His gray hair was in place, his uniform looking like it came from the photo in the Navy Uniform Regulations manual. Traeps's appearance always annoyed Donchez, he looked like one of those absurdly handsome older men that graced the casts of women's soap operas or vitamin-supplement commercials.

"Sir, we got a sniff of something odd with the KH–17 spy platform making a Mediterranean pass at dawn over Cyprus. As soon as we had it the Air Force sent out an RF–4 recon jet to take a closer look." Traeps laid a second photo on the table next to the first.

Donchez puffed while studying the first photo. The high-altitude satellite shot was a grainy God's-eye view of the sea taken shortly after sunrise, judging by the elongated shadow of the object shown in the center of the shot. That object was cigar-shaped, bulbous at one end, tapered on the other. The more telling information was the shadow, which formed the shape of a vertical surface. A fin. A submarine conning tower. Donchez dropped the satellite shot and picked up the second photo, a highly enlarged glossy. The black-and-white shot revealed much more detail than the first photo, this one clearly showing in a side-looking view the shape in the water—the unmistakable shape of a submarine, every detail clear, including the windows set into the conning tower, even the men standing in the cubbyhole at the top of the sloping fin. Donchez looked up, anger creasing his features.

"This submarine. Is it the UIF's acquisition from the Japanese?"

"Yessir," Rummel said. "Destiny-class, type-two nuclear."

"Wasn't this submarine on the target list a week ago? It should have been sunk next to its pier."

"That's right, sir, but there was a spot of bad weather and some higher priority targets. The sub was rescheduled to be hit tomorrow. Bad timing, I'm afraid. She . . . she got underway yesterday."

"Nice catch for naval intelligence," Donchez said bitterly. "I want a report why that little fact escaped our attention yesterday. So what's this got to do with the Firestar?"

Rummel answered. "The jet crashed into the sea about a mile from the submarine. We're assuming a connection between the two events. The submarine was probably detailed to pick up the pilots of the Firestar."

Donchez stared at Rummel. "And who were the men flying in the Firestar?"

"We don't know, sir."

"But you have a pretty good guess for me."

"Conjecture, Admiral."

"Let me in on it, if you would, Fred."

"Sihoud, sir."

"Where did the sub go?"

"Continued heading east toward Kassab, then submerged. We have more photographs if you want to see—"

Donchez shook his head. "What you're telling me, gentlemen, is that for the last twenty-four hours I've been doing my level best to knock out General Sihoud, and the result of the fleet's effort is his escape to a submarine that is now god-knows-where, and Sihoud is not only gone but we can't find him. Is that your conclusion?"

"Afraid that's it, Admiral," Watson said, "but we've got a plan—"

"I'm sure you do, Dee. I'd just love to hear it."

Watson gestured to the wall chart.

"We've got two well-positioned units in the Med to track this Destiny. The carrier air group *Reagan* off Tripoli is escorted by the Improved Los Angeles-class submarine *Phoenix*. We can use her to plug the gap at Gibraltar and make sure the Destiny doesn't make a run for open ocean. Then we've got the *Augusta* off Cyprus in the east. She can scour the Med from east to west. Between the two units we'll pick up the Destiny. I'm expecting her to make port in Kassab or somewhere in North Africa to unload Sihoud to a field command where he can get back to his ground campaign."

"Taking *Phoenix* away from the *Reagan* is risky," Donchez said. "Leaves the whole battle group vulnerable in case the Destiny tries something. Let's not forget, the Destiny may be a third-world export submarine, but it's built by first-rate designers. Some folks think it's as good or better than a *Centurion*. Besides, why the hell would Sihoud run for the Atlantic? That would do nothing for his war effort. He needs to get back into action. Let's leave *Phoenix* where she is."

"Good point, sir," Traeps said. Donchez glared at him, not liking the ass-kissing.

The vice CNO for operations, Admiral Dee Watson, shook his jowls in disagreement. "Admiral, I'm only a skimmer puke," he said, referring to his own operational days as a surface-warfare officer, the surface ships known derisively as "skimmers" by the submarine force. "But if we keep *Phoenix* with the battle group, Barczynski's gonna have more evidence for his ten-billion-dollar-self-licking-ice-cream-cone allegation."

Donchez thought it over. The chairman of the Joint Chiefs of Staff, Gen. Rod Barczynski, was a vigorous opponent of aircraft-carrier battle groups, noting how often carrier aircraft and carrier group ships seemingly had little purpose except to protect the carrier itself, hence the self-licking-ice-cream-cone epithet. It was a distortion, of course, but in the battle for defense dollars plenty of nasty tricks had been played by one service against another. Watson was on-target in bringing up the political result of a tactical decision, yet to hell with politics when there was a war to win. Except there was more here. Sihoud had escaped in a submarine that nobody knew anything about. Its capabilities were matters of conjecture. There was the priority of killing Sihoud, and the possibility of his escape was unacceptable. When weighing the idea of Sihoud's escape against any danger to the aircraft-carrier battle group, it seemed clear that the risk was worth the insurance.

Donchez changed his mind. Sihoud must be caught. "Dee, we'll do it your way. Get *Phoenix* to patrol the far western basin at Gibraltar. Get every antisubmarine warfare aircraft in the Med in the air, the P–3s out of Sigonella and the *Reagan*'s Vikings."

"For now, sir, that leaves most of the Med in the hands of the *Augusta*. *Augusta*'s closest by far to the position of the Destiny class. If we catch it, *Augusta* will be the one to do it." Watson looked unhappy, as if he wanted more firepower.

"Who's in command of *Augusta*?" Donchez asked.

"Rocket Ron Daminski," Watson said, a smirk making an appearance on his face.

"Jesus, that Destiny doesn't stand a chance," Donchez said. "Rocket Ron Daminski . . . is he still the terror of Squadron Seven?"

"The same," Traeps said.

"He's a blunt instrument." Watson said. "I recommend we use him. Daminski's orders should tell him to sink the Destiny submarine on initial contact."

"Tell him to give us a situation report before he puts her on the bottom, just in case. I guess that's it, gentlemen. Get *Augusta* and Daminski in trail of the Destiny. If Rocket can find that sub, it'll be on the bottom fifteen minutes later. Give him some help, John, and get those P–3s and Vikings up in the air looking for the Destiny. Let's detach one of *Reagan*'s ASW frigates. I don't care what it takes, but sink that submarine. Daminski's authorized all force necessary. And have the watch officer call me at home the minute we've got something. You two should get some rest yourselves. You're no good to me dead on your feet."

Central Mediterranean

Commodore Sharef frowned down at the deck from the surface-control space on top of the fin, ten meters above the curving hull. Perhaps under different circumstances he would have been less agitated—it was shaping up into a beautiful morning, the sun rising higher in the winter sky, the deep blue water of the Mediterranean so clear that Sharef could see the hull shape underwater from the elliptical bow forward to the X-tail aft. And the air smelled so *clean* after being locked inside the *Hegira* for the last twenty-four hours. There was something invigorating about being on the surface, even though the surface was the submariner's enemy. As if to remind him of the danger, the sound of distant aircraft engines came whining into his ears. He looked up and saw nothing. Even the binoculars were unable to locate the jet—it must have been a high-altitude transport . . . he hoped.

Sharef shouted down to the deck, his voice unhurried but clipped. "On deck! Get those men below! Now!"

The rescue team had just pulled the second man in from the raft. One of the men was younger and healthy, the second bent and weak, needing help just to stay on his feet on the curving deck. The deckhands and the survivors pushed into the hatch set into the port side of the fin and went down the ladder to the control room below. Sharef leaned over and saw that the last man had secured the hatch fairing in the side of the fin. The only men left in the surface-control space were deck officer Omar Tawkidi and Sharef. Sharef glanced at his watch and ordered Tawkidi below. Sharef lifted the panel doors, the cubbyhole at the top of the fin vanishing, the fin again streamlined and continuous. He checked for loose items, binoculars or flashlights, anything that could bounce or rattle around to cause noise, and finding nothing, lowered himself down into the hatchway and shut it. Twenty steps down at the joining of the fin to the outer hull there was a wide space in the vertical tunnel. Sharef checked the hatch set in the side of the fin and, satisfied it was secure, lowered himself into the command-module access-hatch. When his head was clear he pulled down the hatch to the fin tunnel and spun the hatch wheel, engaging the heavy dogs. He continued down the ladder all the way to the deckplates and operated a hydraulic control lever. The lower hatch, stowed in the overhead, rotated into position below the upper hatch, engaged its own dogs, and rotated into place. The ship was now rigged for submergence.

Sharef stepped though the doorway into the control room and blinked in its dim light, looking for Tawkidi.

"Deck, are you ready to submerge?"

"Yessir."

"Take the ship down to 100 meters, heading east at dead-slow. Continue the heading for ten minutes, then do a computer self-delouse. I want a report on the status of the delouse."

"Yessir. Ship control, dead slow ahead, ship's depth 100 meters."

"Where are the survivors?"

"Your stateroom, sir. Captain al-Kunis is with them."

"Any idea who they were?"

Tawkidi took a deep breath.

"You won't believe it, Commodore. I think you'd better see for yourself."

Sharef hurried out of the control room, down a narrow passageway between the computer space to starboard and the radio room to port to the door to his stateroom. He opened the door and found himself looking into the face of the Sword of Islam, Gen. Mohammed al-Sihoud. A part of Sharef's mind realized he should be snapping to attention, but he simply stood there, looking from Sihoud to his first officer al-Kunis, to the second survivor, Rakish Ahmed.

Eastern Mediterranean
USS *Augusta*

The door opened slowly, the hinges groaning as it came open. The light from the passageway was bright enough to make the eyes ache even under sleep-swollen lids.

"Captain, sir? Noon meal is being served, sir. The officer of the deck thought you might want to go down to the wardroom."

Commander Ron Daminski tossed aside the sweaty sheet and sat up in his narrow rack. The room seemed to swim around him. The chronometer showed it to be 1125 hours Greenwich mean time. As he ran his blunt fingers through his hair he tried to remember when he'd fallen asleep. Ten hours before. He should have felt refreshed, recharged, but instead felt heavy and tired and old. He squinted up at the mess cook.

"Tell the officers to go ahead without me." Daminski knew he was breaking with tradition, but somehow it seemed dishonest for him to be joking and talking with the officers at a meal and then reprimanding them for their inattention to duty a half-hour later. For his entire tour aboard, he had rarely eaten in the wardroom although protocol still demanded that he be invited, in case he changed his mind. He knew inattendance at the meals was taken as a sign of aloofness, perhaps of arrogance, by the junior officers, but that was his style and he was unable and unwilling to change.

"Aye, sir. Would you like me to bring your meal up here for you?"

Daminski yawned, wondering if he looked as bad as he felt. What would Myra think of how he looked, he wondered. God, Myra's letter—where was it? He found it on the scrunched bedclothes and tucked it into the waistband of his gray boxers.

"Huh? Oh, no. I'm not hungry, Seaman March." Just go away, he thought. Let an old man wake up.

The door shut slowly. Daminski stood, his knees popping. At the thought that a shower would help him wake up, he tossed the boxers in the laundry bag and stepped into the cramped head between his stateroom and the XO's. There was a small stall, a phone-booth-sized shower and a tiny sink. The whole affair was covered with sheet stainless steel except for the deck. Daminski walked into the shining shower and turned the water on full cold, convulsing as the spray hit him. He turned it back off and lathered up without water—there were no running water showers on Daminski's ship, not when each drop had to be distilled from seawater and most of it made for the reactor and steam plants, not for hotel usage. Once soapy, he turned on the water again, mixing in the hot, and rinsed off, the force of the water a vigorous massage. He cut the water, now feeling cold in the steel vertical coffin. He wiped the walls down with a squeegee and toweled off.

In the mirror above the sink was the pale sun-deprived face of a man too far past his prime, the wrinkles now deep in his forehead, a forehead that gained more real estate each year as the hair vanished. His graying hair was too long, almost shaggy. He dried it and brushed it straight back. He considered growing his beard back; in the three weeks left in the patrol he could have a well-filled-in beard that would mask his chin's growing jowls. He shook his head. Captains should be cleanshaven, he'd always maintained. He dragged the razor across his face, brushed his teeth with the baking soda in the tube. Back in his stateroom he put on fresh boxers and T-shirt and a new poopysuit, a black coverall with American flag patches sewn on the shoulders, his name over the left pocket, an embroidered gold dolphin emblem above his name. Then his black Reeboks and he was ready for another day at sea.

But he'd been wrong that he'd be cheered up by the shower, he thought as he unzipped the poopysuit and slid Myra's letter against the skin of his chest. The heaviness was still with him, just cleaned of its surface scum but as solid and substantial as ever. There was always one man who could cheer him up—Terry Betts, the torpedoman chief. Betts should have finished lunch by then. Daminski left his stateroom and padded down the steps to the torpedo room two levels below, down in the belly of the forward compartment.

He walked into the aft end of The Room—the crew's name for the space that was cavernous and open when empty of torpedoes and cramped and tight when the ship was loaded out. On this run, *Augusta* was carrying a full load. Daminski walked down the narrow aisle between the weapon racks, running his crooked fingers along the flanks of a Mark 50 torpedo. The weapon was cool and shining in the bright lights of the room, her Astroturf green paint gleaming. Stencilled black letters near the tip read MK 50 MOD ALPHA WARSHOT SER 1178. Back over his shoulder Daminski could hear the sound of a man grunting with exertion as he lifted weights. The torpedo room was one of few spaces available for exercise, though the crew spent much of their spare time in their coffin-sized racks sleeping away the patrol. The more they slept, the shorter the run would seem.

Senior Chief Terry Betts sat on a cushioned bench at the forward bulkhead of the room at the torpedo local-control console. A two-liter bottle of Classic Coke was set in a special holder on the console, Betts sipped the soda from an *Augusta* coffee mug. He was a huge bear of a man, his gut protruding almost half the way to his knees. His thick forearms stuck out of the rolled-up sleeves of his poopysuit, a custom-tailored one made to hold his tremendous frame. Daminski smiled as he approached the grizzled chief.

"Terry. You're awake. Something wrong?" Daminski's face was suddenly alive with humor.

"Me? I heard you'd been down ever since the launch, there, Rocket." Betts took a long pull on his Coke.

"That's Captain Rocket to you, Senior Chief." Daminski and Betts went back decades to the USS *Dace,* an old dinosaur Permit-class submarine when Daminski had been a green ensign torpedo officer and Betts had been the division's first class petty officer. The two had always played squadron softball in the spring and football in the autumn as long as they were both stationed in Norfolk. Whenever Daminski was bored he liked to relive old games with Betts, bringing back the glory of that one perfect touchdown, or the time the softball had flown what seemed a quarter-mile away.

Daminski sat down next to Betts and let out a whoosh of breath, the feeling of heaviness sneaking into him in spite of Betts's presence.

"We still looking at going home in three weeks, Cap'n?" Betts asked.

"I guess. Not that there's much to come home to."

Betts studied a Mark 50 torpedo on the central rack.

"Myra got another bug up her ass?"

"Worse than usual. This time she—"

A phone at Betts's side whooped. Betts scooped up the handset, the black telephone dwarfed in his massive fist.

"Torpedo room. Betts . . . yeah, he's here. Hold on." Betts handed Daminski the phone. "Conn for you, Skipper."

"Captain."

"Off'sa'deck, sir. Request permission to come to periscope depth, sir."

"Whatya got?"

The officer of the deck gave the ship's course, speed, and depth and the distance to the surface-ship contacts being tracked. Satisfied that the ship wouldn't collide with some rustbucket tanker bound for Naples, Daminski ordered the ship to periscope depth. The submarine would remain submerged, hiding under the cover of the waves, interacting with the world above only, extending the radio mast to listen to the satellite transmission of their radio messages, extending the periscope to avoid a collision. Daminski handed the phone back to Betts. Even as the big torpedoman chief reached over to replace the handset in its cradle, the deck inclined upward to a fifteen-degree angle as the OOD drove *Augusta* up toward the surface 500 feet overhead.

Betts asked again about Myra. Daminski thought about finishing the story, then thought better of it, dismissing the impending breakup of his marriage with a wave of his football-damaged hand.

"Hell with it, Terry. The real reason I came down is that you're looking kind of wimpy these days. I think the fat's gotten into your arms there. What do you say? Loser buys the keg."

Betts stared down his nose at Daminski. Daminski was fond of frequenting the bars on the piers and arm-wrestling anyone who was foolish enough to take him on, but he had always had the intelligence never to challenge Betts.

"Captain, I will break your arm, and then you'll bust me to third class."

"Come on."

Betts picked up the bench and carried it to the starboard weapon rack, to the free space where no weapons were stowed. He bent and brought a tool chest to the opposite side of the corner of the rack, kneeled on his box, brought his huge arm down on the rack and stared at Daminski.

The deck had leveled off and was now rocking gently in the waves near the surface. Two decks above, the OOD would be on the periscope while the BIGMOUTH radio antenna reached for the sky, picking up the radio traffic from the orbiting communications satellite. The GPS navigation system would be swallowing a data dump from the navigation satellite, pinpointing their location in the wide ocean to within a few yards.

Daminski kneeled down on the toolbox, his knee protesting from three operations to repair damaged cartilage. He put his elbow on the rack, his ham hand only two-thirds the size of Betts. The two men grasped hands, Daminski's fingers so crooked that his middle finger had to be straight to allow him to clasp his other fingers around Betts' hand.

"Giving me the finger, huh?" Betts asked, sounding serious. "That'll just piss me off and you'll have a compound fracture."

Daminski was grinning, his lips pulled back so far every tooth in his mouth showed, a war face he had cultivated since his days on the *Dace*. It did nothing for Betts, who two decades before had watched Rocket Ron practicing the face in the mirror.

"On three," Betts said, his face already looking slightly red, his wrist tense, ready to cock when the contest began. "One, two, three!"

The two arms jumped, the tendons and muscles straining. Sweat broke out on Betts' forehead. Daminski's face muscles trembled. Two, then three men in the compartment silently gathered around.

Betts' fist had cocked slightly inward, pulling Daminski's hand in an unnatural twist. Daminski's arm, however, had not given an inch, still ramrod straight, if anything allowing his hand to twist while still pushing for angle. But the senior chief had over a hundred pounds on the captain. Both arms began to shake, slightly at first, then more pronounced. Daminski's hand began to travel backward toward the rack surface as Betts bore down on him. In one grunt Daminski recovered, almost all the way to the vertical. A shrill rip sounded in the room as Daminski's poopysuit shoulder seam let go. Daminski grunted as his arm began to force the massive chief's hand backward, perhaps an inch.

The phone from the control room whooped, making Betts jump slightly. Daminski sensed an opportunity but Betts took a breath, tensed his arm, pushing the smaller Daminski's back to the vertical, then farther. Daminski's hand was slowly sliding down toward the rack.

One of the men in the room picked up the phone. "Captain, it's for you, sir. Officer of the deck."

"Tell him to wait." Betts took advantage of the interruption and pushed Daminki's hand farther down, now almost at a forty-five-degree angle, halfway down to the rack. Daminski kept fighting, his breaths wheezing.

"Captain says to wait, sir," the phonetalker said. "Yessir, wait one." Then to Daminski, "Captain, OOD says there's a flash radio message for you, personal for the captain. He says he needs you in control. Now, sir."

Daminski looked up at Betts, who was smiling.

"I'd better go, Chief."

Betts' hand kept pushing on Daminski's, but the effort to get the captain down had cost him. Daminski's hand was fighting its way back up.

"Yeah, you'd better get up there," Betts said, taking a gasping breath between each word.

By then Daminski's fist was almost at the vertical again.

"On the count of three, let go."

"Okay."

"One," Daminski said, eyes closed, still struggling against Betts' bulk. The ship's deck took on an angle again as the submarine left the danger of the surface and returned to the arms of the deep, beneath the thermal layer, where only an extraordinarily lucky warship would be able to detect them.

"Two," Daminski wheezed, his fist now cocking against Betts', driving the huge arm downward toward the rack. Betts' face was red, his eyes clamped shut, his teeth biting into his lip. Daminski's arm began to move Betts' down. Betts began to give out a groaning sound. Daminski took one final breath and forced his arm toward the rack. Betts' hand shook. After a final moment, Betts let go and Daminski drove the huge fist down to the rack. Betts slipped off the bench box, holding his arm and gasping.

Daminski stood. "Three. You okay, Terry?"

"Screw you," Betts said from the deck as four torpedomen tried to pull him upright. "Sir."

Daminski laughed, fingered the rip in his uniform and headed for the stairs to the middle level.

"Next time for sure, right, Senior?"

Betts got to his feet and stared at Daminski. "You won't survive the next time, Skipper."

Daminski waved at Betts and moved up the stairs, taking the second flight to the upper level, turning the corner and heading aft to the control room, amazed at how much better he felt, Myra's letter almost forgotten. Almost.

Officer of the deck Lt. Kevin Skinnard stood on the raised periscope stand, a slim man in his late twenties with traces of acne on his cheeks below his deep-set eyes. His face looked haunted by lack of sleep as he held out a metal clipboard to Daminski, the radio messages printed out from their trip to periscope depth.

Daminski opened the clipboard cover and read the message.

261157ZDEC

FLASH FLASH FLASH FLASH FLASH FLASH FLASH FLASH FLASH FLASH

FM   CINCNAVFORCEMED

TO   USS AUGUSTA SSN–763

SUBJ   RETASKING

SCI/TOP SECRET—EARLY RETIREMENT

PERSONAL FOR COMMANDING OFFICER//PERSONAL FOR COMMANDING OF-
FICER

//BT//

1. MISSION RETASKING FOLLOWS EFFECTIVE IMMEDIATELY.

2. USS AUGUSTA ORDERED TO INTERCEPT AND SINK UNITED ISLAMIC
   FRONT DESTINY CLASS TYPE TWO NUCLEAR SUBMARINE UNIT ONE AT
   FIRST DETECTION.

3. SUBJECT UIF SUBMARINE UNIT SURFACED BRIEFLY AT 0635 LOCAL AT
   LATITUDE NOVEMBER THREE FIVE LONGITUDE ECHO ZERO THREE
   ZERO. UNIT PICKED UP DOWNED PILOTS, PROCEEDED EAST AND SUB-
   MERGED.

4. INTENT OF UIF SUBMARINE UNKNOWN. DESTINATION/MISSION ALSO IN-
   DETERMINATE. HOWEVER, ANALYSTS BELIEVE GENERAL SIHOUD MAY
   BE ABOARD AS A RIDER.

5. P-3 PATROL AIRCRAFT FROM SIGONELLA WILL BE PATROLLING IN
   SEARCH OF UIF SUBMARINE. ANY DETECTION WILL BE PUT ON COMM-
   SAT TRAFFIC WITH ELF CALL TO PERISCOPE DEPTH.

6. USS AUGUSTA ORDERED TO TRANSMIT SITREP TO CINCNAVFORCEMED
   IMMEDIATELY ON CONFIRMED DETECTION OF UIF SUBMARINE. AFTER
   SITREP TRANSMISSION AUGUSTA AUTHORIZED WEAPON RELEASE FOR
   SINKING OF UIF UNIT.

7. AFTER UIF SUBMARINE CONFIRMED SUNK USS AUGUSTA ORDERED TO
   PROCEED TO NAPLES ITALY FOR PATROL REPORT DEBRIEFING TO COM-
   MEDFLEET.

8. GOOD LUCK TO YOU AND YOUR CREW, RON. GOOD HUNTING.

9. ADMIRAL J. TRAEPS SENDS.

//BT//

Daminski smiled, signed the message, glanced at the chronometer
and jotted down the time. He handed the message board to OOD Skinnard and moved down to the chart table, shuffled down in the locker
portion for a new chart of the Mediterranean and marked the spot of
the Destiny-class' surfacing with a blue pencil dot. He grabbed a time-
distance circular slide rule and spun the wheel several times, then drew
a circle in the sea with the compass center on the blue dot. Skinnard
checked his calculation and nodded. Daminski pointed to the chart.

"Course two eight five at flank until we're here, then slow to ten knots
and do a large sector search. Notify the ops boss to do his homework on
the Destiny-class and tell him we'll be briefing the officers at 1400."

"Dive, make your depth eight five four feet. Helm, all ahead flank,
right two degrees rudder, steady course two eight five," Skinnard ordered.

Daminski frowned at Skinnard for a moment. The youth was the sonar officer, and Daminski was about to see how good he was.

"Skinnard, you got a sonar-search plan for the Destiny-class?"

The lieutenant didn't blink. "I reviewed it myself two days ago, Captain. It's current. My sonarmen will have it loaded in five minutes. If that sucker's out there, we'll snap him up."

Daminski's frown didn't ease but inside he was smiling. The kid had given the right answer, and it was because he was trained right—Daminski-trained.

"I know you will," Daminski said, his face close to Skinnard's. He turned and walked to his stateroom, whistling tunelessly. A lousy day had turned out pretty fine, after all. He rubbed his right shoulder and bicep and grimaced. At least he could shoot the Destiny submarine without it ripping his arm out of the socket. Damned Betts. Next time he'd lift a few weights before challenging his beefy torpedoman.

7

THURSDAY, 26 DECEMBER

Eastern Mediterranean
USS *Augusta*

The door to sonar smashed open. The sonar chief turned and stared at Captain Daminski, his hair drawn back, red wraparound glasses shading his round eyes. Chief Bruce Hillsworth, Royal Navy, was on an exchange program, his usual assignment to the HMS *Triumph*, an attack submarine of the Trafalgar class. After going to BSY–1 BATEARS sonar school in San Diego, Hillsworth had reported aboard *Augusta* for a temporary assignment to assist the regular sonar supervisor. But the irreverent Brit had proved so adept at his job that, at Daminski's insistence, the Navy had approved his top-secret clearance and proposed to the British Admiralty that he be allowed to complete a three-year tour.

Daminski slammed shut the door to the sonar shack, violating the rig for patrol quiet that required doors to be shut gently. Hillsworth ripped off his earphones and glared at the captain, then spoke, his South London accent oddly exotic in a navy dominated by descendents of early twentieth-century immigrants and great-grandsons of the Confederacy.

"Sir, if you insist on slamming the door I shall be obliged to ask you to leave my sonar compartment."

Daminski clapped Hillsworth on the shoulder. "Aw, your queen wears combat boots."

Hillsworth's nose tilted toward the overhead. "Is there anything in particular I might be able to help you with, sir?"

Daminski looked around the room and took it in, as if he were seeing it for the first time, or perhaps the last. The space was quiet, the sonar-display consoles humming, ventilation ducts purring, the room dimly lit by blue fluorescent lights and the green of the console video screens. A wall speaker played the sound of the selected beam of the spherical sonar array, the volume turned low enough to make the ears strain to hear the sound of the merchant ship's propeller off in the distance. The faraway whooshing of the screw blades sounded lonely, mournful.

"I want to see the sonar search-plan for the Destiny-class."

Hillsworth nodded, took off the headphones and led Daminski to the computer in the forward corner of the cramped space. Daminski paged through the software, looking at the expected tonal frequencies predicted from the Japanese-constructed ship. Little was known about her sound signature. When the ship had left the Mitsubishi shipyard in Yokosuka the Improved-Los Angeles-class submarine *Louisville* had trailed her out, doing an "underhull," a periscope surveillance of the new ship as it ran on the surface. The video of that observation had given naval intelligence a more complete picture than if they had gotten a tour of her drydock. When the Destiny-class submerged, the *Louisville* stayed with her, circling her in what was known as an SPL (for sound pressure level recording). The wideband-width tape recordings were analyzed for weeks at NAVSEA until the resulting sonar search plan was created. That plan noted the various pure tones eminating from the Destiny submarine as a function of distance from the contact and the angle of the ship itself. Sonar detection in the BATEARS BSY–1 suite was done primarily by narrowband detection, listening in a narrow slice of ocean for a particular pure frequency, a tonal. Reducing the space listened to and the frequencies listened for cut down on the near infinite amount of data the sonar computers would otherwise have to process to find the enemy sub. But the plan depended heavily on what tonals the target submarine transmitted.

Daminski frowned. "This SPL is a year old," he complained.

"Afraid so, Cap'n."

"This might not sound anything like the Destiny does today."

"It might."

"No way, Chief. This data was taken on Destiny's maiden voyage. God knows our boats sound completely different from sea trials to a year later after we've fixed all the shipyard's screwups and eliminated all the sound shorts. I think we should open up the tonal gates."

"Sir, you'll be doubling or tripling the volume of data. It'll slow us down. Might not scoop up the rascal at all."

Daminski turned from the computer screen and looked up at the overhead. "I can't help thinking they're somehow ahead of us. There's something we haven't thought about."

The phone rang from the conn.

"OOD for you, gov'na. Says you're requested in the officer's mess for a briefing. Probably about our friend the Destiny."

"Yeah." Daminski sighed. "Don't forget opening those gates, Chief. At least a couple hertz."

"I'll consider discussing it with the weapons officer, if you don't mind, sir."

Daminski laughed, noting Hillsworth's rigid insistence on following the chain of command, even knowing that the weapons officer would take his orders from Daminski.

"Keep listening for this asshole, Chief."

"As ever, sir," Hillsworth said, strapping his headset back on.

Daminski left sonar, shutting the door gently this time, and walked down the passageway to the amidships ladder, to the middle level. He ducked into the wardroom, which was packed with the ship's officers, took his place at the head seat at the leather-covered table and waved at the navigator and operations officer, Lieutenant Commander Tim Turner, to begin the briefing.

Turner was of medium height, his most noticeable feature his oddly coifed hair—odd for a thirty-three-year-old—moussed nearly vertically from his forehead in imitation of a current rock star. His face made him look ten years younger than he was, but the baby face and outgoing, amiable personality covered an explosive temper. The only time the *Augusta* crew had seen evidence of that temper was when Daminski had pushed him too far, yelling in the lieutenant commander's face over a problem with the routing of the radio messages. Turner had blown up, telling Daminski where he could shove the message board. Surprisingly, Daminski had backed off, apologized, and walked away. It almost seemed Daminski had been deliberately trying to get Turner to lose control, just to see where that boundary was for future reference. Ever since then the two men had gotten along very well.

"Good afternoon, gentlemen," Turner said. "This briefing is SCI top secret, codename: *Early Retirement*. Everybody cleared for this, Jamie?"

"Yessir," the communications officer said, checking the room's attendees against his clearance list.

"Okay. A few hours ago we received a flash transmission to intercept the United Islamic Front Destiny-class submarine, reported to be in this area." Turner pointed to a chart he'd taped to the wall, showing an ellipse drawn in the eastern Mediterranean basin between Cyprus and

Crete. "Our mission once we detect and classify the contact is twofold. First, we transmit a message to the CINC that the Destiny is there. Then," Turner said, "we sink it." Turner tapped the chart again. "We're heading out at flank speed. In another two hours we'll slow to ten knots to lower our own ship's noise to do a large area sonar search. The handouts Jamie's passing to you are the details of the sonar search-plan with the Destiny's tonals and SPL results. Also in the handout is a print of the Destiny-class nuclear submarine."

Daminski flipped past the sonar search-plan to the blueprint of the enemy submarine. The ship was odd-looking to an American submariner's eyes. It looked like a fat torpedo, rounded at the bow, cylindrical over its length with an abrupt tapered stern, the aft end having the strange X-tail rudder/sternplane combination with the even stranger ducted propulsor water turbine instead of a screw. But the strangest part of the ship was the sail, or fin, as the UIF forces called it. The fin height was nearly the same as the diameter of the hull, the structure poking up thirty-five feet.

"As you can see, this vessel is radically different from our own designs, and a major departure from Russian designs as well." Turner was lecturing now and obviously enjoying it. "Unlike our own philosophy, there is no spherical or bow sonar array. The bow is taken up with torpedo tubes like a World War II boat. The tubes are actually outside the pressure hull, containing canned weapons. So the tubes are one-shot deals and there's no reloading and no reload machinery—makes the ship simpler and lighter with fewer pressure-hull penetrations. It's got thirteen large-bore hundred-centimeter tubes and eight small-bore fifty-three-centimeter tubes. Even with no reload Destiny can kill you twenty-one times over.

"This ship is a double-hull vessel, great for taking torpedo hits without getting hurt. Plus, the inner hull is a simple cylindrical elliptical-headed pressure vessel. They've minimized hull diameter, the main drawback to a double-hull ship, by making ballast spaces fore and aft of the pressure hull. And get this, gents: the pressure hull with its four compartments has only one of them manned. The reactor and steam plants are so automated that they run everything from the control room up front under the fin. There's no shaft penetration to the hull because the propulsor is turned by an oil-enclosed AC motor—only electrical cables penetrate the hull. The motor is damned quiet, as is the low-speed propulsor. The reactor is liquid metal cooled with MHD pumps—whisper quiet, and there's no reduction gearing since it's electric drive. The turbine generators are reported to be screamers at a dual frequency at about 155 hertz. For sensors the ship has huge hull sonar arrays, damn near covering the whole hull. Her ears are a lot bigger than ours, which sort of makes up for the lack of a spherical array up forward."

Jamie Fernandez, the communications officer, raised his hand. Turner recognized the young ensign.

"Sir, the Destiny-class—do we know the actual name of this particular ship? The Moslems don't call it the Destiny, do they? And what do we know about the ship's captain? How will he react when we approach him? What does the intelligence say?"

"We don't have data that specific—"

"Those are bullshit questions, Fernandez," Daminski's voice boomed. "The answer is *it doesn't matter* who the hell the captain is or what the hell they call their damned ship. Our job is to put it on the bottom." Daminski looked at the officers. "Come on, let's get our stuff together here. Go on, please, Mr. Turner."

Turner continued, finishing with the intelligence they did have about the ship—submerged tonnage, speed, depth capability. After another quarter hour Turner finished and looked at Daminski.

"Anything to add, sir?"

"Just a couple things, Mr. Turner." Daminski stretched and snapped his fingers for a cup of coffee. The engineer, tall lanky Mark Berghoffer, the Pennsylvania Dutch farmboy with the foghorn voice, leaped up, grabbed an *Augusta* coffee mug from the rack, splashed the hot brew into it and placed it before the captain. Daminski slurped loudly, then. "Here's how I see it, guys. Feel free to jump in if I'm wrong. I think we can take this dude by sneaking up on him. Those big hull arrays will leave a hell of a baffle area in his stern, and the surface flow will be noisy from the propulsor. The ship itself is damned good, but I'm betting the crew is unfamiliar with their platform and they're poorly trained. We've been at sea a hell of a lot more in the last six months than these people. Once we get a sniff of this guy we're ordered to do a situation report. I'll preload the damned thing in a radio buoy and poop it out the signal ejector so I don't have to go to periscope depth in the middle of the approach. Then I'll put out a horizontal salvo of four Mark 50s, wait for the detonations, then we go on to Naples for a night of beer, Italian food, and Italian women. Any questions?"

There were none. The briefing broke up. Daminski sat in the end seat for some time, finishing his coffee, staring at the intelligence profile of the Destiny-class, and thinking about Fernandez's questions: who *was* the Destiny's captain? And what the hell *did* they call the ship? And what would Destiny's captain do if he detected their approach? Questions for which Daminski had no answers, and felt he should have.

Arlington, Virginia
Pentagon E-Ring
Joint Staff Special Compartmented Facility

Admiral Donchez glared at the air force security guard at the fortified entrance to the joint-staff headquarters. Even the navy's number one admiral had to produce his ID card, his Pentagon bar-coded SCIF-access card, and have the photo-images on the cards compared to his face by two on-watch sentries before he could gain access. At last the sentries admitted Donchez into the maze of corridors leading to a large briefing room. Before Congress had mandated this joint-service fever, this room had been the War Room, the information presentation facility for presidents and cabinet members and congressmen and generals. Now that the post-cold-war world's threats were different, the joint staff had gutted and remodeled the room, making it look more like a movie set than the old functional war room. The joint staff briefing room was large but so packed with computer consoles as to seem cramped except for the table in the center of the room. The black table was ten feet wide and sixty feet long, the surface illuminated by a hanging contraption in the shape of a large racetrack shining fluorescent light down on the slick marble surface. The room's north and south walls were electronic wall charts, their images driven by the computer consoles on the east and west walls. Off to the side of the large briefing table was a smaller table, seating only twelve, where the chairman of the Joint Chiefs liked to have his meetings. The entire facility was a SCIF, special compartmented information facility, built to elaborate specifications that attempted to prevent eavesdropping. These included the prohibition against windows or ventilation ducts leading to the rest of the building; the computer consoles were networked only with each other and to a barrier computer. Only the barrier computer was allowed to communicate with the outside world through sanitized phone lines and data cables. The barrier then scanned incoming data to ensure that it was virus-free. A second computer system was devoted solely to monitoring the barrier, making sure its integrity was maintained. Every phone in the room was a secure-voice unit, all passing through the modules of the barrier computer.

All this seemed fine for tactical or war-fighting strategy meetings, but JCS chairman General Rod Barczynski also favored the room for administrative meetings. Thirty-five years of living and fighting in tanks had made the general uncomfortable with rooms with windows and curtains and wood tables. Donchez could understand but still felt odd discussing, say, the latest uniform change in the war-fighting environment of the joint-briefing facility. Except, of course, this morning's briefing was no administrative function. Barczynski wanted answers. Dick Donchez's career had been filled with sessions like these. To Donchez, success was not a matter of avoiding failure but of making the right decisions and taking the correct action when staring failure in the face.

Behind Donchez were his commanders-in-chief—John Traeps, the CINC naval forces Mediterranean, and Kenny McKeigh, the CINC naval forces Atlantic—as well as his aide Fred Rummel. Vice CNO Watson was minding the store in Flag Plot. Donchez sat at the table across from the general and his staff, Donchez's CINCs seating themselves beside him. He looked up at Barczynski.

"Afternoon, General," Donchez said. "Having a good vacation?" Donchez referred to Barczynski's penchant for getting outdoors away from D.C. on weekends and holidays. Being at work on the Christmas holidays, war or no war, was not his style.

"I've had a lot better, Dick," the general said.

The general's physical appearance made him seem an unlikely character to be in command of the nation's military. He was a large man, his barrel chest presiding over an equally broad paunch, but somehow Barczynski didn't seem fat, just big. Someone seeing him at the grocery store would think him a boilermaker or a longshoreman. He had a habit of taking off his uniform jacket and rolling up his shirtsleeves, and when he did his thick forearms bulged from the shirt. Barczynski had a way of looking a man in the eyes with disarming directness, especially when asking—rarely ordering—that an action be taken, his eyes smiling, the laugh lines coming, as if to say I know you can do this, will you help me out? Those eyes also had the ability to get the truth from subordinates trying to cover their trails, and tails. They could also mesmerize bosses, disarming opponents. And they worked wonders with the press, who loved him. There were rumors that when he retired he could win a presidential nomination. He was one of few officers able to weld a caring attitude for his men with a relentless commitment to the mission at hand. Officers and enlisted men alike would do things for Barczynski that they would never agree to do for anyone else, taking the unglamorous missions, hardship tours, the army's dirty jobs. As a way to reward the men who worked hard for him, he was fond of building esprit de corps by throwing keg parties; wherever he had been assigned in his career he could always be found after hours in the officers' club, usually with a Heineken in each giant fist, surrounded by younger officers. But his physical appearance and beer diplomacy masked a penetrating insight and a tactician's mind unrivaled by most military academicians.

Donchez himself had enormous professional and personal respect for Barczynski as well as liking him as a friend and fellow officer, the two senior officers friends for the past several years. But even so, Donchez was wary of the army officer because he felt he was short on understanding of navy operations. Barczynski's working knowledge of the fleet had come from joint-command operations during which he'd come back with a distaste for carrier battle groups, the navy's starting offense. Over the last few years Donchez had convinced Barczynski of the utility of submarines, the usefulness of SEAL team commandos, the gunboat diplomacy of Aegis cruisers, the punch of an amphibious assault by a battalion of Marines, and the value of sea-launched Javelin cruise missiles, but the general still balked at Donchez's insistence that carrier air wings were worth their price tag, the general more comfortable with land-based air force fighters and bombers, which he'd been familiar with since his West Point graduation. Donchez had continued to press, and Barczynski had grudgingly gone along with the navy chief's tactical recommendations, but as far as carrier battle groups were concerned, they were something that Barczynski tolerated rather than supported.

Barczynski looked at Donchez now and started in abruptly. "Dick, what's this I hear about Sihoud getting away? I thought your SEALS were there to stop that. Do you know how tough it was to get Dawson to buy in on this assassination thing? We promised him results. So far we've got nothing."

"Sir, I'm not sure what you might have heard from your sources. The missile attack did fail and the SEALS missed Sihoud's departure from the bunker—he must have taken off before the Javelins hit, because the SEALS verified that nothing was left. We believe Sihoud made an escape on a Firestar fighter that flew out over the Med and dropped him off at a submarine. The UIF's Destiny-class submarine." Donchez showed him the photos.

"This Destiny sub. It's a diesel boat, right? Your guys can find it and kill it?"

"I'm afraid it's a nuke, sir. Japanese built, state of the art, although it's just an export-level unit—God help us if the Japanese ever decide to make their own wars with their own hardware."

Barczynski was not amused. "Go on, Admiral."

"The ship is run by Egyptians, Iranians, Iraqis and Libyans. We believe they are not very well trained, not operating as a smooth team—"

"You've got a bunch of your subs in the Med to get this guy, right?"

"We've got two front-line units, both Los Angeles-class attack submarines, one guarding Gibraltar at the mouth of the Med, the other sweeping the eastern basin to the west looking for the Destiny sub. We've got a few dozen antisubmarine patrol aircraft in the air, some of them from the *Reagan* battle group. We'll get him."

"Where's he going? What's he doing?"

"We think he's hiding from us for a while, then he'll redeploy with one of his theater commanders, probably North Africa. But we'll get him . . . Sihoud's a dead man."

"I hope so, Dick. The president wanted to know what happens after Sihoud is gone. Sihoud's got three damned good field generals, the theater commanders. Even with him gone Bobby Kent at CIA thinks the generals can still run a pretty good war."

Donchez handed over a file, the cover of it busy with classification stamps and banners.

"That's Operation *Early Retirement* Phase Two, General. We'll take out each of the theater commanders. CIA agrees with my staff that once the lower echelon generals are out of the picture—"

General Felix Clough, U.S. Air Force, walked in. Air Force chief of staff Clough was young to be a general, even in the Air Force. Most of his academy classmates were still colonels, some majors. Clough had a round face, made academic-looking by his wire-rimmed glasses. Like Barczynski, he was a broad-framed man, though taller than the JCS chief, but on Clough the paunch looked more like fat than Barczynski's muscle. Clough had come up the Air Force's ranks first as a nuclear missile silo commander, then as a scientist. He had met Barczynski twenty years before at a seminar and the two had for some reason hit it off, the Air Force allowing Clough to be Barczynski's liaison officer for several assignments. Donchez had nothing against Clough personally, but at the Pentagon Clough was his worst nightmare, an Air Force general officer with a doctorate who thought he knew all there was to know about military systems. For Clough, life was simple: Trident submarines were wasteful and easily replaced by Air Force silos and B–2 bombers. Carrier air power existed only because of pork-barrel politics and was clearly inferior to long-range, stealthy, fast and lethal Air Force fighters. The Marine Corps was redundant, its functions easily replaced by the Army, the Air Force and the Navy doing its unglamorous but utilitarian function of transporting troops to the battlefields. Donchez suspected it was Clough who had coined the "self-licking-ice-cream-cone" term concerning aircraft carrier battle groups, "missile silos lost at sea" for Trident submarines and "the Navy's army" for the Marines. Unfortunately Clough had Barczynski's ear.

Donchez continued as Clough sat down. "The lower-echelon generals," Donchez said, glancing pointedly at Clough, "once killed, will drain the UIF Combined Armed Forces of so much talent that defeat should be nearly immediate. The battlefields will be chaos—"

"They usually are," Barczynski said. But the point wasn't lost on Donchez—the Army general had been in battlefields before, in Vietnam and Iraq, risking his life, while Donchez . . . though not by his choice . . . had not.

"Sir, once the Navy's SEALS knock out Generals Ben Abbas, Ramadan, and Ihaffe this war will be a mop-up."

Clough smiled at Donchez.

"Well, at least your people will get to do something over there."

Screw you, Donchez thought as he returned Clough's smile.

"Dick, that should be it. Let me know about Sihoud."

"Aye, aye, sir," Donchez said, standing.

"Oh, one thing," Clough said to Barczynski while waving Donchez to a seat. "Didn't you want to ask Admiral Donchez about the testing of the Vortex missile? I heard that the Navy's doing a live fire with two submarines tomorrow."

Donchez took a deep breath, sitting back down, wondering what business of Clough's the Vortex missile could be, except that it had a track record of failure that Clough could use against the Navy.

"I thought this was a war briefing, General Barczynski, or I would have brought the videos and charts and graphs of the Vortex program."

Barczynski put both hands up, as if to separate Donchez and Clough. "Hold on, hold on. Dick, what's the deal with this live firing exercise? This Vortex is going to kill someone if I read these reports right."

Donchez's jaw clenched. He already had had to answer for the failed operation to kill Sihoud, and now Clough was kicking him when down, dragging out the Vortex program. It would have been easier to tolerate if the Vortex had been someone else's brainchild, but it was Donchez's personal dream, his legacy to the Navy. And so far the program had been one problem after another. Donchez opened his briefcase and took out a folder, thinking back over the last two years and the long road to the Vortex's operational test.

"General, here's the short course on the Vortex missile program. After we had that unfortunate incident under the polar icecap a few years ago when we lost the *Devilfish,* we wanted to develop an antisubmarine weapon that would be as effective as the old Russian Magnum, the big 100-centimeter nuclear-tipped torpedo. We were somewhat disappointed in the Mark 50, frankly, although it did well against the Chinese fleet during Operation *Jailbreak* back when *Seawolf* liberated the *Tampa.* But those were surface ships we were firing at, not submarines. The ASW standoff weapon, the Ow-sow, also used against the Chinese, was a big break, but it turned out to be a surface ship killer, not that effective against a sub. In the meantime the opposition submarines were getting faster. The Japanese Destiny-class, for example, can do damned near forty-seven knots and the Mark 50 only about fifty. On a good day, the Destiny submarine can run long enough in a tail-chase so that a Mark 50 runs out of fuel, effectively outrunning our torpedo."

"Does that mean we won't be able to sink the Destiny?"

"No, sir. We have a tactical advantage against the Destiny. He can't run from a torpedo he doesn't know has been launched."

"This Vortex—it was your invention, wasn't it, Dick?" Clough asked.

Donchez understood Clough wanted to equate the Vortex test failures with Donchez personally.

"The concept was mine, yes. The weapon that eventually was named 'Vortex' introduces a new era in torpedoes, General Barczynski. It is a hybrid weapon, half-torpedo, half-missile, a solid-fueled missile that travels underwater for its entire run to the target. It goes 300 knots. It cannot be outrun. And its warhead is five times the size of the Mark 50's, over seven tons of PlasticPac explosive. The yield comes close to the kiloton TNT level with conventional explosives. It's the ultimate submarine-versus-submarine weapon system."

"Except that it blows up when you try to launch it," Clough added.

"Felix," Barczynski said tonelessly. "Go ahead, Dick."

"The early weapon tests were, I grant you, troubling. We found the rocket fuel had to be hot-launched—ignited inside the launching tube—otherwise the missile lost stability, but in-tube ignition means the tubes have to be incredibly strong. Also, the solid fuel is more volatile than typical rocket fuel and we had problems slowing the combustion rate. On launch the pressure transient in the tubes exceeded the design pressure and led to a longitudinal stress failure—"

"What does that *mean?*" Barczynski asked.

"It means the launching tubes blew up," Donchez said, "in nine out of twelve static launches. We completed a detailed study of the failure mode and did a total weapon redesign. The new missile was named the Mod Bravo, and in its two static tests it has performed perfectly. Tomorrow's Mod Bravo test will be a sea-launch from the USS *Piranha,* a decommissioned 637-class attack submarine, against the old *Bonefish,* which is a diesel sub set up to be a test drone."

"You're launching this Vortex from an old attack sub? Is that wise, with all the tube explosions? Couldn't that sink the boat?"

"That won't happen, sir. Besides, the firing ship will be unmanned. It's fully instrumented. If something were to go wrong, we'd be able to determine why without the problem hurting anyone."

"Setting up *two* drone submarines is rather expensive, isn't it, Admiral?" Clough flipped through papers. "I think I have some budgetary figures here—"

Donchez stood and addressed Barczynski.

"If there's nothing else, sir, I'll be following Operation *Early Retirement* in Flag Plot."

He had scanned out of the room before Clough could say anything else.

CHAPTER

8

FRIDAY, 27 DECEMBER

Tongue of the Ocean, East of Andros Island, Bahamas
Atlantic Undersea Testing and Evaluation Center (AUTEC)
Exercise *Bonecrusher*
USS *Piranha*

Captain Michael Pacino stepped down the tight ladder to its landing in the gyro control space, jogging left to the door to the torpedo room. In his early forties, slim to the point of gauntness, and tall, Pacino's six-foot-two height made him duck as he cleared the stair landing. His hair, once black, was streaked with early shades of gray at the temples. His eyes were a penetrating blue-green, the skin around them wrinkled from years of squinting out periscopes. He wore cotton khakis, the only insignia the eagles on his collars, the submariner's dolphin pin over his left pocket and a round brass capital-ship command pin beneath the pocket button. His jaw clenched as he walked into the room, making him appear angry or intensely determined.

Pacino looked at the room, fighting back a sense of *déjà vu*, the voices of the past loud in his ears. The USS *Piranha* was identical to his former command, the *Devilfish*, every detail matching the memories he had tried hard to forget—the layout, the paint colors, the cramped interior, the poorly arranged control room, even the smell, that odd mixture of oil and diesel exhaust and ozone and sweat, edged with battery acid. Pacino couldn't help wondering what his *Devilfish* looked like at that moment—had the old girl imploded from the depths, or had she flooded completely through the open bridge hatch as she sank in 11,000 feet of freezing Arctic Ocean seawater? Had she come to rest on the ocean bottom keel down, or heeled over miserably, or was she perhaps vertical, her tail impaling the sandy bottom like a spear stuck in the ground? The questions were always ringing in his mind, but never more insistently than now that he was in *Devilfish*'s sister ship, the submarine class leader and prototype, the *Piranha*, Richard Donchez's old command from the early seventies.

Somehow it was appropriate to test Donchez's Vortex missile from the ship that he had once commanded so long ago, back when Pacino's father—Donchez's friend and academy roommate—was alive and in command of the *Stingray* one pier over. The present intruded on Pacino's thoughts when his tour guide, a tanned lieutenant commander, introduced the weapon-test director.

"Dr. Rebman, this is Captain Michael Pacino, the skipper of the *Seawolf*, the submarine that will be doing the next Vortex test with a manned submarine when this test is complete. Dr. Rebman is from the Dahlgren weapons lab, he's the Vortex program manager."

Rebman was a dark chubby man wearing an expensive gray suit, the clothes seeming out of place in the surroundings of machinery and equipment. He had a mustache and goatee, perhaps an attempt to minimize his fleshy lower face but which made him look rather devilish and ridiculous all at once. When told Pacino commanded the *Seawolf*, Rebman's face lit up with delight.

"Captain! Wonderful to make your acquaintance! I was just asking about you and the *Seawolf*. How is the Vortex tube installation going?"

Pacino shook the limp sweating hand. He did not smile.

"The shipyard is behind schedule," Pacino said, his voice toneless. "The Vortex tubes have some problems."

Rebman frowned. "Maybe I should come over after the test firing and take a look. Would you show it to me?"

"I suppose," Pacino said, looking around the torpedo room at the port side where the Vortex missile tube had been installed. The tube had replaced both port torpedo tubes and extended aft from the forward bulkhead to the rear bulkhead of the room and beyond, the laundry space ripped out to accommodate the massive weapon. The sheer size of the missile was one reason Pacino and the crew of the *Seawolf* disliked the system—just one Vortex tube on the *Piranha* had taken over the lower level. On *Seawolf*, the three-tube launching system had hogged most of the starboard torpedo room, taking up space that could have stored twenty-five weapons. *Seawolf*'s normal fifty-weapon loadout had been cut in half, only to make space for three weapons that tended to blow up their launching tubes. Pacino shook his head, then looked at Rebman, who for the last minute had been giving a passionate lecture on the Mod Bravo and how it would be different and how it would revolutionize submarine warfare.

"Don't you agree, Captain, that just one 300-knot underwater missile would be all you'd need to sink an underwater adversary?"

"Dr. Rebman, if you're really interested in what I think, here it is. We rarely kill a bad guy with just one shot. Combat isn't like that. And it would be nice, if it's not asking too much, if the missile could be launched without blowing up the launching platform." Rebman's face tightened. "Well, I'm going back to the *Diamond*. Good luck, Dr. Rebman."

Pacino leaned on the wooden handrail of the *Diamond* and stared out at the shimmering blue-green sea; with the sun rising over the Bahamas to the east, the sleeping Andros Island behind him to the west, the scene could have been pictured in a travel agent's vacation brochure. The Tongue of the Ocean AUTEC submarine test range was one of the few submarine facilities in the world with such splendor, but it had been chosen for advantages unrelated to the beaches and the transparent Bahamian waters. The facility had been chosen because it was a bathtub of deep water surrounded by a ledge of shallows and islands—the shallows ensured that no prowling opposition submarines could spy on the tests, yet the tongue, the bathtub of deep water, was sufficiently broad that sub-versus-sub exercises could be held without fear of running out of room. The entire bathtub was instrumented with a three-dimensional sonar system linked to a DynaCorp Frame 90 supercomputer capable of immense data storage and rapid processing. Nearby Andros Island was worthless as a resort because, except for Andros Town, it was a rock resembling the surface of the moon, if the moon had scrubby undergrowth. On the shore facing east toward Tongue of the Ocean, DynaCorp's Sound Surveillance Systems subsidiary had set up a compound, a small town housing the technicians, naval officers, engineers, scientists, and salvage divers needed to run the test facility. Other than a weekly plane from Palm Beach, the island was isolated from the world, which the Navy saw as another benefit. Pacino had spent two nights on the DynaCorp compound with nothing to do but drink in the prefab building used as an officers' club. He was glad to see the test finally get underway; it was time to get back to the *Seawolf.* There was much to do and little time to do it, including getting the ship out of the drydock and ready for the first manned live firing of the Vortex missiles. And to turn over command of the ship to her next captain, he reminded himself, a thought he did not want to face. Giving up *Seawolf* would feel like giving up his son . . .

"Captain Pacino," Dr. Rebman's voice called, "you might want to see this from inside."

In a covered deck space behind the pilothouse a command center had been rigged in what had been the crew's mess. Behind Pacino, through several large windows installed in the bulkhead, a dozen men could be seen peering into eight oversized video monitors. Pacino walked into the space, almost immediately breaking into a sweat, the air conditioning inadequate to keep up with the men and the video screens and the heat of the Caribbean sun. On the forward bulkhead, four of the monitors showed the interior of the gutted target submarine *Bonefish,* one camera in the rear of the boat pointing forward, another forward pointing aft, one showing the topside deck looking aft toward the conning tower, one below the deck level; the only thing discernible inside the empty boat were the strings of temporary lights and the pallet of batteries that powered them. Every bulkhead, console, valve, pipe, and cable had been removed from the old boat so that the hull could be seen. *Bonefish* had no engines but did have a rudimentary depth-control system. Her forward motion would be controlled by a tug with a cable to *Bonefish's* bow, the tugboat expendable and under command from the *Diamond.* The video signals from the cameras were obtained remotely in the *Diamond's* control space using telemetry. The camera's video data was transmitted along fiber-optic lines to a telemetry module inside the remote-controlled tugboat. The cameras would roll aboard the *Bonefish* even after missile detonation and the sub was on her way to the bottom.

The scientists intended to study how the ship sank, what the hole looked like, how the ship died when the Vortex hit it, all in an attempt to judge the effectiveness of the warhead. The remains of the hull would be salvaged and evaluated by materials experts. The 3D sonar data would be evaluated and presented, showing the path of the weapon, whether the unit had been stable after launch, whether its trajectory to the target had been straight and controlled or serpentine and reckless.

Not all the data was coming from the target. The firing ship was also under the eyeballs of the DynaCorp technicians. Two of the screens showed flickering images of the interior of the *Piranha,* viewing the fat and long steel Vortex launching cylinder from several angles. The tube was covered with strain gauges and what looked like miles of wires, trying to find out how the tube behaved under the stress of the missile launch. The visual and electronic data would be conveyed to the outside world by means of cables leaving the submarine at the aft end of her sail to a data buoy floating on the surface, which would transmit the images and tube-strain information to the *Diamond* via data link. The buoy had a long reel of cable with a tension spring, so that no matter where in the bathtub the transmitting sub went, the *Diamond* would continue to receive data. The data buoy also received control signals to the *Piranha's* maneuvering system from the *Diamond's* control space; at the aft end of the hot room a control console had been placed with room for two technicians. These men drove the *Piranha,* changing her speed, depth, and course from the wraparound console.

In the past, data would have been collected from the weapon as well, the warhead replaced with a data recorder, a black box, that would tell the researchers what the torpedo had seen at each second of its trip to the target and the ensuing pursuit and "explosion," the final detonation replaced with a turnaway maneuver. But in this test, the missile's tremendous kinetic energy at 300 knots was so extreme that after it passed the target, it would continue on—there was no way to shut down a solid-fueled rocket—and in continuing it would smash into the far sheer wall of the bathtub, taking out hundreds of thousands of dollars of sonar sensors. The weapon-test scientists had elected to allow the Vortex to detonate its warhead to study the effects on the target, but also to act as a missile self-destruct system to preserve the bathtub's sonar array.

Pacino watched as the control crew orchestrated the test, the snatches of conversation blending into each other, rising into a slow crescendo as the launch time approached. Over the next hour the *Bonefish* left the surface, sinking into the clear Tongue water under the control of the towing control tugboat. At the command of the technicians at the *Piranha* control console, the firing ship submerged and slowly cruised toward the launch point. The morning test preparations continued until the sun was high in the cloud-streaked sky. At last the missile firing was on its final countdown.

Pacino, his summer-weight khaki shirt now soaked with sweat, took a position at the oversized windows facing the Tongue and waited. Dr. Rebman joined him, the suit coat now replaced with a starched white lab coat. The countdown was initiated, and as it reached zero Pacino watched the sea where the tugboat towed the target. At the count of zero, launch point, the room grew silent, all eyes but Pacino's watching the video monitors.

He saw a slight rush of foam at the distant point where he had imagined the firing ship to be, then moments later the sea at the target bearing erupted in a column of water that blasted upward in an odd spherical shape, barbs of spray coming out of the curving dome of the explosion. The water continued to rise, forming a mushroom cloud that dwarfed the *Diamond,* the cloud spreading and rising into the air, then raining down on the sea below. Then the sound came from the distant explosion, the roaring power of it rattling the glass of the windows, slamming Pacino's eardrums, the full bass of the detonation pounding him. Pacino smiled, unable to contain the exhilaration of it, already bringing his hands up to clap, and turned to the men in the room, expecting the crew to be as exuberant at the success of the test.

Instead he saw long, incredulous faces staring at two video monitors as a tape player replayed the scene. Rebman was bent over a control console, shouting into a headset. The video scene rolled, the Vortex tube of the *Piranha* in the center of the picture, until Pacino could see the tube burst open in slow motion, then the explosion as the missile's flaming exhaust filled the torpedo room. The camera apparently died at that point, the picture turning to snow. On the screens on the right videos played in a closed loop as the target ship's cameras recorded the death of the ship—apparently the missile had sunk the *Bonefish*. But it had also put the *Piranha* on the bottom. Another tube rupture.

Rebman slammed the headset down and rejoined Pacino at the window. Without a word Pacino walked out to the weather deck and leaned on the wooden railing, staring out to sea where the tugboat floated, no longer towing anything but a frayed-ended cable. Rebman followed him out.

"At least it sank the target," Pacino said.

Rebman said nothing for several minutes.

Finally the scientist said, so quietly Pacino had to strain to hear him, "This is the end of the program, we've tried everything. The Vortex program is canceled."

But was it really dead? Knowing Donchez, Pacino had to wonder . . .

After a few minutes the *Diamond* turned and headed back to the DynaCorp compound's piers.

Two hours later Pacino was on a Navy DC–9 flying for Palm Beach, wondering how long it would take the shipyard to tear out the Vortex system from *Seawolf*. It would probably take three or more months to return the ship to her pre Vortex condition, and by then he would no longer be captain. True, he would be going on to a plum assignment— who could take issue with promotion to rear admiral and the job as commander submarines, Atlantic Fleet? But still, he would have liked to take *Seawolf* out to sea just one last time as her commander. This business with the Vortex had taken that from him. Driving submarines was a young man's job, Pacino finally concluded, and now forty-two years old, it was time to move on, and the sooner he accepted that the sooner he'd adjust to driving a desk. It was time to give up playing with toys, he tried to tell himself. And didn't really believe it.

At Palm Beach International, on the way to the commercial jet to take him to Norfolk, he was intercepted by an ensign in service dress blues.

"Admiral Pacino?"

"Captain, son, just captain."

"Message says 'admiral,' sir. But anyway, Admiral Donchez sends his regards and requests your presence at the Pentagon. There's a Falcon jet waiting for you, sir."

"Do you know what this is about?"

"Something about a weapon test, sir. That's all I know."

The jet's approach to National Airport in Washington was spectacular, the flight path taking Pacino over the Pentagon. He looked down on the odd building, wondering what Donchez had on his mind about "a weapon test" that couldn't wait one more day.

FRIDAY, 27 DECEMBER

Central Mediterranean
CNFS *Hegira*

"General, let me go over our discussions so far so that I can make sure Captain al-Kunis and I fully understand our mission," Commodore Sharef was saying.

Colonel Ahmed waved him on, nodding.

"You do not intend to return to the battlefields. Instead you are leaving the war to your field generals and staying aboard while we transit the Atlantic to within strike range of Washington, D.C. While en route we assemble the three Scorpion warheads into three sea-launched Hiroshima cruise missiles. Once in position we launch the Hiroshima/Scorpions at Washington, then withdraw back to UIF soil, where you will reestablish yourself while Western Coalition forces withdraw. This is all correct?"

Sihoud looked at Ahmed, who nodded and answered for the general, who was still suffering from broken ribs, a punctured lung and a laceration along his lower back.

"That is correct, Commodore."

"Then let me point out a few difficulties, if I may. Number one, we may never make it out of the Mediterranean. The sea is filled with coalition naval forces, including an American aircraft carrier battle group."

"A few torpedoes and we're out," Ahmed said.

"American carrier battle groups always sail with one, sometimes two nuclear submarines. Attack submarines. Hunter killer subs. Subs designed to kill other subs, like ours."

"You have torpedoes aboard?" Sihoud asked, speaking up for the first time, his resonant voice filling the room.

"Yes, General," Sharef said. "And if I am against one submarine, I *might* be able to evade an attacker, *if* I know he is there. If his sensors are better than mine, and if his engines are quieter than the sea around him, he could possibly attack us before we could respond. It is a horse race, General. Anyone who claims to predict the outcome of a naval battle of evenly matched forces is a liar." '

"You are afraid?"

"There is risk, here, General Sihoud," Sharef said. "Where there is risk there must be rational decisions. Only you can make those decisions. If I minimize the problems and the risk, as your aide here does, I do you a disservice."

Finally Sihoud's face broke into a wide smile. "You are right, Commodore. We will all listen until all problems have a satisfactory conclusion. Please go on."

"All we can do against an enemy submarine is stay as vigilant as possible and maintain absolute ship silence. That means no working on the weapons systems until we are clear in open ocean."

"Agreed," Ahmed said.

"Number two," Sharef went on, "the Scorpion warheads must be assembled, involving highly radioactive components and high explosives. I am counting on Abu-i-Wafa to use sufficient controls so that we do not irradiate the crew or blow the things up. Number three, these warheads might not work. There is nothing I can do about the functions of the weapon, so for this I will assume the missiles will function perfectly. And that brings us to problem number four—how do we get these missiles loaded into the tubes, given that the tubes do not penetrate the pressure hull and are encapsulated one-shot designs?"

Sharef gestured to al-Kunis, the Libyan first officer, to spread out the ship's blueprints.

"The solution Captain al-Kunis and I propose is to blow the water out of the forward ballast tank and weapon area free-flood, and cut open the tube caps on three Hiroshima missile tubes. We'll set up a rig to maneuver the missiles out, where we'll open them up and install the new warheads, then reinstall them in the tubes and weld the end caps back on."

"Sounds easy enough," Abu-i-Wafa said.

"Think again," Sharef said. "Working in a ballast tank is no holiday, particularly when the ship is at-depth. The tank is open to the sea at the bottom of the ship. Anything could send the water rushing in, a small leak in a vent gasket, a sudden maneuver. The ship will be at maximum speed to keep sufficient water flow over the bowplanes to keep the ship submerged in spite of the buoyancy of the ballast tank, so any slight turns could bring water in. There are no work platforms, no lights, no ventilation. It will be dangerous. And in the end it *might* not work—the tube may fail at launch from being inexpertly welded. General, this is a gamble."

"Yes, Commodore, all important things in war are. Anything else?"

"Yes sir. Problem five. Even if we conquer all the other obstacles to this point, there will be the American fleet awaiting us on the far side of the Atlantic."

"But how will they know we are there? Can't we stay invisible?" Abu said.

"Abu, we surfaced to pick up the general. They saw us then. They know we are somewhere in the Mediterranean, and they probably suspect the general and Colonel Ahmed are with us now. The subs attached to the carrier battle group will be coming after us, and if we survive the inevitable encounter with them, they will still know we are no longer in the Mediterranean, if only because we will not be surfacing there in the next one or two weeks. That leaves the Americans wondering, and soon they will put up a fenceline of ASW ships and subs and airplanes to catch us coming in. If they sink us, not only do they stop the launch of the Scorpions, they score a hit on General Sihoud . . ."

"Commodore, there must be something you can do to lessen this risk," Sihoud said.

"There is. I propose we avoid the east coast of America. Mr. First, the North Atlantic chart, please." Al-Kunis pulled out the chart of the North Atlantic, the projection showing the arctic circle and the lower rim of the Arctic Ocean. "The range of the Hiroshima missile will allow us to shoot well before we reach the coast. If we have the weapons ready we could launch in mid-Atlantic. Since I expect that preparing the missiles will take longer even than our pessimistic projections, I suggest we follow the great circle route to the southern tip of Greenland in the Labrador Sea. Captain al-Kunis has marked our proposed track in black tape. As you can see, we come in missile range of Washington here well south of Greenland, and if we follow the track shown up the Labrador Sea to Baffin Bay, we stay in range until we reach Godhavn, Greenland. That leaves us the excellent escape route north into the Arctic Ocean, back around Greenland, and south to Gibraltar. At this time of year the polar icecap extends south all the way to Baffin Island, with drift ice down into the Labrador Sea. No surface fleet will be able to pursue us there. By the time we emerge east of Greenland, they will have called off the search, Washington will be a radioactive nightmare, the Western Coalition will be in retreat, and we will return having accomplished the mission. Of course the possibility is high that attack submarines will be sent after us, most likely post launch. But I am confident we can defeat their ships if we encounter them singly, and if we detect them before they detect us."

"Then we are decided," Sihoud said, rising. "If there is nothing else I will retire for the evening."

"Good night, sir. And, General, I wonder if I and my first officer might have a word with Colonel Ahmed."

Sihoud waved and left the room. Ahmed turned to Sharef.

"Colonel, I have other concerns that I wanted to address with you."

"Go ahead, Commodore," Ahmed said.

"I wanted to see you first on this, but if your response isn't what I'm looking for, I'll take it to the general," Sharef said slowly.

Ahmed frowned. "I'm sure we can work out whatever's on your mind."

"I'll be direct with you, then, Colonel. You and General Sihoud have unlimited access aboard the ship. You can go where you please, talk to the men, even be in the ballast tank while the Scorpion insertion is done if you want. You can look at the navigation plots, hear the radio messages, ask any questions you please. The mission is yours to command, and this ship is completely at your disposal."

"Thank you, Commodore."

"However, Colonel, while you may give me orders and change my mission at any time, the way I carry out that mission is not your business. I retain command of this vessel, and only I direct when and how weapons are launched, how enemy ships are engaged. If you or General Sihoud attempt to give me rudder orders on this run you will find me quite deaf. Can you and the general accept that?"

Ahmed was quiet for some moments. When he spoke, he seemed like a man trying to remain calm.

"I will put the matter to General Sihoud." Ahmed hurried out, shutting the door quietly behind him, as instructed when he and Sihoud first came aboard.

Sharef turned to al-Kunis and smiled.

"You and your fellow Iranian do not seem to see eye to eye," al-Kunis said, reaching for his tea, the skin at his eyes crinkling as he sipped the brew.

Sharef considered that. Captain Abdullah Latif al-Kunis was thirty-seven, slightly taller than Sharef, almost as thin, with dark skin and a thick but tightly trimmed beard. His eyes were remarkably large. He rarely spoke without considering each word. At first Sharef had thought he would be a liability in combat, or any real-time situation; introspective people rarely seemed to have the quick reactions needed for military duty. But al-Kunis had surprised him with his ability to act decisively in tight situations, giving clipped but quiet orders from the periscope platform. He was a Libyan from Tripoli and had been a submariner on Foxtrot-class diesel boats all his career, commanding the Libyan Foxtrot sub *Al Khyber* for two years just before the Treaty of Algiers had united the Islamic states. He had been selected to be a staff officer in Ashkhabad for several years, where he had first met Sharef. When plans were made to acquire a Destiny-class submarine, Sharef had asked for al-Kunis, raising eyebrows at fleet headquarters that he did not pick another Iranian Navy officer. As far as Sharef was concerned, al-Kunis was the best man for the job, an able seaman and a good, innovative officer. Like Sharef, he had never married, although at the ship's recent port call at Tripoli there had been a woman there to see al-Kunis off. She could have been a girlfriend, fiancée, or sister. Sharef hadn't asked, and al-Kunis hadn't volunteered.

Sharef turned his thoughts back to Ahmed. "Ahmed is a smart man but he is a pilot and sees things differently. To a flyer, soaring over the earth, everything is easy. To a submariner, confined to a steel prison with no windows, nothing but the Second Captain computers to tell us what is outside, nothing is easy. But give him a year underwater and he might not make a bad officer."

"You heard he lost people in the bombing of Chah Bahar."

"I was sorry to hear it," Sharef said, bending over the Mediterranean chart. "So, where are the American submarines?"

Captain al-Kunis joined Sharef at the chart and jabbed his finger at the west point of Sicily, where it pointed toward Cape Bon, Tunisia, near Tunis on the North African coast. The gap, the Strait of Sicily, was only 150 kilometers across, the submerged navigable channel only thirty kilometers wide.

"Here at the Strait of Sicily. A few boats patrolling north and south here would pick us up. They may have patrol planes here as well. If they have the submarines to station a choke-point patrol . . . Maybe they weren't prepared. What if we transit through the Strait of Messina between Sicily and the boot?"

"Too shallow," al-Kunis shook his head. "The strait is filled with ferry boats, the channel is too tight. Running aground or colliding with a ferry boat isn't worth the risk. I'd take the Sicily-Tunis choke point."

"If we make it through, then what?"

"Gibraltar. If it were up to me, I'd station a fleet there to catch us on the way out."

"But they don't know we're leaving the Mediterranean."

"You must hope that, Commodore."

Sharef nodded, shut his eyes, and stretched. "I'll be in control. Write a procedure for the ballast tank work on the Hiroshima missiles. When you're done see to it that the navigator has our intended track plotted and laid into the computer. And check the sensor computers every hour and make sure our younger officers are vigilant. I do not want to be detected by an American submarine without warning. After control I'll be going down for a couple of hours. Both of us should be in the control room when we pass through the strait."

USS *Augusta*

The deck trembled slightly with an insistent vibration, the power of the ship's propulsion shaking the submarine as it plowed through the Mediterranean at flank speed, the electromagnetic speed indicator reading thirty-nine knots on the airplane-style console of the helmsman's panel. *Augusta* had been running at flank for over thirty hours, ever since the flash message had come in at noon the day before. The sprint put her sixty nautical miles short of the Strait of Sicily.

Commander Ron Daminski leaned over the chart table aft of the periscope stand in the control room. A pencil was clutched between his teeth, his broken fingers stabbing the buttons of a calculator, missing several times, causing the captain to curse under his breath. Above him on the periscope stand Lt. Kevin Skinnard leaned on the handrails and watched. The captain took the dividers, measured out a distance on the nautical mile scale, and walked them across the chart, drawing several pencil marks at the narrowed water between Sicily and Tunisia. Finally Daminski stood erect and squinted at the chart.

"What do you think, Skipper?" Skinnard asked.

"I'm half-tempted to set up a barrier search in the strait. I have the feeling he'll be coming through it."

"I don't know. Why does anyone think this guy is transiting from the east basin through the strait? What's there for him in the west basin? I'm beginning to think we humped the pooch coming this far west."

Daminski looked up at Skinnard and grinned. When he'd come aboard, Skinnard had been a shy quiet officer, almost a yes-man. After a few months of Rocket Ron he had developed the same intimidating style Rocket employed, whether learned by imitation or more likely from knowing the captain would accept no yes-men.

"Okay. You're the Khalib. What do you do?"

"Submerge here off Crete, wander east, maybe hang out in the southern seas of the eastern basin, and when the heat's off, come ashore in Egypt or eastern Libya."

"You're thinking he's going back to the Cairo front."

Skinnard nodded.

"I don't think so," Daminski said. "This guy's headed for the western front in Morocco. If he were headed for Cairo he'd be there by now. Plus the jet wouldn't have gone so far into the Med to find the sub. So he gets his butt to Morocco, hoping by the time he gets there we've forgotten about him."

"I still wonder why he's in a sub in the first place. He knows we're out here."

"He's hiding. Biding his time. He'd pop up in Marrakech and surprise the hell out of everyone if we weren't on his tail."

"So why the Strait of Sicily? This boy can go forty-seven knots." Skinnard took up a time-distance circular slide rule. "That's twenty-six hours' transit from his dive point, which put him in the strait at lunchtime today. That was six hours ago. If he was going though the strait, he's long gone."

"Skinnard, you're a sub skipper hiding a VIP government official aboard, with orders to hide and make your way to Morocco. What speed do you order up so you don't get caught, you don't make too much noise? Flank speed, forty-seven knots?"

"Um, no, sir. Probably ten or fifteen knots, take it easy and keep the noise down."

"Right. Which means we'll get to the strait at least a few hours before the Destiny."

"But, sir . . . you never mentioned this in your briefing."

Daminski paused, knowing he was caught but not betraying it. "No, Skinnard," he said, acid in his voice. "Do I have to tell you my every thought?"

"No, sir." Skinnard smiled, knowing Daminski was putting him on. "So, sir, you want a barrier search?"

"Damn straight. Southwest to northeast bowtie pattern right here." Daminski sketched a bowtie shape on the chart straddling the deep channel of the Strait of Sicily. "In another hour slow down to four knots, rig ship for ultraquiet, and stream the thin-wire towed array. And station the section tracking team a half-hour before you're there. We'll set a nice trap for this son of a bitch."

"Yessir," Skinnard said, watching as the captain half-limped out of the control room, wondering how the hell they would catch a lone submarine in the wide Mediterranean if the boat chose to stay in the eastern basin. If Daminski was wrong it would be a long dry patrol. And if he was right, and the Destiny-class was as good as the intelligence seemed to suggest, it would be a short patrol. A very short patrol.

Skinner took the microphone hanging above the periscope platform by its spiral wound cord.

"Sonar, Conn," he barked, "report all contacts."

Pentagon E-Ring
Suite of the Chief of Naval Operations

Since Pacino could remember, Admiral Donchez's offices had always been fairly ornate but the splendor of the CNO suite was too much to take in with a glance, especially since the admiral had been all over him since he walked in, plastering him with questions about his health, his ship, his family, everything except the reason he had summoned him to Washington. Pacino puffed on the Havana cigar Donchez had pulled from the humidor, the smoke filling the room with a mellow haze. An aide brought steaming coffee.

"Like the coffee, Mikey? It's imported special from Colombia."

"It's great, Admiral," Pacino said, looking at Donchez, noticing that age had finally seemed to be catching up to his father's old Academy roommate although his enthusiasm seemed undampened.

"How's it feel to be Admiral Pacino?"

"I'm still a captain, sir. I've got a few months before I'm confirmed. *If* I'm confirmed."

"A few more months and you'll be working on your second star. Aren't many admirals these days wearing the Navy Cross. Which reminds me, you're out of uniform without it."

Pacino glanced at his chest, the rows of ribbons four tall, the gold submariners' dolphins presiding above the ribbons, the capital-ship command pin beneath, the ribbon for his Navy Cross absent. Although Donchez would disagree, Pacino had always considered the medal something of a consolation prize for surviving the sinking of the *Devilfish*.

"You know, Admiral, I think I'd trade the star for a chance to keep command of *Seawolf* for another year. I don't suppose you could arrange that . . ."

"Navy's got other plans for you, Mikey. Besides, commanding the Atlantic Fleet's sub force will make you forget about the Seadog. Besides, your replacement—Joe Cosworth, right?—will do okay and it's time someone else got to drive the finest sub in the force. You can't hog it forever."

"I suppose so." Pacino looked at the older man, wanting to ask him how the war was going but, imagining the answer to be painful, restrained himself.

"Well, on to business. I heard Dr. Rebman packed it in. You saw the Vortex test? What did you think?"

"Well, sir, on the positive side, there was nothing left of the target after the missile hit it. The explosion made a mushroom cloud—I felt like I was on Bikini Atoll watching a nuclear test. There would be nothing left of an enemy sub after getting chopped up by a Vortex."

"I knew it. The torpedo is obsolete. The Vortex can blow a bad guy to hell before he even knows he's been shot at. This will make the Russian Magnum torpedo look crude."

"Yessir."

"Anything else?"

"I assume you heard, sir. The *Piranha* sank. The Vortex blew up the launching tube on the way out."

"I know. And I also know you've thought of how to fix that problem."

"Excuse me, sir?"

"That's why I sent you down there. You're a Ph.D. mechanical engineer. You probably scratched a couple of equations on an envelope and figured this whole thing out."

"Sorry, sir, but I just rubbernecked at the test like everyone else."

"Come on, Mikey. I know you hate the Vortex. It takes up damn near all your torpedo room and it's too volatile, like sleeping with a grenade."

Pacino looked into Donchez's eyes. His exact words had been "sleeping with a grenade with the pin pulled," but Donchez had been close enough.

"Mikey, with this weapon you don't need a room full of fifty torpedoes. One shot does it. With six Vortex missiles you can kill six submarines, every time. In the old days you'd shoot horizontal and vertical salvos and hope like hell the target drove into the search cone. This thing doesn't have a search cone—the whole ocean is the search cone. Now tell me how to make the thing work."

"Equalize the tubes . . ." Pacino had, of course thought about his answer ever since the test, figuring he might have such a confrontation with Donchez. He still hated the damn thing, though.

"What?"

"You've been launching a solid rocket in a closed-ended cylinder with tons of water at the muzzle end. The tubes are blowing up just like a gun barrel would if the bullet had too much gunpowder. Relieve the pressure at the aft end by piping the thing to sea pressure. When the rocket fuel ignites, instead of a pressure wave that ruptures the tubes, it blows steam out the relief piping and blasts out of the tube. Tube pressure stays within stress limits. It's pretty obvious, I figured your design team had rejected it for some good reason."

"That's all? Just open vent piping at the breech end?"

"Well, it's more than that. I did do a few calculations—" Pacino looked at Donchez, who smiled. "The vent piping would need to be full-bore, the diameter of the entire tube. Instead of a launching tube you need a launching *duct* with the missile in the forward end. On missile launch the exhaust gases pass out of the aft end of the duct and out the pressure hull, and rocket thrust carries the missile out the duct."

Donchez leaned back. "The Vortex program is saved—"

"Not exactly, Admiral. The tubes already take up half the torpedo room. The duct tube extensions would take up another thirty feet of length, with three-foot inner diameters. That's a hell of a lot of space. There's no room aboard. You'll have to design a whole new class of submarine to hold these pigs, because on the LA-class, with the duct work there won't be room for reactors or people or electronics. The Vortex is just too damned *big.*"

"Or we could put the tubes outside," Donchez said.

"Yeah, and take the hit in speed and sound emissions. We spent hundreds of millions making *Seawolf* the quietest submarine that technology could build, and now you're going to put a bunch of tubes and pipes and supports and valves topside to put out flow-induced resonances. For the fleet of submarines we have, it just doesn't make sense."

"I suppose you're right, Mikey. I'm sorry I called you out over the holiday," the old man said heavily.

"Sir, the Vortex is still a damn good weapon system," Pacino said, figuring he could afford to be generous. "The problems can be fixed, but it'll take the *next* generation of submarine to do it. You're just ahead of the current technology."

Donchez waved him off, his face a mask.

"Thanks for coming, Mikey."

An hour later Donchez's Falcon jet lifted off National's southwest runway and headed for Norfolk Naval Air Station. Pacino poured himself a Jack Daniel's over ice and shut his eyes. He felt badly for Donchez. A man who had been his father's closest friend and who had played a big part in his own career, a man who had brought him back from deep black despair three years ago after *Devilfish* went down and put him in command of the Navy's top-of-the-line attack submarine, the *Seawolf.*

The whiskey was good, but not good enough to make Pacino feel much better.

10

FRIDAY, 27 DECEMBER

Strait of Sicily
USS *Augusta*

The ship was rigged for ultraquiet.

The fluorescent-light fixtures throughout the forward half of the ship were switched to red to remind the crew to tread lightly and maintain ship silence. The port side of the steam plant was shut down, including one main engine and the turbine generator as well as a half-dozen pumps serving that half of the propulsion plant. Reactor main coolant pumps were running in superslow speed, reduced frequency, barely moving the water through the reactor core. The screw turned at bare steerageway, a mere thirty rpm, giving the ship just enough forward propulsion to maintain submerged depth control.

The watchstanders on duty were wearing headsets, all plugged into ship control phone circuits, while the shipwide PA system was locked out, its use having the adverse potential of being heard outside the hull. Hard-soled shoes were prohibited. The galley was shut down. A tray of cold cuts and a plate of white bread had served for evening rations, although the coffee machines still brewed at full power. Showers were secured. The evaporator, maker of pure water from seawater, was shut

down. The ventilation system fans were on slow, the normal bass booming sounds of the ship almost silenced.

Behind the ship the TB–23 thin-wire advanced towed array of the
AN/BSY–1 Busy One sonar system trailed on a cable a mile-and-a-half
long, the noise from the *Augusta* ahead distant and faint. The towed
array's electronic ears strained for noise, listening for the specific tonal
frequencies expected to be emitted from the Destiny-class submarine
predicted by Daminski to transit the gap of the strait at any moment.
While the towed array searched for tonals, the spherical array in the
ship's nose cone, a steel ball fifteen feet in diameter covered with hydrophones, listened to the noise of the ocean, hearing broadband noise just
as a human ear would. Backing up the spherical array were six hull
arrays, large sets of hydrophones arranged on the skin of the ship, each
somewhat disadvantaged by the interference of own-ship's noise from
within the pressure hull but useful all the same.

On the chart table in the cramped control room, the strait took up
half of the large table, the illuminated crosshair of light, the "bug,"
shining upward onto the chart surface, driven by the table's servomotors
in scale to the ship's actual motion through the sea. For the last hour the
bug had traced a bowtie pattern across the strait, a barrier search. Any
shipping coming through the strait would be detected. For the Destiny
submarine, the question was not whether it would be heard but whether
Augusta would hear Destiny before Destiny heard *Augusta*—if the
Destiny were heading west as Daminski maintained.

In the control room Lieutenant Commander Mark Berghoffer, ship's
engineer, presided as officer of the deck. He paced the deck of the
control room, stopping every few minutes at the chart table to ensure
the ship held to the bowtie search pattern, then at the sonar repeater
screen above the Position One console of the attack center's firecontrol
system, finally leaning over Ensign Jamie Fernandez's Pos Two screen, a
god's-eye-view of the strait with *Augusta* in screen center.

Commander Ron Daminski, never one to sit on the sidelines, had
been camped out in sonar ever since arrival at the strait. Sonar chief
Bruce Hillsworth, clad in his Royal Navy sweater with the embroidered
submarine dolphins on the breast, had grimaced in disgust, finally putting the intruder to work. Daminski sat at the forward console of the
four panels, wearing a set of headphones, his hands resting near a touch
keypad. Hillsworth, also wearing headphones, hovered over him, directing Daminski to flip through the computer displays, occasionally
having Daminski adjust the cursor ball to a particular bearing to listen
to the broadband noise. The other three display consoles of the BSY–1
sonar system showed graphs of noise intensity versus frequency, searching through the frequency gates for the expected tonals of the Destiny-
class target. Chief Hillsworth scanned the frequency buckets, allowing

each frequency search to integrate over five minutes, more if there were a spiking frequency, but so far every tonal gate had shown nothing but random noise.

The ocean around them was empty.

Daminsky looked at the broadband display as a bright line traced its way down the short-time screen. He squinted at the trace, moving his hand over the cursor ball, moving the spherical array beam to the bearing of the trace. When the cursor line was superimposed over the trace, Daminski shut his eyes and listened.

All he could hear was the frantic sound of the snapping of shrimp. He turned and looked at Hillsworth, face wrinkled in frustration.

"Just a bunch of fish getting it on."

"Don't worry, Cap'n. He'll come. And when he does, we'll hear him."

"Let's hope we hear him before he hears us," Daminski said, returning to his sonar search.

CNFS *Hegira*

The normally open control room was jammed with the majority of the ship's officers. The room was dominated by the circular periscope platform with the observation seat that could rotate on a circular track during periscope exposure. Now at depth, the control seat was folded down into a compact box with a cushion on top, the box serving as the captain's command seat.

Commodore Sharef had called battle stations for the passage through the strait, bringing twelve men into the packed room. He stood at the computer chart display table. He was the battle stations attack officer, as tradition demanded. First officer al-Kunis stood next to him, acting as the battle coordinator, responsible for the functioning of the entire team. On the periscope stand was Commander Omar Tawkidi, the navigator and third in command, who was stationed as deck officer. Lieutenant Commander Aby Haddad, the ship's senior watch officer, was the junior deck officer. Reporting to the four senior officers were the main functions of weapons control, ship control, reactor control, and sensor control. At each of the stations two officers sat at the Second Captain console displays, except at sensor control, where four officers scanned the computer analyzed data coming in from the large hull arrays and the gyrostabilized linear towed array.

As the ship approached the mouth of the strait Commodore Sharef ordered the ship to dead slow ahead, just enough velocity to keep the towed array from dragging. He and al-Kunis took up positions in the sensor-control corner, watching the displays of the sonar system.

"Anything?" Sharef asked Sublieutenant al-Maari, the sensor-control officer at one of the displays. The sublieutenant turned toward Sharef, the young man's earphones half-removed from his right ear. He shook his head and returned to his display.

"Deck officer, put in a Second Captain delouse."

"Yes, sir," Tawkidi said, turning to the ship-control console. "Ship control, ten clicks and prepare for a delouse. Reactor control?"

"Reactor is ready," the mechanical officer reported.

"Ten clicks," the ship-control officer reported.

"Engine stop. Reactor control, commence delouse," Tawkidi called.

The term delouse was handed down from old Soviet tactics, which the UIF's Combined Naval Force had inherited with the Victor III submarine acquisitions. It referred to the Russian tactic of an attack submarine escorting a ballistic-missile submarine out of port. To ensure that no lurking American attack submarines were trailing the ballistic-missile ship, the Russian attack-escort sub would perform a detailed antisubmarine search of the sea in the vicinity of the ballistic-missile ship, an attempt to "delouse" her. The tactic had lived on in the Destiny-class, in which the Yokogawa Second Captain computer was able to perform a self-delouse by shutting down the entire propulsion plant, allowing the sonar systems to hear unimpeded by own-ship's noise.

At the reactor-control console the mechanical officer inserted the command shutting down the reactor, dropping control rods into the liquid metal cooled core until the unit went subcritical and ceased heating the circulating liquid metal. The magnetohydrodynamic coolant pumps cut off, halting the liquid sodium flow, the conductive sodium acting as an emergency cooling system, keeping the core from melting from its residual heat. In the next compartment aft, the turbine generators spun down, their steam from the boilers now lost. Large automatic cutoff valves then shut, isolating the steam headers. The condensate and feed pumps in the lower level shut down next. The electrical power grid, responding to the loss of power input from the turbine generators, began drawing current from the battery in the farthest aft compartment until the ship was running on battery power alone. The *Hegira*'s main machinery silent, the ship coasted submerged, her computer systems straining to hear the sounds of the ocean, the signal-to-noise ratio now dramatically improved as the submarine drifted in the strait 400 meters deep.

All but the smallest thousandth of a percent of the ocean's noise was meaningless, random noise or biologics—fish. And what nonrandom noise the computers did hear was inevitably merchant shipping. The merchant ships outnumbered the warships five hundred to one. There was the occasional warship, detected at long range from a bottom bounce, but rarely a submarine, since submarines accounted for less than one of every fifty of the world's warships. Most submarines were short-range diesel boats designed for coastal defense. It would be odd to find a nuclear submarine as the first detection of the patrol, if this strange mission could be called that.

Sharef inserted several keystrokes, a new trace coming up on the screen in white, this trace the anticipated noise of a Los Angeles-class American attack submarine. The traces on the five- and ten-minute histories, with own-ship's noise subtracted out, were fairly similar to the expected white curve. The curves would never completely coincide, but just the slightest similarity was usually enough to classify the target. In this case the data was evident.

"Definite contact, Commodore," Tawkidi reported from one of the display consoles farther forward. "Seven-bladed screw, no cavitation, high-pressure, high-flow pumps, electrical turbine tonal at sixty-one cycles. The contact is submerged, bearing three one zero. Range is distant. The detection may be a surface bounce—we've got a good sound channel down to 700 meters."

Sharef glanced at the ship's chronometer. It had taken twelve minutes to integrate the sonar data to find the submarine waiting for them. The one disadvantage of the *Hegira*'s power module was its small battery. With the tremendous load of the Yokogawa Second Captain supercomputer and minimum ventilation loads, the battery could only last for a twenty-minute delouse.

"Battery power, reactor control?" Sharef asked.

"Twenty percent remaining, sir."

Sharef frowned. "How long?"

"Maybe another five minutes, sir," the mechanical officer reported. "Then we'll have to bring the reactor back up."

"Deck officer, can you keep the contact once we restart the plant?"

Tawkidi frowned over the sensor consoles, the other four watchstanders there concentrating on the screens, al-Kunis and Sharef's presence making the area crowded.

"Yes, I believe so, Commodore. The computer has a definite trace now. The contact, as distant as he is, will stay within a few degrees of the bearing of initial contact. We can work with that, sir."

"Very good. Restart the reactor and maneuver the ship for a range on the target, then prepare for torpedo attack."

Within a few moments, the reactor plant systems were back on line, the computers were able to stay locked onto the target's sonar emission. Sharef drove *Hegira* across the line-of-sight to the target submarine and established a parallax range of ninety-two kilometers, an extremely long-range detection at the very limits of sonar reception.

"How close do you want to come before we shoot, sir?" al-Kunis asked.

"Close enough so that we do not miss. Be patient, Mr. First. We will get to a range of forty kilometers, then launch."

Sharef and al-Kunis moved to the chart table, watching the bearing to the target plot out on the chart, the flashing dot indicating the target over ninety kilometers away at the northwest mouth of the strait. Sharef ran his hands though his hair, wondering how many more submarines he would have to find before he could make good the escape from the Mediterranean.

"Status of the weapons?" Sharef called to the deck officer.

"Large-bore tubes two through six are equalized to sea pressure, bow cap doors open, Nagasaki torpedoes spinning up now," Tawkidi reported, glancing at the weapons status display. "We'll be ready to launch in less than one minute."

"Very good. Equalize and open bow cap doors to tube eleven and spin up the Dash Five."

Tawkidi gave the orders to the officers seated at the weapon panels, then looked at Sharef. "You think we should use our only evasion device?"

At that moment Ahmed and General Sihoud walked into the room.

"Warm up the Dash Five evasion unit," Sharef said, looking at the visitors. "We need it."

USS *Augusta*

Daminski concentrated on bearing one one zero, the selected spherical array broadband beam. The sounds of white noise were piped into his earphones, the sounds of the ocean a slushy mix of rushing sounds from the waves, distant schools of dolphins, hissing from shrimp, the rumble of ocean floor and perhaps Daminski's inner ear itself, the noise from the sea much like the inside of a conch shell held to the skull. He was about to rip the earphones off for a few moments when his shoulder was tapped.

The radioman of the watch stood behind Daminski's high-backed seat holding a clipboard. "Your draft contact message, Captain. OOD said you wanted to load a message into a SLOT buoy." SLOT was shorthand for submarine-launched one-way transmitter, a baseball-bat-sized buoy that could be put out of a signal ejector, float to the surface and transmit a UHF message to the satellite without requiring the sub to come up to periscope depth.

Daminski knew this was cheating but so be it. He had been ordered to send a detailed contact report when he detected the Destiny. Before the encounter the Pentagon wanted to know that Destiny's location had been pinpointed and reported so that if anything went wrong, they would know where to send the next unit to sink the UIF submarine. Orders to transmit were an incredible burden on a submarine trying to sneak up on an adversarial contact. Transmitting a contact report meant going up to periscope depth in the middle of a shipping lane, putting up the BIGMOUTH antenna, and transmitting a message that might take five minutes to write, confirming the position of contact and all the other bullshit data the sidelines officers wanted: signal-to-noise ratio, first detected frequency, target bearing and range, target course and speed, on and on. The ship would take needless minutes and make unnecessary noise ascending to periscope depth, transmitting, and descending again before the attack could be started.

But then, orders were orders, which was why Daminski had decided to cheat, writing a contact report in advance, anticipating contact and preloading the message in a SLOT buoy that he could launch from test depth with no more interruption of the attack business than the push of a button, then get on with sinking the UIF submarine. After all, the only thing the topside sailors *really* needed was the information that *Augusta* had contact at the approximate position and that the attack was underway. Anything else they could find out when it was over.

Daminski scratched a few lines on the clipboard.

DATE/TIME: TRANSMISSION LOG AT DETECTION OF UHF BUOY

FLASH FLASH FLASH FLASH FLASH FLASH FLASH FLASH FLASH FLASH FLASH

    FM   USS AUGUSTA SSN—763

    TO   CINCNAVFORCEMED

    SUBJ   CONTACT REPORT

SCI/TOP SECRET—EARLY RETIREMENT

//BT//

    1. CONTACT REPORT FOLLOWS.

    2. POSITION APPROXIMATE IN STRAIT OF SICILY LATITUDE NOVEMBER THREE SEVEN DEGREES ONE THREE MINUTES LONGITUDE ECHO ONE ONE DEGREES TWO ONE MINUTES, MODIFIED BY POSITION OF UHF BUOY.

    3. COMMENCING ATTACK.

    4. FURTHER DETAILS TO FOLLOW.

//BT//

Daminski reread the message. He especially liked "commencing attack."

"Show it to the officer of the deck, then code it into the SLOT buoy. I want that buoy loaded in the signal ejector in five minutes."

"Aye, sir." The radioman took the clipboard and vanished. Daminski strapped his earphones back on and turned to the console. He was interrupted again, this time by Chief Hillsworth.

"Captain, I think you'd better check this," he said, punching keys on Daminski's touch pad. The lower waterfall display of the broadband spectrum blinked out, replaced by several graphs of sound intensity against frequency. The graph with 154 hertz in the center looked like a child's sketch of twin peaks.

"A doublet," Daminski said, "right where the old SPL said it would be, minus one cycle. Good thing we opened the gates, right, Chief?"

"We'd have found it anyway, Cap'n."

As the men watched, the twin hills on the graph grew in height, the hills becoming mountains, then columns, then spikes. No fish or natural phenomena made frequencies that pure. The tonals were man-made. It was a machine. A submarine.

"Nice nipple erections on that freak bucket, eh, Chief?" Daminski asked, not averse to bugging the proper Hillsworth. "Can I make the report?" Hillsworth nodded. Daminski pulled the boom microphone to his mouth.

"Conn, Sonar. New narrowband contact, designate Sierra Four, showing a double frequency at one five four hertz, approximate bearing one three zero. Contact is a submerged warship."

"Sonar, Conn, aye. Captain to control."

"On the way," Daminski replied to his boom mike. "Meanwhile designate Sierra Four as Target One. Launch the contact message radio buoy and man silent battle stations, spin up all four Mark 50s and open two torpedo tube outer doors."

"Captain, Conn, aye."

Daminski handed Hillsworth the earphones, stood up and clapped the chief on the shoulder, then left the sonar room, shutting the door quietly behind him.

11

FRIDAY, 27 DECEMBER

Strait of Sicily

The baseball-bat-sized SLOT buoy rested inside a tight tube on the flank of the forward part of the ship. It had not waited long when the tube's insides filled with seawater, the pressure increasing until it matched the outside sea pressure of the Mediterranean. A few seconds later the muzzle door opened; there was no more light in the tube than there had been before. Another moment, and the lower end of the tube pressurized with flowing seawater at a higher pressure than the seawater outside. The SLOT buoy was launched from the tube, the force of the ejection and its own buoyancy carrying it to the surface over 500 feet above. For several minutes the buoy rose in the dark seawater, the pressure around it easing as it drifted upward. The buoy breached the surface, the upper few inches of the unit drying out in the sea air, open-circuiting a sensor that eventually caused a whip antenna to flip up into the moonlit sky. The transmitter inside began sending Daminski's contact message to the UHF communications satellite above, repeating the message over and over until an hour later the battery was exhausted and the buoy shut down, flooded, and sank back into the depths of the sea.

High overhead, in a geosynchronous orbit, the Navy's CommStar communications satellite received the message the first time it was transmitted, logged in the time, and seeing the message priority as FLASH, interrupted its other tasks and retransmitted the message to the COMMSAT in orbit in mid-Atlantic, which then relayed the message to the U.S. Navy communications facility deep inside the Pentagon. There in the special compartmented communications center, an annunciator alarm went off on a computer console, alerting the watchstander of the flash message. Immediately after the message printed out the senior chief radioman made a call on a top-secret cleared phone to the office of the commander in chief of naval forces Mediterranean, Admiral John Traeps. Traeps's aide, a lieutenant commander, ordered the message taken to Flag Plot, where Traeps was conferring with the CNO. The printout was hand-carried to Admiral Traeps and Admiral Richard Donchez in Flag Plot. Traeps read it, initialed it, passed it to Donchez, who commanded the position be plotted on the electronic wall chart. Within thirty seconds a flashing blue dot appeared on the chart's Strait of Sicily, the dot labeled USS AUGUSTA SSN–763 SUBMERGED OPERATIONS; beside it a flashing orange dot's label announced UIF DESTINY UNIT ONE.

Traeps had called a radioman over to take a message. Traeps handed him the message from the *Augusta,* with orders to copy the message to the USS *Phoenix,* now on station guarding Gibraltar and the entrance to the Atlantic, to the *Reagan*'s ASW Viking jets, and to the Sigonella Orion ASW patrol turboprops.

Donchez looked up at the chart and nodded. Within the hour he should be calling Barczynski to tell him the good news.

USS *Augusta*

In the control room, officer of the deck Mark Berghoffer looked expectantly at Daminski, who had just shouldered his way into control from the door to sonar. Daminski began giving orders faster than they could be acknowledged.

"Off'sa'deck, I have the conn. Helm, all ahead one third, turns for five knots, left ten degrees rudder, steady course two four zero. Dive, make your depth 1,000 feet. Give me tube status, off'sa'deck . . ."

The deck inclined downward as the helmsman pushed the control yoke for the sternplanes to the full-dive position. As the deck leveled off, the room began to fill with men, all four consoles of the attack center manning up with officers on headsets, phonetalkers backing up the ship-control station, plotters working manual plot tables to back up the computers, executive officer Danny Kristman arriving as firecontrol coordinator, Tim Turner taking over as battle stations officer of the deck, Kevin Skinnard manning the attack center's Position Two, Jamie Fernandez beside him at Pos One, the weapons officer Ron Hackle at the firing panel. Daminski checked his watch—battle stations had been fully manned within two minutes of his arrival at the conn. Not bad.

As the watchstanders settled in, information began its flow to put a torpedo on the contact. Three minutes after Daminski's maneuver to the west, Skinnard dialed in a trial range and speed of the target. His estimate of target course was good, assuming the Destiny was heading through the strait going outbound, making it going northwest.

"XO," Skinnard called on his boom mike to Kristman, the battle stations firecontrol coordinator, "I have a curve and a fair solution based on narrowband TMA. Range 43,000 yards, target speed eighteen knots."

Kristman appeared over Skinnard's shoulder and looked at the dot stack, then turned to Daminski.

"Captain, based on narrowband TMA, we have a firing solution."

"Sonar, Captain," Daminski called, "any broadband detects yet?"

"Conn, Sonar, no," Hillsworth replied.

Daminski turned to Kristman. "I hate to shoot on a narrowband solution."

"I recommend we shoot a horizontal salvo now, sir. We don't know what this guy's detection threshold is. He could counterdetect any second."

"Yeah, but if we shoot early and he hears the fish or the launch transient, he'll turn tail and run and we miss our chance. For *Early Retirement.*"

"If we don't shoot and he gets off a shot first, we'll be the ones running."

Daminski glanced across at the Pos One geographic plot, made a decision. "Attention in the firecontrol team," he said, his football-huddle voice grabbing the attention of every watchstander in the room. "We have a narrowband solution to Target One and I'm putting out a horizontal salvo of Mark 50s down the strait. The range is distant, so to conserve weapon-fuel usage we'll use a slow transit speed with a shallow depth run to enable. That will also keep the torpedoes quiet as they do their run. Everybody got that? Be ready for a counterfire if this guy sees us first. Carry on." Daminski turned to Kristman again. "Torpedo presets, XO—offset the torpedoes by one degree, run to enable 25,000 yards, low-to-medium active snake. Give me a readback."

Daminski watched the firing panel until the torpedoes were programmed, then took a last look at Skinnard's dot stack. The solution was tracking. It was time to shoot.

"Attention in the firecontrol team. Firing point procedures, tubes one and two, Target One, horizontal salvo, one degree offset, one minute firing interval."

"Ship ready," officer of the deck Tim Turner reported.

"Weapons ready," firing panel operator Ron Hackle called.

"Solution ready," Skinnard said from Pos Two.

Daminski looked around one last time. In another five seconds he would have ordnance in the water aimed at another submarine. This wasn't an exercise, this was the real thing. Daminski called out the start of the launching litany.

"Tube one, shoot on generated bearing."

"Set." Skinnard on Pos Two, sending the firecontrol computer's estimate of the target position, course and speed into the torpedo.

"Standby." Hackle on the firing panel, rotating the trigger to nine o'clock.

"Shoot!" Daminski from the conn.

"Fire." Hackle, taking the trigger to the three-o'clock position marked FIRE.

The air in the room seemed to detonate in a reverberating blast, smashing Daminski's ears as the high-pressure air from the piston ram vented inboard, the air sent to pressurize the water tanks surrounding the torpedo tube, which then flushed the torpedo out of the tube. The watchstanders yawned in unison, clearing their ear passages from the pressure pulse.

"Conn, Sonar," Hillsworth's British accent declared on the firecontrol phone circuit, "own-ship's unit, normal launch."

"Firing panel lined up for tube two, sir," Hackle reported.

"Tube two, shoot on generated bearing," Daminski repeated.

"Set."

"Standby."

"Shoot!"

"Fire!"

The deck jumped beneath Daminski's feet and his ears slammed again.

"Conn, Sonar, second-fired unit, normal launch."

"Weps, cut the wires on units one and two and shut the outer doors."

"Aye, sir, wires cut on one and two . . . outer doors shut on one and two."

"Open muzzle doors tubes three and four," Daminski said impatiently, cursing that it was taking so long to get out the salvo, but the tube banks could line up only one tube from each side at a time.

"Three and four open, presets loaded, ready for launch."

"Firing point procedures, tubes three and four, Target One," from Daminski.

"Ship ready."

"Weapons ready."

"Solution ready."

"Shoot on generated—"

Hillsworth's worried voice cut through Daminski's order: "Conn, Sonar, loss of Target One!"

"Sonar, Captain, say again."

"Sir, we've lost Target One. He's vanished."

CNFS *Hegira*

Ahmed walked slowly into the control room, glancing uneasily at Sihoud as he noticed how crowded the room was, almost the entire crew seated at the consoles or standing over the seated men. As crowded as the room was, it was eerily quiet, the only sounds a slight high-pitched whine from the three dozen computer consoles in the room. Something was definitely wrong. Ahmed's voice was hushed as he addressed Sharef.

"Commodore, what—"

Sharef impatiently waved Ahmed to silence while bending over a video display. Ahmed studied it, unable to make out anything useful in spite of being trained in the latest fighter cockpit computer weapons systems.

One of the ship's more senior officers, a commander with TAWKIDI written on his breast pocket, appeared next to Ahmed, as if it were his duty to brief Sihoud and Ahmed. He spoke in a hushed tone.

"We've detected a hostile coalition submarine in the narrows up ahead. Probably an American Los Angeles-class. He's blocking our exit. He probably does not know we are here."

Sihoud said nothing, just stood frowning at the computer screens and the officers' backs. Ahmed tried to find the general's eyes but Sihoud didn't acknowledge him.

"What are we going to do?"

"We aren't close enough yet. In a few minutes, when we are closer, we'll be launching a Nagasaki torpedo salvo at the coalition sub."

Ahmed frowned. "Why can't we fire the torpedo now?"

"We can, but the captain does not wish to give away our position by firing—torpedoes are noisy. If we launch from too great a distance, the target may hear and turn to run. A torpedo in a tail chase sometimes catches up, but sometimes it runs out of fuel before it can go into attack mode, and the sub escapes."

"Then chase him and fire again."

"We might not detect him again," Tawkidi said.

"Why not? You have this time," Ahmed said, his voice rising.

Sharef turned and glared at him. Ahmed felt his face flush.

"The sea does funny things with sound," Tawkidi said. "Detecting him now may be easy, but detecting him six hours from now may be impossible when the sun heats the water near the surface and changes the temperature profile and makes the biologics become active."

Ahmed shook his head. It was like being told his aircraft radar only worked on good days.

". . . torpedo launch transient . . ." an officer at one of the panels said quietly to Sharef, his earphone removed from one ear. "Incoming torpedo from the target, sir."

Sharef picked up a set of headphones and listened while staring at another display panel, the patterns on it different but still meaningless to Ahmed.

"Prepare to insert a computer delouse," Sharef commanded. "Select the Dash Five in tube eleven. Ship control, engine stop."

"Ready, sir."

"Engine stopped."

"Insert the delouse!" Sharef ordered.

"Shutting down now," the mechanical officer called to Sharef from the aft starboard corner of the room. "Reactor is shut down. Battery life is thirty percent."

The ventilation fans spun to a halt in the room and the heat of the computers and men immediately caused the temperature to soar. Sweat broke out on Ahmed's forehead, a drop forming on the end of his nose, his armpits wet.

Conversations in the room stopped. Nothing seemed to be happening, except the officers continued to stare at the computer videos.

"Tawkidi, what the hell is going on?" Ahmed asked, careful to keep his voice down.

"The Coalition sub launched a torpedo at us. We were wrong about him not hearing us." Tawkidi himself stared at the video screens, never looking at Ahmed or Sihoud.

"And? Why did you shut down the reactor? Won't the torpedo hit us?"

"It might." Tawkidi held his finger over his lips, silencing Ahmed. Ahmed finally saw Sihoud turn and look at him.

"Status of the Dash Five?" Sharef glanced at the bulkhead chronometer.

"Unit is warm, sir, bow cap open, emissions set at ninety decibels. Commodore, this is the only unit. If he shoots again, we have no more."

Sharef nodded, outwardly certain-looking, inwardly doubting one Dash Five on a journey like this would be enough.

"Shoot tube eleven."

"Fire eleven . . . tube indicates normal shot."

"Turn the Dash Five to course one zero zero, increase the emission to 120 decibels."

"Turn inserted, sir, passing north, passing east, steady on one zero zero, emitted noise at 120 dee bee."

Another prolonged silence in the room. The ship was airless, hot and incredibly humid. Ahmed's face and hair were soaked, the sweat filling his eyes. Suddenly he was acutely aware that there was a half-kilometer of seawater between him and the sky above.

"Turn the Dash Five to one four zero and increase to 130 decibels," Sharef ordered. The officer on the panel acknowledged, played with the computer, and reported his results.

"Second torpedo launch from the target, Commodore."

"Commander," Ahmed said to Tawkidi, "please tell us what's going on without my having to beg you, if you please."

"The commodore launched an evasion device programmed to sound like this ship—the Dash Five—louder than this ship but otherwise identical. Meanwhile the propulsion plant is shut down and quiet and we drift silently while the Dash Five confuses the torpedoes."

"Aren't you going to shoot back?"

"First things first. Once the incoming weapons are fooled, we'll shoot. Otherwise the enemy sub could steer the torpedoes and hit us. The commodore invented this tactic. It is brilliant, if untested."

Ahmed traded a glance with Sihoud. Sharef was using a combat tactic not invented by the Japanese—how good could it be?

"Bearing rate to the incoming weapons?"

"Constant bearing, sir," al-Kunis reported, frowning.

"That means the weapons are still coming for us. They haven't picked up the decoy yet," Tawkidi whispered.

Ahmed felt a wave of nausea rise in his stomach and continue upward until a band tightened around his forehead.

We're dead, Ahmed thought.

Daminski ripped off his one-earphoned headset and dropped it on the deck as he shouldered past the attack center consoles to the forward starboard corner of the control room. He grabbed the accordion door curtain separating control from sonar and pulled it open, the door ripped half off its track.

"What the hell is going on?" his voice loud and razor sharp.

"Nothing, sir. Afraid that's the problem," Hillsworth said to the sonar display screen. "Target One dipped below threshold signal-to-noise ratio. We've lost him."

"What about the one-fifty-four doublet?"

"Gone. Maybe he turned to an aspect that shields the turbine generators. Bloke might be running, giving us his screw. The propulsor might interfere with the tonal reception."

"If he's running you'd hear him on broadband."

"With a conventional screw, maybe. With this ducted water turbine, who knows? Why don't you chase him down the bearing line? He might turn up."

"Okay, I'll drive southeast." Daminski turned to leave, then faced Hillsworth at the door, pointing his crooked finger in the Brit's face. "Get on it, Chief. I want that son of a bitch back on this screen. Make damned sure you listen up for units one and two—they might pick up the target before we do."

Back in control, XO Danny Kristman handed Daminski his headset without a word. Daminski strapped it on.

"Attention in control," he snapped, "check fire tubes three and four. We've lost the contact because he's running from the units. We are pursuing him out the strait. When we regain contact we'll launch the second two units. Carry on. Helm, all ahead full, left two degrees rudder, steady course one four zero."

Daminski crossed his arms across his chest, waiting for sonar to redetect the contact. And waiting was not something Rocket Ron did well.

"Battery's low, Commodore."

By now the sweat pouring off Ahmed's face had soaked the chest of the coverall he'd been issued by al-Kunis. He tried to tell himself it was the oppressive wet heat in the crowded tomb of the control room, but he was honest enough with himself to accept that fear accounted for much of the sweat. A fear made worse, far worse, by his inability to save himself with his own action. He tried to avoid Sihoud's eyes; their violet irises contained no comfort, only mirrors of his own anxiety.

"How much longer?" Sharef asked.

"I'm showing zero. We've got to restart the power unit now or I won't even have enough current to pull the control rods out of the reactor core." The mechanical officer, Quzwini, was on the opposite corner of the room from Sharef and spoke in a hushed voice, almost a whisper, but his report cut through the room.

"Sir, incoming torpedoes are speeding up," al-Maari called from the sensor console beside Sharef.

"Give me another minute," Sharef said over his shoulder to Quzwini while concentrating on a screen.

"Computer's going down in twenty seconds, sir."

"Bearing rate?" Sharef asked al-Maari.

"Zero, constant bearing, still driving toward us . . ." al-Maari said, straining to hear in his headset, his face suddenly vexed. "I've got a ping, sir. Both weapons are pinging."

"Commodore, I've got to restart the plant, now!"

"Wait, Quzwini."

"The Dash Five has detected the pings . . . and is pinging back with the enhancer."

"Shutting down the computers now, Commodore."

"I said *wait,*" Sharef said sharply.

"Sir—"

"I'm getting severe cavitation from the torpedo screws," al-Maari interrupted. "They've gone to maximum speed. Now I have a right bearing drift, increasing, sir. The torpedoes are drawing right. They're going after the Dash Five decoy, both of them!"

"Restart the reactor!"

Ahmed felt a sigh of relief whooshing out of him—until the computer screens died and the lights went out and the remaining fans wound down. Five hundred meters underwater, the ship lost power.

12

FRIDAY, 27 DECEMBER

Strait of Sicily
USS *Augusta*

"Conn, Sonar, own-ship's units one and two are active and homing."
Hillsworth's report was calm, controlled. "We have return pings from
the target bearing one four four. Unit range gates are narrow."

Daminski smiled, raising his hands as if he'd just made the saving
tackle.

"Attention in the firecontrol team. We're not waiting for a solution.
I'm putting two Mark 50s down the bearing line to the target, high-
speed transit, run to enable 10,000 yards, active snake search. Firing
point procedures, tubes three and four, Target One, horizontal salvo,
one-half degree offset."

Daminski received the readiness reports and ordered the tubes fired.
Hackle took the trigger to the firing position twice; twice the deck shuddered and the atmosphere in the room blasted its pressure pulse pain-
fully into the ears of the watchstanders. Once the weapons were
launched Daminski slowed the ship to five knots, hoping to hear the
contact better in case it evaded again. But Hillsworth had it nailed, both
from the ping returns from torpedoes one and two and from broadband

and narrowband contact. The UIF Destiny-class submarine was doomed.

Daminski wondered for a moment if he should reload the tubes, all four now empty. Loading would create noise that could lead to the target hearing them well enough to put a counterfired torpedo down the bearing line. Leaving them empty, however, meant that he had nothing in his tubes to shoot a surprise contact, a second hostile submarine coming out of nowhere.

The UIF had only one Destiny submarine. Their Victor IIIs were bottled up in port and were either broken down or louder than was good for them. And there was no way this enemy ship would counterdetect the *Augusta*.

This was why they paid him command pay, Daminski thought, and made a command decision—leave the tubes dry and reload later.

Battle lanterns, large flashlights in waterproof boxes, came on, barely holding back the thick darkness in the control room. Ahmed felt the evening meal trying to rise in his throat. He forced it back down, the taste bitter.

"Ship control," Sharef said, his voice commanding and sharp from the forward starboard corner of the control room, "have you got depth control?"

The ship control officers at the console stared at a row of old-fashioned electrical instruments illuminated by the battle lantern behind them. How the instruments worked, Ahmed could only guess; perhaps they had their own battery pack behind the panel. Ahmed considered Sharef's question in the dim room surrounded by helpless navy officers and blank screens. A loss of depth control would mean that they were . . . *sinking.*

"Hydraulic backups are functional, Commodore," a very young officer said from the left seat of the two. "Depth 510 meters, negative depth rate. Air bottles are fully charged."

"Keep the ship above 800 meters with air bubbled to the negative tanks, but minimize air use. Keep the angle zero within seven degrees."

"Yessir."

Sharef checked his chronometer in the light of a battle lantern.

Ahmed considered asking what was going to happen but thought better of it when he saw Sharef glaring at him in the dark airless space. Sharef leaned over the dead chart table and drummed his fingers on the horizontal video-screen glass.

Ahmed checked his own watch, wondering how long the ship would float in the sea, powerless, while the Coalition submarine and its torpedoes were out there, searching for them.

* * *

Daminski frowned at the report from sonar, his eyes meeting Kristman's. Ron Hackle, the weapons officer at the firing panel, turned around and joined in the silent conference of consternation.

"Say again, Sonar," Daminski said slowly, trying to think.

"Captain, Sonar, the first two own-ship units are at the bearing to Target One, active pinging range gates so narrow that the torpedoes are within a hundred yards of the target. But that situation continues. The torpedoes sound like they're in reattack."

"Ron, what's that mean to you?" Daminski asked the weapons officer.

"The units are on top of the target, sir. They should be detonating. Instead they're going into reattack."

"Why the hell would two units go into reattack?"

Daminski leaned over the firing panel to look at the Pos Four display of data from units three and four, which were still attached by thin electronic wires to the torpedo tubes and from there to the firecontrol computer. It was unfortunate that he had had to cut the wires on units one and two in order to line up the tube banks to shoot three and four; the data from one and two would likely solve this problem.

"What do the units say?"

"Still on the run to enable," Hackle said.

Daminski turned to the conn and mumbled to himself. "Units one and two on top of the target and going into reattack mode. Reattack mode. Which means they lost the target and are turning to find it again. But they keep pinging, so they reacquire the target, but then lose it and go into reattack again."

Daminski paused and looked at Kristman. "Why would a unit go into reattack?"

"Bad proximity sensor," Kristman said slowly. "The unit hears the target, homes on it, but can't detect an iron hull or doesn't hit the hull directly, so it swings back around for another approach. Goes into reattack."

"One unit with a bad proximity sensor, okay. Two weapons? I don't think so. What if the sensor is good? Why would it go into reattack?"

"Blip enhancer? Or active countermeasures?"

"What?"

"The target could broadcast an active sonar ping that matches the incoming sonar pulse, with a frequency shift, timed to fool the torpedo's range gate."

"Like sending a return back early so the weapon thinks he's closer than he is."

"It's possible."

"Take a hell of a computer and a sonar system to do that," Daminski said. "And a damned quiet boat. Even then, it might work against one weapon, but against two? Or four?"

"What if we switched off the active on units three and four? That way they can't get confused."

"Do we have the signal-to-noise ratio we need to switch them to passive sonar mode?"

"Hillsworth'll know."

"Sonar, Captain, have we got enough SNR to switch units three and four to passive search mode?"

"Captain, Sonar, yes."

"Do it."

Hackle's fingers flashed over the panel, stabbing variable function keys, changing the display to a new menu showing torpedo presets. In the menu he changed the search mode from active to passive, programming the second-fired units to search for the target by listening only rather than pinging active and listening for the return.

The men in the room were quiet, waiting for the second pair of torpedoes to enable, to begin their search for the target. The wait took several minutes. Daminski stood behind Hackle and Kristman, wondering what the hell he'd do if the second units went into reattack.

Sharef had stared at his wristwatch on and off for the last ten minutes. Every time he did Ahmed watched him, waiting for the commander to *do* something. But nothing happened.

Sharef's thoughts would have confused Ahmed. Sharef was thinking about the Persian rug in his stateroom, about its intentional imperfection. The imperfection that had been woven into it as a symbol of mankind's humility before Allah, who was insulted by the thought of human perfection. And to Sharef, the imperfection of the *Hegira* was her battery, a battery much too small to allow the ship to hide under the acoustic curtain of a delouse maneuver. But unlike the rug, the submarine's imperfection would have consequences. It might end up killing them all. Maybe that would please Allah, Sharef thought, a bitterness edging his thoughts. He looked at his watch and up to see Ahmed staring at him. He flashed the air force officer a humorless smile. Ahmed frowned.

The deck sloped ominously downward, the ship in a dive. Sharef had ordered the man at the ship controls to let the ship dangle and not fix the angle unless it threatened to exceed seven degrees, but even a quarter degree was detectible to Ahmed, and one degree set off alarms in his mind that the ship was sinking. Five degrees felt like a ramp. With the deck at a five-degree dive, the forward end of the room was a half-meter lower than the aft end.

Finally Sharef moved behind the ship control consoles and spoke to the youngster in the left seat. The order made little sense to Ahmed:

"Bubble one and three, bring it up at point five per second, start your flood at a hundred, maintain thirty to twenty-five meters."

"Yes, sir. Bubbling one and three now."

A muffled sound of rushing air could be heard for a few seconds.

"Quzwini, lay below to the auxiliary diesel panel and prepare to snort."

The mechanical officer turned over the power plant consoles to a lieutenant and hurried out of the room. Ahmed searched the patches of dark and glare for Commander Tawkidi, finding him at the sensor console area leaning on one of the stations.

"Now what, Commander?"

"We're coming up to periscope depth to restart the reactor."

"Why don't we do that deep?"

"Battery's dead. We need electricity. Once we get near the surface we'll put up the snort mast and let the diesel engine breathe. The diesel generator will give us enough current on the grid to restart the reactor plant."

"Oh. But it will be loud, won't it? Will the enemy hear us?"

"Yes. But that is the commodore's decision."

The deck leveled off, then began inclining the opposite direction, the aft end sinking. The boat drifted upward, the deck continuing its slow oscillations. Ahmed felt his frustration intensify at how ridiculous it was to have lost power and drift in the sea at the most critical moment, when they were under attack by an enemy submarine. If they survived this madness he intended to ask Sihoud to have Sharef fired.

Two decks below, in the aftmost bulkhead of the command module in the equipment room, Commander Ibn Quzwini took a seat at the auxiliary diesel console, his battle lantern lighting the dead gauges. His walkie-talkie radio on his belt squawked.

"Quzwini, raise the snort mast."

Quzwini took the cover off a hydraulic control valve, careful to keep any leakage inside the cover from spilling on the deck. He grabbed the knob of the valve lever and pushed it up and to the right, then locked it into position. A hiss and a thunk sounded from the overhead as the high-pressure hydraulic oil forced the snort mast out of the fin and extended it high over the hull.

Ten meters above the command module, the submarine's fin neared the surface in an attempt to reach the air, to bring it into the ship to feed the hungry diesel. The snort mast, a pipe with a water-sensing valve at the top, pointed to the waves, finally broaching the surface and extending toward the night sky.

"Control, Quzwini, snort mast is up."

"Depth is two seven meters."

"Mast is broached. Draining the induction manifold."

Quzwini manipulated several more hydraulic controllers that operated large shutoff valves in the piping from the snort mast to the diesel engine induction. He was careful, since flooding the diesel with seawater would ruin their chances of restarting his reactor in the next minutes. He lifted a metal cover from a high-pressure air station and operated a valve that would blow out the water from the exhaust piping. Finally the engine was ready. He hit an air valve that rolled the massive engine, ensuring the bearings were lubricated with oil before he started the diesel. He reached below the panel and pulled a plastic cover off an electrical knife switch, the circuit connected to several car batteries housed inside the console, the electricity that would energize the field coils of the generator and allow it to produce power. He rotated the knife switch, flashing the field, then smashed his palm against the start button set in the air-control valve manifold.

Immediately the high-pressure air flowed loudly into the diesel intake manifold and turned the machine, the heavy engine accelerating slowly until it was at speed. Quzwini, going more by feel than any operating procedure, stabbed another air-control valve, commencing diesel engine fuel injection, hoping the engine would continue to roll. Its own compression would have cylinder temperatures high enough for ignition. Reaching again by feel, he cut off the high-pressure starting air just as he heard the engine roar to life, the sound loud even though the beast was three compartments aft. The deck trembled as the machine came up to speed, the sound violent and painful. He watched the output voltage meter, coaxing the machine under his breath, watching the needle rise from the zero peg and climb steadily until it stopped at 250 volts. Quzwini wiped his forehead with his sleeve. The diesel had made it up. Normally he would nurse the engine, giving it twenty minutes to heat up and stabilize the bearing oil temperatures and jacket water outlet, but this was no training exercise.

He popped a cover off a large electrical breaker and punched the red button marked CLOSE, then watched the battery bus voltage meter needle zip up to 250 volts. Up on the main panel he checked the engine speed and diesel voltage. The engine had held now that it was loaded with the current drain of the dead battery. He stood and walked forward along the panels of the Yokogawa Second Captain supercomputer until he reached the 400-hertz motor generator control cubicle, one of the power generators for the computers. He shut its breaker and shone his flashlight on its voltage and current meters. The motor generator set came up to speed in the steam module compartment, supplying the computers with their odd 400-cycle AC power. He stepped to the 120-volt 60-cycle panel and performed the same function for the computer's 60-cycle power generator. When it came up to speed he shut a breaker and reported to the control room that they could restart the Second Captain.

He took a walk back to look at the diesel panel, scanning its instruments one last time. Time to get back to the control room and restart the reactor.

He grabbed his battle lantern and started the walk. By the time he reached the stairs, the overhead lights had come back on. He hurried back to the control room's aft starboard corner, acknowledging Sharef's smile, then sat in the control seat. The reactor core display took some time coming up on the console, but finally the Second Captain had warmed up and the display showed core status. Quzwini selected the electrical distribution network on an adjacent console and pointed to his subordinate to energize the main ship service AC motor generator set. Lieutenant Kutaiba, the propulsion officer, brought the machine up, energizing the high-voltage AC bus network. Quzwini now had power to his control rod drive motors, and he stabbed the soft response key that was configured to commence reactor startup.

Two modules aft, in the reactor bay, the rod drive motors began pulling control rods out of the uranium core, the power module that had once been eyed by Sihoud as raw material for his desired nuclear weapon, but the fuel would have taken over a year to reprocess with an entire reprocessing plant to isolate the uranium—the reprocessing plant itself would have taken over a year to build, so Sihoud had left the Japanese-constructed core alone and searched for nuclear weapon material elsewhere.

Within three minutes the core was in the power range, the steam headers were warm, and Quzwini had begun spinning up the turbine generators. As soon as he brought the first electrical turbine onto the grid he shot orders at Kutaiba to secure the snorting operation. The diesel engine aft shut down, the absence of its reassuring roar making the ship unnaturally quiet. There was a clunking noise as he lowered the snort mast. Quzwini continued bringing the power module up, finally putting the propulsion turbine generators on-line. He turned to Sharef.

"Sir, the plant is back, propulsion AC motor is ready."

"Dead slow ahead, dive to 500 meters," Sharef ordered. He left his spot behind Quzwini and turned to al-Kunis in the sensor area. "Find the submarine as soon as you can. Weapons officer, reapply power to the Nagasaki torpedoes in tubes one through five."

Hillsworth shook his head as he held his headset's earphone to his skull.

"Conn, Sonar, Target one has shut down, last bearing one three eight. I still have four units between bearings one three five and one four zero, all four in reattack mode. And sir, I'm getting diesel engine noises from astern, edge of the starboard baffles."

In the control room Daminski stared at the firing panel. The weapons that still had their wires connected had acquired on the target, gotten close enough to go to final warhead arming, then lost the target and gone into reattack. Not one detonation. And now sonar reported a loss of the target and a diesel engine noise from astern. From *behind* them.

Daminski turned to look at Kristman, ideas forming themselves in his mind, all of them colliding and sparking as they swooped through his head.

The torpedoes went into reattack close to the target.

Both passive and active homers.

Reattack. Couldn't find the target.

Target shuts down.

Diesel engine startup from the baffles.

"Cut the wires tubes three and four, shut the outer doors, drain the tubes and reload one through four!" Daminski shouted to Hackle, his voice oddly loud, as if he had become half-deaf. "Helm, right five degrees rudder, all ahead one third!"

"What is it, sir?"

"Fucker fooled us with a goddamned *decoy, that's* what. That's why the units kept going into reattack. They can't get a proximity signal on a decoy. Now that asshole is snorkeling from his launch position—must have shut down his reactor to run silent and something went wrong, tripped a battery breaker. Hackle, get those torpedoes loaded and open the outer doors, tubes one and two. Helm, steady course one four five. Attention in the firecontrol team. The diesel engine is redesignated Target Two. Target One is a decoy and will be dropped from firecontrol. Give me a two-minute leg to Target Two before we maneuver, then we'll shoot another salvo at him. Carry on."

"Conn, Sonar," Hillsworth's voice shouted, "diesel engine transients designated Target Two have shut down. Loss of Target Two, last bearing, three one five."

"Status of the tubes, Hackle!"

"Sir, we've drained down and are loading a Mark 50 into tube one now, it'll be another three minutes before we're connected and spun up."

"Goddamn it. Get those fish loaded."

Daminski was furious at himself for leaving the tubes unloaded. It would take five minutes to warm up the weapon gyros and shoot them, if he had a firecontrol solution, which he didn't with Target Two shutting down.

"Sonar, Conn, what's the status of Target Two?"

"Still nothing, sir."

"Son of a bitch."

"Regained contact on the Coalition sub, Commodore. He's maneuvering. Towed array range is crude but workable at eight kilometers. We have the target bearing and range set into the torpedoes in one through five."

"Status of the weapons?" Sharef asked.

"Nagasaki torpedoes warmed up, bow caps open, target solution programmed, sir."

Sharef nodded. "Shoot tubes one through five."

"Firing one . . ."

The deck trembled with the power of the tube launch. Four more times the deckplates vibrated. Finally, Ahmed thought, Sharef was fighting back.

"Tube launches complete, tubes two through five and seven," al-Kunis reported. "All weapons running normally."

"Ship control, turn to three four zero, ahead sixty percent, maintain depth 500 meters."

"Yessir, turning to three four zero, sixty percent."

"Shut the bow caps on one through five, warm up six and seven and flood the tubes."

Ahmed watched, approving.

The first Nagasaki torpedo left the tube under the pressure of a gas generator at the breech end. Some moments before it had been divorced from the electrical power from the mother ship. The tube had fed in the target's data as well as the run speed and search pattern to be used on the target. The expanding gases at the base of the tube pushed on the aft end of the weapon, hard, pushing it into the cool curtain of the Mediterranean water. As the elliptical head of the torpedo left the envelope of the submarine's bow, the water flowed into a duct set low in the weapon's nose, spinning a small water turbine on jeweled bearings. The turbine generated a minute current in a generator that energized a small electromagnet in a relay; the magnet shut the relay contact in the engine start logic circuit, providing the computer with a signal to start the weapon's engine.

The pressurized peroxide fuel flowed out of the opened fuel solenoid valve into the combustion chamber, expanding into vapors as it entered the annular-shaped chamber with the ring of spark plugs. The plugs arced from the high-voltage current of the onboard battery, igniting the peroxide vapors, which soared in temperature at the inlet vanes of the axial turbine in the aft end of the torpedo. The gases spun the turbine and passed out the flapper exhaust valve into the surrounding sea. The spinning turbine turned a shaft connected to a ducted water jet propulsor, similar to the larger unit of the *Hegira*. The torpedo accelerated to its shallow depth cruising speed on the intercept course to the target, its sonar ears listening hard for the sounds of a gear-driven screw.

* * *

"Conn, Sonar! Torpedo in the water, bearing three one nine! Second launch, two torpedoes—no three—Conn, Sonar, we have multiple torpedoes in the water, all screws cavitating!"

"Helm, all ahead flank! Maneuvering cavitate!" Daminski shouted. "Dive, make your depth one three hundred feet. Off'sa'deck, load Mark 21 evasion devices in fore and aft signal ejectors. Helm, right half degree rudder, steady course one three zero."

Daminski watched the control room crew follow his orders until the ship was on course, running from the incoming torpedoes. This was a moment he had dreaded—at the business end of an enemy torpedo with nothing to do but run and hope they ran out of fuel. His stomach filled with acid.

"Conn, Sonar, how many torpedoes?"

"Sir, five torpedoes. Bearing rate zero. They're getting louder, Captain."

Daminski, in spite of trying to keep his mind from the memory, had been in this position before, but always in the attack simulators in Norfolk and Groton, rooms set up to look exactly like 688-class control rooms, with the same attack-center consoles and plots, a room adjacent to the simulator the sonar display room. If the overhead lights were blacked out, a crew could almost believe they were in an actual control room fighting the targets that appeared as diamond symbols on the firecontrol consoles. In the simulators, the computer "target" frequently fired torpedoes at the attacking submarine, turning hunter into prey, testing the approach officer's wits to see how well he could evade the torpedo—put the incoming weapon in the baffles due astern, or on the baffle edge if he wanted to be fancy and track it on broadband sonar and run at flank speed.

The reason Daminski hoped to forget was compelling. He had been shot at by the computer over twenty times in the last five years. In those twenty times, his ship had never survived. The computer's torpedoes always killed him. In the postattack mop-ups he had always wanted to know why the counterattacks were so lethal . . . "Maybe you're getting too close to the guy, Commander," a fire control chief had told him. "Shoot him from a longer range and if he shoots back the torpedoes might run out of fuel." "Yeah, and he'll hear mine and evade. I don't think so." "Suit yourself, sir." "Does anyone else survive being shot at? Any of these other 688-jockies on the Norfolk piers? Guys who shoot further out?" "You want to know the truth, sir?" "Give it to me straight, Chief," Daminski had asked, wondering if his own tactics were truly flawed. "Commander, nobody survives. Unless the torpedo coming at you is so far off your bearing that it goes the wrong way, or so grossly flawed that it won't detonate, or a *long* way away when you first hear it, that's it. A sixty-knot long-range torpedo coming down your bearing line will almost always nab a forty-knot submarine. Of course, you might be up against a slower running torpedo. But I doubt it." "Thanks a load, Chief," Daminski had said.

Nobody survives.

Screw him, Daminski thought. When *Augusta* pulled back into Norfolk he'd look that chief up and demand a beer. Several beers. And an apology.

FRIDAY, 27 DECEMBER

Strait of Sicily

"Torpedoes are closing, all five in the baffles."

The deck shook as *Augusta* ran from the weapons. Daminski looked at the speed indicator, wondering how he could go faster.

"Off'sa'deck, status of the signal ejectors?"

"Mark 21s loaded, ejectors ready."

"Launch fore and aft."

"Aye, sir."

The two signal ejectors pushed out baseball-bat-sized noisemakers, one of them set to blow a large cloud of bubbles to confuse active sonar, the second programmed to make loud broadband noise, much like that made by the ship's screw as she plowed through the water at maximum speed.

"Get me the engineering officer of the watch on the JA," he said to Kristman. Kristman grabbed a phone handset and barked into it, then held it to Daminski. "EOOW, unload the turbine generators and pick up the loads from the battery. Take the mode selector to battleshort, then open the throttles to a 150 percent power, you hear me? And take T-ave to five twenty, that's right. Repeat that back . . . and listen, be damned sure you don't lose an AC bus—the last thing I need is to lose a main coolant pump. Do it."

He handed the phone back to Kristman, who nodded approvingly.

Daminski glared at the speed indicator, which slowly climbed from thirty-eight knots to forty-two. Daminski had given orders that might breach the fuel elements and melt the core, and all he had gotten from it was four lousy knots. Parasitic drag, he thought abstractly. Daminski climbed the periscope platform and grabbed a sheet of paper from the navigator's pad, scribbling on it for a few seconds, then pausing. For a few moments he put his hand into his coverall suit and fingered the letter from Myra, then shook his head and finished writing. He looked for Kristman and called the executive officer to the conn periscope platform, away from the men at the attack-center consoles. He pulled the XO close.

"Danny, send for a radioman with a SLOT buoy. Have him code this in quickly. Load it forward." Kristman reached for a phone, intercepted the radioman entering control and gave him the paper without reading it. The young radioman left in a hurry.

The next item on his mind was the tubes. He still might be able to get off a counter-fire, even without a solution on the target.

"Weps, what's the status?"

"Sir," Hackle's voice seemed higher than usual, with just a suggestion of a tremble. "One and two are dryloaded. Mark 50 power is on, self-checks still in progress. Recommend flooding tubes and opening outer doors."

"Flood one and two and open the outer doors."

"Sir," Kristman said, touching Daminski on his shoulder, "we'll have to slow to shoot the units. Twenty knots, maybe twenty-five."

"Do you really think they'll have a problem?" *Augusta*'s tubes were located far aft of the bow and were canted outward ten degrees, making the torpedoes leave the ship at an angle. At forty-two knots of forward velocity the weapons would get so much side force from the slipstream that they might bend or break. The standard operating procedure declared nonemergency launches be made under twenty knots—like a war-shot torpedo launch was ever routine . . .

"You heard about the flank-bell launch from *Trepang*, didn't you? One torpedo broke in half. The second one did fine. But those were exercise shots without warheads. You bust a warshot in half, it'll blow the compartment wide open."

"Our Arab friends might already have taken care of that. I'm more worried about the health of the torpedoes. A broken Mark 50 won't kill a target very well." Daminski faced the attack center. "Weps, what's the goddamned status?"

"Outer doors open one and two, self-checks complete, ready to fire. Except for the solution, sir."

Daminski leaned over the Pos Two panel and changed the mode from the dot-stacker to line-of-sight, an odd configuration showing two rowboats, one at the bottom representing own-ship, the one at the top the target. Daminski put the bearing of the target due astern at bearing 320, with a range of 20,000 yards, course northwest heading out of the strait.

"There, now you've got a solution. Keep that in."

"Conn, Sonar, we're getting active sonar from one of the torpedoes."

"What's the range gate look like?" The range of a torpedo could be guessed by how often it pinged active sonar. Long ping intervals meant the receiver had to wait to get a return ping over a large distance, rapid pings meant the torpedo needed to wait only seconds for the ping return and was close. The more rapid the pings, the closer the weapon.

"Ping interval is prolonged. Range is probably two thousand to three thousand yards."

A nautical mile, Daminski thought. He was a mile to a mile and a half ahead of the weapons. He was going forty-two knots. Allowing for a fifty-knot torpedo—no, he'd give it fifty-five knots—that meant he had between four and seven minutes till the torpedoes caught up.

"Listen up," he said to the watchstanders, "we'll be launching the counterattack now, then launching a radio buoy in the signal ejector telling the boss we've been attacked and to watch out for the Destiny's shutdown-and-hide tactics. I'm going to order us to slow to twenty knots to launch, then we'll throttle right back up and keep running. Ready? Helm, all back two-thirds, mark speed two one!"

The helmsman rang up the order on the engine telegraph. Back aft in the maneuvering room the throttleman answered the bell, shut the forward turbine throttles and opened up the astern turbines. The ship shook hard, as if rattled by the hand of a god. A bookcase above the chart table dumped its contents to the deck, one of the volumes hitting the plotting officer in the head on its way down.

"Speed two one, sir," the helmsman called.

"All stop! Snapshot tube one!"

"Set," Skinnard called.

"Standby and fire," Hackle said, rotating the trigger. The blast of the tube firing sounded more violent than the previous four.

"Snapshot tube two."

"Standby and fire." The second tube fired. Daminski shouted over the second blast, "All ahead flank, maneuvering cavitate, 150-percent reactor power, T-ave five twenty!"

The deck trembled again with the power of the screaming main engines. The speed indicator needle climbed slowly, too slowly, to forty-two knots.

"Conn, Sonar, both own-ship units, normal launch."

"Sonar, Captain, what's the pulse interval?"

"Sir, active sonar from the torpedo has shutdown."

"Jeez, what the hell does that mean?" Daminski mumbled to Kristman. "Danny, have we got that radio buoy loaded?"

Kristman nodded. "Loaded forward, tube flooded, muzzle door open."

"Shoot the forward signal ejector."

Daminski looked around the room at the watchstanders, trying to maintain his war face. There was nothing more he could do. He had shot back at the enemy submarine. He had warned CINCNAVFORCEMED that they were on the business end of five UIF torpedoes. He had launched evasion devices, for whatever good they would do. And he had taken the reactor far over the redline, overpowering it as far as he dared without melting the core or breaching the steam piping or blowing open a turbine casing.

He had *Augusta* running for her life.

He had always wondered whether he would want to know in advance if he were going to die. He had decided he would want five minutes warning, no more. Not enough time to worry about it, just time to think about the children and perhaps make peace with the angry Catholic Church God of his youth. Maybe say goodbye to the good things in life, tip back a Coors or down a shot of Wild Turkey. He tried to remember the last time he had made love to Myra but it was a blur. He fingered the letter from her, imagined her face. He had a momentary memory, sharp as a new razor, of the faces of his three little children, then one of his father, his dad angry even in this reflective memory—

"Conn, Sonar, active sonar from one of the torpedoes."

"Range gate?"

"Sorry, Cap'n, the unit is pinging a ramp wave in continuous."

Daminski shared a look with Kristman. The incoming torpedoes were so close that one of them was transmitting a continuous waveform, getting a precise fix on *Augusta*'s location.

There was only one thing he could do, Daminski thought. If he did an emergency surface, he might get above the ceiling setting of the weapon, or perhaps it would blow its warhead at the bubbles the ballast tanks left behind. And even if they got hit, maybe if they made it to the surface he could save some of the men, maybe not all, but some.

"Chief of the watch, emergency blow fore and aft! Diving officer, take her up, twenty degree up-bubble!"

The COW slammed two large stainless-steel levers into the overhead while the diving officer ordered the ship up. The room filled with the blasting noise of high-pressure air as the bottles emptied the air into the ballast tanks, pushing out the seawater and making the ship lighter.

The deck tilted up, the helmsman overreacting, the ship coming up in a thirty-degree angle before the diving officer could push the control yoke forward to get the bubble back to twenty degrees. The depth indicator numerals spun as the ship climbed out of the depths, heading for the surface, her speed aided by the buoyancy in the tanks, the speed indicator reading forty-five knots, then forty-six. *Augusta* was screaming for the surface.

But even over the noise of the roaring emergency blow system, Daminski could hear the wailing sonar system of the lead torpedo in pursuit. The depth indicator unwound, 500 feet, 400, 350, but the screaming siren of the torpedo sonar system grew louder. Daminski could hear the torpedo's screw itself, a whooshing sound just outside the hull. He turned away from the depth indicator on the ship control panel. It had spun to sixty feet as the bow of the ship blew out of the water, climbing at her tremendous velocity until the sail came out, then the long length of black hull, her underside painted a dull anticorrosion red, until gravity dragged her back, the deck already coming back to level as the ship fell back into the sea, the splash raising a cloud of water vapor in a 300-foot diameter around her. Her downward momentum then carried her under again, the hull vanishing from the surface, only the upper half of the sail breaking through the waves.

It was at that moment that the first Nagasaki torpedo detonated, the weapon having followed the target as it went shallow, as it the torpedo had expected it. The explosion was centered below the reactor compartment, the explosive force directed upward, breaching the hull and rupturing a steam generator and its main coolant piping, the seawater smashing into the compartment. The second Nagasaki detonated farther aft, beneath the turbine generators of the aft compartment, the hull breaching there too, the water filling the space. The third torpedo was a dud, the detonation from the second knocking the detonation train off, the preexplosive failing to detonate the high explosive and the unit disintegrated. The fourth torpedo impacted the aft section of the forward compartment, blowing a twenty-foot gash in the lower level, the blast smashing through two decks and tearing apart the navigation space aft of control before the water came flooding in. Daminski had a quarter-second to turn and see the deckplates flying upward in slow motion as the blast disintegrated the aft part of the room. The last torpedo detonated at the flank of the forward compartment, forward of the control room. The wall of water from the aft of control had washed its way to the plot tables by the time of the last explosion and its unmerciful water came blasting in from the forward end.

The lights went out as the plot table came off its mountings and smashed into Daminski, who would have hit the deck but instead splashed into seawater. He expected the impact of the table to kill him, but he was still conscious as the darkness came, not from death but from the seawater shorting out the battle lanterns.

Five feet to port, Dan Kristman was knocked into Tim Turner by the force of the invading wall of water, the force of their collision breaking bones, Kristman's ribs and Turner's arm and collarbone. The two officers flew forward into the ship control seats, knocking Turner out, snapping Kristman's neck, the bodies collapsing into the rising water.

Kevin Skinnard, sitting at Pos Two, was carried through the door to sonar and into a sonar-display console, the glass screen spider-webbed by the impact of his head. He was stunned but conscious when the unit blew sparks all around him as its power supply shorted out in seawater, an arc flashing in front of his face before the water filled the room, the battle lanterns in sonar surviving and illuminating the submerged room with a dim smoky light. Skinner tried to move, to swim, the water forcing its way into his lungs paralyzing him with shock. He had a fraction of a second to recall childhood nightmares of drowning, seeing ships sinking in deep water, wetting his bed after seeing a movie about the *Titanic,* upset too because his teddy bear was soaked. His father had preached confronting his fears, and as an adult he had, going into submarines in part to show himself that the fear of deep water—which he'd never told any of the SUBLANT shrinks about—had been overcome. Now he knew that fear had finally come for him. Eventually the pressure of the increasing depth burst his lungs, the bubbles rising sideways toward a bulkhead instead of up toward the overhead. The ship must be rolled nearly horizontal, he thought. It was his last thought.

In the control room Daminski felt himself pinned beneath the plot table and what he guessed was the deck beneath the attack center. The pressure around him increased, squeezing on his chest until his lungs gave out, breath forced out of him, water filling his body. In a part of his mind that still functioned he remembered how deep the sea was beneath him, the memory of the last fathometer report from Turner—over 900 feet there at the mouth of the strait. He had time to wonder whether he'd still be alive when the hull hit the sea floor before that thought and all others slowly faded . . .

The broken hull of the *Augusta* hit the rocky bottom of the Strait of Sicily at terminal velocity, seventy knots, going bow down. Two of her Mark 50 torpedoes detonated from the shock of the crash with the bottom. The impact split her into three pieces, the damage already done by the four torpedo detonations. For several minutes the reactor core spewed steam in protest against its loss of cooling, but soon the seawater brought the fuel temperature down, and the reactor merely put out hot water. The rush of bubbles from the hull took more than an hour to stop, the sea finally calm at the wreckage site, the water again quiet.

Nine hundred feet above, a SLOT radio buoy finished its last transmission, flooded and sank, coming to rest on the ocean floor a mile north-west of the wreckage.

Fifteen nautical miles to the northwest, aboard the UIF submarine *Hegira*, the report was received that the target had gone down. Several junior officers and Rakish Ahmed smiled until Commodore Sharef fixed them with a burning glare.

The two torpedoes launched from the target sub before it was hit had gone far off-course, eventually running out of fuel and sinking, and when they did, the last pieces of the *Augusta* came to rest on the ocean floor.

14

FRIDAY, 27 DECEMBER

Burke Lake, Virginia

Donchez pulled at his starched collar, cursing the bow tie of his dinner dress blue uniform, and asked the bartender for a Canadian on the rocks. Alone for the first time in the last half-hour, he took a moment to look at the house too grand—pretentious, perhaps—to be a mere house. General Clough called it his "lake cottage," a reference to the fact that he owned at least four residences, his old money put to work for him tonight as he entertained the entire Joint Staff from the chief petty officers and master sergeants all the way to General Barczynski himself. Clough stood in a far corner of the high-ceilinged living room, near one of the four couch arrangements, talking to two of Donchez's admirals, John Traeps and the visitor Roy Steinman up from Norfolk, the commander of the Atlantic Fleet's submarines. There were times, Donchez had to admit, when Clough's political skills were impressive; he might even have liked the man had the general not decided to attach his service's survival on the decline of the Navy—or perhaps his war was declared not on the Navy but on Donchez himself, as the ring of admirals around Clough would suggest. In the end, it didn't matter. All jobs, even chief of naval operations or chief of staff of the Air Force, were temporary.

Of course, even if he and Clough had a hot war between them instead of just broken diplomatic relations, Donchez would still be at the party, not out of obligation or ambition, not with any sort of duplicity or hypocrisy, but because of the odd military multiple-personality each of them had. Many times the military had reminded Donchez of an old cartoon that began with a sheepdog and coyote punching in a time clock, exchanging pleasantries until the work began, then each going through a day of murderous conflict, the coyote attacking the dog to get the sheep, the sheepdog defending, and after a dozen explosions of TNT and mishaps with crossbows and boulders on pulleys, the end-of-shift whistle blew, the combatants punching out the time clock, each hoping the other had a nice evening and planning their bowling outing. So many times in Donchez's career that had applied, his old executive officer on the *Thresher* literally shouting in his face at 1600, only to invite him for a beer at the club at 1730. The odd schizophrenia had repeated itself in his own leadership, when he had been XO of *Dace* and had to get the attention of one of the talented but inexperienced junior officers, finally raising his voice in a younger man's face—as he frequently had to Ronny Daminski—then continuing the man's training after-hours in the officers' club, laughing about the incident over a beer, and then beginning the same routine the next day when Daminski had messed up again. Even now, he and Clough and Barczynski could have their differences, even acidic conflicts, and still check their jobs at the door. They were, after all, in the same game, brethren of the same system, at the moment united against the Muslims on the other side of the globe and against all other enemies.

Barczynski walked up now, his collar unbuttoned, his hairy throat poking through, a Heineken dwarfed by his paw, a grin on his face. The two men chatted for several minutes. Barczynski finished an old tank story before Fred Rummel caught Donchez's eye from the end of the room, waving urgently. Donchez excused himself and walked with Rummel to the lakeside patio. Rummel shut the French doors behind them, a light snow falling in the mid-evening and beginning to accumulate on the cleared stones of the patio. Rummel looked around, then pulled a crumpled piece of paper stamped TOP SECRET, with the code words *Early Retirement* under the TS stamp. Donchez initialed the sheet with Rummel's pen, then read the last message from the *Augusta*.

DATE/TIME: TRANSMISSION LOG AT DETECTION OF UHF BUOY

FLASH FLASH FLASH FLASH FLASH FLASH FLASH FLASH FLASH FLASH FLASH

FM   USS AUGUSTA SSN–763

TO   CINCNAVFORCEMED

SUBJ   CONTACT REPORT

SCI/TOP SECRET—EARLY RETIREMENT

//BT//

1. CONTACT REPORT NUMBER TWO FOLLOWS.
2. POSITION APPROXIMATE IN STRAIT OF SICILY AT DETECTED POSITION OF SLOT BUOY.
3. USS AUGUSTA ATTACKED DESTINY SUBMARINE WITH MULTIPLE MARK 50 SALVO. WEAPONS DID NOT DETONATE, WE SUSPECT, BECAUSE DESTINY HAD RELEASED A FULL-SPECTRUM DECOY THEN SHUT DOWN REACTOR AND STEAM PLANT TO HIDE WHILE WE SHOT AT DECOY.
4. DESTINY BATTERY CAPACITY LOW OR HE HAD DC ELECTRICAL PROBLEMS. REDETECTED DESTINY SNORKELING JUST PRIOR TO HIS LAUNCH OF APPROX FIVE LARGE BORE TORPEDOES. ALSO, DESTINY EMITS A 154 HZ DOUBLET.
5. CURRENTLY RUNNING FROM UIF TORPEDOES. WILL ATTEMPT COUNTERFIRE, BUT HAVE LOST CONTACT ON TARGET WHOSE LAST POSITION WAS IN OUR BAFFLES. PROBABILITY OF A HIT ON DESTINY SUB CONSIDERED LOW.
6. IF AUGUSTA SINKS, IN THE NAME OF OUR LOVE FOR OUR FAMILIES PLEASE TELL THEM AS MUCH OF THE TRUTH AS YOU CAN, AS SOON AS YOU CAN.
7. CDR. R. DAMINSKI SENDS.

//BT//

Donchez looked up at Rummel, his face pale.

"Who knows about this?"

"Message center crews, CINCMED and SUBLANT watch officers. They sent it on the SCI fax in your staff car. It's only been seven minutes since it was first transmitted."

Donchez read it again. "Get Traeps and Roy Steinman out here."

Rummel returned with the admirals. By then Donchez had read the message from Daminski twice more. When the admirals arrived, Donchez handed the message over for them to read. Steinman, the slow-talking New Orleans submariner with the young face, spoke first.

"Daminski could be going down right now while we're reading this. We need to find out what happened to him. Then we need to sink this SOB."

"*Phoenix* is at Gibraltar," Traeps said. "We could bring her up and ask if she heard anything."

"Get a DSRV to Daminski's last position," Donchez ordered, wondering where the nearest deep submergence rescue vehicle was. "If *Augusta* went down, we might get someone out."

Steinman shook his head while Rummel hurried back to the staff car. "I know you're right, we've got to do that, sir, but if Daminski was on the wrong end of five Nagasaki torpedoes he didn't stand a chance. We just completed an intel estimate we got from an insider at Toshiba. The Nagasaki can do seventy knots on a high-speed axial turbine and has a range of seventy-five nautical miles. It's a big sucker, three feet in diameter and fifty feet long. Most of that is warhead. If it's launched against you . . . well, I recommend we copy this message to the *Phoenix* so she knows about this playing-possum tactic. She might have to get out of the way if this sucker is as good as Rocket Ron thinks." Or, he added silently, like he thought.

"Let's wait on the death certificate until we hear more, Roy," Donchez said. "John, get on a secure line to your watch officer and have him call *Phoenix* up to periscope depth and get a report from her on anything she heard from the bearing to the Strait of Sicily. Go ahead and copy *Phoenix* on this message but have it marked personal for commanding officer."

Admiral Traeps left through the house to the front, where Donchez's staff car waited. Steinman reread the message. He looked up at Donchez, the moon reflecting off the teardrop-shaped lenses of his glasses.

"Did you note that line about telling the truth?" Steinman looked out over the lake, swallowing hard.

"I agree with Rocket Ron. If we lost *Augusta,* I want to tell the families immediately."

"How are we gonna do that, sir, let the world know a third-world sub put one of our best on the bottom?"

"I'm hoping your *Phoenix* can take care of the Destiny."

"At least Sugar Kane knows more than Rocket Ron did about this guy's tactics."

"Kane?"

"David Kane, captain of the *Phoenix.* Crew calls him Sugar, a title I regret to say I thought up. Kane was a junior officer of mine back on the *Archerfish.* "

"Small world," Donchez said. He'd never heard of David Kane. "Your man Kane. Is he good?"

"He knows his stuff," Steinman said cautiously, knowing Kane wasn't Donchez's blood-and-guts kind of sailor. Kane was a politician, ever tuned to his own advancement—he'd always looked like he belonged on Wall Street wearing a $2,000 business suit than oily smelling khakis on a nuclear submarine. But his squadron commanders and crew seemed to love him. Kane was a crowd-pleaser, adept at saying what his bosses and juniors wanted to hear. He was a new generation of captain, and Steinman wisely kept that to himself, knowing a single misinterpreted remark to the CNO could torpedo a career. Besides, Kane *was* good, he was just good in a self-serving kind of way.

Traeps and Rummel returned by the stairs to the patio from the lawn by the lake. They were covered with snow.

"You'd better check this out, Admiral."

Donchez held the faxed message Rummel handed him up to the porch light and read. It was from the *Phoenix*. The meat of the message dashed his hopes.

SONAR DETECTED MULTIPLE DISTANT EXPLOSIONS ALONG BEARING LINE TO STRAIT OF SICILY. SUBSEQUENT TRANSIENTS BELIEVED TO BE HULL BREAKUP. USS PHOENIX REMAINS ON STATION EAST OF GIBRALTAR WITH NO FURTHER DETECTS.

Donchez held out the message to Steinman.

"Let's get Barczynski," he said. "We'll have to come up with a story on this. I don't want this UIF thing brought out, not till we kill him. Roy, I guess lost-sub cover stories are your responsibility. Sorry."

"I know, sir. We'll have a statement ready for the morning. We'd better get going on the notifications. I guess I'd best visit Daminski's wife myself."

"I'll do that, Roy," Donchez said. "He was one of my boys from the *Dace*. Maybe you could see to his XO and wardroom."

Steinman nodded, trudging back into the house.

Donchez walked around to the front, where his staff car was parked, following the path made by Traeps and Rummel. The car's engine was idling, the big black Lincoln bristling with antennae. The front door of Clough's house opened and Barczynski came out, his overcoat thrown over his shoulders. After asking Donchez what was up, the look in Donchez's eyes telling him the matter was grave, he read the messages, Daminski's and Kane's.

"General, we've got this message going out to the second sub in the western Med. He knows how the enemy fight their ship and he'll be ready. Sihoud and the Destiny will be on the bottom—"

"Dick, I'd like to believe that. But I heard the skipper of *Augusta* was a damn good man. An expert at getting top performance out of a crew."

"He was one of the best," Donchez said, thinking *he ought to be, I trained him myself*. "His professionalism shows in his last message, sir. He knew he was a dead man but he took the time to tell us how to beat the Destiny." Donchez looked hard at Barczynski. "I want to declassify that *Augusta* sank, General. Tonight. We couldn't keep a lid on it too long anyway, she's due back in a couple weeks. It'll give us a black eye if we let the next of kin celebrate New Year's and wait on the pier and we tell them then she's been gone since December. We sat on sinking news back when *Stingray* went down in '73 and the press and the families beat the hell out of us. And rightly so."

"Dick, we can't be saying anything about the Destiny sub—"

"We won't. Steinman's working on a story now. *Augusta* sank because of a faulty torpedo or a flooded main seawater system or any of a thousand things that can sink a submarine. It's known to be a dangerous business. We've lost three nukes in the past, sir, we've done this before, I'm sorry to say."

"I don't want any salvage divers coming up next week saying we lied."

"We won't say where she sank. Besides, she's down in 900 feet of water. It'll take a while. By the time any salvage vultures are down there, we'll have the Destiny on the bottom. Then they can dive for Sihoud's bones." He had to believe that.

"Okay, Dick. Do it your way."

Donchez got into the car, Rummel at the door ready to shut it.

"And, Dick—"

"Yes, General?"

"I'm very sorry."

"So am I, sir. So am I."

Virginia Beach, Virginia

Myra Daminski blew out a breath of exhaustion as she sat at the kitchen table, the kids finally, after a long fight, in bed and quiet. She sipped at the coffee, the milk she'd dumped in it making it a chocolate-brown color. The sudden glint of a policeman's cruiser lights from outside the dining room window didn't surprise her—it was the Friday night between Christmas and New Year's, and the neighborhood parties were in full gear, the music blaring from the house across the street. Someone had probably complained. She flipped through a book, finally finding the page, the one all about comfort in confusion over a trying, or dying, marriage. The doorbell rang. Annoyed, she marked the page, put the book down, and walked through the hallway while straightening out her thick black hair.

She opened the door, expecting to see people who'd come to the wrong house for the party, but stared into the pressed uniform of a Virginia state police trooper, behind him two men in dark uniforms, the driveway blocked by a large black car behind the trooper's cruiser. She turned on the outside light and immediately saw that the men in black uniforms were navy officers.

"Mrs. Daminski? I'm Admiral Dick Donchez. Could we come in?"

She opened the door wider, the men came in.

"I just made a pot of coffee, come on into the den, have a seat." She ran into the kitchen, reaching for the coffeepot.

"Ma'am, I think you'd first better listen to the admiral," Fred Rummel said.

Myra Daminski looked up, her hands on the island countertop.

"It's about the *Augusta*," Donchez said, his voice deep, gravelly. "Two hours ago the ship went down in the Mediterranean during an exercise with another submarine. We have reason to believe the entire crew was lost. I'm sorry . . ."

Myra's eyes glazed over. Donchez wondered if she was registering the news.

"We headed down from D.C. as soon as we could. I'm the Chief of Naval Operations. Ron was an old hand on my former submarine *Dace*. He was a fine officer and a good friend of mine. I can't tell you . . ."

The words seemed to rush over her. A lump formed in her throat as she wondered if the letter she had written him had gotten to the ship before it sailed from Sardinia. She hoped it hadn't and would be returned to her.

"What happened?"

"We're not sure yet. We're doing everything possible to find the crew. If any survived we'll know in a few hours. We'll be taking a deep submergence vehicle down tonight. But I don't want you to get your hopes up, Mrs. Daminski. The other sub in the exercise radioed that it heard hull breakup noises on sonar."

Myra looked up to see her son Joe in his pajamas, standing in the foyer at the base of the stairs.

Later, in the staff car, Donchez looked out the window at the dark trees, thinking about Myra Daminski's reaction—or lack of reaction—and the tears of the boy. Mrs. Daminski had been rocking him in a big chair in the den when they had left. Myra's face was, well, set. Stoic? perhaps.

For the next half-hour Donchez himself was lost in memories. Daminski arm-wrestling in the wardroom, Daminski drinking beer at a ship's softball game, Daminski arguing with the burly torpedoman Betts, Daminski teaching the younger officers the torpedo-tube interlocks. The first time he heard Betts call him Rocket Ron, and the way the crew took up the name, Donchez trying to put a stop to it, the nickname a violation of military discipline but finally giving up as the moniker stuck. The day Lieutenant Daminski showed up in Donchez's XO stateroom to ask for emergency leave to see his dying father, the tough macho lieutenant suddenly seeming vulnerable, almost stuttering. Daminski's wedding to his first wife, an event for all the ship's officers, the wardroom ganging up on the strutting Daminski and carrying him kicking and fighting to the pool and dumping him in, Daminski sputtering to the surface, a grin on his face as he climbed out and ran after his attackers, his once starched service dress whites soaked. The weeks of shock

Daminski went through when the marriage foundered the next year, the junior officer burying himself in his work.

When Donchez was done remembering, he turned his thoughts to what he had to do. Somewhere in the Med the UIF Destiny submarine lurked, a ship quiet enough to escape the detection of an Improved-Los Angeles-class sub's BSY-1 sonar system, so quiet when its reactor was shut down that it didn't register over the own-ship noise of the LA-class. The Destiny had the acoustic advantage, a nasty situation in which the opposition sub was quieter than the U.S. boat. That situation had never arisen in the old days, even with the Russians—American subs had always been quieter, stealthier—until the Russians had built the Omega-class attack submarine, the one Donchez had spent so many nights worrying about until he had sent *Devilfish* to find it. And its then commander Pacino hadn't been able to hear the Omega until he was directly beneath it, the Omega surfaced at the polar icecap.

There was only one American submarine quieter than an Improved-Los Angeles-class, and that was the *Seawolf.* And there was perhaps only one submarine captain who was in the same league as Rocket Ron Daminski, and that was Captain Michael Pacino, *Seawolf*'s captain. Pacino was due to rotate off, accept his first star and replace Roy Steinman as COMSUBLANT. And *Seawolf* lay in a shipyard drydock as the Vortex tube installation finished, the yard just now getting a high-priced work order to reverse course and rip the tubes out after the failure of the system in the Bahamas.

"Fred, get me Pacino on scrambled satellite voice. He should be home in Sandbridge Beach. Then get me Stevens."

"Stevens, the NNSY shipyard commander?"

"Yes." He waited.

"Pacino." Pacino's voice was distorted through the scrambled voice circuit.

"Mikey? It's Dick. I'm afraid I have some bad news."

BOOK II

ATLANTIC BREAKOUT

15

SATURDAY, 28 DECEMBER

Portsmouth, Virginia
Norfolk Naval Shipyard
Graving Dock 4

Captain Michael Pacino stood at the railing of the dock and stared down at the mess.

Several tons of ugly scaffolding hid most of the wide hull of the *Seawolf*. The mass of equipment staged at the ship's starboard flank obscured most of that side of the ship. A platform with handrails had been placed on top of the conning tower. Forward, the plastic sonar dome had been removed, the large sphere of the BSY–2 Advanced BATEARS sonar looking bare and exposed. Scaffolding had been erected around the equator of the sphere. The deck of the ship that was visible was a bright green, the color of the inorganic zinc primer put on the sandblasted hull. Hoses and temporary ducts snaked into the hatches. A large hole, a hull cut, gaped forward starboard, part of the work for the Vortex tubes.

Although the ship had been committed to the drydock solely for the insertion of the Vortex tubes, a drydock availability came around so seldom that the shipyard had not been able to resist taking advantage of the opportunity to invade the ship for other projects. The sonar hydrophone change-out project was an example, an alteration not scheduled for another two years but put into motion now since it might be difficult to schedule later. And as usual, once the main work was complete it would probably be some minor target-of-opportunity alteration that would delay the vessel from leaving the dock.

Pacino's mouth was set in a tight grimace. Seeing his ship in the dock filled him with a kind of gut pain. The ship belonged at sea, not under the hands of a thousand uncaring shipyard workers. The sun had risen above the surrounding buildings, the dirty old brick of them still dark on this Saturday morning, the morning after *Augusta* went down, the morning after Rocket Ron went down. Pacino tried to push back the thought even as he began to think it. After seven, and no sign of shipyard activity. Pacino glanced at his watch, saw the approaching shadow and looked up to see Captain Emmitt Stevens, the shipyard commander, turned out in starched khakis, gleaming white hardhat, spit-shined shoes. Pacino turned and gave him a halfhearted salute. Stevens looked ready to take a bite out of Pacino.

"Captain," Stevens said, "another dock availability ruined by the ops guys."

"Excuse me?"

"Once again one of my schedules is blown to hell by COMSUBLANT. I got a call from Admiral Steinman last night. The brass wants your boat out pronto. Immediately if not sooner, I think Steinman's words were. I'll be damned, Patch. We had a lot to do on this work order, and now we're just doing a hurry-up-button-it-up-and-get-her-to-sea for some goddamned exercise for Steinman. All I hear are complaints from you guys that your ships don't work. Well, dammit, this is why."

Pacino regarded Stevens, the older man gray at the temples, his hair combed back swoopingly up over his ears and under the hardhat. Stevens was an EDO, engineering-duty type, one of the crack whiz kids at MIT in the naval architecture program when Pacino was there trying to start his master's work, Stevens worldly and wise when Pacino was still trying to find the bathroom. Pacino wondered how much he could tell Stevens, then decided that in spite of security, if the shipyard commander knew what was up he might get the ship out faster, or better.

"You heard about *Augusta?*"

Stevens expression changed in a flash. "Rocket Ron. Yeah, I heard. The yard that did him last, New Hampshire, is standing by. Shipyard commander might get his chops busted. Rumor has it that it wasn't a weapon problem. Some sort of depth-control trouble from the depth-indication panel they put in last spring. From what I heard, the depth indicator showed him shallow when he was deep and he plowed into the bottom and ripped open the hull."

"Emmitt. Rocket didn't go down from a faulty depth gauge. And the reason *Seawolf* is going out in such a hurry is because of Rocket Ron. We're going to take care of the problem that put him on the bottom."

As the calls from the admiral rang in Stevens's head, the urgency to abandon the dock work was now apparent.

"Jesus. Patch, listen, I . . . we'll have you out of here in no time. Buttoned up and good as new. Better. We'll be flooding the dock by Tuesday."

"Emmitt, I know I shouldn't even have to say this, but I will anyway. This conversation never happened."

"Absolutely." Stevens had already turned to get the yard forces mobilized.

"And, Emmitt." Stevens turned. "We flood the dock tomorrow at sundown. By Tuesday it may be too late."

"That's impossible."

Pacino just stared.

"Tomorrow. Right. comsublant says Tuesday, Pacino says Sunday. Fine, Patch, you got it."

Fifteen minutes later the shipyard workers appeared from nowhere, swarming over the vessel. Ten-story-tall cranes on wide rail tracks rolled up, their alert horns wailing in the dawn. The dock loudspeaker blared. Workers in the dock below shouted at each other. Pacino, satisfied, nodded and walked to the gangway.

Western Mediterranean
Strait of Gibraltar
USS *Phoenix*

The western basin of the Mediterranean narrowed to a corridor eighty miles wide and 200 miles long at the entrance to the strait at Gibraltar where southwestern Spain reached out but did not quite reach Tangier in Morocco. The basin looked like the head of a seahorse—at least, it did after one had stared at the chart long enough—the island of Mallorca forming the horse's eye, Gibraltar forming the point of its nose. The long-pointed snout, the narrow corridor, was filled with shipping, now mostly military cargo vessels transporting supplies to the Coalition Third Armed Force along the Atlas Mountain Front in northern Algeria. Lurking beneath the surface ten miles east of Gibraltar was the U.S. nuclear submarine *Phoenix*, waiting in search of the Destiny-class submarine. Farther to the east, two U.S. destroyers cruised the blue water, both streaming towed array sonar systems, both hearing nothing. Between the destroyers and the *Phoenix* four Orion P-3 patrol turboprops

flew back and forth from Barcelona to Algiers, laying a barrier of passive listening sonar buoys, monitoring the buoys for man-made noise
and doing low flyovers with the magnetic anomaly detectors energized,
seeking the Destiny. Farther east, just west of the islands of Sardinia and
Corsica, Viking S–3 carrier-based jets cruised the sea, dropping their
own sonobuoys and streaming their own MAD probes. So far all forces
had come up with exactly nothing. It was as if the Destiny submarine
had dissolved in the saltwater after her attack on the *Augusta.*

At her barrier search point, *Phoenix* was sailing slowly east at two
knots, bare steerageway. The Flight I Los Angeles-class submarine was
quite similar to *Augusta,* so much so that a civilian might wander the
ship for hours without being able to tell the difference. But *Phoenix,*
commissioned back in 1981, was thirteen years older than the Improved-
Los Angeles-class submarine *Augusta,* and since she was from the original flight of SSNs in the 688 class, she had no vertical launching tubes up
forward for the Javelin cruise missiles and her depth-control planes
were mounted on the sail while *Augusta*'s had been installed forward as
bowplanes. With her older BQQ–5D sonar system and outdated CCS
Mark II firecontrol system, *Phoenix* was practically in a different class
than the *Augusta* with her BSY–1 coordinated combat system. In addition, *Augusta* had had advanced technology-quieting, making her noise
signature a small fraction of *Phoenix*'s. But even though *Phoenix* was an
old girl, she was still, in the hands of Kane's crew, capable and formidable, as long as she would never be called on to fight an Improved-L.A.-
class.

As dawn broke over the western basin, *Phoenix* continued her barrier
search, turning to the south in the box pattern, the ship rigged for ultraquiet, the section tracking team manned and waiting in the control
room, two torpedo tube doors open, two torpedoes powered up and
ready.

Somewhere ahead of them the Destiny submarine hid, its weapons
responsible for the death of over 120 men, their graves at the sea bottom fresh.

In the control room the watch had just been relieved, the ship smell-
ing of eggs and bacon and coffee being served on the deck below. At the
starboard chart table aft of the periscope stand Commander David
Kane leaned over the chart, his submarine coveralls pressed, the American flag patches brand new, the embroidered gold thread of his submarine dolphins shining in the bright lights of the space. Kane walked a set
of dividers across the chart and did a mental calculation. He looked as
fresh as if he'd had twelve hours of sleep, but he had been awake over
thirty hours, the only sign of his fatigue in his eyes—he blinked frequently when he was tired, and at the moment he was blinking rapidly.

Kane, forty, looked a vigorous thirty-five, tall and dark, his face tanned, his chin and cheekbones sculpted, his eyes penetrating and deep blue. He was lean and muscled from hours of working out at the pier gym in port, from running in place between the main engines at sea. Kane was an officer predestined for success, marked from his first year as a midshipman at the Academy. He was a three-striper, the company commander, the first semester of his senior year. The second semester he had worn six stripes as brigade commander, the highest midshipman rank at Annapolis. Every formation he had stood before the tourist crowds, his gleaming sword drawn, his modelworthy looks giving the formations a surreal recruiting-poster quality.

His midshipman room for three years had had a large sign nailed to the wall, the sign stolen by his classmates from a mall boutique and presented with mock fanfare. It read NOT JUST ANOTHER PRETTY FACE. But deep inside Kane sometimes had his doubts, wondering if he had made his achievements honestly. He had never taken his success for granted, had always gone the extra mile for the Navy, always pushing himself.

When he was thirty-seven he had been the youngest submarine captain on the Squadron Seven pier and on the entire east coast. To earn that job he'd given up shore duty between his navigator tour and his XO job, a decision that had nearly cost him his marriage. He had gone to great lengths to placate his wife Rebecca, because he genuinely loved her but also because she was a large factor in his success. Becky was blonde and beautiful, had even posed for *Playboy* when Kane was a first-class midshipman. At a late-night bull session, the copy of the magazine dog-eared from the examination of the midshipmen, Kane was found staring at the photo spread. One of his classmates suggested he write the woman, and he had, enclosing not only photographs of himself as the six-striper, the brigade commander, but the beery and excessive testimonials of his friends. Amazingly she had written back, telling him she was a student at Hood College north of D.C. A year later they were married in the Academy chapel; a year after that they had their first child, the second on the way two years later. Through it all Becky had remained gorgeous, able to charm the most hardened admiral at the Navy functions. Kane thought about her often, missing her when he went to sea. And whenever the stress at sea rose to a high level, Kane reacted by thinking more and more about Becky; the act of thinking about her had become his own barometer of tension. The more he saw her face, the deeper the shit he was in. And he was thinking about her now almost nonstop.

Kane's reflection was interrupted by the appearance of his executive officer, Commander Carl B. "CB" McDonne. McDonne was a huge man, his blue coveralls stretching over a huge stomach; the crew joked behind his back that every single body part of McDonne was fat. His bulk was impressive; his head balding, his features rough and mismatched, his voice loud and caustic. McDonne noted with perverse pride that he was the "absolute ugliest officer in the Silent Service." He filled every room he walked into with his nearly spherical body *and* his razor-sharp intelligence. CB McDonne was acknowledged by the crew to be "heavy," the respectful submarine term for knowledgeable, but he could be arrogant too, with a sarcastic style. He might have been hated throughout the ship if not for his saving grace: his sense of humor was explosive and hilarious and irreverent. When he felt the mood he could convulse a roomful of officers.

There were times when Kane was certain that the admiral in charge at NAVPERSCOM who had sent him McDonne was a comedian—Kane could have searched the fleet for ten years and not found a worse match for his XO than CB McDonne. Still, the XO had his moments, thanks to his encyclopedic knowledge of the boat and tactics. He was excellent at training, drilling the lessons into the officers. And strangely, McDonne was almost as good working a crowd as was Kane himself, his profane manner checked at the door of formal Navy functions. Kane had photos of McDonne at ship's parties, his menacing look gone, a pleasing and jolly smile beaming out at the junior officers. McDonne was fundamentally different outside a nuclear submarine. If he could just manage to leave Becky Kane alone at their parties he would be redeemed in Kane's eyes, but McDonne had a thing for Becky's still impressive blonde beauty, and he just couldn't quit.

All things considered, Kane and the ship functioned adequately with CB aboard, and Kane had heard from on high that he had amassed points with the brass for taking CB on without complaint. Kane looked up now at McDonne as the XO pushed in the forward door, his sides touching the port and starboard doorjambs as he stuffed himself in.

"I just got out of radio," McDonne said. "You'd better see this."

McDonne passed Kane the metal clipboard with the last message from the *Augusta,* the printout straight from the computer buffer after *Phoenix* had ascended to periscope depth ten minutes before on a routine trip to retrieve her message traffic from the COMMSAT. Kane read the message and staring at the chart to the Strait of Sicily, his suspicions of the previous evening correct—the Destiny had sunk *Augusta* and might be coming their way.

McDonne looked disappointed in Kane's reaction.

"What do you think about that?"

Kane looked at McDonne, his expression flat.

"I think, sorry to say, Rocket Ron made a mistake and paid for it."

"Do you think the Destiny will come this far west?"

Kane shook his head. "No. He's got to be going to the Atlas Front. That sub'll broach its sail close in to the Algerian coastline, drop off Sihoud, then fade back to its port at Kassab. Two hours after he ties up to the pier a squadron of Stealth bombers will blow him to scrap metal. No, I doubt we'll even catch a sniff of him."

"That'd be a damned shame," McDonne said. "I'd like to put a Mark 50 right down his throat."

Kane nodded, thinking that he had trained for this tactical situation his entire adult life, and now it might happen for real, outside of the sterile world of exercises. The sub had put Rocket Ron's *Augusta* on the bottom of the Med, and no mere amateur could ever hope to do that. The Destiny-class submarine must be good, good enough to blow apart an Improved-688. Kane couldn't help worrying about the chance an old Flight I 688 boat had against the Destiny.

"You know, XO, *Augusta* was damn near brand-new. She had all the latest stuff. Almost as good as a *Seawolf*-class for acoustic detection range. And the Destiny plowed through her like she was a World War II diesel boat."

McDonne nodded.

"Skipper, we know their tactics. He puts out a decoy, shuts down and hides. And when we attack the decoy he comes out of the baffles and shoots a volley."

"So, CB, how the hell do we know if we're following the decoy?"

"I guess the contact that shoots the torpedoes is the real submarine."

"So we don't know where he is until he puts weapons in the water, and if he's shut down we still might not hear anything but the torpedoes —and by then it's too late. Still think we've got an advantage?"

"We're in trouble."

"All we can hope for is that the Destiny makes a mistake or puts out a machinery rattle."

"Wait a minute, sir. Ron fired off a volley of torpedoes at the Destiny. Maybe one of them hit him."

"Did sonar have any explosions?"

"No . . . listen, Captain, if you think the Destiny will drop Sihoud off at the Algerian coast, maybe we should head east along the shoreline."

"Can't. CINCNAVFORCEMED was specific—guard Gibraltar. Kill the Destiny if he tries to come through. If he's farther west, the P–3s or the Burke-class destroyers or the Vikings will nail him with sonobuoys, maybe force him our way. Maybe put a hole in him with a Mark 52."

"I think I'll stop by sonar on the way to my stateroom, make sure the senior chief knows what we're up against. I'd just as soon not die in my sleep."

"Get some rack, XO."

"Good night, sir."

For a long time after McDonne ducked into sonar, Kane stared at the chart, wondering where the Destiny was hiding. And what his mission was.

Western Mediterranean

The *Hegira* had passed Minorca and was approaching the invisible line linking Barcelona, Spain and Algiers. As the ship got closer to Gibraltar the sea began to narrow from 300 kilometers to 150 kilometers. It sounded broad but it was beginning to feel like a bathtub—land to the north and south, enemy fleets east and west.

Sharef walked from the chart table to the sensor consoles. The sea around them was filled with sound, bad news. The electronic chart table was taking feeds from the sensor consoles as the sensor officer, Lieutenant Jadi, identified the source of the noise and its bearing and range. From the analysis of the Second Captain the sounds to the north and south were the screws of destroyers of the American Arleigh Burke-class, capable of pulling deeply submerged towed array sonar systems—ships to stay away from. Farther to the west were ominous splashes and high-pitched wailing noises, most likely sonobuoys dropped from anti-submarine patrol aircraft. Again, an area to avoid. Sharef had maintained a serpentine course on the approach to Gibraltar, assuming that the Coalition forces knew he was there after the sinking of the American 688-class submarine. The westerners would be very angry and ready to sink him.

He wondered if they suspected he was bound for the Atlantic. If they knew Sihoud was aboard—and how could they not, with the endless time on the surface recovering him and Ahmed?—they might postulate that he would be dropping the general off in the North African campaign raging in Algeria.

Sharef looked around at the humming control room manned with the A-crew of extended combat stations watchstanders. Half the ship's complement was on watch, the B-crew sleeping, waiting for their turn to take over the watch. Next to full combat stations it was the ship's maximum state of readiness. Once Sharef had ordered the manning of the extended combat stations, the watches had stood twelve hours on, twelve off. It was well into Sharef's second watch, and he was exhausted. He returned to the chart table, thinking that he was probably wearing a path on the deck tiles between the sensor consoles and the table.

The plot table showed the tracks of the destroyers, which seemed to be driving along a north-south barrier seach, and the approximate locations of the sonobuoy drops farther to the west. The worst of the ASW search looked like it was behind them. All that was between them and open ocean was the Strait of Gibraltar. Of course, that was a narrow choke point ideal for catching a transiting sub, but could they guess *Hegira* was bound for the Atlantic?

He should have felt complacent but he didn't. Something would be waiting for them. He drummed his fingers on the chart table's glass surface, noting that his entire last watch there had been no sign of Sihoud or Ahmed.

"Commander Tawkidi, what are Sihoud and Ahmed doing?"

Tawkidi checked his watch; it read 2035 hours, Greenwich mean time.

"When we came on watch at 1900 they were playing chess in the first officer's stateroom. Should I check on them, sir?"

"No. But I wonder, do you think Ahmed ever wins? And if he does, what does that say about the general?"

Tawkidi smiled.

"I doubt Colonel Ahmed is stupid enough to win. Losing at chess with the general would be the best chess."

Sharef nodded and turned back to the sensor consoles.

Ten meters forward, through the doorway to the central passageway past radio and the computer room, Sihoud and Ahmed both hunched over a chessboard spread out on the first officer's desk. Ahmed bit the inside of his cheek as Sihoud advanced his queen to striking distance of Ahmed's king. Ahmed let out a breath and looked at the General.

"I resign, General."

On the chessboard, Ahmed had lost all but a knight, a rook and the king. Sihoud retained nearly all his own men.

"Let's switch sides, Rakish, and continue playing."

"If you say so, General, but it is hopeless."

It took Sihoud thirty moves, but an hour later Ahmed found himself boxed in by Sihoud's few pieces.

"Check and mate, Rakish. See, you could have turned it around."

"No, General, only you could have," Ahmed replied. "I don't know how you do it."

"You are too bloodthirsty, my friend," Sihoud said, his resonant voice still commanding when hushed in the gloom of the stateroom. "You willingly trade a bishop for a knight, a queen for a queen, fighting a war of attrition. You'll never see me do that. If under threat, I withdraw and wait. There is a time for aggression, a time for patience. You should ask Allah for patience, Rakish."

Ahmed had already put the game away, his mind far from chess. "General, what do you think of this mission, the sinking of the American submarine? You never said a word to Sharef, nothing about risking our lives by turning off the power. Those U.S. torpedoes could have ripped us to pieces. I wonder about Sharef's competence."

"Commodore Sharef has been doing this for a long time, Rakish. What would you think if he told you how to fly a supersonic fighter?"

"Point taken, sir, but still . . . he does not seem aggressive enough. He let that sub get close enough to hear us and shoot at us before he let off the decoy. Then he ran out of power and had to run that diesel—my ears still ring from the noise—and practically begged to be shot at."

"Sharef knows when to be patient and when to be aggressive, Rakish. He would make an excellent chess player. Perhaps I should challenge him when we are in open ocean."

"I would like to see that, General."

"You asked my thoughts about the mission."

"I would like to know what you think, General."

"Can you make the Scorpion warheads functional?"

"The missiles will function. But I wonder about Sharef's ability to get the weapons in the tubes and make the tubes work."

"He will make it work, and the missiles will deliver their plutonium payloads. After that, General Ramadan will sign the peace treaty with the Coalition and the UIF will prosper for many, many years."

"General Ramadan . . . but what about *you,* General?"

"I have my doubts that even Sharef can escape the Coalition anger once the missiles are fired." Sihoud waved off Ahmed's protest. "Enough of this talk of gloom. Let us fix our attention on the mission. We have much to do before the missiles can be launched. I suggest we get some sleep."

"We'll be passing through Gibraltar in the morning. We should be in the control room."

"I'll see you at change-of-watch. Sleep well, Rakish."

As Colonel Rakish Ahmed walked down the narrow stairs to the stateroom he was borrowing, his thoughts lingered on Sihoud's words about not surviving the mission. It occurred to him that it no longer mattered if he lived or died, as long as he could drop the weapons on the American capital to avenge the deaths of his wife and son. After that he didn't care if he died. He recalled Sihoud's words about his blood-thirstiness, but he pushed them aside. The westerners who now raped the United Islamic Front deserved death, lingering and painful.

Sandbridge Beach, Virginia

It had been dark for hours when Pacino's engine coughed to silence in the carport under the pilings of the beach house. He climbed the stairs, fatigue making his footsteps heavy. He dropped his briefcase and his khaki jacket in the foyer, intending to head straight for the liquor cabinet, but his wife had beat him to it, leaning against the bar with a double on ice in her hand. He took it from her, the whiskey burning down his throat.

"Where's our boy?"

"In bed for hours." She ran her slim fingers across his forehead, her skin chilled from the glass. "Are you okay?"

Pacino shut his eyes.

"The ship's a wreck. Somehow we're going to get her to sea before midnight tomorrow."

"You never told me what the big rush was about. Another phone call from your Uncle Dick?"

"Did you see the news about the *Augusta?*"

She sighed. He noticed the crinkle at the bridge of her nose that only came when she was disgusted or angry or confused . . . or deeply frightened.

"I saw it. It was awful. All those men drowned. All because of a shipyard mistake. And now you're rushing the yard to finish up, and the same thing could happen to you. *Why* are you in such a hurry?"

"I can't believe Rocket Ron is dead," he said, ignoring the question. "God, I'll miss him."

"Rocket Ron? You didn't even like him! I lived though a year of pure hell when you were his engineer. You were ready to drain his brake fluid one day, remember, you came home at noon in the middle of the week, swearing at the Rocket—"

Pacino smiled at the memory.

"Yeah. I knocked back half a fifth that day."

"I had to put you to bed. What was it he said that set you off?"

Pacino was no longer in the room but back in his stateroom on the *Atlanta,* the ship he had been assigned to seven years before as engineer. The captain had been Rocket Ron. A surprise reactor-board inspection team had come aboard, worked the ship over for two grueling days, then left giving the ship an "Above Average" rating, the highest mark they ever gave, a cause for a major celebration. Rocket had opened the stateroom door holding the board's report. Pacino had smiled in anticipation of Rocket's congratulations.

"The board said the radioactive spill-drill team didn't decontaminate the man in the tunnel," Daminski said.

"He frisked out clean—the drill monitor screwed up—"

"I don't want to hear your excuses, Pacino." Daminski pointed his finger in Pacino's face, an eighth of an inch from Pacino's nose. "Your goddamned team fucked up and it's because *you* failed to train them. If I can't count on you to do that what the *hell* can I count on you for?"

Daminski went off then, slamming the door behind him. Pacino stared after him, astonishment giving way to fury. He found his car keys and left the ship. He sped home, went into the house and was blind drunk by the time Janice arrived home. After that he remembered nothing until the next morning, when he felt like a pile-driving hammer was smashing into his head at each heartbeat.

On the boat that morning he found Daminski in the control room talking to a chief. When he finished, Pacino started in, knowing he was taking his career into his hands.

"Captain, you were out of line yesterday. That spill team—"

Daminski interrupted, his voice quiet. "I know, Patch. And I'm sorry I hollered at you. You did an excellent job and you should be proud of yourself."

Daminski turned, his shoulders stooped, and walked into his stateroom.

Pacino didn't know which bothered him more, the chewing out or the aftermath of contrition.

Not that it mattered now, he thought, looking at his wife's eyes. She still waited for an answer.

"I don't remember," he said.

"But I still want to understand," she continued. "You never liked him and now you're full of grief. What do you know that I don't know?"

"We all spent that whole tour on the *Atlanta* hating Daminski and bitching every second about what a hardass he was and how miserable he made our lives. But when he left it was all the crew could do to keep their eyes dry. At that change of command there was a real sense of loss. See, Daminski, somehow, made us bigger than we were. He challenged the man in every sailor and officer aboard. The best was never good enough for him. We used to say that heaven would regret the day he died, because he'd chew Saint Peter's butt for the gates of heaven showing dust and improper maintenance. And now that he's gone I look back and I see that he was a sort of second father to every man he ever commanded. A stern sonofabitch of a father, but underneath, he really cared."

"Great," she said. "So what's the big rush for you?"

He was about to tell her when it suddenly seemed a bad idea. He shouldn't have told Emmitt Stevens, except that Emmitt needed some real motivation. Janice had nothing she could do with the truth except worry.

"It's nothing, Jan. Just more Navy bullshit. You were right the first time, a call from Uncle Dick. He can't stand to see the *Seawolf* in the dock. And who am I to argue with him? I was the one who told him I wanted to take her to sea one last time before I was relieved. This is probably his Christmas present to me. I'll be back in an hour."

Before she could question him he left the room, went out of the house to the beach and started walking in the surf, wondering what Rocket Ron really said to Saint Peter.

CHAPTER

16

SUNDAY, 29 DECEMBER

Strait of Gibraltar

Ahmed stood in the crowded control room. The screens, as before, were
filled with cluttered patterns of light and color. Four of them in the
sensor area were devoted to what appeared to be graphs with curves
tracing contours across horizontal axes, the curves forming mountains
and valleys that wiggled slowly as he watched.

Commodore Sharef was hunched over the displays. Sihoud was not in
the room, preferring instead to stay in his stateroom and study the
tactical maps of the North African Atlas Front. It was difficult for
Sihoud to stay in the control room when the information presentations
were indecipherable and the officers too busy to tell him what was going
on. As for Ahmed, he was suspended far below the surface in this iron
lung driven by men he had no experience with, had no control over and
had no reason to trust other than that they wore a uniform similar to his
own. He felt a trickle of sweat fall down his forehead and into his eye.
He turned away, wiping the stinging eye, and leaned over the computer-
driven plotting table to look at the plot between the shoulders of two
mid-grade and one junior officer. The plot showed the contour of the
narrowing sea-lane between Spain and Morocco, depth shown by the

shade of blue—darker in the center of the channel, lighter as it neared the shoreline—a pulsing red mark located a few kilometers east of the narrowest part of the strait.

"What's the red mark?"

Commander Tawkidi answered, his eyes remaining on the plot.

"Another submarine. Los Angeles-class American, like the last one we encountered."

"What are we going to do?"

"We?" And at that moment Commodore Sharef spoke, his voice loud

"Commander, a moment please."

Tawkidi held up a hand to Ahmed and walked to Sharef at the plotting table.

Sharef's voice was low now. "The American is at the limit of our sensors, Navigator. I propose we shoot now, before he has a possibility of detecting us. The torpedo will come onto his sonar screens before he knows we are in the area and force him to run west into the strait. There's a chance that a navigation error could cause him to wreck but he will certainly be hit."

Tawkidi looked down at the sketchpad Sharef had been doing calculations on. "Sir, the hostile sub is over ninety kilometers distant. That is almost outside the range of the weapon. It can only cover 180 kilometers at search speed, 140 at attack velocity."

"But if we launch at search speed, seventy clicks, and are lucky, the weapon will approach close to the 688 sub before it is detected. The best case is perhaps twenty kilometers range before the 688 hears the torpedo. The 688 runs, the torpedo locks on and speeds up to attack speed and runs at 130 clicks toward the target. If the target runs at his maximum speed of seventy clicks the torpedo intercepts and kills the target twenty minutes later, with a total run of 115 kilometers, well under the 140 limit. I agree that's the best case. Now, if detection range is poor at, say, thirty-five kilometers, the torpedo intercepts and kills the target with a run of 135 kilometers, still well below the 140. And that assumes he detects the torpedo and starts a high-speed run away from the weapon. If he is not good enough to hear our unit, the relative intercept speed is even higher. It is a good risk."

"And if he counterfires?"

"After the launch we'll drive off the track by five kilometers, then delouse. Once we're shut down, an incoming torpedo will not detect us."

"A delouse without a Dash Five? I don't think those tactics will—"

"At this long range it will do. And if it does not we will have time to restart."

Tawkidi scribbled on the pad. "Sir, torpedo-run time to the target is about an hour and twenty minutes. We can't stay shut down that long. We only had forty minutes last time."

"The battery did not have a full charge. It will last longer, perhaps an hour, now that it has had a deep discharge and the full-current recharge. We'll wait twenty-five minutes prior to the delouse and restart before we fully drain. Is that satisfactory?"

"Aye, sir. We're ready to shoot." Tawkidi knew when to say yes.

Sharef's voice grew loud in the tight room. "All watchstanders, a moment please. We have classified the submerged contact as another 688-class American. To avoid an attack I intend to fire a single weapon now at long range, move off the track, and shut down propulsion with a delouse maneuver. When the 688 is on the bottom we will proceed into the Atlantic. We will warm up a second weapon and keep it standing by in case. Questions? Very well. Weapons officer, open tubes nine and eight to sea and warm up the weapons, report when ready to fire. Deck officer, maneuver the ship to the south. I don't want to approach the target any closer than we are now."

"Aye, Captain. Ship control, one degree right rudder, steer course south."

For what seemed a long time to Ahmed nothing happened but the flashing of displays on the weapon-control screens. The room's only noise was the humming of the computers and the low growl of the air handlers. After several minutes the torpedoes were warm.

"Range to the target?" Sharef requested.

"Ninety-one kilometers," Lieutenant Commander Mamun, the weapons officer, reported from the weapons panel.

"Shoot tube nine."

The deck shook as the heavy Nagasaki torpedo left the ship for its distant target.

"Ship control, right five degrees rudder, steer course north. Reactor control, prepare to insert a delouse."

Sharef walked to the sensor-console area and looked at the two banks of console displays devoted to the target submarine. Nothing had changed—they apparently had not heard the launch. The next two displays on the neighboring console were monitoring the torpedo on its slow-speed approach to the submarine far over the horizon. Now there was nothing to do but wait the forty-five minutes or hour until the two machines detected each other. One would run, the other speed up and chase. When the hunter had killed the prey, the passage to the Atlantic would be wide open and *then* it would be time to think about how they would assemble the Scorpion warheads in the Hiroshima missiles. And once that problem was solved, all that remained was to get within range of Washington and fire the missiles. Sharef briefly wondered whether he would ever get *Hegira* back to base after the missiles had done their job. Better not to think of that, he told himself.

Meanwhile, ten kilometers to the west, the Nagasaki torpedo drove on toward its target.

USS *Phoenix*

Edwin Sanderson was a big man, frequently asked how he stood being confined in a submarine. He wasn't exactly flabby but was well on his way to developing a gut, standard issue for chiefs in the submarine force. Too many second helpings of bacon and eggs, too few exercise sessions in the torpedo room. His hair was now more gray than black. His gray penetrating eyes tended to show red after hours of staring at the sonar consoles. When he was angry many a senior officer had backed down to him. When off-duty or drunk or amused he could crack a grin that made the face radiate goodwill around him. His wife joked that it was his infectious smile that had charmed her into his orbit, but that if she had seen his anger when they were courting she would never have married him.

As for whether he felt confined in the sub, in truth he was more at home at sea—his routine restricted to the sonar display room, the sonar equipment space, the chief's quarters and the crew's mess—than at his Ghent home. His home life was enjoyable, he had a pretty wife, now showing some weight on her previously thin frame, two sons, one in high school, the star center on the basketball team, the other in junior high who hadn't quite found himself. It wasn't that Sanderson didn't enjoy being in port, it was just that his wife and sons seemed to *own* the house, and he was a frequent visitor. Home was a busy port, he was a cargo ship that pulled in from time to time. The family welcomed him when he'd return from a run at sea, but after two days he felt like he was under-foot. Life had led him to the sea and made him a chief then, and he loved it.

At sea the actions of the men around him seemed centered around him. The ship to him was a giant mobile ear, built so that sonarmen could listen to and interpret the sounds of the sea, most of them random, others man-made and sinister. The rest of the vessel, her reactor and steam plant, her control room, her weapons, even her crew were all subordinate to the task of listening to the sea. This submarine, built for a dozen select sonarmen, was more, he felt, his than the captain's. After all, he was the chief sonarman, the one man declared by the Navy to be the best aboard at listening to that symphony of sound in the sea, best at leading the men who would listen under his instruction, best at attending to and fixing the monstrous ear and the surrounding equipment, best at directing the young officers who drove the ship in a way that would make his equipment listen optimally.

His title said it best—Senior Chief Sonarman Sanderson. He sat now at the aft display console of the BQQ–5D sonar set, the seat just forward of the sliding curtain to the control room, where he could see the other consoles and talk to the officer of the deck in control without using the speaker system or the cumbersome boom microphone. As usual, he was dressed as if they had just pulled into the Norfolk carrier piers: starched khakis, his submarine dolphins gleaming above two rows of ribbons and his boomer pin, his nametag shining over his right pocket, his chief's emblems new, his shoes shining. He always dressed this way at sea, never opting for the relaxed coveralls and sneakers of shipmates. Some said it was because in his khakis he retained his authority, his formality, while in a poopysuit he would become just another crewman. The closest to a friend Sanderson had, a first-class petty officer named Smoot, insisted that the khakis were more comfortable to the chief, but Sanderson himself knew the first reason came the closest. In his more mellow moments he realized he had a streak of arrogance about him, but he maintained even to himself that it was a selfless arrogance born out of service to his country—after twenty-six years in the Navy he was the best sonarman on the goddamned east coast. If he had limits they were only that he had to use the aging BQQ–5D sonar suite instead of the advanced BSY–1 of the Improved-688 boats, and that he was sailing aboard an older 688 submarine instead of a much quieter 688-I class. But even so, he would pit his ship and his sonar against any in the fleet—if exercises meant anything he and the *Phoenix* were a match for any warship afloat or submerged.

Sanderson regarded the waterfall display of the Q–5 through squinted eyes. His fingers moved across a touch pad and called up the TB–23 thinwire towed array, selecting the beam going transverse across the array that looked east-west now that the ship was headed north. Any intruder sailing into the strait from the western basin would first show up on that beam, long before the broadband spherical array heard it. The question was, were they searching for the right frequencies? Captain Kane had referred to a 154 hertz double tonal, something from the message from the sunken *Augusta*, but the information was tainted—after all, how good could tactical data be from a crew that had gotten their butts shot to the bottom of the Med?

It did not occur to him that what happened to *Augusta* could happen to the *Phoenix*. He could not, after all, afford even to consider this.

He dialed up the athwartships beam's frequency gate, spanning from 148 to 158 hertz, waiting to see the double tonal of the Destiny submarine. He stared at the graphs for two minutes, three, four. There was no doublet.

Frustrated, he flipped the display back to the waterfall broadband display of noise versus bearing, putting north in the center of the tube. The detected noises at an instant were shown by bright dots, each direction except the astern "baffles" heard all at once. The data of that instant dropped down as the next second of data flashed up, and then both data lines dropped again as the next sound information came in, making the screen traces fall downward, earning the display its name. The display was split into three pieces. The top trace was only twenty seconds from the top to the bottom, where the data dropped from view The middle section was five minutes deep, taking a set of data 300 seconds to drop from view. The bottom area was the long history trace, displaying the last half-hour of waterfall data. The displays were an ingenious means of interpreting sound data because most of the ocean's noise was random and would go from north to southeast to west instantaneously. The display of this random noise would resemble snow on a TV screen, but a man-made noise, a ship, would continue to generate noise from a single bearing, the continuing bright traces forming a vertical line at the bearing of the sound emission.

Sanderson blinked at the short-time display at the top, concentrating on the bearings to the east. As he watched a slight trace appeared at 087, then winked out. Shrimp or whales farting, Sanderson thought, but kept watching. A moment later the trace returned. The five-minute-history display showed the two traces at a consistent bearing—east.

"Sonar, Conn," Sanderson's earphone buzzed. "Coming around to the west in one minute."

"Conn, Sonar, no," Sanderson said into his mike, leaning over the console. "Ted, get Smoot up here fast," he ordered Seaman Worster. "Joe, select the athwartships beam of the thinwire and dial up the high freqs. Bill, you take the next lower buckets. Red, you take the 200 sector with a single bucket looking for the 154." Sanderson had put the sonar crew onto the new trace, trying to squeeze every bit of data from it the computer could process.

"Sonar, Conn, say again?" Lieutenant Commander Schramford, the ship's engineer, sounded incredulous.

"Conn, Sonar, we've got something. Maintain course north." Sanderson said it as if it were an order. He counted the seconds until Schramford made it to the door. It took only two before the heavy curtain between sonar and control slid open, Schramford's beefy face glowing greenish in the backwash from the sonar consoles.

"What have you got?"

Sanderson tore off his headset, a flare of anger coming into his eyes. "Goddammit, Eng, if I knew I'd let you maneuver, now wouldn't I? Give me as much time on course north as you can while I look at this trace. Go on."

Schramford was an older officer who, although he had his hands full with the chief engineer job, still stood watch at least four times a week and was one of the ship's better tactical minds. He disappeared, presumably to check the chart and whisper on the phone to the captain. Sanderson put his headset back on and rotated the cursor ball set into the console panel to the direction of the noise, which was intermittent but getting stronger.

He tried to block out the sound of the whining of the video screens and the roar of the air handlers, reduced now with the rig for ultraquiet. He projected his consciousness out into the sea, thinking of himself as being at one with the ocean, a thought that his buddies in the chief's quarters—the goat locker—would ridicule as having come from California, but the thought still helped him detect the target, or whatever it was that was making the faint trace at 087, now 088. As Sanderson listened he heard a slight undulation in the sound, a flushing sound. He listened for a few more seconds, then opened his eyes, thinking he knew what he'd heard.

He got up from his seat and scanned the six screens of the other consoles, seeing the picture develop on the sonar traces at each individual frequency. Smoot entered with Seaman Worster.

"What's up, Chief?"

"Listen to this. Let's see if you hear the same thing I did."

Smoot, a tall thin man in his thirties with black hair and a mustache and goatee, pulled on a headset and shut his eyes, weaving slightly on his feet from fading sleep. After a moment he opened his eyes wide and scanned the consoles, then met Sanderson's eyes.

"Pump jet propulsor."

Sanderson smiled, then looked up to see Schramford's face.

"Sir, we've got a submerged contact, bearing zero eight eight, distant, with a pump jet propulsor. You can maneuver back to the south and make sure you turn to the right. I don't want to lose this guy in the baffles."

"You got it, Senior."

"Captain know yet?"

"He will in ten seconds."

Lieutenant Commander Tom Schramford, U.S. Merchant Marine Academy Class of '84, now chief engineer of the USS *Phoenix* and this watch's officer of the deck, barked the order to the helmsman to put on ten degrees right rudder and order up all ahead two thirds and steady on course south. Satisfied that the ship was turning, Schramford picked up a phone mounted on the overhead at the periscope platform and pressed a toggle switch. Fifteen feet forward, the buzzer rang next to Captain Kane's rack.

* * *

Kane's eyes opened and he reached for the phone beside his rack, the buzzing noise from the conn halting as he answered. "Captain."

Tom Schramford's voice seemed close in his ear; Kane could almost feel the engineer's breath against the side of his head, whistling into his ear as the younger officer said the dozen words that pumped adrenalin into Kane's system and catapulted him from the rack: "Sir, we've got a submerged contact bearing east. You'd better come to control."

"Man silent battle stations," Kane said. "Spin up the idle Mark 50s." He hung up on Schramford's acknowledgement.

He slid into his poopysuit in one smooth motion, slipping his feet into docksiders left at the foot of the rack, tightening his belt as he pulled a brush through his hair and splashed a handful of water on his face from the tiny basin under the mirror on the bulkhead, toweling off and tossing the towel into the sink before going through the door to control. He could feel the dozen pairs of eyes on him, the men in the section tracking team looking for decisions.

He stepped up on the periscope platform, scanned the room for data, simultaneously listening to Schramford's report. He took in the ship's position in the channel, the bearing and bearing rate to the contact, the lack of a 154-hertz tonal—odd—and the faint broadband detect on a pump jet propulsor. After a moment, while the battle stations crew manned the attack-center consoles of the CCS Mark II firecontrol system and the manual plots, Kane stepped into the portal to sonar and looked in on Sanderson. The senior chief nodded at Kane and turned back to his console. Kane scanned the consoles, from Sanderson's going forward, seeing for himself that no tonals were appearing in the frequency gates, just the intermittent broadband streak on the waterfall display from the array in the nose cone.

Schramford tapped him on the shoulder. "Captain, battle stations are manned. We've been steady on course south for almost three minutes. The bearing rate is in, and the Mark II, Ekelund calculation and Hewlett-Packard all agree—range to the contact is 64,000 yards."

"What? That's over thirty miles. That's got to be a record for a submerged broadband detect with no tonals . . . Target course?"

"Two seven zero. He's driving due west for the strait."

"What's the firecontrol speed?"

"It's out of line, sir. We must need another leg."

"Why?"

"His speed is showing up as forty knots. Too high for the Destiny without him making a lot more noise and sending out a few tonals. We're just getting a lousy speed solution with the data this intermittent and the contact that distant."

"Wait a minute," Kane said, looking over the Pos Two operator of the

Mark II console. The screen's dots—FIDUs, fixed interval data units, sent over electronically from the BQQ–5 sonar—were lining up straight as a ruler. Kane reached out for the speed knob on the board beneath the screen and dialed in a more reasonable target speed, down to fifteen knots. The dot stack, the neat vertical line, skewed into a messy ">" sign, the bottom portion of the date representing the leg when the ship was on course north, the top portion after the maneuver, the data during the maneuver useless and out of alignment. The target motion analysis, the TMA, could have been done poorly but one maneuver had been north, the second south, with the target coming in from the east— supposedly yielding an ideal solution that should have been good enough to fire on and score an easy hit. Kane dialed the speed higher without looking at the target-speed readout. He turned the knob until the dot stack was back in line, going nearly vertical. The target speed readout said 41.4 KNOTS.

"That's no submarine," Kane said, bolting for the door to sonar.

"What?" Schramford stared after him.

Kane slid the curtain aside and looked into Senior Chief Sanderson's eyes, ready to tell him the target was going too fast, too silently to be a submarine. Sanderson's mouth was already open to speak.

"Cap'n, we're doing TMA on a fucking torpedo!"

17

SUNDAY, 29 DECEMBER

Strait of Gibraltar

Kane turned and shouted to the helmsman.

"*Right full rudder, all ahead flank, steady course west!*" He made the periscope stand in three big steps, grabbed the microphone and tried to keep his voice level. "Maneuvering, Conn, cavitate."

"*CAVITATE, CONN, MANEUVERING, AYE,*" the overhead speaker replied.

The deck trembled and heeled over to a fifteen-degree angle with the vortex from the turn, the ship sliding into a violent snap roll, ship control becoming difficult as the angle increased and the rudder began acting like a diving plane.

"Helm, ease your rudder to right five degrees." The ship still shuddered through the turn, a small sonar display above the helmsman lighting up as the screw cavitated, boiling off sheets of steam as the men in maneuvering opened the throttle wide to one hundred percent reactor power.

"Right five degrees, helm aye, maneuvering answers ahead flank, passing course two six zero, ten degrees from ordered course." The helmsman then reversed the rudder, fighting the gyrocompass, the deck angling crazily to the other side, then leveling off. "Steady two seven zero, sir."

"Chief of the watch, call on the phone circuits, torpedo in the water."

"Aye, sir."

Kane fought his way through the battle stations bodies to the navigation plot. Schramford had the last range on the torpedo plotted as well as their position. The blue dot denoting the torpedo seemed perilously close in scale to the mouth of the channel.

Kane felt the deck vibrating beneath his feet, the twin main engines putting out maximum speed. The *Phoenix* had been in a drydock overhaul two years before for a nuclear refueling. The core had been removed through a gaping hull cut and replaced with the General Electric S6G–Core–3. The new core had a thermal output almost twice the power of the Core–2 that had previously powered the ship, the doubling of thermal power seen at the shaft as an increase from 35,000 to 47,400 horsepower. After all that, the additional power was good for only an additional five knots on account of parasitic drag—even if screw power had doubled, the counterforce from skin friction would have quadrupled. But an extra five knots were worth the $10 million investment, Kane thought, when a Nagasaki torpedo—manufactured at Toshiba with the highest quality—was running up your ass.

The speed indicator read out thirty-nine knots. Kane measured on the chart, looked up at McDonne, who was rubbing red eyes while strapping on his headset.

"This fish can go seventy knots. Why was it only doing forty?"

"Trying to sneak up on us, or still on its run to enable. Or maybe it hasn't detected us yet."

"That'd be a trick, with us flanking it through a snap roll. If it can't hear us by now it wouldn't hear a train wreck." Kane pulled on his boom microphone and single earphone and spoke into it. "Sonar, Captain, any changes in the torpedo sound signature?"

"Captain, he's in the baffles and we've lost broadband," Sanderson's voice announced, his annoyance clear through the circuitry. "I'm trying to get a look at the end beam of the towed array now and we've been listening hard to the caboose unit."

"Captain, aye." To McDonne: "If he goes forty or forty-one or forty-two knots to our thirty-nine, with his range at thirty miles, he may run out of fuel before he catches us. We could keep this tail chase going for days if he had the fuel."

"Sonar, Conn," Kane said to his mike, "any detection of the torpedo?"

"Conn, Sonar, wait."

In the sonar display room Sanderson put his face in each console screen, keeping his eyes on it for less than a second, then moving on to the next. "Captain, we tentatively hold the torpedo on the caboose unit broadband." The tail end of the TB–23 towed array had been modified to hold a neutrally buoyant teardrop-shaped broadband hydrophone array added for situations like this when the sonar crew would need to track something in the astern baffles, but the unit was small, its output difficult to interpret, its reliability suspect. "We don't have anything on the towed array end-beam. There are no detectable tonals. And we can't give it a turn-count with the pump jet propulsion. Until the weapon goes active it's impossible to see if it's closing, unless you want to wiggle the array, and I don't recommend doing TMA on the torpedo."

Kane was thinking he'd just heard the longest speech the ordinarily taciturn senior chief had ever given. He checked the chronometer bolted above the attack center, the red numbers reading 2039, almost 9:00 P.M. zulu time. The torpedo had been first detected just twelve minutes before. Kane turned to McDonne, who stood between the attack-center consoles and the conn's elevated periscope platform.

"XO, if that weapon sped up to seventy knots when we went to flank, how long to intercept?" Kane waited. The question translated to: *If that torpedo knows we're here, how long do we have to live?*

McDonne looked over the H-P computer and down at his own distance-time slide rule.

"Sir, fifty-eight minutes to intercept from detection point. That's fifty minutes from now."

Schramford looked up from the aft sector of the conn, where he'd been peering over the tactical plot. "Captain, I think I can give you an extra six minutes. That would be another four miles down the line, maybe enough to make this torpedo run on fumes."

"Another six minutes, Eng? What're you talking about?"

"We'll take the core to the design limit, maybe further. I might get another couple thousand horsepower at the screw. We'll overpower the core, take average temperature to 530 or 540, pick up the grid on the battery—"

"Don't waste time telling me, for God's sake," Kane said. He'd skipped the engineer tour, serving as a weapons officer and navigator, thinking of himself as more a tactician and a leader and a seaman than a technocrat, privately referring to all things related to the mysterious reactor plant as "neutron shit." "You're the engineer, get back there. I relieve you of the deck. Get Houser up here to replace you."

Schramford was gone, announcing that the captain had the deck and the conn. Kane now thought about Daminski's last message. The fleet commander would need to know that the enemy might be trying to break out into the Atlantic, and if the worst happened—the admiral would need to know.

"Get a SLOT buoy ready, XO. Copy this for coding into the buoy."

McDonne spoke on his mike to radio, then looked up at Kane. "Addressee, CINCNAVFORCEMED. Priority, flash. Subject, contact report." McDonne's pen flashed over his clipboard. "Message: 'One, position approximate at—' "

Mike Jensen, the navigator, spoke up from the port plotting table: "Two miles east of the narrows at Gibraltar."

"Copy that, XO? 'Two, USS *Phoenix* detected single incoming Nagasaki torpedo from the east at long range on faint broadband, no tonals. Estimated time of torpedo intercepting *Phoenix*, 2130 zulu. Am now attempting to outrun UIF weapon. Three, request ASW aircraft vectored to this position to ensure Destiny does not break out of Med en route Atlantic. Four, due to suspicion that Destiny unit is westbound, intend to mine exit of Gibraltar with salvo of Mark 50 torpedoes in circular passive patterns, ceiling settings set to avoid damage to surface shipping. Five, *Phoenix* reports negative, repeat negative acoustic advantage against Destiny class. If we survive Nagasaki and if passive circle Mark 50s fail to hit Destiny, intend to clear datum for Faslane, Scotland and reload. Six, Commander D. Kane sends.' Got it? Code it in, flood and launch.

"Weapons officer, status of the Mark 50s in one and two?"

"Ready in all respects, sir," Lieutenant Commander Chris Follicus intoned from the weapons-control panel at the end of the line of firecontrol consoles. Follicus, a chunky man with thick eyeglass lenses that made his eyes appear large and liquid, was sharp and quick, some would say glib. Kane had started to think of the weapons officer as something of a bullshit artist.

"Set both for medium-speed run to enable, passive low-speed circular search patterns, ceiling one five zero feet, search depth 400 feet, active homing on acquisition. Tube one unit will orbit 5,000 yards from launch at bearing zero eight five, tube two 10,500. And make tubes three and four ready in all respects."

Kane waited for Follicus to make the presets, then climbed the step to the conn platform.

"Attention in the firecontrol team," Kane announced, two dozen pairs of eyes locking onto him. "We're sprinting away from a torpedo launched by the Destiny submarine, but confidence is high that we can outrun this thing." Right, he thought. Until it speeds up to seventy knots and cuts us to pieces. "While we're running I intend to put out some weapons of our own. We don't know where the Destiny is, except that it's east of us in the Med's western basin. I believe this torpedo shot is an attempt to get by us and break out into the Atlantic." God knows why, he thought, and how would he prove it if asked by the admiral? He had no answer. "So to counter the Destiny's out-chop we're going to fill the gap at Gibraltar with Mark 50 torpedoes set for circular searches. If he comes out while the Mark 50s are still alive he'll get hurt bad. On the plots, I want the orbit points and shutdown times of these weapons plotted and kept up to date so we can plan the weapon deployment. That's all, carry on."

There was a brief lull in the action while Kane waited for Follicus to run the weapons' confirmation of the presets. It was only a matter of seconds but seemed an hour. The stark reality of it was only now reaching Kane that inside an hour he might be dead on the bottom of the Strait of Gibraltar. If he could act he could almost forget that, but waiting was hell. During that wait the thought intruded that he should live as if today were the last day of his life, a notion he had always sarcastically met with the comment *If today's my last day on earth I'm buying a Porsche Turbo on credit and driving it to Atlantic City.* On the business end of a Nagasaki torpedo, the remark no longer seemed so witty.

Kane's contact message was relayed at highest priority through the eastern Atlantic communications satellite to CINCNAVFORCEMED's headquarters at the old Sixth Fleet compound in Naples, Italy. The NAVFORCEMED watch officer, a mustang lieutenant, held a secure phone to his ear, and while waiting for Admiral Traeps scratched a tactical message to the airborne antisubmarine forces in the western basin directing them to Gibraltar.

Four P–3 Orion ASW patrol turboprops received the NAVFORCEMED flash transmission. One ignored the order, already departing station, low on fuel and empty of sonobuoys, its replacement en route from Sigonella. The remaining three throttled up, climbed and headed west, reaching their destinations and cruising back toward the dark water of the strait. The moon had been full but had vanished behind dull unremarkable clouds that seemed to boil up from nowhere and everywhere. The first four-engined plane shut down the two inboard turbines and feathered the props, swooping low over the water sixty nautical miles east of the narrowest point of the strait, turning slowly as it steadied on a southern course, leveling its wings and slowing further until it almost seemed suspended over the water. Silently, at five-second intervals, the cylindrical sonobuoys fell out of the underside of the fuselage, plunking into the water in a neat row, the splashes lost in the powerful thrumming of the props.

A few moments later, twenty miles west of the first plane, the second P–3 arrived on station, dropped a load of sonobuoys and circled back around. The third took station off Tangier at the opening of the mouth of Gibraltar, laying its sonobuoy field just as the USS *Phoenix* passed under it. The buoys laid, the P–3s orbited the drop points at sufficient distance that the buoys' sonars would not be impaired by the noise of the planes' engines but not so far that radio reception would be impacted. They settled into north-south elongated orbits parallel to the sonobuoy fields, cruising close enough to the surface so that their MAD probes could reach down into the sea in search of anomalies in the earth's magnetic field, the iron hull of a submerged submarine able to focus magnetic lines of force just as a lens bends light waves. The MAD probes detected nothing, but that wasn't unusual since the probes were useful only at extremely short range.

While the P–3s had been turning toward Gibraltar, two pilots and a sonar tech climbed into the Seahawk LAMPS III antisubmarine helicopter on the rolling aft deck of the Burke-class destroyer *John Warner* and ran through the laminated start-up checklist in record time, the twin turbines whining and then howling to idling revs, the clutch catching and spooling up the main rotor. The chopper shook as the rotor passed through several resonance points, then steadied as the blades sped up to idling revolutions. The pilot's radio headset crackled, a distorted voice from the *Warner*'s combat information center, the pilot's reply competing with the roar of the turbines and the beating of the main rotor as the Seahawk lifted off the deck, the bull's-eye painted on the dark surface barely visible in the overcast night as the *Warner* shrank below and astern. Thirty miles south, an identical helicopter turned west and soon joined the first, the two units ready to drop dipping active sonar sets at the first sniff from one of the P–3s.

Two hundred feet beneath the surface, between the farthest sonobuoy field to the east and the central field, the Destiny-class submarine *Hegira* picked up speed, her ship-control console's display of gyrocompass bearing showing a course of 278, west northwest.

Commodore Sharef frowned, the unexpected tasting sour in his mouth. The close pass of the antisubmarine warfare turboprop plane to the west ahead of them glowed angrily red on the display screens of the second sensor console, the other screen showing the approach of a helicopter's rotors. The sensors were filling up with the sounds of the aircraft, then with the wailing pings of the sonobuoys. Anger filled him, anger directed at himself. Somehow the American 688 submarine had managed to call in this airborne circus above them. Worse, there had been no explosion from the Nagasaki unit, and time was dragging on. If the torpedo did not explode soon it would run out of fuel. He'd lost the American unit on the sensors, the ship now outside their detection range and quieter than the sea, which was now a damned poor sonar environment with all the aircraft engines. Sharef looked at Tawkidi, who seemed even more upset, since it was the younger man's recommendation to shoot closer in.

Sharef decided he had no choice. He could not launch another Nagasaki without knowing the location of the American unit. The Nagasakis had such large fuel tanks that the weapon would wait and circle if it had no target, preventing Sharef himself from getting through Gibraltar since the torpedo would then find the *Hegira* and sink her. He could not stay here, not with the angry aircraft buzzing above. The longer he stayed, the greater the chances of being detected, and then destroyed. He could not turn back into the Mediterranean. To do that would leave his mission incomplete, nor could he put in a delouse reactor shutdown and wait. Waiting would only give the Coalition naval forces time to reinforce the curtain of ASW planes—and soon, ships—at Gibraltar. He had to bet that the Nagasaki he'd already launched was still in hot pursuit and not waiting for another target; he had to run the gauntlet through the strait, and he had to do it now.

"Commander Tawkidi, announce full-combat stations. Ship control, ahead thirty clicks, depth 100 meters. Weapons control, open doors seven and eight to sea and warm up the weapons. Sensor control, watch carefully for signs of the American 688 submarine and the previously launched Nagasaki unit—I don't want to be chased by our own torpedo if it lost the American. Reactor control, be ready to go to emergency ahead if any of the aircraft launch homing torpedoes."

Sharef stood at the computerized plotting table to see if he could make it to the Atlantic. He tried to strangle the thought that the mission might soon be over.

USS *Phoenix*

Lieutenant Victor Houser arrived from maneuvering, his normal battle station duty aft as engineering officer of the watch. Houser was unofficially the leader of the stable of junior officers aboard, the senior lieutenant. As most late first-tour officers were, he was cocky and young and full of himself, tough and aggressive. The boat's folklore still repeated stories of his pugnaciousness even when he was a nub, a neophyte officer. He was a Southerner hailing from Atlanta or western panhandle Florida depending on the day he was asked, his accent thick, slow, drawling. Crew members and officers in the same compartment with him would unconsciously imitate his speech just as fighter pilots once imitated the slur of test pilot Chuck Yeager's West Virginia twang. This echoing of Houser's accent, if in Kane's earshot, even had Kane speaking in an Atlanta cadence.

Houser was only slightly shorter than Kane, his height all in his legs. His hair was a light brown or dirty blond, long on top, sticking straight into the overhead, and at his neck stretching almost to the bottom of the collar. He had a double chin, odd since there was not another ounce of fat on the young man. He compensated by being the first man to quit shaving at sea and grow his U-boat beard, sometimes cheating and refusing to shave the two days before the ship would get underway. The beard now was fully grown in, his fleshy chin safely hidden. He was wearing, as usual, his own uniform at sea, eschewing khakis and submarine poopysuits for well-worn jeans, high-top Nikes and one of his dozen Hawaiian shirts, the pattern guaranteed to be the brightest thing in the compartment, and a multicolored belt holding his radiation dosimeter, the gaudy belt looking to Kane like Houser had stolen it from a Barnum and Bailey clown. Kane put up with the unreg outfit out of respect for Houser's abilities and the sense that Houser, with his perhaps overdose of "personality," was something of a ship's mascot, a good luck charm, not to be trifled with.

Houser worked for Tom Schramford as main propulsion assistant and assistant engineer, the traditional job of the senior lieutenant, responsible for most of the mechanical components of the propulsion plant and thirty-five nuclear enlisted men. In his own way he was one of the most tactically inspired junior officers Kane had ever known. As MPA he was brilliant, thick with the mechanics who worked for him, talking street engines and hot rods when not troubleshooting some problem with *Phoenix*'s machinery. As one of Kane's officers of the deck, Houser was good if rough around the edges, driving the ship like a sports car. Kane could always tell when the aggressive Houser was driving—dishes broke from his angles and snap rolls, cooks cursing from spilled soup pots and table settings dashed to the deck. Kane would chew him out for his maneuvers, knowing inside that Houser could fight the ship better than many of the department heads.

Houser's relationship with Senior Chief Sanderson was not smooth. Their mutual disrespect was the stuff of shipboard legends, the two men not so much oil and vinegar as dynamite and matches. Houser had been sonar officer when Sanderson had arrived aboard, the sonar chief expecting a red carpet and immediate obedience to his royal proclamations as captain by proxy, including all officers of the deck and his entire chain of command from the sonar officer to the weapons boss to the XO and even the captain. That attitude went nowhere with Houser, the lieutenant quickly informing the senior chief that in his opinion, according to Navy Regulations, and by God the last time he checked, officers outranked *all* enlisted men, no matter how many ribbons and hash marks and stars they wore on their service dress sleeves. After a week butting heads Kane had a choice between transferring off the most able, though admittedly prima donna, sonar chief in the known universe or giving Houser, his best junior officer, a new job. On the afternoon of

Sanderson's eighth day aboard Houser took over as main propulsion assistant and the ship had sailed smoothly ever since.

Except when Houser was officer of the deck, as he was now. Another reason he was aft as engineering officer of the watch during battle stations and Schramford, the engineer, who normally should have been the EOOW, was instead officer of the deck. Now with Schramford aft cranking up the reactor, Houser mounted the conn and looked down at the displays and the status board and the plots, pulling on a headset as he did.

"Sonar, Conn," Houser's acerbic voice rang on the communication circuit, "what's the status of the incoming torpedo?"

Sanderson's reply was equally caustic.

"Still incoming."

"Any idea of range? Or speed?"

"Conn, Sonar, no."

Schramford's voice came on the circuit next. "Conn, maneuvering, we're overpowering the reactor now, limited by main engine bearing temperatures, reactor power steady at one three eight percent."

"We're getting . . ." Kane craned his neck and peered at the speed indicator, noticing the deck's vibration seemed about the same . . . "forty-two knots. Is that all she has, Eng?"

"Sir, any more and we'll melt the mains or grind up the reduction gear. As is we'll sustain some core damage and higher radiation levels."

"Eng, you get me away from this torpedo and I'll buy you a brand-new plant," Kane said.

"Captain, presets loaded and confirmed," Follicus broke in.

"Very well, Weps," Kane replied. "As soon as we're done shooting, get the crew working the reload."

"I've already told them, sir."

Kane stepped back from the attack center to the periscope stand, where he could see the entire crew in the stuffy room.

"Firing point procedures, tubes one and two."

"Ship ready," Houser drawled.

"Weapons ready," Follicus said.

"Solution input," McDonne said, obviously unhappy at shooting a torpedo without contact on the Destiny, the artificial range and orbit point a gamble.

"Tube one, shoot on programmed bearing," Kane said.

"Set," from the attack-center Pos Two console's Rodney Olson as he locked in the orbit point for the torpedo in the computer, sending it to the torpedo in the tube in the lower level deck.

"Stand by," Follicus said, taking the firing trigger on the firing panel to the nine o'clock position, completing the launching circuit in the computer.

Two decks below a small solenoid valve opened in an ultrahigh-pressure air line leading to the firing ram, a large piston with the high-pressure air on one side and water on the other. The air side of the ram became loaded with the air at over 3,000 pounds per square inch, the surface area of the piston translating the pressure to a force of 200 pounds per square inch as it pushed against the water on the other side of the ram. The water side realized the same pressure spike, the pressure in the torpedo tanks soaring, the water spilling into vents in the aft end of the tube, rocketed the torpedo from the tube. In little more than a second two tons of Mark 50 torpedo had been accelerated to three g's and cleared the tube. The ejector ram, now at its end position, came to rest, the air side venting inboard in a tremendous crash, pressurizing the entire ship and temporarily deafening the torpedo-room crew in spite of their Mickey Mouse ear protectors.

In the control room David Kane's eardrums slammed from the pressure of the torpedo launch. Before his hearing returned to normal he barked the next order:

"Tube two, shoot on programmed bearing."

Seconds later the second torpedo left its tube and turned back around to the east on a medium-speed run to enable.

For the next fifteen minutes, the Nagasaki torpedo gaining steadily on it, the *Phoenix* launched torpedoes every forty-five seconds, the weapons leaving the ship and turning back around to head east.

After twenty-three torpedoes had been launched, Follicus turned around to face Kane and McDonne.

"Sir, the last torpedo is loaded in tube four. Should we shoot or save it?"

McDonne spoke up, knowing Kane would want a recommendation.

"I say save it, Captain. Never know when we'll need an insurance policy."

Kane decided he'd be damned if they found a spare torpedo in his hull's wreckage . . . if it came to that.

"No, XO. Firing point procedures, tube four."

When the last weapon had left the ship, leaving the torpedo room empty, the torpedoes en route to or already at their preprogrammed hold points waiting for the emergence of the Destiny, sonar chief Edwin Sanderson clapped his hands against his headset, his eyes nearly bulging out of his head.

"Conn, Sonar," he called, his iron control lost for a moment as he spit out the words—"Nagasaki torpedo is going active. Range gate shows it's within 2,000 yards."

18

SUNDAY, 29 DECEMBER

Western Mouth, Strait of Gibraltar

The guidance-and-attack computer of the Nagasaki torpedo had half the power of an American-made Cray supercomputer but also took up only a cubic meter of space aboard the thirteen-ton torpedo. The sonar system of the weapon was sophisticated and sensitive, able to hear a surface warship fifty miles away, a submarine thirty to forty in ideal sound conditions with a target radiating a typical amount of noise. The power of the computer was used mostly in sifting the several hundred thousand gigabytes of sound data it picked up from the sea, including tonal frequencies in a narrowband processor, all the analysis done in real time, just as *Hegira*'s Second Captain system did, except that instead of displaying the data, the torpedo's computer relayed the analysis to the target-interception subroutines. The interceptor programs calculated the swiftest interception course and speed to the target—the torpedo attempted to avoid unproductive tail chases, instead aiming itself toward a point in the ocean where the target would be in the *future,* a sort of smart football aiming not for the wide receiver but where he *would* be at the exact time of reaching the field. In this case the target parameter calculation was predictable since the target submarine had put the torpedo due astern. The Nagasaki could only aim for the target and order the propulsor to spin at maximum speed, giving it 128 clicks of forward velocity to the target's mere seventy-seven.

The speed advantage had the torpedo steadily closing the distance to the target, gobbling up the sea between hunter and prey. The weapon had, in effect, been patient, content to drive in at maximum thrust and click off the minutes, waiting as the target grew nearer and nearer. Still, it was not easy being patient with the knowledge that the target was just ahead; had the unit been a cheetah pursuing a gazelle, its mouth would have been watering furiously at this point.

Soon the target was within two kilometers, the range determined by driving in a slight wiggling course to see how the bearing to the target reacted. The short range caused the targeting functions to activate the unit's sonar set—passive listen-only sonar was fine for pursuit of a loud contact but not good enough for the exact placement and detonation of the six metric tons of shaped-charge plastic explosive in the warhead. If the torpedo attempted to hit the target with passive search sonar, with this high closing speed, it could experience a bearing error that would cause the unit to go sailing past the target and have to turn around and continue the chase. The active echo-ranging came on, illuminating the sea around it with a powerful medium-pitched sonar pulse, transmitting the pulse at power high enough to generate steam vapor bubbles at the nose cone. After the pulse the torpedo went silent and listened for the return, which came back a fraction of a second later, the sound distorted by the target submarine's rotating screw, the frequency downshifted to a deeper pitch by the target's motion away from the sonar pulse. The target position in the computer's mind needed to be adjusted slightly, the range a bit farther than the torpedo had originally thought.

The target position established, the torpedo began its final arming actions, preparing the high explosive's fuse for detonation. The targeting program called for another data point, the sonar transmitter complying with another loud ping. The target was now at one point five kilometers. A software interlock closed a contact in a relay of the fuse's arming circuit, preparing the system to detonate with the last signal in the circuit: the proximity magnetic sensor. The target's wake from its large-diameter propeller began to buffet the torpedo, its signal to dive to a slightly deeper depth to avoid the screw vortex and get under the target's hull amidships. The roar of the screw ahead and the turbulence of it became more violent. Another ping, another range. Less than a kilometer now.

The target was too close to ping a pulse and get a meaningful return. The sonar switched to a ramp transmission, a police-siren sound going slowly from a deep pitch to a high-pitched wail, then dropping down to the low pitch. The receiver was able to get the return from the target at the same time the transmitter put out the signal. The range closed to 400 meters, shrank rapidly to two shiplengths, the target screw vortex pounding the Nagasaki with turbulence.

The torpedo drove on, closing quickly, in the last seconds of its life.

USS *Phoenix*

Senior Chief Sanderson's face was blotchy red as it tended to be when he was angry—which he now was—or scared—which he also was. He tried to keep his voice steady as he made the report that he considered his last.

"Conn, sonar, incoming torpedo has switched active sonar to a continuous ramp pulse. He's inside a thousand yards and still closing."

"Conn, aye," Kane's hurried voice replied.

Sanderson reached to pull off the sonar headset, thinking the torpedo explosion would deafen him, then figured it didn't matter . . . he'd be dead before he heard the detonation.

Aft, in the control room, Commander Kane spoke on a phone, his voice rushed and loud, no longer showing his trademark cool.

"Eng, open your throttles wide, I don't care if the mains fly out of the fucking casings, and do it now!"

The hull vibrations increased suddenly to a violent shaking as the screw's thrust bearing 200 feet aft lost its oil film and made metal-to-metal contact, threatening to shear off the shaft. In maneuvering, several beads of sweat ran down Tom Schramford's forehead as he glared at the reactor power-meter needle as it climbed to 150 percent and hit the top peg, deep into the red zone, the reactor compartment's high radiation alarm flashing on the reactor control panel. The reactor core was coming apart, he thought, the bomb-grade uranium no longer separated from the cooling water by a sheath of zirconium cladding, the clad now rupturing as the fuel elements overheated. The main engines shook hard aft, the bearings hot, the boilers now putting out steam and water, unable to deal with the huge steam demand and still supply dry steam, the water droplets impinging on the main engine turbine blades, threatening to break off a blade. And a thrown blade would blow open the casing, blast the compartment with steam and roast the men aft.

Schramford didn't like his orders but would have done the same himself if he'd been in command. It was too loud aft with the complaining drive train to hear the sonar from the incoming torpedo, but forward in the control room David Kane's ears were filled with the wailing knell of the weapon.

Kane had tried everything, putting the reactor in the red, running as hard as he could. He wondered if he should emergency blow to the surface, then rejected the idea. From the sonar tapes of *Augusta*'s sinking, he suspected that an emergency blow had been Rocket Ron's last action, and it had not saved him. The bubbles from the ballast tanks had probably made them an even bigger target, or the blow had slowed them down.

Kane was out of alternatives. He could only wait. Sensing the eyes of the men around him, he kept his war face on: a deep frown, narrowed eyes, jaw muscles clenched. His vision of Becky's face was starkly real. He blinked her away and looked over at the ship-control console, abstractly wondering how fast the ship could go full out. The electromagnetic log speed indicator read 42.9 knots, the last twenty percent of reactor power barely able to push them another 1.5 feet per second faster.

The torpedo's sonar grew louder, then stopped, just before the explosion.

The Nagasaki was fifteen seconds away from detonation when the alarm was received in its upper functions from the self-check module reporting low pressure in the port and starboard fuel cells. A half-second after the alarm sounded the drive turbine began to spool down as the last drops of fuel flowed into the combustion chamber, the chamber cooling, the drag of the water almost immediately bringing the propulsor speed to windmill velocity. With the loss of the turbine, the AC and DC power generators winked out, dropping electrical power to circuits and systems across the board with minor exceptions that were supplied by the onboard battery.

The torpedo, too long in its tail chase, had run out of fuel, but even this eventuality had been planned for. There was just enough power left to complete the final relay contacts in the fuse-arming circuit, just enough consciousness remaining in the weapon's dying brain—in an imitation of a human reflex—to order the detonation of the high explosives. The torpedo's computer intelligence blacked out, but not before the relay in the detonation circuit clicked home and the trickle of current found the fuse, igniting it into incandescence and detonating the high explosive.

At the time the torpedo was 125 meters astern of and twenty meters below the target submarine's screw, tantalizingly close but too far to guarantee a kill. The fireball from the six-ton explosive blew outward, the shock wave reaching far out for the hull of its intended kill.

The disruption of the ocean region where the torpedo had once been was momentary, and within seconds the violence of the explosion was replaced by bubbles of combustion gases and a shock wave expanding outward in a forceful pressure pulse, its power smashing into the aft hull of the submarine target. Although the pressure pulse was cruel, the sub's hull was not cut in two, not ruptured, not even cracked, the high-tensile HY–80 steel holding against the stress of the pressure wave as its hammer slammed into the vessel. Had that been the end of the explosion's effect, the submarine would have sailed on.

But hull integrity was not sufficient by itself to allow survival in an underwater six-ton plastique explosion . . . the pressure pulse did three things to the sub that made her survival doubtful, perhaps impossible.

The first was to blow the horizontal stabilizer surfaces upward from the blast angle, coming as it had from below. The sternplane surfaces' hydraulics were overcome by the force of the shock wave, the force of it rotating the surfaces up on their massive hinges, the ship lucky that the sternplanes were not completely torn off.

The second was to shake the ship in such a violent acceleration that the electrical breakers all opened, from the smaller scram breakers providing power to the reactor's control rods to the main grid turbine breakers and motor generator output breakers supplying the vital loads, even the battery output breaker. As the circuit breakers were jostled open the ship's electricity was completely lost, the reactor one of the biggest consumers of its own electrical output, the system eating thousands of horsepower in the coolant recirc pumps and the two dozen other pumps that circulated the power plant's various fluids. It was, in effect, the vessel's heart failure at the same time as a central nervous system shutdown, brain death.

The third result was more a response to the first effect and an aftermath of the explosion: the force that had smashed the sternplanes upward from the tail section of the sub had compressed hydraulic oil in the cylinders that pushed the sternplane surfaces, the oil returning to the air-loaded accumulators, the pressurized oil embued now with more energy than the air pressure after the explosion. The high-pressure oil set up a hydraulic pendulum, the same sort of hydraulic pendulum observed by sloshing back and forth in a bathtub, the rising water on one end inevitably bound to rush to the other end. Now that the explosive power of the detonation was dissipating, the force pushing on the sternplane vanished. The high-pressure oil rushed from the accumulators unchecked, back to the cylinders that controlled the sternplanes, now unopposed by the seawater force on the sternplanes, likewise unopposed by the actions of the sternplanesman in the control room, the youth slumped in his control seat dazed and on the border of consciousness. The cylinders forced the sternplanes back down to the full-dive position and kept them there.

The final result was a jam dive—the ship speeding ahead at over forty knots, the sternplanes in the full-dive position, inclining the ship downward at high speed heading for crush depth, her dead reactor unable to pull her back, her dazed crew no longer capable of pulling the ship out.

In the control room, Kane watched his ship's lethal dive toward the bottom.

The explosion of the Nagasaki torpedo was picked up by several dozen sonobuoys floating below the orbiting P–3 Orion at the western strait mouth. The sonar technician shared a look with the ASW officer. The explosion detections were all at the position of the submarine contact they had tracked as the 688-class USS *Phoenix*. There was nothing the airplane could do except continue the effort to find the Destiny—class if and when it outchopped the Med. The ASW officer, hoping for good luck, and needing to do something, ordered the spinup of the Mark 52 torpedo nestled in the weapon bay beneath the wings. When the torpedo was warm, its computer asked for target coordinates. The ASW officer, frustrated, was unable to answer the question.

CNFS *Hegira*

Sharef looked back to the chart table to see their progress through the strait, debating with himself whether he should increase speed, finally deciding against it out of unwillingness to generate a louder sound-signature with the aircraft so close. Behind him, on the fifth and sixth sensor-display consoles, lines of noise intensity jumped and danced as the ship's hull arrays picked up the propulsors of the American Mark 50 torpedoes orbiting at the mouth of the strait, as yet unnoticed by the officers at the consoles, who had been suddenly distracted by the indication of a dozen sonobuoys that had just splashed into the water above them.

Sharef's mouth opened to order evasive action when Tawkidi, his eyes wide, his characteristic calm cracking, announced the next jumping graph on the display, much worse than sonobuoys:

"Low aircraft overhead, sir, looks like he's got a positive detection."

Two sonar techs and the ASW officer of the mid-channel P–3 Orion leaned over the central console, reviewing the incoming data from the last field of sonobuoys dropped five minutes earlier.

"That's *him*," the sonar tech said.

"One last volley, about here," Lieutenant Commander Quaid said, speaking into a lip-mike intercom to the pilots up forward.

The plane turned, pulling many more g's in the turn than its ungainly turboprop appearance would indicate. Quaid held himself on a handhold as the plane lumbered back around to the south, watching the displays as the next round of sonobuoys dropped out of the plane's belly and splashed into the water below. The console display curves filled the display, the lines incomprehensible to the uninitiated but full of detail and luscious information to the fraternity of flying antisubmarine warriors.

"Definite contact, Destiny submarine. Lock-in solution, shift to internal power and prepare to drop."

"Weapon ready, solution set."

"Skipper, ASW, target located and confirmed. Right turn now to zero one five. Request release."

"Turning now . . . on zero one five. Permission to release."

"Drop!"

"She's down."

The aircraft, glinting silver in the moonlight, dropped its payload into the strait, the torpedo looking like a large bomb as it separated from the P–3 and dived nose-first toward the black waves, a parachute popping astern to slow its entry into the water. A flash of phosphorus foam, and the torpedo vanished.

The Mark 52 torpedo was still, in effect, groggy, half-asleep as it hit the water, but the sudden deceleration jolted it into full electronic consciousness. It immediately began listening to its seeker sonar as it dived to 300 feet and turned two complete circles. Its computer had been loaded with the bearing to the hostile submarine, but targets had a nasty habit of evading once they heard the heavy splash of a Mark 52 hitting the water. The unit turned, on its first circle hearing something to the west, ignoring it to make sure there wasn't another target closer, its electronics trained to discriminate between cheap decoys and real submarines. Now at 300 feet, the unit turned again past west and heard the target again, somewhat fainter this time. The torpedo abandoned its second circle and spun the propulsor to maximum speed while pinging with active sonar.

The return came back, solid, hard. The target was directly ahead, the range minimal. The weapon sped up to fifty-three knots and bore down on the sub, diving slightly to a depth of 450 feet, the depth of the target. As the target grew closer, the torpedo shortened the pulse-repetition frequency. It would be a short run. In anticipation, the unit armed its warhead and continued speeding toward the target.

"Loud splash, bearing of the aircraft at one one two, sir," Tawkidi reported, his voice level but unnaturally loud in the hushed room. "We've got a propulsor, definite torpedo in the water . . . and the unit is active and closing."

"Reactor control, emergency ahead, maximum power to the point of nucleate boiling in the exit plenum, transfer loads to the battery and disable the overload protection in the propulsion motor breakers. Ship control, steer two six five, depth 200 meters, report speed."

Sharef had ordered reactor control to put out maximum power short of melting down the fuel assemblies, the calculations for emergency-ahead speed predicting a speed of eighty-eight clicks. Shared did not smile as the display wound out to ninety-three clicks, since the American airborne-launched torpedoes could do well over ninety-five clicks, perhaps even 100. Sharef continued heading west, out of the Mediterranean with its flocks of aircraft launching torpedoes and their damned sonobuoys toward open ocean and the Atlantic. The torpedo was still driving up on them but it was small. Sharef hoped that it would not harm them too badly. Still, no commander took a hit without evading. At that moment he devoutly wished for another Dash-Five evasion device.

"Commander, report status of the SCM."

SCM was sonar countermeasures, a torpedo-deception system designed by the Japanese shipbuilders, a sort of ventriloquist sonar pulse generator built to fool an incoming torpedo and make it explode too early, the transmitters mounted in the two lower X-fins aft. The sea-trials test results on it had been inconclusive, but in a torpedo tail chase the SCM sonar received the pulse of a torpedo sonar, listened for how often the pulse came in, then on the next ping-listen cycle the SCM would transmit an identical pulse back to the torpedo. The SCM transmission was designed to be heard by the torpedo before it heard the echo return of its own original transmission bouncing off the sub. It was simple in concept but close to impossible to make it succeed at sea. The problem that came up first was making the ship able to transmit a ping that exactly matched the torpedo's ping, then changing it so it would sound like an echo return, adjusting the timing and frequency of the bogus echo so that the torpedo would be fooled into thinking the target was nearer, farther, slower or faster than it actually was. The system required the most sensitive receivers, the most perfect transmitters and the dedication of an entire supercomputer.

All these requirements had been worried over for years, the final hurdle for the computer. Computing resources were most at a premium during a torpedo evasion. Sensors were straining to hear another threat or locate another target, weapons systems were programming the counterfire, reactor systems were controlling the potentially dangerous core as it approached its design limits, and ship-control systems were preparing to maneuver to evade—there simply was not time or machinery to do the intense calculations needed to put out the ventriloquist sonar pulses. The Japanese, as usual, had relished the chance to solve a seemingly impossible technical problem and had installed a separate compact supercomputer tied into a new hydrophone array on the X-tails. The system was expensive and not guaranteed to work, but about half of the tests had shown impressive results.

As they ran from the torpedo, Tawkidi and Sharef had been too involved with the incoming torpedo and activating the SCM system to notice what lay ahead: the minefield of two dozen Mark 50 weapons circling and quietly waiting for the Destiny submarine.

David Kane's mind was operating on parallel tracks, and if he were not seconds from disaster he might have found the effect fascinating, the sudden expanded mental capacity the result of the rush of adrenaline and his own sense that he probably had less than thirty seconds to live.

Phoenix's deck had plunged to a steep down-angle as a result of the diving-angle on the sternplanes. One part of Kane's mind acted as a recorder and impartial observer, seeing that the inclinometer mounted above the ballast-control panel was off the scale, which would be over a fifty-degree down-angle. A grease pencil on a string suspended from the OOD's status board hung very nearly horizontal relative to the deck—the ship was headed damn near straight down, a fact Kane could swear to if for no other reason than he and the other battle stations watch-standers had fallen to the forward bulkhead, the cluster of almost two dozen bodies at rest against the door to the forward passageway, the door to sonar and the ship-control station. The sternplanesman was out cold after being slammed into his control yoke by the hit he took from XO McDonne, the safety harness either failing or unused. The diving officer was the man next in line to save the ship, his duties to supervise ship's course and depth and angle, this incident fitting right into his job description, but who was not up to the task. Usually the DO sat behind the flight-deck-style controls, behind the console that separated helmsman/sternplanesman from the fairwater planesman. He had been knocked from his seat by the impact of several plotters and a phonetalker, the pile at rest against the ship-control panel, blocking view of the plane indicators and depth gauge. Houser, the OOD, was apparently missing, but could have been under the pile of bodies. Which left Kane himself, who was initially on the conn and had slid down the deck and hit someone else, too pumped up to experience the shock or surprise he would have expected.

It was obvious to Kane that the ship was dying and had only seconds to go before changing from a submarine to a submerged debris field. The ship had been going full-out at the time of the Nagasaki detonation, the initial blast giving them a slight up-angle, then suddenly pushing them into a dive. The reactor had tripped, that much was obvious from the loss of the ventilation system. The ship would now plunge until it exceeded crush depth, at 1,300 feet below the surface, a trip that would probably take only a few seconds. Once below 1,300, the sea pressure outside the hull would become greater than the ship was designed for, the enormous force built up from the weight of the water above. The submarine force had lost three nuclear subs to the crushing pressure; the first, the *Thresher* in 1963, went down on sea trials and made a crater when it hit the bottom. There was not much left of her intact, just a square mile of ocean bottom scattered with wreckage.

If the water was not deep enough to crush the hull, the ship would hit bottom and rupture like an egg hurled to the kitchen floor. A fleeting mental vision flashed through Kane's mind, that when the Russian submarine *Komsomolets* sank a decade before, it had hit the rocky bottom of the Norwegian Sea so hard that it broke into several pieces, two of her own torpedoes detonating from the violent impact.

Kane next saw the chart as if it were suspended in front of his face, blocking his nightmare view of his submarine. The mouth of the strait had a very rocky bottom with scattered patches of sand. And the depth was only 225 fathoms, a little over 1,300 feet. The good news was that at least the ship wouldn't implode from sea pressure, but the bad news was it would end up worse off than the *Komsomolets*. These thoughts all ran through Kane's mind in less than a few seconds, and during that time the ship dived over 210 feet deeper.

The second track of Kane's mind was devoted entirely to action, most of it reflex. Years before at submarine school an instructor could walk by in the hallway and casually say "jam dive," and Kane would have shouted back *"all back full, emergency blow forward, full rise on the bowplanes."* Immediate actions. All automatic. All useless here . . . because ordering up "back full" meant the ship needed propulsion to back down with the screw and pull the ship out of the dive, and there was no power; because ordering an emergency blow meant reaching the ballast-control panel, a mere twelve feet away, twelve feet of obstacles, piled bodies, control seats, consoles, with no walkway now that the ship was vertical; and to get full rise on the planes, the fairwater planesman might as well have been as remote as the ballast panel.

At least the ship-control panel's sternplane control yoke was close. Kane, at that point thinking about *Komsomolets*, reached for the helmsman, who was still slumped against the wheel, his harness dangling toward the panel. The young man's face was pressed up against the yoke, his nose broken, his eyes swelling shut. Kane grabbed the boy's arm and pulled him away hard enough to tear muscle and break an arm —all those tall tales about fear-crazed mothers lifting thousand-pound tractors off their wounded children were absolutely true, Kane discovered, as the boy's body sailed across the room from what felt like a gentle shove. With his other hand Kane grabbed the sternplane yoke and pulled it back hard enough to slam it back to the stops, his own muscles shooting sharp pains into his shoulders. He wondered if the hydraulics were still working, but the yoke had the solid feel of being connected to the hydraulic oil control manifold.

Two hundred feet aft the main hydraulic oil system accumulator, only half charged, pressurized the lines leading to the sternplane control ram. The accumulator would have been recharged by the hydraulic oil screw pump, but the loss of power had shut it down. The result was a dangerously low pressure capacity in the system. The header came up in pressure and gallantly tried to move the massive sternplanes, but the loss of pressure was too much. The emergency system, having waited years with nothing to show for it but an occasional use in a drill, filled the gap, its accumulator discharging as pressure plunged in the main system, operating a redundant ram on the other side of the rudder. With the power of the emergency system, the sternplane surface rose from full-dive to full-rise in the same amount of time, as if the entire system were completely healthy.

Kane looked at the half-dead ship-control panel, seeing the internal battery-supplied instruments displaying the sternplane angle easing, then rising. He found the ship's angle display, the "bubble," and watched to see if the ship would respond in time. The angle began coming off the deck, the forward bulkhead that had been a floor a moment ago now rotating so that it again became a wall, the men falling off it onto the true deck. Kane held onto the control yoke and blinked as the display reeled off the depth: 1,150, 1,200, 1,250 feet and still diving. He had succeeded in taking the steep down-angle off the ship, but not in checking its downward momentum. The depth gauge spun off 1,300 feet, crush depth, and Kane couldn't watch it anymore.

But it was not crush depth that claimed the *Phoenix*. Thirty-five seconds after Kane first grabbed the control yoke, the ship slammed into the rocky bottom with the kinetic energy of a hundred-car freight train smashing into a cliff wall at eighty-five-miles-per.

Kane hit the ship-control panel, gashed his head open, slid to the deck and tasted blood as it spilled into his mouth.

19

SUNDAY, 29 DECEMBER

Eastern Atlantic
West Mouth, Strait of Gibraltar

"How close?" Sharef asked, leaning over Tawkidi's seat at the sensor-control panel. The incoming airplane-launched torpedo had been following them for three minutes now.

Commander Tawkidi, combat-stations deck officer, looked up from the sensor-control section, his eyes widening in surprise, then showing triumph. His headphones had just transmitted a booming roar from the bearing to the Nagasaki torpedo and the American submarine some fifty kilometers distant to the west.

"What is it?" Sharef demanded.

"The Nagasaki torpedo just detonated!"

Sharef leaned closer. "Any indication of the American submarine?"

Tawkidi searched, putting off for a moment the monitoring of the incoming American torpedo.

"No hull breakup noises yet but there are no indications of its reactor or steam plant—wait a minute . . ." Tawkidi listened, his eyes shut. A second faint rumble came through the headphones. "I think the target just imploded or hit the bottom, Commodore. If he wasn't dead before he is now."

Sharef nodded solemnly. Sinking another submarine could never be a time of joy for him, the submarines of the enemy forces sharing more with him than any landlubber in his own nation, men who knew the deprivations of being at sea for weeks, the lack of companionship from family or friends, fighting the sea, existing in the Spartan environment of the ship, the deep-diving vessels built to accommodate the equipment, not the needs of the crew. He forced himself to remember that they were Americans, brothers of the brutal men who had blown his *Sahand* to the bottom of the gulf, killing so many of his shipmates—and then he felt nothing for them, neither pity nor hatred.

Out of the corner of his eye Sharef saw General Sihoud and Colonel Ahmed standing near the door to the forward passageway. He ignored them and returned to the tactical chart, then to Tawkidi's console at the sensor panel. The American torpedo continued closing and he began to feel a sense of unreality, as if he were disconnected from the scene. He had tried to tell himself that these could be his last minutes but somehow he remained unconvinced. Every man had a time to die. Sharef still believed it was not yet his time. But then, he wondered if he would know when it was time.

Tawkidi's enthusiasm faded as the Second Captain displays filled with the curves of dozens of sonobuoys pinging at them and the aircraft engines orbiting overhead.

"Now how close?"

"A kilometer, maybe less."

"Enable the SCM."

"SCM is up and enabled in automatic. It needs a few more pings before it will be able to reproduce the false echo."

"It better start working before that torpedo gets any closer."

The pinging of the torpedo began to sound through the hull, sharp and high-pitched. A second ping rang through, louder now, suddenly answered by a distorted-sounding pulse that was at a lower pitch but otherwise a copy of the original. The noises continued, the torpedo pinging a high pulse, the ship's SCM sonar answering with a deeper, throatier false echo. As the minutes passed, the torpedo's pulses became more frequent until the pings from the weapon and the *Hegira*'s ventriloquist system merged into one long loud groaning sound, as if the two machines were sounding mating calls to each other. Sharef and Tawkidi glanced at each other, then over to Sihoud and Ahmed. The general seemed serene, Ahmed looked angry as they faced being hit by an American torpedo.

The moaning sonar pulses continued, lasting for one endless second after another. The sonar display above Tawkidi's head showed the danc-ing broadband signatures of the orbiting Mark 50 torpedoes shot by the American 688-class, the traces as yet unnoticed in the tense room, per-haps because the weapons showed no tonals, perhaps because even their broadband sonar noises were whisper-quiet, but more likely because the men at the sensor consoles were so focused on evading the incoming weapon. It was then that one of the broadband traces jumped as one of the American Mark 50 units now ahead of them by five kilometers sensed their presence, pulled out of its circular hold pattern and sped up to meet them.

Less than two shiplengths astern, the SCM's deception pulses had convinced the American Mark 52 torpedo that the ship was immediately ahead. The outgoing pulses were transmitted, immediately answered by a downshifted echo return, the lower pitch the result of the target run-ning away and lowering the pitch of the return. The torpedo looked for a sign of iron with its hull-proximity sensor but there was no hull present where the sonar signals expected it. It searched its mind for the answer to such a puzzle—a strong sonar pulse echo with no sensation of an iron hull—and the computer realized the problem. Obviously the iron-hull sensor was not functioning, but the closeness of the target's hull could be deduced from the sonar pulses. And there was no sense allowing a valid target to escape merely because the hull sensor had open-circuited.

The torpedo, satisfied with its built-in logic, exploded, 480 meters astern of the *Hegira*.

By the time the Destiny-class submarine exited the western mouth of the Strait of Gibraltar, seven of the torpedoes launched earlier by the *Phoe-nix* had run out of fuel. Spent, the units flooded with seawater and sank to the bottom, some imploding from the deeper depths of the Atlantic, a few breaking apart on the rocks of the sea floor. Every few minutes thereafter another one or two torpedoes became exhausted and exe-cuted their self-destruction sinkings. The Destiny's track leading from the strait passed through a wide gap between still-active torpedoes, six of the weapons too far from her to pick up her acoustic emissions. Her track brought her within acoustic range of four remaining torpedoes. Three heard her—or perhaps thought they heard the Mark 52 torpedo in pursuit of her—but the fourth experienced a mechanical problem and continued circling until it too ran out of fuel.

The first of the three Mark 50s to detect the Destiny was six nautical miles northwest at the time of detection. The second and third were slightly closer, one to the south at five and a half miles, the other to the northeast at just under five miles. The unit to the south confirmed the target by wiggling and sensing the shift in the bearing to the sounds, then accelerated to its fifty-knot attack speed, computing a lead angle to position itself to a point in the sea where the target would be thirty minutes in the future, the calculated time of interception. The unit to the northeast did the same, its interception time slightly less with the Destiny's approach vector. The torpedo to the northeast of the Destiny also sped up, its calculated contact time shorter.

There was little time and much to do for the closest Mark 50. It hurried through its arming sequence, sensitized the hull proximity detector, made a few course corrections and depth corrections, and watched as the target zoomed in.

CNFS *Hegira*

The explosion of the aircraft-launched torpedo shook the ship, the impact smashing into the stern. The force of the hammer blow jarred every compartment and deck. The men aboard experienced the impact as a booming roar and a trembling sensation, a shaking of the deck. Sharef, standing at the tactical plot table, waited for the explosion to smash him into the glass-topped table or hurl him into the overhead. He waited for the water to come roaring in to take his life, and likewise he waited for the panicked thoughts and fears and visions to fill him as they had long ago on the *Sahand* when he had thought he was dying. But the roar of the explosion died out and left only quiet. Sharef remained standing, his knuckles white where he had tightened his grip on the table's handholds. The trembling of the deck calmed almost as soon as it had come, its violence concentrated in its first quarter-second. The ship was dry, and the slight tremble in the deck suggested they were still moving at emergency-ahead speed.

They had survived.

Sharef did a quick inventory of the control room. The Second Captain consoles were still alight with displays, only a half-dozen dark and disabled. The Japanese designers had been worried about this moment, because the ship was completely controlled by the Second Captain's supercomputer process-control modules in the lower level with their operator-control consoles in the control room. They were not shockproof, in fact were highly vulnerable to the slightest accelerations. This ship was so different from the old Victor III he'd last commanded. The ex-Russian ship, renamed the *Tabarzin,* had been almost entirely hardwired. Computers were unavoidable, but the late-1980s vintage ship had been designed with a stark distrust of microprocessors and process controllers. As a result the old sub had been bulletproof, a bucket of bolts that could be taken into combat with confidence. But this ship, so automated and filled with electronics, seemed unprotected. To Sharef, who had seen what damage a ship could experience before dying, the idea of losing computer control in the first few seconds of taking hostile fire was unacceptable. He had voiced his concerns to the shipbuilders, and surprising him, the Japanese had listened, stopping production for a week to interview him and then conduct shock testing. The results of the shock tests were not good—a minor explosion from a torpedo distant enough to spare the hull would still take out the entire Second Captain, requiring wholesale replacement of bubble memories and microprocessor cards. The Japanese, though, had recovered quickly, replacing the computer-process controller cabinets with larger units that had layers of thick gel to cushion against shock. The tests were redone with mixed results. With the gel filling, the Second Captain computers could take a mild shock, but more intense impacts would begin causing damage. In the time left to them the computer designers added redundant components to the circuits, standby boards and cards and microprocessors, kept warm and on-line and ready to be switched into the process train in the same instant as the loss of the primary component. The dual-pressure hull of the ship could take a huge torpedo before flooding, but without ship-control computers the ship could only surface and surrender *if* the Second Captain died.

Sharef watched the consoles, waited for the remaining displays to wink out. None did. He turned aft to the weapons-control area and put his hand on Lt. At Ishak's shoulder. Ishak was the computer-systems officer, a bright young man who understood electronic entities far better than he understood people.

"What's the damage?"

Ishak had already rolled his seat to the Second Captain master console in the aft port corner of the room. The master console could review the health of the entire system and reprogram it if required. Ishak interacted with the console, and watching the electronics engineer talk to his system—his face took on the intensity of a man talking to his loved one. He spun in his chair, his face bright, ready to report the system still healthy, when he was interrupted by Tawkidi at the sensor-control area.

"Commodore, multiple torpedoes in the water! Bearing abeam to port to abeam to starboard!"

The mid-channel P–3 Orion patrol turboprop that had launched the Mark 52 torpedo continued following it as it pursued the Destiny submarine. The Mark 52 was easily tracked, its broadband noise signature loud and steady. The Destiny faded in and out. The P–3 had used up three-fourths of its load of sonobuoys tracking the UIF sub, and it would not be long before it would need to be relieved on-station. The west mouth P–3 had been notified of the attack but could not help out from its position sixty nautical miles farther west, where it orbited as it tried to find the *Phoenix*. And from the position of the explosion of the Nagasaki torpedo there was no sign of *Phoenix*, not even the sound of her reactor cooling on the ocean floor. It was as if she had buried herself in the earth's crust and vanished. The western P–3 continued the search, standing by in case the eastern aircraft needed help.

Meanwhile, a flash message had been transmitted to CINCNAVFORCEMED detailing the situation with the exchange of torpedoes, the apparent loss of the *Phoenix*, the pursuit of the escaping Destiny, and the need for further ASW assets at the entrance to the Atlantic to prosecute the target. Soon after the CINC's receipt of the signal, the Burke-class destroyers searching the Med's western basin were vectored to Gibraltar and ordered to outchop into the Atlantic. Several S–3 Viking ASW jets lifted off the deck of the USS *Reagan* deeper in the Med, the jets banking hard in their turns to the west as they deployed to help the P–3s. At Sigonella Naval Air Station, three more P–3s, all fueled and loaded out with Mark 52 torpedoes and sonobuoys, rolled out onto the runway and lumbered off into the night, but it would be some hours before they would reach the strait.

Within the next fifteen minutes the Mark 52 torpedo caught up with the Destiny submarine and exploded. The sonar techs and the ASW officer in the P–3 above got their hopes up, but when the bubbles and turbulence finally stopped, there had been no sign of a hull breaking up. Two sonobuoys placed farther west radioed their signals, the screen display on the tech's console showing that the Destiny submarine continued on its path heading west. By the time the P–3 had throttled up, banked hard and overflown the positions of the reporting sonobuoys, the Destiny was gone.

The sonar tech slumped into his control seat, his eyes shut, then suddenly sat up straight again and looked to the ASW officer.

"Mr. Quaid! I've got three traces of torpedoes. American Mark 50 torpedoes. They're all at attack velocity."

Quaid leaned over the console, frowning.

"Where'd they come from?"

"Must have been launched by the *Phoenix* and we didn't pick them up when they were slow in transit, or maybe they were passive circlers."

"Maybe *Phoenix* will get her revenge yet."

"Too bad it'll be posthumous," the tech mumbled.

"Too early to call that. What've you got?"

"Multiple weapons, look like they're several miles apart, all of them homing toward the same spot at once."

"Good, maybe we've got a chance for at least one hit. Let's set up a sonobuoy field inside the triangle of the torpedoes and hope for the best."

Sharef knew the order he had to give.

Computers were wonderful, supercomputers even better, and the Second Captain system was everything a submarine could ever want, making control of the ship and the sensing of the seas around the ship easy and natural; the system conquered the task of blending man and machine into one organism, mating the human instincts and reflexes of the machine, until the interface between them blurred to the point that the entire ship was an extension of his well-trained crew. But could a mere box of integrated circuits be trusted to drive them from harm without *any* human supervision? The question was now more than academic— the procedure called for Sharef to turn command over to his computer counterpart and let go.

He was surrounded by incoming high-speed torpedoes bearing down on the *Hegira* from three directions. If Sharef withdrew along the wrong course he might evade a distant torpedo at the cost of driving into a close one. When the bearings to the torpedoes were known and plotted, conventional wisdom dictated the submarine commander drive his ship in a direction that would bisect the largest angle between the bearings to the weapons. But that would be suicide if the ship drove into the closer of the incoming torpedoes. Range to the torpedoes was crucial information, but doing target-range analysis, wiggling the ship in long slow maneuvers, was not possible with only seconds to impact with a close torpedo. The ship's sonar systems, with the exception of the ventriloquist SCM sonar countermeasures suite, were entirely passive listeners— pinging an active sonar to find torpedo range was just not an option.

The Destiny-class submarine designers had known she would someday be outnumbered, and expected if the sub ever got into combat that several weapons would be vectored in at her from other submarines, from aircraft, from surface ships. The Destiny was conceived as a one-ship fleet, and as such was required to have the computer systems made capable of fighting multiple threats from multiple bearings.

The standard operating procedure in the case of multiple inbound torpedoes from around the compass was simple. But Sharef still did not like it. The procedure called for turning his ship over to the Second Captain, which would do course target range analysis by driving the ship through a rapid wiggle, perhaps an S-curve, then, having a feel for the torpedo ranges, calculate the ship's best course to evade, even if it meant driving almost head-on into the most distant weapon.

It required an act of faith, the one quality Commodore Sharef had a severe shortage of, cynicism setting in on the day of the *Sahand* sinking.

But Sharef was no fool, and valued his ship and his crew and his mission, and he gave the order. He shared a momentary look at his first officer, Captain al-Kunis, who had remained silent through the entire day's combat as his function required—he could not participate by UIF regulations and Islamic tradition—the second-in-command's lot in life was to stand beside the commanding officer, remain silent and be ready to take over if the captain fell. Until that moment he would not involve himself, only observe. But it was clear that al-Kunis felt Sharef's thoughts about total trust in the Second Captain system, the doubt in the first's eyes a dark shade.

"Deck officer, engage the Second Captain in ship-control mode."

"Ship control, engage the second," Tawkidi ordered the ship-control console operators. Sharef watched as the operators keyed in the system, their training anticipating the order and the functional menu screen already called up on their displays, the ship a single keystroke from computer control.

Sharef grabbed a handhold set into the side of the plot table just as the Second Captain took command and put the rudder over. The deck inclined rapidly to the left as the computer threw the ship into a violent maneuver. The ship shuddered. From below came the sound of dishes falling out of a cabinet and shattering on the galley deck. As suddenly as the first maneuver, the Second Captain shifted the rudder, the deck rolling back to starboard, one man at the reactor control consoles thudding to the deck, sheepishly crawling back into his control seat. The deck then leveled and steadied, the ship's S-curve complete. Sharef looked at the ship-control console and saw that the ship was driving up northwest, heading 262 degrees true, almost exactly between the torpedo at 194 and the one at 330. Those fish must be roughly at equal ranges, Sharef thought, which made sense, because the range at which a torpedo could detect them should be a constant. Then again, the chart also told a story, the land too close to allow the Second Captain to drive them back east, which was also part of the computer's evasion routine.

Now under Second Captain control, there was little to do but wait and monitor the system for gross failure. The Second Captain would continue to monitor the weapons, perhaps even sending the ship suddenly into another maneuver to test for range or to check on a weapon coming in from astern in the main sonar's blind spot. As yet there had been no torpedo sonar pulses showing up on the sensor displays, but then evading three torpedoes was not like running in a tail chase from one. The SCM ventriloquist was again enabled in automatic, but it would be useless trying to fool three torpedoes at once. And the system would not do well against a weapon closing in on them from an angle.

Sharef became aware of the officers looking at him, searching his face for signs of confidence or despair, trying to see if their captain saw hope or defeat. Sharef knew the psychology of his men, the same as any crew. A crew without hope could not function. But his face had made him a liar, because just as before he had felt it was not yet time to die, he had a sensation that perhaps now it was.

20

SUNDAY, 29 DECEMBER

Western Atlantic
USS *Phoenix*

Lieutenant Commander Thomas Schramford had been *Phoenix*'s chief engineer for almost three years. Before that he had served as an engineering-division officer on the *Hartford* in each of the aft divisions—electrical, reactor and mechanical—then rotating to the new construction submarine *Tampa* while she was built at DynaCorp's Electric Boat's Groton yards. While spending his two years watching *Tampa* progress from a single hoop of structural HY–80 to a fully fitted-out combat submarine he learned the 688-class in such detail that every cable, valve, microelectronic processor, pipe and panel were engraved in his memory. On the wall above the engineering officer of the watch's desk was a large print of the piping and instrumentation systems of the plant, from the core's main coolant piping to the last condensate pump pressure control valve. As part of studying for the engineer exam, Schramford had to be able to reproduce it from memory, and he still could. If need be he could have started up the reactor from memory—in spite of the fact that Operating Instruction 27, Normal Reactor Startup, was over 120 pages long, not including the steam plant startup procedures.

Of all the men aboard, Schramford was one of few in the aft compartment who had escaped serious injury or loss of consciousness from the collision with the bottom—the others who remained conscious were dazed or trapped under bodies or equipment. He was conscious but his mind was dulled with pain from striking his groin on something, the terrible ache ballooning up through his abdomen. He clamped his eyelids shut and bit his lip, trying to fight the pain, but for some time the pain won, and after seconds or minutes or hours the ache eased but continued throbbing, sapping his strength.

The ship was quiet, the roar of the turbines gone, the air handlers shut down, the reactor inert. There on the deck of the maneuvering room, Schramford found his thoughts turning to the reactor core. The ship had been steaming full out just before the loss of all electrical, and the reactor went from over 150 percent power to zero. But nuclear reactors never just turned off. The radioactivity of the core remained after the bulk of the reactions were stopped, adding tremendous heat to the coolant loop, in this case heat equivalent to running the core at fifteen percent power without cooling. Uncooled, that power would soon melt the reactor, possibly find its way out the bottom of the pressure vessel and then eat through the hull itself.

The ship's designers had planned for such an emergency; the emergency cooling system, XC as it was abbreviated, was a brilliant set of pipes, valves and a seawater tank that could cool the core using the trick that hot water rises and cold sinks—natural circulation. No moving parts. Had it been lined up, Schramford would have had no worries, but it had been locked out in its configuration for at-sea operation, the procedure designed to prevent an inadvertent XC initiation when at power, since an unintended cold-water injection into a critical reactor could cause a core runaway. But now, with no flow and no XC, the reactor vessel would be stewing, its temperature rising, certainly boiling the coolant. Once the water was driven from the core and replaced with steam, the fuel would melt and the ship would die. Schramford's mind, groggy and full of pain, filled with three words—Three Mile Island.

Schramford slowly climbed to his feet and searched the darkened space for an emergency air-breathing mask, finally retrieving one from an overhead cubbyhole. He strapped it on, the black rubber straps a spider across his face until his chubby features poked into the Plexiglas face mask. He reached up to plug in the hose, clipped the regulator to his belt and breathed in. Almost immediately his head cleared, and his first thought was that this was a bad sign. The atmosphere was contaminated, the scrubbers and burners and oxygen bleed gone since they had hit bottom. It could be worse . . . the battery might be dumping toxic clouds of chlorine gas into the ship or one of the weapons might be leaking fuel. A Javelin cruise missile rocket motor burning would fill the boat with hydrogen cyanide, in which case Schramford and the crew would already be dead.

As engineer, Schramford was responsible for acting in this miserable situation. He heard in the background the damage-control code he had drummed into his junior officers and chiefs since his first day aboard: *Save the ship, save the plant, then save the men* . . . Surrounded by men struggling to breathe the ship's poor air, he knew his duty was to the ship first. He pulled a battle lantern from the bulkhead, disconnected his mask hose and hurried forward to the ladder and down one level, juggling the lantern in one hand while descending and trying not to get tangled in his air hose. A large man, he had little enough wind as it was without dashing down a ladder holding his breath. He plugged in at a middle level manifold and puffed for a few seconds, then unplugged and ran into the portside hatch to the reactor-compartment tunnel, unlatching the heavy door as he went and plugging in his hose as soon as he arrived.

There in the tunnel was the primary-valve station for the valve-op system and several XC valves. Schramford opened a toolbox and took out a large wrench and tugged off the large antileakage cover from a XC–9, then put a special ratchet wrench on the valve stem and pulled on it with all his strength until the valve finally moved. He kept cranking until the valve opened completely, dumping the pressure off the top of another valve deep in the radioactive reactor compartment. When that valve came open the hot-leg water could flow up to the seawater exchanger and the cold leg could flow down. Schramford found the seawater valves to the tank, opened all four and sagged against the bulkhead to regain his strength. Through the thick shielded bulkhead he could hear the forceful flowing noises in the XC piping, and then the boiling of seawater in the heat-exchanger tank as the core gave up its heat. The core protected, Schramford could now equip his crew with air masks, then head forward to see to the captain. Once the ship's force were outfitted in masks he could restart the reactor and the skipper, he hoped, could get them the hell out of there.

Portsmouth, Virginia
Norfolk Naval Shipyard
Graving Dock 4

The sun dipped beneath the line of maintenance buildings and warehouses lining the dock. The drydock floodlights had been lit for a half-hour, only now noticed as the daylight faded. Captain Michael Pacino stood at the lip of the dock leaning on the rusted handrails and looked down on his ship. The dock was finally empty of equipment other than a few manlifts, the *Seawolf* now mostly intact and looking like an ungainly whale in a huge dry bathtub. The blue light of welders' arcs flashed in his eyes on the ship's starboard flank, the flickering reflected against the sheer side of the dock as the six men welded along the seam of the Vortex-missile hull cut. The work replacing the curving piece of steel plating to cover what was earlier the gaping hole of the hull cut was only in its first hour; the HY–100 steel of the hull was almost two inches thick. Even with the half dozen men welding, it would be dawn on the next day, Monday, before the weld would be completed, and another several hours before the X-rays were taken and evaluated. The X-rays of the weld would probably show several imperfections that would call for grinding out and rewelding. The repairs could take till mid-afternoon Monday. The confirmation X-rays would take them to Monday night, and only then would the men be out of the dock. And only then could the ship be painted.

The ship looked almost foolish in the dock with the bright green paint of the inorganic zinc primer coat turning the sub into a cartoon character. There were always the inevitable chants of the crew about "we all live in a green submarine" until the yard got its paint gear loaded in the dock and could paint on the intermediate and final coats. The ship would gleam a menacing black on the upper surface, a dull red anti-barnacle coating on the bottom, the line between black and red ruler-sharp as if detailed out by the best body shop in town. Without paint, the ship would be so covered with rust that seawater valves and torpedo-tube doors would start to hang up. The salty seawater would literally begin eating the hull. The paint job would take another full day, delaying *Seawolf* until Wednesday morning.

There was just not enough time. Pacino needed to be underway sooner. He pulled a walkie-talkie radio from his belt and called the ship. The duty officer came up almost immediately. Pacino ordered him to call for the shipyard commander to come to the dock. Maybe there was still a way, Pacino thought.

The welding continued, the blue flickering light of it forming dancing spots in Pacino's vision. The sun had vanished by the time Emmitt Stevens's shipyard pickup truck drove up and he got out, his hollow face set.

"Captain," Stevens said. "Ship supe says we'll be painting by this time tomorrow. We should be able to flood the dock Wednesday."

"No."

"Look, Patch, I know you want out, but—"

"Emmitt, the weld will be done by dawn. As the last bead is in place I want the dock flood valves opened. *Seawolf* will be at sea by sunrise."

"You can't do that! What about X-rays and repairs?"

"How good are the welders?"

"Come on, Patch, that's HY–100. It doesn't weld like mild steel. Even with the best welders on the coast we'll have two dozen flaws, that's if we're lucky. The repairs will take half a day, the retests another half day and the paint job most of Wednesday—"

"Skip the X-rays and the repairs. There won't be any paint job. We'll go to sea green."

"Mike, listen to me. You're making a *big* mistake. I can't guarantee a weld like that without tests. You could spring a leak the first time at test depth—a bad one—and we'd never hear from you again. And that's not all the weld could be fine for the first ten excursions to test depth, but the eleventh could be fatal. Or it could be fine in warm water, but diving into colder temperatures could make a flaw brittle-fracture. It could go with no warning, no chance to emergency blow. You're risking your neck, your crew's necks."

In the drydock floodlights Pacino's eyes focused on a sight far from the dock below.

"Wrap the welds and flood the dock. My crew will be ready to go by 5:00 A.M."

Stevens sighed. "You got it, Patch. Jesus, though, good luck."

Pacino didn't answer.

Eastern Atlantic
CNFS *Hegira*

Commodore Sharef didn't need to see the updated displays to know that the *Hegira* was about to take a torpedo hit. The torpedo that had been ahead of them to the west had started out too close. Its intercept speed, combined with the ship's initial closing velocity, had caught them. The computer initially predicted impact at four point five minutes after initial detection. The update was tracking.

Sharef turned away from the displays and stepped to the forward bulkhead of the room to where Rakish Ahmed and Sihoud were standing. Ahmed had borrowed a crewman's jumpsuit. Sihoud had reclaimed the silk *shesh* he had been wearing when they had picked him up, the rip in the garment's hem now sewn up. Sharef idly wondered who had done the sewing. Hard to imagine the Khalib himself doing a seamstress' job. Sihoud's dagger gleamed on his belt. In spite of the general's inspiring size and presence, Sharef felt it was a charade. His instincts told him the general was frightened. Not that fear was dishonorable, because if there was a time to feel it, this was it. Had he not been nearly killed on the *Sahand*, it might have been different, but he had seen the deaths the enemy missiles had brought, and the idea that the same could happen to these men now filled him with a resolve that precluded fear.

"General. Colonel. In less than a minute the first torpedo will hit us. We have done everything possible to avoid it, but with three weapons coming in from all around we were not likely to evade them all. I wanted you to be prepared for the impact."

"Is there nothing else you can do, Commodore?" Sihoud asked.

"There is one option, to surface and count on the torpedoes having a ceiling setting to avoid surface-ship traffic, but that will slow us down and the weapons will easily catch up. Our own Nagasaki torpedoes were designed to find a surfacing sub that much easier from the clouds of bubbles put out by the surfacing systems. It is not a good gamble, General. We have a better chance of the attacking torpedoes running out of fuel than we do of evading by surfacing. Other than that, all we can do is run."

"You said less than a minute," Ahmed said. "How long now?"

"Twenty seconds," Tawkidi said.

The SCM system began groaning out false sonar signals even before the incoming sonars could be heard through the hull. Sharef moved to Lieutenant Ishak's master console. He dropped to one knee, hearing the seconds ticking off in his mind, but tried to keep his voice level.

"Lieutenant, have you told the Second Captain our intended route to the North Atlantic?" The ship's navigation plan, worked out with the officers when the mission was first explained, had them sailing a great circle route toward the range circle around Washington, D.C. The plan had called for them to intercept that 2,900-kilometer circle centered on the American capital at a glancing angle to the northeast, the better to have a longer time en route to assemble and install the Scorpion warheads in the Hiroshima missile airframes. That route would also keep their path heading more toward Greenland than the east coast of America, in case they were tracked or detected sporadically during the trip—making a beeline for Washington would alert the Western Coalition if they were tracked, and the West would expend all possible efforts to sink them. Sharef was convinced that the West had not yet awakened to the situation, that what they faced now were half-measures intended to find Sihoud. If the Americans had the slightest idea that the ship carried a doomsday weapon pointed at their capital, the entire combined navies of the West would hunt him down like a dog.

"Sir, the great circle path toward Greenland has been inserted into the Second Captain since the briefing, but that will not help us if the missiles are not assembled."

Sharef nodded. The Second Captain was perfectly capable of driving the ship to within missile range of the target and launching the weapons without help from the crew, as long as the system was properly programmed. But without fully assembled and complete missiles, the Second Captain would drive them to their destination but would be useless in hitting the target. It was essential that the weapons be assembled as soon as possible. After the missiles were ready, the mission would practically be accomplished, because at that point the mission no longer needed the crew, just an intact ship and healthy Second Captain—

It was then that the American torpedo caught up with them.

The Mark 50 torpedo found the pressure hull of the target, notwithstanding the odd sonar pulses coming from its stern, the noises sounding something like echoes but not at the correct angle or frequency. The torpedo had closed the target from an angle since it began homing, and just as the onboard computer had thought, the target submarine had ended up at precisely this point in the sea at the time of interception. The iron proximity sensors set into the Mark 50's flanks tingled as the hull of the target grew closer, until finally the Mark 50 drove directly under the giant hull of the target, the huge diameter of the hull seeming to be flat at the bottom. The shaped charge of the torpedo automatically was adjusted to blow maximum force in the direction of the hull. Within milliseconds of detecting the hull the high explosive blew. The torpedo underwent a metamorphosis from solid object to pure-energy fireball.

The fireball erupted upward and ruptured the steel outer hull of the target, the pressure wave going further and blasting apart the exterior reinforcing hoop frames and steel plates welded onto the framing. The blast's intrusion into the inner hull blew the interior of the compartment to wreckage and pressurized the compartment to a level approaching its design basis, the force threatening to rip a hole in the other side of the cylinder or tear the compartment from the neighboring one. But as fast as the pressure wave came, it was spent, the energy that had breached both the hulls and pulverized the interior of the compartment now expended and attenuated. The pressure level in the compartment fell, the gas by-products of the explosion leaving through the five-meter-wide hole in the inner hull, the gases replaced by the cold seawater that flooded the space except for a small gas bubble trapped in the upper cylinder of the compartment. Thirty seconds after impact, the damage of the blast was complete.

The submarine outer hull was left with a twenty-meter-wide hole that extended into a hoop-wise rip around almost the entire circumference of the ship. The inner hull of the aftmost compartment was ruptured, the interior equipment—the diesel generator and the battery—blown to pieces. The outer hull's aft conformal sonar array was obliterated. The interior high-voltage cables for the propulsion AC motor were severely damaged, and the SCM sonar-fooling ventriloquist electronics and sonar array were no more. However, the other inner-hull compartments

were undamaged, the stern control X-planes remained intact and functional, and except for the structural rip in the outer hull, the ship was
otherwise unharmed. Propulsion had been lost from the shock of the
blast, and the ship's electrical systems were down without the DC battery, but the computer systems of the Second Captain survived, their
circuits still complete, their internal power systems still supplying the
current for continuing electronic consciousness.

But the men inside the *Hegira* did not move, and half of them no
longer breathed. The lights in the control room were out, only the glaring bulbs of the emergency lighting system energized, the blood running
on the deck turning brown as the minutes turned into an hour. The
room had not served its masters well, the seats in the room mostly
rolling swivel chairs, the only bolted-down control seats those of the ship
control officers. The other men had been standing or sitting in the rolling seats when the torpedo detonated. The bodies in the space flew like
marbles in a shaken jar. Physically, except for the blank screens of the
Second Captain consoles, the room was intact. The men were the difference. Before there had been almost two dozen in the control space, the
room normally large and uncluttered but made cramped by the entire
ship's crew of officers jammed in. Now there were piles of bodies thrown
about by the intense g-forces from the explosion. Four men had died
almost instantly in the blast, more in the ten minutes after, the result of
strangling from a pileup of bodies or drowning from blood spilling into
lungs. The unconscious living and the dead lay on the floor, no spark of
intelligence in the ship except the core processors of the Second Captain
in the process-control modules on the lower level.

After two minutes of waiting with no commands from the human
crew, the core module of the Second Captain took action, as it had been
programmed to do. Its first action was to power up the peripheral modules made inactive by the loss of AC power. The remainder of its systems were fed off a motor-generator that was powered by the reactor's
electrical grid, and the reactor was down. Almost a third of the system
was functional at the end of this action, including the ship-control modules, the air-quality systems and reactor-control cores.

The Second Captain took inventory of the condition of the reactor
plant and began the reactor startup recovery routine. While the control
rods came slowly out of the reactor core, an American ASW patrol
plane orbited above the spot where the torpedo had detonated. The
Hegira did not hear the plane, the sensor-control processors still dormant. Astern of her, two other torpedoes closed, still in pursuit from
before.

Sixty nautical miles west of the *Hegira*'s position, the *Phoenix* still lay
inert on the bottom, her systems shut down, a few souls struggling for

survival inside. After initiating emergency-core cooling, Tom Schramford intended to shut his aching eyes for just a moment. If he had realized he was suffering from a severe concussion he would have kept going, but his minute rest was now into its twentieth minute with no sign of ending soon.

Up forward, Commander CB McDonne opened his right eye and watched the world swirl around him, unaware of where or even who he was. A few minutes later he felt his tongue, which hurt like hell and was stuck hard to the roof of his mouth. When he tried to move it, it sent pain to his brain that went a long way toward shaking off his lethargic state. At least it brought him the realization that he was the executive officer of a submarine in serious trouble. He tried opening both eyes and saw only a dim tangle of feet and limbs, poorly illuminated by a battle lantern that had clicked on by itself when the power had gone down. McDonne tried to breathe and felt another streak of pain shoot through his ribcage. He took another breath and pushed outward at the pile of bodies. He barely seemed to notice at the time that some were warm, some slick with blood, others cold and stiff. He gathered himself, got to his feet. He bent to the men and began pulling them apart, careful to avoid moving broken limbs or men who looked like they might have broken their backs or necks. The kid at the helmsman's station had taken the control yoke on the forehead. The diving officer, originally seated behind and between helmsman and sternplanesman, had plunged forward onto the deck. The chief of the watch, originally at the ballast-control panel to port, had smashed his head on the BCP, his head spun nearly around to face his back.

Houser was in the pile that McDonne had pulled himself out of. Also in the pile were the three officers originally at the attack-center consoles. All were still breathing. Captain Kane was in the pile, and seemed okay if bruised, his face swollen and covered with dried blood from a forehead gash. His nose looked like it was broken. McDonne pulled the weapons officer, Follicus, off the heap. He was alive but dead white. After separating the bodies, all of them at the forward end of the room, McDonne stood again and felt faint. He figured that it must be from the exertion, but then wondered about the atmosphere in the ship. It had a pungent acidic taste to it, more than the smell of blood—the air had to be contaminated. With no power, the ship's air would soon be totally polluted. It might already have near-toxic levels of carbon dioxide, maybe even chlorine if the battery compartment was taking in seawater. He moved aft to the damage-control locker and pulled out a dozen masks, plugged in one for himself and began strapping them onto the faces of the men who remained alive. As soon as he felt his initial taste of uncontaminated air, the ache in his head vanished and he had a new energy, and with it, a new series of thoughts, all bad. Such as the reactor fuel assemblies melting; without the emergency cooling system it might now be fried to a radioactive crisp. He might already be dying from a lethal dose of radiation and not feel it. The ship might be flooding, or would be unable to ascend from the bottom if the propulsion machinery were broken—after slamming into the bottom that hard how could the systems be intact?

And if the ship turned out to be paralyzed it meant the unthinkable— a submarine escape. Suddenly he wanted to know their depth, searching the ship-control panel for the old-fashioned Bourbon-tube pressure gauge calibrated in feet of seawater. The one on the panel read 1,355 feet, deeper than crush depth by fifty-five feet. To exceed crush depth and slam into a rocky bottom and still make it in one piece was a testimony to the design engineers and perhaps to a supreme being too, if McDonne had been religious. By the end of the day he might well be, he thought, pondering a submarine escape from 1,300 feet.

The whole concept of sub escapes had been rethought after the Russian Navy opened their archives and provided details of submarine accidents. One of them stuck in McDonne's mind, that of the *Kaliningrad,* which sank under polar ice cover. Several men had made it inside an escape pod when the ship broke in half. The cause of the sinking was still classified, but evidently several of the Russian officers had escaped and survived the cold of an arctic storm. The other accident that came to mind was the sinking of the *Komsomolets;* the escape pod from that incident brought a handful of men up from below test depth but they later died of complications. The U.S. Navy opened an inquiry into submarine escapes, wondering if it was missing something by not including escape pods on American subs. McDonne had done some of the work for the study during his shore tour at NAVSEA in Crystal City. The report's conclusion: *"Submarine sinkings generally lead to depth excursions below crush depth and hence to complete hull failure with 100% crew casualties. Hence, installation of escape vehicles is not considered a worthwhile safety investment."* In real English, why put in escape pods when the crew would die in a sinking when the hull imploded?

But there was a positive result—the escape trunks, the ship's airlocks —were redesigned to allow crewmen to leave down the ship's full crush depth, rather than from 400 feet. The escape trunk changeout had been done in that messy shipyard period when the reactor was replaced by the new hotrod core. The installation had taken months, but the escape trunk was now able to function down to 1,300 feet. Still, surviving a free ascent to the surface from a quarter mile deep was unlikely. The bends, the cold, the length of the trip, all would conspire to kill a man. And who would want to leave the ship at 1,300 feet with nothing between him and the sea than a Steinke hood? It would be worse than suicide, it would be madness.

McDonne tried to forget the idea while he strapped emergency air masks on the men in the space. He slapped several cheeks and saw a few regain consciousness. Captain Kane's eyelids fluttered open, blinking away the blood. As soon as he got the men in their masks he unplugged and moved aft through the middle level, wondering what the status of the reactor was, a thought still nagging at him that the ship might well have turned into a tomb if they couldn't get off the bottom.

In the eastern Atlantic, late evening Sunday became early morning Monday as the circling P-3 patrol planes ran out of fuel and departed station to head home, one of the planes remaining as it detected the sound of a Mark 50 torpedo explosion with no sound afterward except that of the other two pursuing torpedoes. But those two weapons were as lost as the lone P-3, never finding their target, searching until they ran out of fuel and shut down. After another half-hour on the search with no sign of a hull breakup, the ocean empty, the P-3 was so low on fuel it had to divert to Rota, Spain. The replacement P-3s arrived an hour into the morning, but by then the sea was calm and quiet except for the lonely noises of a few passing whales and a school of clicking shrimp.

Several messages were transmitted to CINCNAVFORCEMED, which at first ordered the aircraft to continue the search, but the fleet of P-3s could not be maintained airborne indefinitely. Between maintenance problems and crew fatigue, the planes' numbers steadily dwindled. By sunrise Monday, only the Burke-class ASW destroyers patrolled the area, and they heard exactly nothing.

The DSRV deep-submergence rescue vehicle *Avalon* and the supporting equipment and crew that had been flown to Naples for the *Augusta* wreckage-site search was called away just as submergence operations had commenced. The *Avalon*'s mission was redefined to go down to the hull of the USS *Phoenix.*

Assuming she could be found.

21

MONDAY, 30 DECEMBER

Eastern Atlantic

David Kane opened his swollen eyes and tried to focus. The light was too dim. The headache was worse, compounded by the straps of the mask cinched around his head. It took him some five minutes to rise to his knees, another several to find a seat where he could rest. While he sat on the control seat for attach console position one, not a soul stirred in the dim room. Finally he decided to remove the mask and fumbled with the rubber straps for some minutes before it came off. His first breath of the ship's air sent him back to the deck, its high carbon-dioxide level like a nail in his skull. Eventually he struggled back into the mask. He didn't remember what had happened.

Forty feet aft and fifteen feet below Kane, Executive Officer McDonne leaned over the prone figure of Tom Schramford. McDonne slapped the engineer's Plexiglas mask. Schramford was alive but showed no response. McDonne hurried on to the aft compartment to check the damage to the reactor plant. It had to be healthy or they would have to try a dead-stick ascent to the surface with the emergency blow system, and if that didn't work . . . wait for rescue. The alternative of a submarine escape, McDonne had decided, was just not viable.

McDonne moved into the compartment through the large hatchway and felt the stuffy, humid heat of the shut-down steam plant as it cooled, its only heat sink the atmosphere of the compartment. He entered maneuvering first, sickened at the sight of the blood on the panels. The crew aft had taken the grounding as hard as the control-room crew. McDonne pulled the cold body of the electrical operator off the panel, his hands covered with congealing gore that he wiped on his coveralls as he stared at the panel in the dim light of the battle lantern. He rotated a selector switch on the panel near a DC voltmeter, selected the battery and held his breath. If the battery were still okay the trip up would be less awful. The needle zipped up to 280 volts. McDonne let out his breath, reached down to the console and snapped the battery-breaker switch to shut the breaker and bring up the DC grid.

Immediately the lights overhead flickered on and blasted brightness into what had been a nightmare tomb of the sunken submarine. McDonne didn't stop there. He shut the breakers to the DC fuses, then the breakers to the motor-generators, the machines on the deck below that were as big as his car, each built to convert DC battery power to AC to run the minimum ship's loads in an emergency with no reactor power. The MG sets spun up, and when output voltage and frequency stabilized he shut the output breaker switches and powered up the AC electrical grid. No fires, no explosions, no sounds of arcs or sparks. The battery had been charged up prior to their arriving on-station to search for the Destiny, so there would be plenty of power to start—as long as the gear was healthy.

McDonne went forward to the reactor-control cabinets and bent to the scram breakers, his belly straining. When that didn't work he plopped down on his rear end and pulled up the large levers shutting the breakers, bringing power into the reactor's control-rod drive mechanisms. The inverter cabinets hummed with the power. Still no fireballs or shorts. He struggled to his feet and walked back to the maneuvering room, reached to the reactor-control panel and snapped rotary switches lining up the system for a restart, then latched the rods with the rod drive-control lever, the central feature of the horizontal section of the console. The rods were soon latched and connected back to their drive motors. Time to start the monster up. McDonne rotated the pistol grip of the rod controller to the rods-out position and waited. It would take five minutes of rod pulling before there was enough reactivity in the core to warm the cooling water. Now what they needed was a healthy steam plant with working turbines, and *Phoenix* would be on her way . . .

Alexandria, Virginia

Admiral Richard Donchez walked the last block to his house, the snow freezing his eyebrows solid, ice caking on the towel around his neck. His breath made vapor clouds around his head in the snowy evening. He walked up to the entrance feeling more tired than usual. With the pace of his job he had worked out only twice in the week before, not so good for a man who had never missed a workout for a dozen years in spite of multiple national-security crises. The air inside the foyer seemed hot and thick. He stepped out of the snow-covered sweatsuit in the entrance, padded to the shower and let his muscles relax in the hot spray. When his skin was red and tingling he turned off the water and got out. He pulled on a fresh pair of chinos, white cotton shirt and a sweater and sank into a deep recliner set before an entertainment center. One click of the remote flashed the news on the screen, the campaign maps showing northwest Africa as the Coalition ground forces ran into stiff opposition. The newscasters asked where General Sihoud was, the Pentagon spokeswoman responding that he was in hiding somewhere in Africa. The phone rang. The secure line to the Pentagon. He listened to the Flag Plot watch officer for ten seconds and hung up. By the time he had changed into his uniform his staff car pulled up.

In the back of the Lincoln Donchez considered using his satellite-secure voice radiotelephone but decided whatever the news was it was certainly bad and he would rather hear it from the watch officer. He turned on the car's television and scanned the channels but there was still nothing new or breaking. Donchez paused for a moment during a special investigation into the sinking of the *Augusta,* watching as the media focused on the mistakes of the Portsmouth shipyard and the failed depth-indication system causing the ship to sink. Donchez hated cover stories, even though there was no way around them. Now the car crunched through the snow at the entrance to the Pentagon, snow falling faster than the ground crews could keep up with it, or they were still shorthanded from the people on Christmas vacation.

His aide Rummel was waiting at the entrance. This time Donchez had no patience for the stairs and they rode up the elevator, then strode down the E-Ring corridor to Flag Plot. Once inside, the somberness of the faces told him the news was worse than he'd expected. He glared at his deputy for operations, Dee Watson, whose face looked even more jowly than usual, the heaviness of the situation in the lines of his sagging face. The commander of the Atlantic's submarines, Admiral Steinman, stared from the video screen above them on the wall, the video link to

Norfolk uncharacteristically sharp. On the neighboring screen was CINCNAVFORCEMED's John Traeps's sleepy face, the time now in the very early hours in Naples. Donchez said nothing. Watson finally spoke.

"Sir, I don't know how to tell you this, so I'm just gonna tell you."

"I hate briefings that begin like this," Donchez mumbled.

"Destiny broke out into the Atlantic and we think the *Phoenix* is down."

Donchez tried to absorb both statements. Why would Destiny move into the Atlantic? Why would she want out so bad as to sink *Phoenix*— and had *Phoenix* actually sunk or was she just missing?

Watson broke back in. "Look at this SLOT buoy message transmission from *Phoenix*. After this we heard a loud transient. Nothing since. Not much different from *Augusta*'s report . . ."

Donchez scanned the message Watson handed him.

. . . DETECTED SINGLE INCOMING NAGASAKI TORPEDO FROM THE EAST AT LONG RANGE . . . AM NOW ATTEMPTING TO OUTRUN UIF WEAPON . . . NEGATIVE, REPEAT NEGATIVE ACOUSTIC ADVANTAGE AGAINST DESTINY CLASS.

"Says here he wanted to fire some Mark 50s in passive circle mode at the Destiny," Donchez said to the camera mounted above John Traeps's monitor. "What happened?"

"Well, sir, we've pieced this together from the reports of the P–3s, S–3s and Burke destroyers. The Nagasaki torpedo hit the *Phoenix*, probably sinking her. Within a half-hour several *Phoenix*'s passive circling torpedoes detected the Destiny west of Gibraltar and chased her northwest. Two of the fish shut down but one got a hot detect and detonated. We heard inconclusive signs of damage but one of the P–3s thought it heard transients ten minutes later. Reactor startup was what the operators reported it sounded like. Then it vanished. There was nothing more heard from the Destiny or the *Phoenix*."

"What are we *doing* about this?"

"We've diverted the DSRV *Avalon* from the *Augusta* search to go down to the approximate position of the loud transient. We might find *Phoenix* there—"

"And what about the Destiny?"

"We've directed all ASW assets in the Med out into the Atlantic to search, but the circle of probable detection continues to expand as time goes on. It could be anywhere in 20,000 square miles—"

Watson interrupted. "And with her acoustic advantage over the 688-class I think it might be a lousy idea to send any more Los Angeles-class submarines to find her. This bastard has mowed down two of the best ships in the fleet. Even if he's hurt I think he can still blow our 688s to the bottom. Do you agree, Roy?"

All the men in the room turned to the Norfolk video console. On the screen, Admiral Roy Steinman's image blinked rapidly a few times, his face grim.

"I'm afraid so, sir. There's no doubt about it. We need the *Seawolf.*"

"Roy, what's the status of *Seawolf?*" Donchez said. "I wanted her underway today and we're running out of today."

"Sir, as far as I know she's still in the dock welding on the hull cut at the Vortex tubes."

"What's the holdup?"

"I'm not sure, Admiral," Steinman said, sounding calm but Donchez knew he was flustered.

"Fred, can we patch in the shipyard on this thing?" Donchez asked Rummel. "If you can, pull up Stevens, the shipyard commander."

Fred Rummel punched buttons on the phone and spoke. The delay seemed endless. Donchez lit a Havana and puffed smoke at the ceiling. Eventually the screen flashed the image of the conference table in Stevens's office. Gathered around Stevens were Pacino and an older admiral with Coke-bottle glasses. Donchez tried to place the admiral, who looked familiar, but came up blank. Pacino's image looked dark— Donchez sensed that he was trying hard to cover frustration. Or anger.

Steinman asked the first question. "Captain Stevens, what's the status of the *Seawolf* and why hasn't she gotten underway?"

Stevens opened his mouth but the nearsighted admiral broke in. "Hello, gentlemen. I'm Admiral Douchet, the Naval Reactors office rep responsible for the yard." Donchez didn't like that . . . Naval Reactors involvement meant trouble. The NR office was a police organization watching over the shipyard, often getting in the way of the real work, the obstacles thrown up in the hallowed name of reactor safety. "As you know, we have welded the hull patch in place but the radiography, the X-rays, have not been taken. I found out today that the captain of the *Seawolf* ordered the dock flooded without taking the X-rays, and that is a *gross* violation of quality controls and reactor-safety protocols. I am disturbed by all this and, frankly, at Naval Reactors, we feel that Captain Pacino's disregard for ship safety—"

"Hold it right there," Donchez broke in. "Are you going to sea when *Seawolf* casts off? Are you going to sea with Pacino?"

"Well, no, but—"

"Captain Pacino?"

"Yessir," Pacino snapped, suppressing the beginning of a smile.

"Are you satisfied with the shipyard's work and the quality of the hull-cut weld?"

"Yes, sir."

"Captain Stevens?"

"Yes, Admiral."

"Are you satisfied with the weld?"

"It probably wouldn't pass all the QC work if we did the X-rays, sir. But I think it'll hold up. We'll know for certain after a controlled dive to test-depth."

"Admiral Douchet, what reason do you have for holding *Seawolf* after what you just heard?"

"Procedures, sir. This isn't allowable by any SUBSAFE procedure, and if you'll pardon my saying so, the loss of the *Augusta* from a shipyard error should make all of us more cautious. This is not a proper way to—"

"Thank you very much. Captain Stevens, Captain Pacino, flood the drydock and get *Seawolf* underway immediately. Do you read me?"

"Yes, sir," both said in unison.

"Admiral Douchet, I want to see you in my office at zero eight hundred tomorrow morning. Captain Stevens, I'll be calling on you in four hours. If *Seawolf* isn't gone by then, you are relieved."

"Aye, aye, sir."

"Captain Pacino, get underway and execute your mission."

"Aye, sir."

Donchez broke the connection and looked at each of the men gathered around the screens. In the rush to push *Seawolf* out he had nearly lost focus on the biggest issue of the evening—why was Sihoud going out into the Atlantic?

"Fred, what do you or yours in Intel think of the breakout? What's on Sihoud's mind?"

Rummel hesitated. "I'm not so sure the thinking on that is very clear yet."

"Go ahead anyway."

"One theory holds him going around the horn of Africa all the way to Ethiopia, landing there and surprising us on the opposite flank."

"But Destiny was headed northwest after the torpedo hit her."

"The crew might just have been clearing datum away from the direction they originally meant to go, like they did after they first picked up Sihoud—the ship initially went east instead of west."

"What else?"

"Sihoud might get off sooner along the Atlantic coast of Morocco. He might just be trying to shake our tail."

"Maybe. But the track positions I see on the chart still don't support circumnavigating Africa. Perhaps it's a feint, but let's suppose for a minute that they are really heading away from Africa and deep into the Atlantic. *Why* would they do that?" Donchez scanned the room. He thought about the nightmare every submariner used to have, that a ballistic-missile submarine would be hijacked or taken over by its own crew and cruise to the U.S. coast and launch a missile. The elimination of sea-launched ballistic missiles had ended those fears in some quarters, but the refinement of cruise missiles made the scenario worse. Ballistic missiles were detectable on launch, giving the victim a few minutes' warning. Cruise missiles skimmed the earth below treetop level, arriving with no warning. Hiroshima missiles reportedly flew supersonic at very high altitudes, maintaining stealth with a radar-evasion device. Just as bad. But then, he reminded himself, he was probably just being paranoid. Too many years spent fighting the damned Cold War.

"Well, Admiral," Rummel said, "maybe Sihoud and the Destiny have some new kind of offensive-weapon system, something they could lob at us, something they think will take away our stomach to fight."

"What do you think, Dee?"

"Sir, like my grandmother used to say, 'Maybe so, sonny, but I kinda fuckin' doubt it.'"

"It does seem far-fetched but, gentlemen, there is something here that bothers the hell out of me." Donchez paused and glared at the staff from under his heavy brows. "Dee, I want you to put together a package of SEAL-commando operations. Get Intelligence to give us the probable locations of all UIF weapons-test facilities. Then put in a plan to raid every one of them with the objective of bringing back classified documents and weapon scientists who might know anything about a new kind of offensive weapon or missile or chemical or germ warfare. Or evidence of a UIF nuclear warhead."

"Sir, there might be a hundred facilities including bio labs. And what about the joint directives? Army Special Forces will want a piece of the action."

"I don't care who does it as long as you trust them to get the data. I need an answer in two days. To me that means call the SpecWar guys at SEAL Team Seven and drop them into the weps labs."

"Two days, aye. I hope the answer will be more than a shrug."

"Get on it, Dee."

"Yessir."

"John, tell me, what have we got searching for the Destiny and the *Phoenix?*"

Traeps spoke from his screen, the connection to Naples making an irritating echo. On the plot, Traeps's pointer moved over the western Atlantic to illustrate his prolonged monologue on the ASW effort to find the Destiny. As Donchez listened, he wondered if he should go down to Norfolk and talk to Pacino one last time before *Seawolf* sailed on a mission impossible.

Western Atlantic
USS *Phoenix*

Kane sat in the attack-center console seat feeling his head throb when the overhead lights flashed for just an instant and went back again, then flashed once more, the effect an erie strobe light in the dead submarine. Finally the lights held. The return of illumination to the control room made things worse rather than better, Kane thought, seeing the jumble of bodies. He unwrapped the awkward air hose and crawled on his knees to the men, finding several bodies that were cold, dimly noting that the deck was slick with blood. Some of the men were breathing, wheezing in the ship's dirty atmosphere. Kane decided to get the ones breathing into air masks. The fact that the lights came on meant someone aft was bringing power back up. He thought about calling maneuvering on the phone but figured the nukes would be too busy restoring the reactor to want to talk. He found the air masks and began strapping them on the faces on the deck, wondering if unconscious men would be able to breath in the masks since the regulators didn't deliver air unless the user sucked hard. Still, he'd experimented on a few and they seemed to keep breathing so he went on with it.

When he finished he glanced at his watch—smashed and dead. It had been some time since the lights flashed on. Kane grabbed his hose, unplugged the end, and headed aft. His head still throbbed, his vision seemed less than clear and his lungs hurt from fighting the air-mask regulator. He had forgot to plug in the hose as he moved toward the aft compartment, which indicated how out of it he was—usually that was all an air-mask user could think of, the next air station—and once he nearly had to pull off the mask to breathe, finally finding a plug in the overhead of the crew's mess just before fainting. He stood there, doing nothing but breathing. He forced himself to move on, taking the steps down to the tunnel level, stepped through the hatch, emerged into the aft compartment's middle level and unplugged from the tunnel hose station, dragging the hose up the ladder to the upper level, not sure whether to believe his ears as he got closer to the top of the ladder because he could hear the roaring of steam and the whining of a turbine.

At the top of the ladder he stepped off, took a few puffs from a hose station and moved past maneuvering, freezing in a double-take as he saw that the room was unmanned. Except by the four corpses on the deck. The reactor-control panel and electrical panel were splashed with blood. He looked up from the maneuvering room door and took in the scene of huge CB McDonne rushing by, hose in one hand, steam plant procedure book in the other.

"Captain! Get to lower level and start a condensate pump! Then stand by to start a main feed pump. I'll get you on the Circuit Two."

Kane nodded, body aching as he descended the vertical ladders to the lower level two decks down. When he stepped off the ladder his foot splashed into water. He looked around. The compartment couldn't really be called flooded, but the leaks would need to be pumped, and soon. The equipment was splash-proof but not designed to run under-water. He waded aft to the condensate bay, found the motor starters, pressed the first start button. The pump motor spun up to full speed. He started the other three, then waded forward to the feed-pump bay, wait-ing for McDonne to get a turbine generator up to speed and on the grid so that the feed pump could be started. Finally McDonne's voice boomed through the ship to start the pump. The unit was twice the size of a phone booth and loud coming up to speed. Kane tried to find a phone to see what else needed doing in the lower level. He rang the upper level. No answer.

The nightmare thought struck Kane that something had happened to CB McDonne. Without the XO, he would not be able to finish bringing up the plant by himself. McDonne was an engineer from Purdue, Kane an English major who'd put up with the nuke program just so he could command but never doing more than the minimum to get by. Since his engineer exam he had forgotten half of all he'd ever known and he hadn't been involved in a plant startup in eight years.

But when he reached the upper level, CB was in maneuvering at the electrical panel, concentrating on switching breaker switches. After sev-eral minutes he stepped to the reactor-control panel, adjusted the rod height, then waved to Kane to follow him.

"We're up in a normal full-power lineup. Let's get the burners and scrubbers back on line and clean up the atmosphere. This mask is a goddamn pain." So, he silently added, was their desperate situation.

Book III

SEAWOLF

Monday, 30 December

Portsmouth, Virginia
Norfolk Naval Shipyard
Graving Dock 4

Pacino looked up from the dock as the wind suddenly picked up, nearly blowing off his hardhat. The wind gusted, then calmed, then again roared through the dock. He checked his watch—almost 11:00 P.M. and the water level in the dock had barely risen to the bottom of *Seawolf*'s cylindrical hull after flooding for almost an hour. The ship looked eerie, almost surreal under the harsh floodlights, but also somehow *important,* like a NASA shuttle lit up for launch. The green of the hull added to the unreality. Pacino still could barely believe he was going to sea within hours—the dull disconnected feeling of being in the shipyard with a helpless vessel hadn't left him yet. The frantic mood of the preunderway checklist did not, somehow, feel right here in a graving dock. A pier should be the place a submarine left from to go on a vital mission, not this giant hospital for ships. Still, he felt good that he would get to take the ship down one last time. Up to now he hadn't focused much on the mission. It was all he could handle just to get the shipyard out of his hair, but now that the boat was really cleared for sea he felt a certain familiarity. He had lived this before. This was what he'd been created to do, a task reserved for him alone—that only he could do.

He began to rebuke himself for being so self-important when Captain Emmitt Stevens rolled up in the white pickup truck. Stevens was grinning as he got out and joined Pacino at the dock lip.

"I think you've spent the whole yard availability mooning over your ship from this handrail."

"I don't like seeing the old girl in the dock, Emmitt. It's just not right for a warship to be high and dry like this. And I'm just as out of place here as she is."

"I don't know about that—after the meeting this evening I'd say you can run a shipyard. The way you put old Donchez up to overpowering Douchet, it's too bad you're going to a staff job. You could get a lot done here. We could use you."

Pacino smiled. "I didn't talk to Donchez. He just wants us underway."

"Still, it was good to see that hard ass put in his place."

"Well, in a way he's right, you know. I am risking the crew going down with that weld as it is. But sometimes you've got to take risks . . . What brings you here?"

"Donchez. He'll be here in a half-hour. His Falcon is landing at the naval station at NOB at twenty-three-thirty. He wants to make sure this boat leaves on time. He also said he wanted to brief you personally. This must be some mission, Patch. The CNO comes to wave his hanky as you shove off. How come?"

"My dad and Donchez roomed together at Annapolis. They served on a couple subs together. Donchez took over the *Piranha* when my old man was the last skipper of the *Stingray.*"

Stevens's face went serious. It was common knowledge in the sub force that *Stingray* sank in 1973 when her own torpedo exploded and the flooding took her down below crush depth. There were no survivors.

"I'm sorry, Mike. I had no idea—"

"It's ancient history. Donchez wanted to watch over me when Dad went down but at the same time he didn't want to show favoritism."

"After that China mission I'd say you've done it on your own."

"Anyway, he probably wants to kick my rear end, motivate me. I'd better do a walk-though of the boat. Do me a favor and keep flooding the dock. I want out of here by zero five hundred."

"Will you be starting the reactor in the dock? You know Douchet will have a heart attack—"

"If the plant is ready I'll pull rods here. If not I'll leave with tugs towing me and I'll start the plant in mid-channel. I don't care either way, but at oh-five, we're out of here."

"CAPTAIN, OFF'SA'DECK, SIR," Pacino's walkie-talkie squawked.

"I've gotta run, Patch. Hang in."

"Thanks for everything, Emmitt. I hope I never see this goddamned shipyard again."

Stevens waved and roared off in the pickup.

"Captain here," Pacino said to the radio.

"SIR, ENGINEER REQUESTS PERMISSION TO PERFORM A NORMAL REACTOR STARTUP. AND THERE'S A PHONE CALL FOR YOU FROM MRS. PACINO, SIR. SHE SAYS IT'S URGENT."

"Tell Mrs. Pacino I'll call her back from the security shack in five minutes. And tell the engineer I'll call the engine room on the security line. Captain out."

The radio clicked twice in acknowledgement. Pacino stepped to the guard shack and nodded at the sentry and reached for the phone. The phone buzzed twice before the engineer's voice came over.

"What's the status, Eng?"

"We're nonvisible, sir," Hobart said, annoyed. "We'll have to do a pull-and-wait start-up. We're so low in the start-up range I don't even see reactor power on the start-up meter."

"How long will it take?"

"Could go as long as twenty-four hours. We've been shut down so long the core's barely radioactive."

"Engineer, abort the pull-and-wait start-up and pull rods to criticality. We're a few hours from clearing the dock and I don't have time to wait on the procedure."

"Sir," Hobart's annoyed voice came back, "before I can do that I have to ask, is this a tactical situation as defined by the reactor-plant manual?"

Pacino felt Dave Hobart would have made a hell of a lawyer, but something had called him to the sea and now he wore a poopysuit instead of a vested suit. Despite Pacino's heavy reliance on Hobart's expertise on *Seawolf*'s highly complex reactor systems, he would have to be overridden. Procedures were for peacetime. Hobart was worried that the level of neutron activity in the core was so low that he couldn't see the power level, and by pulling rods he could add enough reactivity to go prompt critical—and blow the reactor apart—before he would be able to stop the runaway reaction. But Pacino knew the protection circuitry would scram the plant if that happened, and even if it wasn't fast enough, it was a risk they had to take. The Destiny out there, somewhere in the Atlantic, didn't give a damn about the health of their core.

"It is," Pacino said, referring to Hobart's question about the tactical situation.

Hobart paused, then: "Aye, aye, sir. Pulling to criticality. We'll note it in the log that you ordered this." Hobart was trying to see if Pacino would forget the dangerous order if he threatened to log it.

"Captain, aye. Also note we'll be heating up with emergency rates once you're critical. I want the plant on line. Immediately."

"Aye, Captain." The phone clicked as the engineer returned to his pre-start-up work. Pacino hung up and dialed his own home at Sandbridge. Janice answered, her voice soft and quiet as it was when she first woke up.

"It's me."

"Michael, Dick Donchez called. He said he wants to meet you here at midnight. And come to think of it, I want to talk to you myself."

"On the way."

Pacino called the officer of the deck on the radio and told him he'd be at home for a few hours, found the executive officer on the phone and turned over the dry-dock flood operation to him, then walked to his car. Walked and wondered what Donchez was doing that required a personal appearance.

Sandbridge Beach, Virginia

The wind blew spray onto the windshield a half-mile from the beach. By the time Pacino parked the old Corvette under the stilted house the car was covered with the slimy saltwater from the restless Atlantic. In front of the house was a black Lincoln with multiple antennae poking out of the trunk and the roof. The rear license plate had the emblem of COM-SUBLANT—Admiral Steinman's car. The windows were blacked out, but Pacino thought he saw the silhouette of someone moving in the front seat. He looked up at the massive beach house, a monument to Janice's old money, and saw that every light in the house was blazing. A fugitive thought stole across his mind, that he should look at the house long and hard because he wouldn't see it again for a long time. He found himself wondering why that had occurred to him, because the mission was a one- or two-week excursion. Three at the most.

When he walked into the house the curtain of warm air was overwhelming after the wet cold outside. He took off his heavy overcoat and went into the central living room to see Donchez and Steinman. And Janice.

"Mikey," Donchez's rough voice boomed. "Long day, huh?"

"One of many, sir."

The three sat down. Janice told Pacino she'd be upstairs, waiting for him.

Donchez pulled out a Havana, shooting an inquiring look at Pacino. Pacino nodded, knowing Janice would be annoyed but also knowing that

Donchez couldn't think without a cigar shoved into his face. Donchez offered one to him and Steinman, and all of them lit up at once.

"Mikey, you've heard about Rocket Ron's *Augusta*. What have you heard about David Kane's *Phoenix?*"

"Nothing. Should I have?"

"Afraid so," Steinman said.

Pacino frowned as he listened to the story. He read David Kane's last transmission, his emotions numbed, but his brain flashing through the tactical problems. By the time the cigars were cold stubs smoldering in the ash tray, he had the ugly picture.

"Mikey, your job is to find the Destiny before he finds you, then kill him with *maximum* possible force. I hate to saddle you with this last, but keep in mind that what has allowed us to come this far in tracking the Destiny are the messages from Daminski and Kane. I want you to try to get through to us what you're up against."

"Anyone have any idea what this submarine is up to? He's got to be doing something other than acting as a bus for Sihoud." Pacino looked from Steinman's face to Donchez's. Whatever they knew, they weren't telling. "Fine. Let me know whatever intel you get."

Donchez and Steinman stood. "We've bothered you enough tonight, Mikey." All three walked to the door. A look passed between Donchez and Steinman.

"I'll be out at the car checking in with the watch officer at SUBLANT," Steinman said. He shook Pacino's hand. "Good luck, Patch. Take this SOB down."

"Watch SUBLANT for me, Roy," Pacino said, trying to smile. "When I get back I want that outfit standing tall and waiting for me."

"I'll be ready to be relieved by the time you get back. Hell, my desk's already half full of your stuff. But are you sure you want a desk job?"

Pacino glanced at Donchez. Steinman waved and took the stairs to sand level two at a time. His shoes crunched through the seashells on the walk out to the staff car.

Donchez stood in the foyer, the cold wind blowing in the open door. "I asked Roy to give us a few minutes alone," Donchez said, pulling out another cigar and bringing it to life with his old *Piranha* lighter.

"The usual pep talk, right, sir?"

"I just didn't want Roy to know what I'm thinking about the Destiny," Donchez said, annoyed at his own transparence. "Which is that Sihoud is up to something, something dirty he'd like to bring home to us here. That sub is invisible and invincible—if you were driving a 688 boat. *Seawolf* is the only thing that can put this guy on the bottom, and only then if you find him and surprise him. If you can't sneak up on him I want you to clear datum and try later. You got that, Captain Pacino? I'm

not just saying this for you, either. We can't afford to lose your boat if
you get impatient."

"Come on, Admiral. I'll make sure I get a clean shot at him."

"I've lost two submarines already, Mikey. Daminski was one of my
j.o.'s in the old days. It hurt bad to lose him. I can't afford to lose a third.
General Barczynski would have a few pounds of my posterior if *Seawolf*
takes a hit."

"Admiral," Pacino said, moving Donchez through the door, "don't
sweat it, I've got the bubble."

Donchez stood his ground in the doorway. "I could send your relief
on this mission. Joe Cosworth. He could do it and leave you free to
relieve Roy at SUBLANT. Janice would like that. Have you considered
that?"

"No way, sir. *Seawolf* is still mine and I'm taking her out one last
time."

Donchez looked over Pacino again, nodded.

"Good luck, Patch. Good hunting. And be goddamned careful."

On the third floor of the house, Pacino looked at Janice's face, knew
what was coming as he grabbed his duffel bag, threw in some fresh
uniforms and zipped it shut.

"He's sending you on a suicide mission, Michael. I heard—they've
already lost two ships, one with Rocket Ron, for God's sake. And now
you're next. He said he'd let Cosworth go, let him."

Pacino waited for a pause. "Honey, you must not have heard Donchez
say that *Seawolf* is the only ship that can knock out the Destiny. We're
driving the best submarine, the best warship, there is. All I have to do is
find this guy and it's over—"

"For him or you?"

Pacino looked at his wife for some moments, taking in her beauty,
even in the midst of the anger.

"I'll be back in three weeks, Jan." He moved out to the balcony
hallway and opened Tony's door, his eight-year-old son deep in sleep.
He kissed the boy's cheek, then walked quietly down the stairs. Janice
followed him out the door to the car.

"I'm sorry . . ." she said, "you're right. You don't need this for a
send-off."

Pacino kissed her. "I know you'll worry, but we'll be okay."

"I know you will, Michael. I know . . ."

He backed the car out into the street and spun the wheels in first gear.
He didn't see her crying in the mirror but he knew she was.

CHAPTER

23

TUESDAY, 31 DECEMBER

Portsmouth, Virginia
Norfolk Naval Shipyard
Graving Dock 4

Pacino felt better the moment he arrived at the dry dock. The dock was completely flooded, the gangway suspended by cables to one of the railroad-wheeled cranes. The dock roared with the sounds of powerful diesel engines, the loudest coming from *Seawolf* herself; a plume of diesel exhaust fumes poured out of the aft part of the submarine's green sail, since the reactor was not yet self-sustaining and the emergency generator had to be run to supply ship's electrical loads now that she was divorced from shorepower. Aft of the sub a tugboat was pulling backward, several lines attached to the caisson, the gate of the dock; soon the tug was halfway into the channel. Two other tugs idled further into the channel, waiting to pull the ship away from the dock and the shipyard and point her to sea. Pacino hated seeing the tugs, the fact that his submarine was still helpless irritated him. Somehow it was wrong for a warship to need a crutch to get to sea. But soon the ship would be plowing the channel with her own muscle, and until then at least she was free of the shipyard.

Pacino crossed the gangway, hearing the blast of the sentry's announcement on the ship's Circuit One PA system, amplified on the dry dock's outside loudspeakers: *"SEAWOLF,* ARRIVING!" Call it vain, but he did love hearing himself announced as he came aboard. He saluted the flag aft and the sentry and stepped onto the green hull. He tossed his bag down the ladderway and lowered himself into the ship, the familiar submarine smell somehow grabbing his attention, the thick vapor of cigarette smoke and cooking grease and diesel exhaust and ozone from the high-voltage equipment reminding him to leave home and Janice and Tony behind and concentrate on the Destiny and the mission ahead. He shouldered his way down the busy passageway to his middle-level stateroom, wondering what the captain of the Destiny was doing at that moment, what he was like, how he fought a submarine. Not that it mattered now, Pacino thought. He'd know from personal experience soon enough.

He took a look around the stateroom. One of the walls had been demolished to gain access to the cables inside, and the yard had only had time to replace the steel structure of the wall but not the outer wood paneling. Pacino unpacked the duffel bag, raided his locker cabinet for his heavy olive drab parka, the early morning cool and wet, the sea-lanes at flank speed promising to turn cool into frigid. He found his blue baseball cap with the gold embroidery thread forming submarine dolphins with the ship's name in block letters, the brim done up in gold scrambled eggs. He grabbed his binoculars and left the room to go to control.

The control room was jammed with watchstanders. He found the executive officer, Commander Jackson "Lube Oil" Vaughn, who had reported aboard only a few months before, when the ship was preparing for the shipyard period; he had yet to go to sea with Pacino. Still, Pacino had full confidence in Vaughn's capabilities, since Vaughn had played a major role in driving his last ship, the *Tampa,* out of the hands of the Chinese communists when the sub had been captured during a close offshore surveillance mission. Vaughn was a tall man who would be thought of as skinny were it not for a very slight but expanding paunch above the belt of his khakis. His face was thin to gaunt, his hair thick if prematurely gray. The gray, Vaughn claimed, was from dealing with a teenage daughter, but fleet rumors held that the escape from the Chinese piers had changed the mostly black mane to nearly white. Vaughn still spoke with a west-Texas accent, his home till the day he left for Annapolis, the home of the high-school sweetheart he had married the day after graduation. Rumor held that he had a tendency to clomp around the ship in cowboy boots at sea, though Pacino had yet to see it in person. Vaughn's nickname "Lube Oil" was a holdover from an incident during his junior officer tour on the *Detroit* when he himself had tried to repair a hopeless lube-oil pump and had succeeded just before flooding the lower level with oil. Vaughn hated the moniker but carried it with good humor.

Vaughn, looking over the BPS–14 radar console, had already, Pacino noted, started on his at-sea beard. Pacino would humor him. After hearing about Vaughn's performance on the *Tampa,* he had requested him as XO but it had taken time to pry him away from a shore tour teaching seamanship at the Academy, where the admiral in command had taken a liking to him and had been reluctant to let him leave. When he had reported aboard it had seemed a shame that it would be too late to go to sea with him, but now Pacino would have that chance. The two men had become close friends, seeing eye to eye on most things concerned with driving the ship and leading the men. So far their differences were on administrative matters, Vaughn a stickler for details, a perfectionist when it came to pushing Navy paper, while Pacino had always been relatively casual about the mountains of paperwork. Two weeks before, Vaughn had tracked Pacino to a remote office in the shipyard to obtain his signature on an oil-and-water report to some obscure squadron bureaucrat. Pacino had wadded up the report and made a hook shot into a trash can. "You ought to try not sending these reports, XO, and see who squawks when they're late. My bet is that you could throw away ninety percent of them and the recipients would never know the difference." But even in this the two had forged a working relationship—while the reports stopped coming across Pacino's desk they still left the ship on time as Vaughn began to sign and send them without Pacino's signature. It was all fine with Pacino, who had high on his list the elimination of much of the submarine's paperwork as soon as he took over as COMSUB-LANT.

Vaughn glanced up now at Pacino, showing pleasure at escaping the shipyard and getting back to sea.

"We're set to bust this joint, Skipper," Vaughn drawled, handing Pacino a briefing sheet with a tabulation of the river's levels and currents, the tides in the sea-lane past Norfolk, and the weather report. "Court's got the conn on the bridge, we're manned belowdecks and the yardbirds are ready to winch us out of the bathtub as soon as you're on the bridge."

"Status of the reactor?" Pacino asked, pocketing the data sheet and grabbing a safety harness and strapping it on.

"Been a while since I asked. Hobart was complaining about your emergency orders but he should be warming the turbine generators about now."

Pacino grinned and reached for a phone handset. "Maneuvering, Captain."

"Maneuvering, Engineer, sir," Hobart's voice replied.

"Where we at, Eng? I want to drive out on our own steam."

"If you'll just hold your horses, there, Captain, I would have called you. We should be switching to a normal full-power lineup in about twenty minutes, then I'll be cooling the diesel. It should be shut down in another hour."

"No. As soon as you unload the diesel, shut it down. The fumes and noise are screwing up the bridge watch."

Pure heresy. Submariners protected the emergency diesel above all else. Hobart paused, obviously unhappy, acknowledged and hung up.

"Must be pretty important," Vaughn said, still leaning over the radar display. "You gonna brief us once we're out?"

"That will take all of two minutes," Pacino said, cinching up the final strap of his safety harness and reaching for the heavy parka. "Once we clear the Norfolk traffic separation scheme, gather the officers in the wardroom. Chiefs too. This will be a trip."

Vaughn turned to the navigator. "Nav, you ready?"

"First fix is in," the navigator said from the plotting table. "It's off by maybe ten feet. Not bad on a global basis."

"See you at sea, XO. Take care of these guys."

Pacino left through the open door forward, the steep and narrow staircase leading up to the upper level, past the galley door to the long passageway set at the ship's centerline. He strapped his binoculars around his neck and climbed the ladder to the hatch set high in the arch of the overhead, the thick steel of the circular hatch rotated up and over by hydraulics. He climbed up, vanishing into the circle of darkness, and emerged into a dimly lit vertical tunnel full of cables and junction boxes and valves. He switched ladders and continued the climb, a dim light filtering down and growing until he reached the top of the tunnel, where he could see grating covering the opening, shoes standing on top of the grating surface.

"Captain to the bridge," he called. The grating was pulled up on a hinge and the men cleared the way. Pacino climbed up into the bridge cockpit, a small cubbyhole on top of the sail crowded with officers and enlisted phone-talkers. He concentrated on the dock below, noting the lines tying them to the pier cleats, the two heavy ones running from the bow to huge winches on either side of the dry-dock entrance, the flow of water in the river. The weather was wet, not from rain but from mist, heavy and clammy, blown by the wind, the millions of droplets visible as they drifted past the glaring cones of the light from the floods. The noise level was near deafening from the diesel, the exhaust note rumbling as it came out of the sail. It would make communicating difficult but Pacino was not willing to wait for reactor power. In the wet weather the exhaust was white and smoky, but at least the wind was from the head of the dock and blowing the fumes away from the bridge crew.

"What's the status, Scotty?" Pacino shouted over the roar of the diesel to the combat-systems officer, young Lieutenant Commander Scott Court, a smart officer with a hundred-dollar haircut and impeccably starched uniforms who always seemed to say the right thing, another politically astute mid-grade officer who had already been marked for early promotion and command, a bit too slick for Pacino's taste. He'd been encouraging Court to get his hands dirtier in the day-to-day operations of his department.

"Good morning, Captain," Court said in his official speaking-to-the-captain voice, "The yard is ready to winch us out on your concurrence. Maneuvering watches are manned. The reactor is critical. We're about fifteen minutes from switching to a normal full-power lineup. Last lines to the dock are seven and eight with the exception of the winch lines. Conning us out is Mr. Pseudo. I'll retain the deck."

Pacino nodded, looked up and aft at the top of the sail. On the top surface a set of temporary steel handrails were set up, the flying bridge. He climbed up the aft wall of the cockpit to the flying bridge and looped his harness' lanyard over one of the rails. He waved to Ensign Ed Pseudo to climb up next to him, the young officer extending the bridge-communication box microphone with him up to the top of the sail. Pacino looked down at the dock and from his vantage point could see the ship below remarkably well—it was not a place for those wary of heights—and down at the head of the dock he could see Emmitt Stevens standing and watching with a visitor next to him. Pacino checked through the binoculars, not surprised to see Donchez standing next to Stevens. The admiral waved. Pacino dropped the binoculars and turned to Pseudo.

"Your ship, Mr. Pseudo. Take us out of here."

Pseudo raised a bullhorn to his mouth "On deck! Take in seven and eight!" He picked up his walkie-talkie and called for the dockmaster. "Dock Four, this is U.S. Navy Submarine. Commence winch-out."

"SUBMARINE, DOCK FOUR, COMMENCING WINCH OUT," the radio squawked.

The motion was barely perceptible at first, but Pacino could see the winches turn, reeling in the lines on either side leading to deck cleats at the ship's bow. Slowly, steadily, the dry dock began to drift away from them. Aft, the rudder began protruding into the river channel. The motion of the ship—a ship that had been a shipyard building for the last four months—was intoxicating to Pacino. Must be the lack of sleep, he thought, but the swaying of the deck beneath his feet made him feel almost drunk. Enjoy it now, he told himself, it's the last underway you'll have with *Seawolf.*

Pseudo ordered the backing signal sounded, six short blasts on the ship's air horn, the deep throaty horn the equal of the *Queen Elizabeth*

II. The stern was far enough into the river to bring on the first tug on the starboard side. The lines were brought aboard to the tugboat and pulled tight to the deck cleats. The dock lip was now even with where Pacino stood, forward on the sail, the land moving away rapidly now as the ship developed momentum. The second tugboat came alongside, aft of the sail amidships on the port side. By the time its lines were fast the bow of the ship was almost clear of the dock.

"Cast off port and starboard winch lines!" Pseudo broadcast on the bullhorn to the deck crew. As the last line was tossed off to the dock the ship was officially underway, no longer bound to the shore in spite of the fact that her power plant was still asleep and she was being towed down the river by tugs. Pseudo barked down at Court, "One long blast on the ship's whistle, shift colors."

The horn blew an earsplitting blast. Aft of Pacino on the top of the sail Pseudo snapped a lanyard hoisting a large American flag to the top of a temporary flagpole. Pacino checked his watch—zero four twenty-five, a half-hour ahead of schedule. A dim shout came from the port side, a request to come aboard. Pacino nodded to Pseudo, who granted the permission, and from the port tugboat an older man with a lifejacket climbed the ladder rungs set into the sheer side of the sail, up over the lip of the bridge and to the flying bridge. The pilot.

"Mornin', Skipper. Name's Jake. I'll be helpin' yuh out today."

Pacino nodded. The use of a pilot had always irritated him. Like the tugs. He could make it out of any port by himself if the charts were good, and Norfolk's charts were dead on. But he had no horsepower until Hobart cranked up the reactor, and as long as the tugs pulled him down the channel, they shared the authority with him. There was only one way to get rid of the tugs and that was to get the reactor. He was about to prod Pseudo to call maneuvering and get the status of the reactor when Hobart's voice boomed out of the communication box.

"BRIDGE MANEUVERING, THE ELECTRIC PLANT IS IN A NORMAL FULL-POWER LINEUP. REQUEST TO COOL THE DIESEL." Hobart still didn't believe Pacino would shut it down without a slow cool, but Pacino hadn't changed his mind. He made a chopping motion across his neck to Pseudo.

"Maneuvering, Bridge, negative. Shut down the diesel now."

"SHUT DOWN THE DIESEL, BRIDGE, MANEUVERING, AYE." Hobart's annoyance rang out through the circuit. Within seconds the loud roar of the diesel exhaust vanished, crashing the bridge into relative silence, the smoky plumes vaporizing. The only sound on the river was the faint hum of the tugboat motors.

For the next minutes there was little to do but watch as the tugs pulled the ship down the river, the predawn scenery of downtown Portsmouth, Virginia, a handful of glowing lights, an occasional passing car.

Jake the pilot chattered on his walkie-talkie to the tugs and tried to make small talk. Pacino mostly ignored him, watching the bridge box, waiting for Hobart. Finally the announcement came:

"BRIDGE, MANEUVERING, MAIN ENGINES ARE WARM, PROPULSION SHIFTED TO THE MAIN ENGINES, READY TO ANSWER ALL BELLS, ANSWERING ALL STOP."

"Well, thanks for the lift, Jake. We'll take it from here."

The pilot looked at Pacino. "We ain't at Thimble Shoals yet, Cap'n. I'm supposed to—"

"I said we'll take it from here. Shove off your tugs."

The pilot shrugged. "You run aground, it's your neck." He climbed back down the sail and into the port tug. The tug crews pulled in the lines and backed away.

"Navigator, Bridge," Pseudo said into his mike, "log that the captain has shoved off the pilot and the tugs."

"BRIDGE, NAVIGATOR, AYE."

"Five knots, Mr. Pseudo," Pacino ordered. "Rig the deck for dive and get the topside crew below."

"Helm, Bridge, all ahead one-third."

The comms box crackled the helmsman's acknowledgement. For the first time in almost four months the *Seawolf*'s screw turned aft, boiling up a white foamy patch. Ahead, the water began to flow smoothly over the bullet-shaped bow until it rose over the first fifteen feet of the top surface of the ship. The foam aft turned into a wake while the deck beneath Pacino's feet shuddered slightly. The tugs had faded several hundred yards behind, their diesels no longer audible above the slight rushing sound of the bow wave. Below on the deck, the topside linehandlers moved quickly, stowing lines in cubbyholes with flush doors, rotating deck cleats into their stowed position, ducking down the hatches. Within a few minutes the deck was clean and streamlined, ready for the ship to submerge.

"Topside's rigged for dive, sir. Last man down."

Pacino scanned the dark river ahead, the channel deserted. "Increase speed to fifteen knots."

"Helm, Bridge, all ahead standard."

The bow wave, a slight wetting of the nose cone forward, now splashed over the top surface of the hull, sliding aft all the way past the sail, the waves of the wake building up and washing aft. The sound of it rose like the surf in a heavy windstorm. Pacino felt the ship's acceleration, felt it all through his body. The heaviness of being in the shipyard had been washed away by the bow wave, replaced with the exhilaration of taking his submarine, his command, back where it belonged—at sea.

The wind from the ship's motion built up, the combined whistle of the wind and roar of the bow wave filling Pacino's ears, the sound of

Seawolf's tremendous horsepower. The ship followed the river until the Norfolk piers passed by on the starboard side, the Squadron Seven submarines lit by floodlights, the ships quiet. Further north, the destroyer and frigate piers, then the cruisers, and finally the giants, the aircraft carriers, their decks towering over the sail. They too faded astern as Pseudo made the turn to the east and entered Thimble Shoals Channel, a slender highway of lit buoys extending southeast to the vanishing point.

"Increase speed to flank," Pacino ordered.

Pseudo smiled. "Speed limit in the channel is fifteen knots, sir."

"Ask me if I care."

"Helm, Bridge, all ahead flank."

"BRIDGE HELM, ALL AHEAD FLANK, AYE, MANEUVERING ANSWERS ALL AHEAD FLANK."

"BRIDGE, MANEUVERING," Hobart's voice rang out, even more peeved now that Pacino had ordered the flank bell without first lining up the circulation pumps. He now had to do an emergency procedure to lower plant power, start the pumps and bring the power back under control. "COMMENCING FAST INSERTION . . . STARTING MAIN COOLANT RECIRC PUMPS . . ."

Aft the screw's foamy wake boiled up as the ducted propulsor doubled its speed. The deck shuddered, more pronounced this time, as the bow wave rose, no longer smooth but full of phosphorescent foam, past the sail to amidships before breaking into the wake. The bow wave kicked up spray onto the bridge, the noise of it growing. The land, now some three miles distant in the widening bay, slipped past faster. By now the ship would be doing twenty-five knots.

"BRIDGE, MANEUVERING, ANSWERING ALL AHEAD FLANK."

The sky ahead of them began to show signs of dawn's approach, the clouds taking on a slight glow. Astern of Pacino the flag flapped in the wind of the ship's motion, the bow wave shrieking, the wet wind deafening. Behind them the two periscopes rotated rapidly as the navigator took visual fixes on the way out, the radar mast rotating once every second. By the time the ship turned south into the exiting traffic-separation scheme, passing Virginia Beach, the sun had climbed above the horizon. Pseudo turned east, the ship finally clear of restricted waters. The land faded astern until only the tallest hotel buildings of the beach were visible. Then they too vanished and the ship was alone on the sea, the early morning vista nothing but dark blue ocean, clouds, patches of sky and the sun. Pacino checked his watch; by noon the ship would clear the continental shelf.

"I'm going below, Mr. Pseudo. Good job driving us out. Continue at flank to the dive point."

"Aye, sir."

Pacino lowered himself to the bridge, clapped Court on the shoulder and took one last look at the seascape, breathing in fresh air before consigning himself to the ship. Always before he had been able to laugh off the voice that said this lungful of fresh air might be his last, but this time there was someone, something out there waiting for him, something with an unknown purpose that was committed to his ship's destruction. And the only thing standing between him and death was skill and heart—his own and his crew's.

He climbed down the ladder into the belly of the ship, chiding himself for thinking too damn much.

24

TUESDAY, 31 DECEMBER

Eastern Atlantic

When Captain Kane walked through the hatch to the forward compartment he felt for the first time since being fired upon by the Destiny that his ship might make it out of the near-sinking after all. It had been an hour since he and McDonne had resuscitated the reactor plant, which now idled at eighteen percent power, and waited for the order to spin the main engines. The atmospheric-control equipment had been started up, burning the carbon monoxide and hydrogen. McDonne had started a high-pressure oxygen bleed and brought the oxygen generator—called the bomb for its production of oxygen and hydrogen from distilled water, the mixture highly explosive—up on the oxygen banks. Kane unplugged his air-mask hose and hurried to the hose station at the analyzer panel, a small cabinet that took air samples and examined the levels of carbon dioxide, carbon monoxide, hydrocarbons and other pollutants. He opened the face of the cabinet and rotated a selector switch to sample forward compartment upper level. All readings on pollutants were normal, though oxygen was high out of specification, which was okay. If anything, the oxygen content would help the crew wake up—those who were still alive. He wondered how many had died. Feeling a sudden anger at the Destiny, he hurried through the other compartment-level readings, all of them the same readouts as the upper level forward. He uncinched the rubber straps cutting into his sweat-soaked hair and pulled off the mask, tentatively breathing the ship's air. He continued forward, stowed the mask in a cubbyhole and climbed the ladder to the upper level.

In the control room he could see that Lieutenant Houser was on his feet, rubbing his shoulder.

"Atmosphere's in spec," Kane said, "Pull the masks off the men and stow them. Find the corpsman or one of his first aid people and let's get the casualties into the crew's mess. Grab whoever you can find conscious to help you."

"Reactor okay, Skipper? Everything up?"

"So far. Full power lineup, running the atmosphere equipment. XO's warming the main engines. He's got the show aft. Once you get the casualties below we'll see who we've got to man the watches, check out the hovering system and see if we can drive off the bottom. Go on, I'll be putting the healthy folks on the gear, see how bad things are forward."

Houser felt like asking where they would go if they got off the bottom, but he moved to his task, pulling one of the plotters up off the deck and taking off his mask.

Kane walked through the forward door to sonar, careful not to step on the prone forms of the sonarmen. He found Sanderson rubbing his forehead, in obvious pain.

"Senior. How do you feel?"

Sanderson started to glare until even that effort seemed to exhaust him. Kane pulled the chief sonarman to his feet and sat him in one of the control seats at the Q-5 console.

"I could use a strong cup of coffee."

Kane slapped his back and went through the forward door into the passageway.

Aft, in the reactor-compartment tunnel, Tom Schramford rubbed his head, and pulled himself to his feet by grabbing onto a length of exposed XC piping. He unplugged the air mask, walked slowly aft and noted the overhead fluorescent lights were on. He emerged into the aft compartment through the tight opening of the hatch, amazed to hear the roaring of steam down the headers, the loud shrieking of the turbines, the curtain of hot humid air stunning and welcome. He went on to maneuvering, looked in and saw blood on the panels, corpses of his operators lying in a heap on the deck, one of them Ensign Michell, the engineering officer of the watch, the younger brother of an acquaintance from his college days. Michell's throat had been opened by an exposed switch or metal panel corner, a substantial puddle of the youngster's blood on the deck. The panel operators, though not as sickening to see as Michell, were just as dead, limbs sticking up into the air in grotesque rigor mortis. Schramford saw that the reactor power-meter needle read eighteen percent, that average coolant temperature was low out of the green band at 499 degrees. He reached for the rod lever and pulled the control rods out an inch, the temperature slowly rising back up into the green band at 502. A lone blinking light shone from the annunciator section on the panel, the alarm face marked HI RAD—RX COMPT. The fuel assemblies must have experienced some melting from the torpedo evasion, he figured, and now the reactor compartment had a high radiation level. He looked over at a panel on the starboard side and flipped a rotary switch several times, saw that radiation levels in the reactor compartment were ten times normal levels. The upper level of the aft compartment, the maneuvering room included, was now a high radiation area. But it was not at a lethal level. At least not yet.

Schramford left maneuvering and found McDonne aft in the upper level between the main engines, reading a gaugeboard. The XO saw him, nodded, "Hi, Eng, you look like hell," and then disappeared behind the turbines to check bearing temperatures.

Schramford returned to the maneuvering room, dragged the corpses out of the room and placed them in the motor-control cabinet space, then went back to maneuvering, found a rag and a bottle of cleaner and began slowly cleaning the blood off the panels.

Forward, in the crew's mess, Houser and the chief corpsman, a chief named Ives with red hair and fair skin covered with freckles, had assembled the casualties, some of the living on the six dinette tables, some on the benches, several on the deck, covered with blankets. Ives counted twenty-two injured too badly to return to duty, half of them from broken limbs, nine still unconscious from head injuries.

In the control room Kane had assembled a skeleton crew of watchstanders at the ballast-control and ship-control panels. A phone on the conn periscope platform buzzed. It was McDonne.

"Skipper, I've checked out the hovering system and the auxiliary seawater systems. I've got Schramford aft. He's got the drain pump ready to clear out the aft compartment. There's some high bilge levels in the reactor compartment we'll have to pump. Do we have a chief of the watch?"

"I've got Henderson stationed. He's got a bad arm and a sprained ankle but he'll be okay."

"Good. Go ahead and have him pump out the compartments on the drain pump. I want to test the trim pump on depth-control one when he's done."

Houser returned to the control room, his Hawaiian shirt covered with blood smears. He stood near the conn while the drain pump came up to speed and dewatered the aft compartment, then the reactor compartment and finally the forward compartment torpedo room bilges.

"Mr. Houser, you have the deck and the conn," Kane said as McDonne walked into the control room.

"Schramford's aft," McDonne said. "He's got enough nukes to watch the plant but not much depth. Manning the plant around the clock will be impossible with a full-watch section. We'll have to double up duty stations."

"The engineer will figure that out, XO. Houser, try to get us off the bottom and let's see if we have any depth control."

Houser acknowledged, grabbing a microphone hanging from its spiral cord from the overhead of the conn.

"Maneuvering, conn, report status of the main engines."

"CONN, MANEUVERING," an overhead speaker squawked. "PROPULSION IS ON THE MAIN ENGINES, MAIN ENGINES ARE WARM, WE'RE SPINNING THE SHAFT AS NEEDED TO KEEP THE MAINS WARM."

"Conn, aye. Chief of the watch, line up the trim pump to depth-control one. You got a level?"

"HOV system lined up, level shows ninety percent."

"Aye, pump depth-control one to sea."

The chief rotated a switch on the ballast-control panel console section. Lights flashed on the display screen as the pump spun up and the level in the tank dropped. The men in the room—Kane, McDonne, Houser and the other watchstanders—stared at the graphics, waiting tensely. The ship would either make it off the bottom now or would require much more persuasion.

"DCT one is empty, sir."

"Shift to depth-control two, Chief," Houser ordered, a frown creasing his face.

The chief selected the second variable ballast tank and pumped it dry. But the ship stayed on the bottom, the depth readout unchanged, still reading 1,355 feet.

"Shift to aux one."

"Pumping aux one."

Fifteen minutes later the variable ballast tanks were dry and the ship remained stubbornly on the bottom. Houser shut down the HOV system operation and joined Kane and McDonne aft of the conn.

"Any thoughts, XO?" Kane asked.

"We must have hit a sandy or muddy spot," McDonne said. "If we'd hit rocks the hull would have been breached. I'm guessing when we hit we made a crater or plowed the mud and sand up over the sides and top of the hull. Hell, we could be half-buried."

"So how do we get out?"

"We emergency blow and put on ahead full," Houser said.

"What about main seawater suction and aux seawater?" McDonne asked. "If we're buried, the seawater suctions will be clogging up and we shouldn't risk a full bell."

"Gotta try something, XO," Kane said. "Houser, do a timed emergency blow, forward first, then aft, with a fifteen-second delay between forward and aft. Give the aft blow thirty seconds, then order up ahead standard. Call the engineer and make sure he knows what's coming."

After Houser told Schramford his intention the men reassembled near the conn. Houser leaned toward the ballast-control panel.

"Chief, emergency blow forward."

The COW reached up into the overhead and rotated the forward lever, the "chicken switch," upward into the open position. The room's silence was immediately broken by the roaring of the high-pressure air into the forward ballast tanks. Seconds passed; the ballast-control-panel area began to fill the room with fog from the ice-cold piping. Houser looked at his watch, then shouted over the noise of the forward blow.

"Emergency blow aft!"

The chief rotated the aft lever; the roaring in the room magnified, a cloud of fog boiling out and rolling over the deck. The deck didn't budge, nor did the depth readout.

"All ahead standard," Houser called to the helmsman, who rotated the engine order telegraph dial on the ship-control panel.

The deck beneath Houser's feet shuddered and shook.

Nothing else happened.

Western Atlantic Ocean
Continental Shelf Off Norfolk, Virginia
USS *Seawolf*

The ship still sailed on the surface as morning became afternoon, the deck trembling from the power of the flank bell and rolling to a ten-degree incline to port, freezing momentarily, then rolling back to starboard, the rocking motion inducing drowsiness. Pacino, standing to starboard of the conn, felt the sleepiness wash over him, the loss of an entire night's sleep consuming his alertness. He forced himself to concentrate, looked over to the port side of the room where the secure fathometer reading showed the bottom dropping out from under the hull of the ship as the submarine crossed the submerged and abrupt downslope of the continental shelf. The phone buzzed on the conn periscope platform. The officer of the deck, Scott Court, pulled the handset to his ear, listened, then handed it to Pacino.

"For you, Cap'n."

"Captain," Pacino said quietly, turning his gaze to the television monitor of the periscope view, the blue ocean and overcast sky seen with the crosshairs and range divisions of the reticle superimposed. The blue of the sea was a startling sapphire color, so bright that it looked like the monitor's color needed adjustment, but the view from the bridge showed that there was nothing wrong with the screen, that the sea's brilliant blue was real.

"Wardroom, sir, Mr. Joseph. The officers and chiefs are ready when you are."

"I'll be down in ten minutes. Tell the navigator to start the briefing without me." Pacino replaced the phone and found Court looking at him from the periscope. "Yes, off'sa'deck."

"Sir, request permission to dive. We're at the dive point, ship has been rigged for dive, watch shifted to control. Fathometer reads 610 fathoms. Ship's course is zero five five, all ahead flank. No visual contacts, no sonar contacts."

"Very well, slow to two-thirds and submerge the ship to 150 feet."

A flurry of orders rang out as the diving officer ordered the chief of the watch to sound the diving alarm and open all main ballast tank vents. The helmsman rang up two-thirds and the engine order telegraph needle chimed back as maneuvering aft slowed to two-thirds. The chief at the ballast panel rotated an alarm lever above the panel, sounding the diving alarm. The klaxon blared throughout the ship, the *OOH-GAH* more realistic, less electronic now that the shipyard had redone the alarm's computer generator.

"DIVE, DIVE!" the chief announced on the circuit one. The diving alarm blasted out a final time.

"All main ballast tank vents open, sir," the chief said after two function keys changed the green horizontal bars on the vent display to red circles. The main ballast tanks forward and aft began to give up their air and flood with seawater, the loss of buoyancy already dropping the top of the hull a foot closer to the waves. Court rotated his periscope view directly ahead and turned the view down to the forward deck. Geysers of water jetted out of the hull, the air-water mixture coming out of the open vents like the spray of a firehose.

"Venting forward," Court called out. He trained the scope aft and looked down on the aft deck, the spray of water from the aft-deck vents reaching higher than the periscope reticle could see. "Venting aft."

"Four two feet," the diving officer called.

On the periscope-view television monitor the afterdeck's surface began to disappear into the white foam and blue sea. A wave washed over the top of the deck, thinned out and washed overboard. The next wave obscured the green paint of the deck for a moment.

"Deck's awash," Court announced.

The ship continued settling slowly into the sea, the diving officer eventually calling, "Six five feet, sail's under," the signal that the ship was completely under, only the number-two periscope exposed above the waves. On the periscope monitor the blue waves grew closer to the view until they were within arm's reach.

"Eight four feet." The waves on the monitor were now mere inches from the view onscreen.

"Scope's awash," Court called as the white foam boiled up over the periscope lens, obscuring all view. "Scope's awash . . ." The foam calmed, revealing the undersides of the waves, the surface of the sea now seeming inside-out, the waves above steadily moving more distant. "Scope's under." The waves in the view had receded until they were just barely visible in the blue haze, finally vanishing, the view filled only with pieces of seaweed floating by in the water.

"Five degree down bubble," the diving officer called, the deck inclining downward as the ship departed the surface.

"Lowering number-two scope," Court said, snapping the grips up and rotating the hydraulic control ring in the overhead. The stainless-steel pole came down into the well.

"Zero bubble, five degrees up on the bowplanes. Depth one five zero, sir."

"All ahead one-third, diving officer, trim the ship."

"I'll be at the briefing in the wardroom, off'sa'deck," Pacino said to Court. "When you've got a trim, perform a controlled dive to test depth. Once that's complete get us back to 600 feet and proceed to point bravo at full." Point bravo was a mark on the chart about 500 miles east-northeast of Norfolk, the agreed-upon hold point in the western Atlantic where Pacino would receive some kind of direction from Steinman and Donchez. Without contact on the Destiny, the mission would be a bust.

Pacino climbed the ladder to the middle level, turned the corner at the galley and walked into the packed wardroom. He made his way to the head of the table, where his seat was waiting, a steaming cup of coffee on the table in a cup with the ship's emblem on it, the snarling wolf's head staring out, the silhouette of a submarine hull in the background. Henry Vale, the Harvard whiz-kid navigator, stood at a high-definition television flat screen, a pointer in his hand, the profile of the Destiny-class submarine displayed on the monitor.

"Go on, Nav," Pacino said. As Vale spoke the deck inclined downward five degrees, the officer of the deck taking the ship down fifty feet at a time to test depth, a test to certify that the hull patch at the Vortex tubes would stand up to submergence pressure.

"Sir, we've been over the Destiny's stats, our instructions to find the

sub and put it on the bottom, and the fact that it has killed two of our
688's. We've all got questions about what the Destiny's mission is and
why it fought so hard to get out of the Med."

"Sihoud's aboard," Pacino said, sipping the hot coffee. The ship-control readout panel set into a cubbyhole next to Pacino's chair read 250
feet. The deck inclined again as Court drove the ship further down. The
hull groaned for a moment. "Destiny might be sneaking him out of
Africa to go around the horn. Or getting him away to someplace he can
hide."

The crowd was speechless, the fact of Sihoud's presence aboard not
yet declassified to the men. Pacino was now unwilling to keep the secret
when he relied on this crew to help find the UIF killer submarine. The
silence was interrupted by a loud pop from above, the hull equalizing
against sea pressure as the ship dived deeper. The deck leveled again for
a few minutes.

"Our op-plan has us driving here," Vale said, the screen changing to a
depiction of the Atlantic Ocean as if the observer orbited thousands of
miles above the earth. A dotted red line curved from Norfolk up to
point bravo. "We'll come up to periscope depth and get our traffic from
the satellite. With luck we'll have a hot tip on the Destiny by then. If not,
we'll hold there in a large area sonar sector search until we sniff him
out."

"Sir," the engineer Dave Hobart said, the sweat streaming down his
fleshy face from being back aft for the drive out of Norfolk, "what good
does it do to hold in the Western Atlantic when the Destiny's coming
out of the Med? Seems kinda messed up, you know? If he's really zipping around the horn we ain't about to catch him in westLant. You
know?" Hobart's speech was always full of "you-knows."

Pacino thought about Hobart's remark, knowing there was some logic
in it based on what he knew but not yet willing to disclose Donchez's
suspicions about the Destiny, about the possibility of it coming west.
Coming . . . with *what?*

"That's the order," Pacino said. "A lot could happen by the time we
get there tomorrow morning. The Atlantic is being scoured by Burke-
class destroyers, P–3 Orions, LAMPS choppers, the SOSUS submerged
hydrophone network and by our spy satellites. Anything pops up, we'll
vector in toward it."

Hobart still wasn't satisfied. "I don't know, Captain, it's still sounding
fishy, you know? For one thing, why doesn't COMSUBLANT send out the
688 squadrons as a barrier sonar picket, all listening together, you
know? Surely they could cover more square miles than we can alone."

Pacino was about to tell Hobart that so far the Los Angeles-class ships
didn't detect the Destiny until it was either right on top of them or had

already sent a torpedo down the track. He was interrupted by the buzz-ing of the phone from the conn.

"Captain, off'sa'deck, sir. Ship is at 600 feet. Request to rig for deep submergence and proceed to test depth." The ship-control repeaters read 600 feet. Pacino had barely noticed the steady down angles and level-offs getting down to that depth. He wondered if the Vortex tube patch would hold up. If it didn't, the mission was over early.

"I'll be right there." Pacino stood. "Time to take her deep, gents. We'll finish this later when we get more data. XO, let's go to control."

Scott Court presided over the control room from the elevated peri-scope platform, leaning on the handrails of the conn.

"OOD, rig for deep submergence and take her down. XO, I'd like you to stay here. I'll be in the torpedo room."

Vaughn nodded and Pacino left through the aft passageway past his and Vaughn's stateroom on the port side, radio and the electronic coun-termeasures room on the starboard. The passageway ended at the com-partment bulkhead, where a dogleg led to the hatch to the reactor-compartment tunnel. Pacino stepped instead down the steep and narrow stairs to the lower level, passing a storage room, the auxiliary machinery space where the massive diesel engine sat dormant, to the door to the torpedo room. The room, previously cavernous when empty and tight when full of weapons, was now so jammed that Pacino could barely make his way past the giant and useless Vortex tubes to starboard. The three tubes, each over three feet in diameter, started thirty feet forward at the room's bulkhead and extended aft all the way to the wall forming the storage space and beyond—the shipyard had cut the storage room in half to accommodate the tubes—and the entire starboard side of the room had vanished, to be replaced by the tubes. Each one was similar to the one that Pacino had visited briefly aboard the *Piranha* just before the test platform's Vortex tube had exploded and sunk the ship. The port side of the room had been left alone but the weapon loadout had been diminished from the previous fifty torpedoes to the present twenty-four, including the three loaded in the port bank tubes. It was a giant step backward. Pacino remembered his words to Donchez and again felt the older man's disappointment at the failure of the Vortex weapons. In the shipyard's haste the tubes and their launching systems remained functional and the weapons had been kept in the canned unreusable tubes in spite of Pacino's insistence that the weapons be removed, the load of solid rocket fuel stored so close to the ship's hull it made them vulnerable to a single torpedo hit. The detonation of the solid fuel would be even more violent than the warhead of a Nagasaki torpedo. Pacino shook his head as he moved slowly forward to the end of the room, where the massive tubes met the hull steel.

There at the forward bulkhead the tubes continued farther forward past the space where there had once been a water-round-torpedo tank, the newly formed void filled with the powerful hydraulic piping and controls needed to open the heavy muzzle doors of the tubes. A torpedoman with a headset had crawled down the accessway formed by interruptions of the piping to the hull, which had been stripped of its foam insulation so that the weld could be watched from the inside as the ship went deeper to test depth. Pacino got as close as he could without crawling down the accessway, shining a flashlight on the weld of the hull patch.

"How's it looking so far?"

"No leakage yet, sir," the torpedoman called.

The torpedo chief, a young health nut named Riesen, stood with a headset at the forward local control panel. He looked aft at Pacino and called, "Going to 700 feet, Captain."

Pacino waved, the hull inclined, groaning and popping from the sea pressure. After reaching 700 feet the deck leveled while the weld was examined for leakage by the torpedomen. After holding for five minutes the ship went deep again to 800 feet, then to 900, until after forty minutes ship's depth was 1,500 feet. Pacino observed the crewmen in the space, noticing their nerves showing, men tugging at collars that suddenly seemed too tight, faces turned upward as if trying to see the surface a quarter-mile overhead.

"THE SHIP IS AT TEST DEPTH," Vaughn's Texas drawl rang out through the ship.

There was a commotion from the hull patch. Pacino moved to see. Several small streams of water, probably pinhole leaks, were spitting water into the bulkhead of the local panel.

"We're getting some leakage here, Captain," the torpedoman said. "Hard to tell exactly where but it's definitely from the weld."

Pacino grabbed up a phone to control. "This is the Captain. Take her up to 400 feet."

The deck angled upward at a twenty-degree angle as Pacino climbed the stairs to the middle level and walked up the ramp of the passageway to control. Court was leveling off at 400 feet when Pacino made control.

"Hull weld leaks," Pacino said, anger at the shipyard rising in his gut.

"You won't be taking us back in," Vaughn said. It was a statement, not a question.

"No. We're staying out. Mr. Court, no deeper than 600 feet unless I have the conn. Post it on the status board."

"Aye, sir."

"Goddamned Vortex tubes," Vaughn said. "Piece of meat."

"You said it," Pacino said. "Off'sa'deck, I'll be in my stateroom. Proceed to point bravo."

In his stateroom Pacino splashed water on his face and changed into a black poopysuit with new dolphins and namepatch. He sank into the deep-cushioned high-back chair at the head of his conference table and shut his eyes for a moment. He took out a journal book entitled *Captain's Night Orders* and scribbled a few paragraphs, stopping to buzz for coffee. The mess cook brought a steaming pot; Pacino dispatched him to take the night-order book to Court on the conn. He changed his mind about the coffee, climbed into his narrow bed and shut his eyes. He thought he should turn off the room lights but sleep sneaked up on him before he could get out of the bed to hit the light switch. It was a relief.

TUESDAY, 31 DECEMBER

Eastern Atlantic
USS *Phoenix*

Houser had to shout over the roar of the emergency blow.

"Secure the blow! All stop!"

The rushing noise of the high-pressure air ceased as the chief of the watch pulled the blow levers back down. The engine order telegraph chimed as its needle rolled to the stop position, maneuvering's answer needle rotating to stop in answer.

"Mark your depth."

"One three five five," the diving officer said, his voice neutral.

"Captain, I say we rock her out with the screw, doing full ahead, then astern. The ballast tanks are full of air now. It's got to be the suction from the mud that's keeping us down."

McDonne frowned. "The emergency blow more than filled the tanks, it should have spilled a lot of high-pressure air out the vents and into the muck or sand. That should have done it."

"Might be a rock or obstruction forward," Kane said. "Let's try a backing bell first and give it a full minute before going forward."

"What speed?"

"Back full."

"Aye, sir. Helm, all back full."

The engine order telegraph chimed again. The deck began a slight vibration, the tremble growing to a shaking force. To Kane it felt like an earthquake. The deck began to tilt into a port list, then inclined forward, the inclinometers showing the angle to be two degrees port, three degrees down, the slope of the deck sounding small but exaggerated greatly by human perception, the few degrees enough to roll pencils off tables and slide books to the deck. The second hand of an old-fashioned brass chronometer ticked slowly around the clockface as the shaking of the hull became more pronounced. Kane was about to order Houser to put on the full bell when the ship lurched.

"Keep backing down."

The deck angled further downward, and with the ship bottomed out, that meant the stern was rising, the ballast tanks' air pulling the stern up. The ship lurched again, this time violently, sending Kane into the number-two periscope, and the deck fell away beneath him to a large down angle. He glanced at the inclinometer, which shook its bubble at around thirty degrees.

"Keep it up, Houser," Kane ordered, a shot of adrenaline hitting his midsection, his heart beating hard. The deck angled further up until he could stand it no more. "Okay, cut it."

"Helm, all stop!"

The ship's speed indicator still showed zero but it didn't work in the astern direction.

"Bubble forward with the EMBT blow," Kane said.

McDonne glared at Kane, but Houser made the order. Once more the chief reached into the overhead and put the forward lever up to the blow position. The high-pressure air bottles blew into the forward ballast tanks.

"High-pressure banks are coming down, sir," the chief said.

"Secure the blow," Houser ordered, shrugging to Kane.

"Houser, put on a one-third bell and get your planes to full rise."

"Aye, sir. Helm, all ahead one-third. Dive, full rise fairwater and stern-planes."

Kane and Houser hunched over the ship-control station watching the depth meter as the ship was ordered ahead. There was a good chance, Kane thought, that he was doing nothing except driving her back into the mud of the bottom, but with a down angle that steep he couldn't keep driving her back. There was no control going backward, the water and screw forces on the sternplanes made them unreliable. The ship could go full vertical, spill all the air out of the ballast tanks and sink back to the bottom like an arrow stuck in mud, and the steam plant would shut down on them, the gravity-draining systems good only for forty-five-degree angles. They would be stuck forever on the bottom, forced into a sub-escape from test depth—a certain death. The deck trembled again, just slightly, the needle on the ship's speed indicator climbing off the zero peg up to one knot, then two. The fairwater plane angle indicator showed the control surfaces mounted on the sail were tilted to thirty-five degrees rise, the sternplane meter showing forty degrees of rise. The down angle of the deck very suddenly leveled and tilted upward, the speed indicator needle picked up to four, then six, then ten knots. The deck continued into its up angle, past thirty degrees, up to forty.

"Take control, Houser, and use ship's speed to fight the buoyancy!"

"Dive, bubble less than five degrees; helm, all ahead full, steady as she goes. Chief of the watch, vent all main-ballast tanks. Dive, bring her up to 500 feet."

Kane glanced at the analog depth indicator. It was unwinding rapidly, the deck's up-angle still at nearly forty degrees, the air in the ballast tanks trying to rocket the ship upward in an uncontrolled emergency surface. The ballast-tank vents indicated open on the ballast panel, trying to let the seawater back in and the air out. The speed indicator climbed, fifteen knots, twenty, until the speed of the ship overcame the huge buoyancy forces, as if the submarine had changed from blimp floating upward to airplane, buoyancy no longer as important as the water force on the control surfaces. The deck angled back down to level, the shaking calming. The depth needle slowly climbed from 650 feet to 500, the speed needle stopping at twenty-five knots.

"Bring her slow, officer of the deck. Ten knots, see if the ballast tanks still have air in them."

The ship slowed as Houser made the order, the depth steady. Kane brought speed down all the way to five knots, with no change in depth. The ballast tanks were again flooded.

"Shut the vents."

"All vents shut, sir."

Kane looked at the panel. All seemed healthy enough to drive home. He felt his heart slowing back down to normal.

"Very well," Houser said. "Captain, ship's course is two nine zero, depth 500. I recommend we come shallow and communicate."

As far as the surface commanders knew, Kane thought, they were dead, a debris field on the bottom. Houser was right. It was time to tell the world that *Phoenix* was back.

"Houser, get the chief radioman in here. I want the gear checked before we go above the layer. We took a hell of a beating. And find Sanderson and tell him I want to know sonar's status. And the firecontrol chief, Gessup, get him up here too. And Jensen, to see how the nav

electronics are doing. Once we get the electronic systems functional
we'll come up and send the brass the word on us and the Destiny."

"Then what, sir?"

"What's Doc think about the injured? A week make a big difference?"

"You're not thinking about Norfolk, are you?" Houser asked. "I've
been with Ives in the mess. Those guys need help fast. Your call, Cap'n,
but if this bucket of bolts belonged to me I'd hightail it for someplace
damned close. Scotland or Liverpool or Rota."

"It will depend on the electronics, Houser," Kane said. "If the ship is
healthy enough to make it transatlantic I'll take the injured off with a
chopper and drive the boat home—this girl's going to need a dry dock
after what she's been through. A pier at Faslane does her no good. And
we're out of the fight anyway with no torpedoes. But if we have no sonar
and no firecontrol, I won't risk the trip."

Kane looked down at the dead computer screens of the attack cen-
ters, suddenly knowing that the vital but vulnerable electronics were
probably total wrecks. It would seem a miracle that the reactor plant
and steam plant were on-line, but three decades before, when Admiral
Rickover himself designed most of the propulsion plant of the USS
Nautilus, the propulsion systems had been absolutely bulletproof, forsaking the then electronic technology of vacuum tubes for mag-amps,
giant iron cores being the state-of-the-art in the late 1930s. Since 1954,
vacuum tubes had given way to transistors, then integrated circuits and
finally microprocessors. Still, the nuclear plants had stuck with mag-
amps, the speed controller on a motor-generator the size of a refrigera-
tor even though the same controller would take up the space of a finger-
nail if done with a microprocessor. The nukes had kept the old-fashioned bulletproof systems, forsaking most microelectronics except the
reactor's safety systems—which had triple redundancy anyway—even
though the designers were pressing hard to save every cubic foot of
volume aboard. Those decisions now seemed rational, since after a
five-g crash against the bottom, the reactor systems had been restarted
without a flaw while the ship's more modern computer systems forward
might never function again.

Sanderson arrived first, looking haggard. Senior Chief Radioman
Binghamton limped in with a splint on his knee. Binghamton was a
shaved-headed muscular Mr. Clean, missing only the earrings and the
height, barely five-foot-four in shoes. He was a man of many styles, able
to shift from humorous and encouraging coach to tough authoritarian.
Not one enlisted man or officer called him "Bingy" to his face, not since
his first week onboard when several radiomen and one chief had found
themselves slammed into bulkheads with Binghamton's large face in
theirs. He was fond of giving advice, especially to those who didn't want

it, like McDonne. But it was a given that every man aboard loved Bing-hamton, with the exception of Edwin Sanderson. Kane had made Bing-hamton chief of the boat, the ranking enlisted man, a move that McDonne pretended to disagree with since both men believed they were the experts at leading the crew. On this run Binghamton had been in an upbeat mood, the word coming down that he would soon make master chief or warrant officer. But now Binghamton's face was full of anger. He kept his silence until Kane was ready. Electronics Mate First Class Edwards arrived, a worried look on his bearded face.

"Where's Gessup?" Kane asked, referring to the firecontrol chief, the man he wanted to tell him the status of the firecontrol system.

"He was getting a cup of bug juice in the crew's mess," Edwards said, "when he just keeled over. Doc says he's got a concussion but he looked like my daddy did when he had his stroke—"

"Okay. Edwards, hang in there." Kane looked at the assembled men. "The reactor is up and we're on the way home, at least for now. I need to know if we can remain submerged and I want to send a message about the Destiny. Radio first. What's the status, Senior?"

"It's hosed, Captain. Every cabinet. I'm cannibalizing components from every system trying to get one up. I think I can get one UHF transceiver going though the BIGMOUTH antenna, but the crypto gear has shit the bed. Anything you say, you better count on the enemy hearing."

"What about a SLOT buoy?"

"All broken to hell. Not one working, and they can't be repaired—no spares."

"How long till you'll be ready to send a message?"

"Ten minutes, but that doesn't mean the BIGMOUTH will work. All I can do is wait till we're ready to transmit."

"Okay, Senior. Get to it. I'll write the message when you've got a functional system. Sanderson, what about sonar? The Destiny is still out there, and I'd just as soon not get ambushed by him again. And I don't want to get rammed by some stupid supertanker when we go up above the layer."

"I need time, Captain. I've got some bad cards that need replacing, and I need to check every hydrophone—"

Kane frowned, knowing Sanderson was a perfectionist, and that there was no time for perfection.

"Screw that, Senior Chief. Change out the bad cards, skip the loop check and bring the system up. I don't care if it's reduced status or broadband-only. I want ears and I want them now."

"I'll do what I can, Captain, but I can't promise—"

"Quit bitching and get it done, Sandy." This was from Binghamton.

Sanderson's face turned red, but he stomped off to the forward sonar equipment space.

"Edwards, firecontrol?"

"Bad disk drive, sir. We're putting in the spare now and it checked out okay. Already switched a dozen cards, doing another dozen now. When we're done the computers will be damn near brand-new. Only thing stopping us is if the spares are bad. We have no more spares, though. If one of these circuit boards dies, that's it. That puts us into an initialization in about an hour after we reload, a half-hour to reload the modules. That's firecontrol up in normal mode in ninety minutes, but it ain't any good without sonar."

"Get going. Nav?"

Mike Jensen, the navigator, had come in when Edwards was talking. Jensen was one of the superstar mid-grade officers, a tall broad-shouldered and handsome black man who had graduated in the top five percent of his Academy class and had been a runner-up for Rhodes scholar before he did physics work at Stanford. His face was swollen and lumpy, making him look more like a boxer than an academic, his right arm in a sling with a splint formed by an inflated tube. He seemed to be struggling against his pain, one of his trademarks his refusal to take any medication or drugs, not even aspirin or coffee. He had probably turned down the prescription painkillers, Kane thought.

"The GPS NavSat looks like it lived. Its self-check put out a few bugs that we're looking at but it's showing the same position it did just before we got hit. The ESGN inertial navigator is dead and gone for good. Wiped the ball. But as the quartermasters say, a pencil, a calculator and a compass can do about as good."

"Okay. How're you doing?"

"Never better. The fractured skull is a nice touch, don't you think, sir?"

"Smart-ass," Kane said. "XO, get me a message draft with Jensen's position and the Destiny encounter."

"Aye, sir."

Forward in sonar Sanderson's broadband display began cascading down the screen as the Q–5 initialization completed. He was at the beginning of a long series of self-checks and didn't intend to tell the conn that they already had rudimentary sonar, not after the tough words spoken in control, but his anger melted when the broadband trace came down the screen with the first noises. The contact was another ship. Close aboard. Submerged.

The Destiny was close enough to collide with.

CNFS *Hegira*

The ship's computer system, unofficially the Second Captain, had a mouthful official moniker—the YEBM-G-Destiny-Hull-1 Distributed Control and Layered Artificial Neural Network Intelligence System, manufactured by Yokogawa Electronic Battle Machinery Corporation. Its architecture had been compared to the human brain by more than one research psychologist. The comparison was perhaps the only way the interfaced, interactive system could be understood by its operators.

The lowest elements of the artificial intelligence were the sensors—sonar hydrophones, electronic countermeasure antennae, as well as valve position indicators, pump running contacts and the nuclear reactor's neutron flux detectors—functioning as nerve cells. The monitoring and control of the ship's basic functions—reactor control, atmospheric purification and life-support, depth-control, weapons-control—were all done by the distributed process-control modules in a function much like the human brain stem, controllers of the human heartbeat and respiration. Surrounding the distributed process-control modules were the higher level functions related to sonar and electronic monitoring. Sonar and EM to the ship were its way of sensing the environment outside, much as vision and touch are to the living organism. And just as a human brain has whole lobe regions dedicated to vision and touch, the Second Captain had a layered modular neural network that had separate nodes associated with the reception, recognition and interpretation of sonar and electronic data. The neural nodes themselves made the supercomputers of the decade before seem crude . . . their logic was not hardwired. The sonar node was capable of simultaneous handling of massive quantities of data in real time, assembling the data into recognizable interpretations of the outside environment by the higher levels of the layered neural network.

The highest functions of the system were the neural artificial intelligence assembler modules, a part of the collected computer totality that were not specifically mentioned in the training or maintenance manuals except in the broadest terms. The assembler modules' relation to the lower layers was similar to human brain frontal lobes, the functions that took the data of the sonar modular neural network and interpreted them, comparing them to data received in the past, generating internal questions that required investigation and analysis.

The assemblers were part of the system tasked with interfacing with the human crew, the advanced artificial electronic intelligence assigned the heavy responsibility of making the crew understand what the system understood, making the crew aware of its interpretations of the environment. The task of interfacing with the crew was the most difficult to design, but in this model, Yokogawa had marched into the frontier of artificial intelligence and extended the science a crucial step.

It would be untrue to say that this level of electronic consciousness was capable of thought, but the unit had a random memory regenerator that reached into the plasma-bubble memory cells for things related to current processing, reaching out across the neural network for associations and previous learning. The unit was not capable of reflection but it did reexamine previous experiences for comparison to present processing and extrapolated such experience into a weighted probability prediction of what future events held in store. It was not capable of confusion, but its processors were designed to suppress action recommendations and slow down neural functions in the event that the comparison of past experience and the prediction of future events were in disagreement with the present reality as perceived by the modular neural networks. When the prediction of reality that benefitted the ship's mission was correct as sensed by the modular networks, the system was programmed to experience a higher neural flux and the release of electrochemicals at certain neural transmitters giving the system the equivalent of self-satisfaction. When the ship's encoded mission was not achievable the system's neural flux was suppressed, turning the processors away from continued attempts to direct analysis at the problem. It had no fear but when the predictor of mission success was perceived as low and system survival was seen as improbable the system's tolerance for risk increased. It also had no way to experience hope but when mission success as seen by the event probability analysis was perceived as high, the assemblers experienced higher levels of neural flux and a release of electrochemicals associated with higher neural connectivity. It had no equivalent to aggression but when the ship's mission was threatened by rapidly developing threats it was capable of understanding, the risk-gradient position moved into the high positive values and the nodes that considered action options became highly stimulated.

The system had only limited capabilities for independent action without input from the crew. It had no real initiative, although when the assemblers were deprived of human input the system reviewed previous experience related to human actions, weighing most heavily the more recent human actions, and the system would consider similar directed action, depending on the current status of the risk-gradient and the outside environment as well as the status of the mission and the seriousness of the threat to that mission. Deprivation of input from the modular neural networks would at first lower neural flux, then begin increasing it to compensate for the lack of processing raw material, much the

way a human deprived of vision and touch and hearing would halluci-
nate in laboratory experiments.

Out of concern for the unknown quality of this electronic increase in
function during sensory deprivation, the ship was wired with internal
microphones. This was a part of the system not revealed in the technical
manuals or in the training courses. One of the modular neural networks
was an analyzer of the human speech inside the vessel as received on
microphones placed in each room of the command-module compartment. These voice recorders were at first justified based on previous ship
designs in which speech records were part of accident investigations,
much as airliners had black-box voice-recorders to analyze the last moments of an airplane that had crashed. Valuable tactical data could be
obtained even from a ship that lost a battle if the entire event could be
reconstructed from recovered voice records. Not all tactical conversations occurred in the control room. Many came about in the captain's
stateroom, in the doorway to the first officer's stateroom, over breakfast
in the officers' mess, in presleep ruminations by the lower ranking officers. In short, the designers had made the decision to wire the entire
ship for sound *without* the awareness of the crew for three purposes.
One was to avoid the sensory deprivation that would cause the system to
fall out of alignment. The second was the same as the black-box designs.
The third was related to the Second Captain. The system's neural artifi-
cial-intelligence assembler modules, the frontal lobes, needed data for
the estimate of the success of the ship's mission and to continue the fight
if the crew died or was disabled. The system's main source for the crew's
estimate of the tactical situation was the input from the speech detectors
in the ship's forward compartment. It was imperfect, and the value of
the eavesdropping system would be in effect only if the entire crew was
lost, but in that unlikely event the Second Captain would carry on based
on what the crew had been doing just prior to their loss, the eavesdropping a sort of programming. If the Yokogawa designers had been able to
wire the captain's brain to detect his thoughts, they might have done
that too.

The system description would lead some engineers outside the Yokogawa enclave to conclude that the Second Captain had an intelligence
very closely resembling a human's, but that needed refinement. If the
Second Captain's artificial intelligence were to be rigorously compared
to a human's it might come closest to being a five-year-old human . . .
a five-year-old capable of advanced thought patterns, highly developed
learning abilities, successful applications of experience-based initiative,
extraordinary adaptability to new situations—in short, a five-year-old
human possessed of considerable brain power. But a five-year-old was
not the person who should be driving a car or flying an airliner, or

directing the actions of the world's most advanced attack submarine. *Unless*, of course, the system concluded that the crew was gone.

In the eastern Atlantic, during the hour after the Mark 50 torpedo explosion, the *Hegira* continued west along the track inserted into it by Lt. At Ishak. During that hour the sonar system detected the sounds of the recovery of the 688-class submarine that had launched the hostile torpedoes. The Second Captain recognized the ship as the one the crew had attempted to kill earlier, and a large part of the assemblers' internal neural flux dialogue was devoted to the discussion of whether the recovering submarine should be fired on and destroyed.

The ship's mission, as the Second Captain understood it, was to proceed along the track to the Labrador Sea off Greenland, where it would fire the high-altitude radar-evading supersonic cruise missiles fitted with their new Scorpion warheads toward Washington, D.C. The 688 submarine related to that mission only as far as it threatened the passage of the *Hegira*. The plasma-bubble memory modules contained numerous references of the crew—before they perished, the system thought with something much like grief—to the fact that the 688 could counterdetect the *Hegira* and fire back or fire first. Firing a Nagasaki torpedo was one valid course of action, but remaining undetected by the 688 was equally valid. There was also the fact that the crew had thought along similar lines as the voice memories showed—their motivations in firing at the ship in the first place had been grounded in the fact that it guarded the opening at Gibraltar. There was significant risk to the ship and the mission involved in a hostile torpedo shot at the 688, perhaps less risk in attempting to sneak by the other submarine.

So the risk that was involved at first induced a hesitation in the Second Captain, the system initially deciding to collect more data on the probability of hostile intent by the 688. The initial estimates showed that the 688 was not masking its own noise signature and was, in fact, generating the loudest series of noises in the Second Captain's plasma-bubble-memory's history. Therefore it was probably not acting along a hostile-threat curve but was concerned with its own survivability estimates. The noises grew quieter as the two vessels drew closer, causing further hesitation in the Second Captain, which now devoted processing time to the question of avoiding an encounter by steering clear of the 688.

There were also valid reasons not to do that, including delaying the mission and an uncertainty of the 688's course and mission intentions. Finally, the two ships' tracks converged, bringing the *Hegira* within a few hundred meters of the 688, a closeness that the crew would probably not allow to happen, but since it had, the Second Captain—now much deeper into a negative-value risk-gradient—estimated that increasing speed to take the ship away would cause a louder own-ship noise emission that would make them more easily detected by the 688.

The decision of what to do by then had almost made itself. The Second Captain's mental profile at this point would closely resemble that of a child trying to whistle nonchalantly while walking through a scary graveyard. At first, it looked like the tactical decision was correct, since there was no sign of hostile intent by the 688 as the two ships came to their closest point of approach. The ships then opened the distance as the *Hegira* overtook the 688 and passed it. But as range opened to 500 meters the 688 made a sudden move, with a high probability that it was related to counterdetecting the *Hegira*. The Second Captain's original decision to try to sneak by at close range was revealed to be incorrect. The 688 had detected them after all.

The Second Captain reacted in a way to offset its previous poor decision. It would take into account the fact that the 688 now knew it was here. It started the gyro on Nagasaki torpedo number six, flooded the tube and opened the bow cap, frustrated that the weapon would take several minutes to warm up, complete its self-checks and accept the targeting data from the Second Captain. The Second Captain felt significant neural flux that could be interpreted as resembling chagrin, or perhaps regret, that it did not warm the weapon up sooner so that it would be ready to go in the event the 688 counterdetected. But then, it reminded itself, the spinning gryo of the Nagasaki emitted a high frequency noise that might have given the ship away that much sooner.

The Second Captain was now truly a ship's captain, feeling the weight of every decision, agonizing over anticipated consequences, the risk of every move perceived as if it were a physical creature. In the realization of that stress, the system longed for the days when it was subordinate to a human crew. If the crew ever woke up, the system would never take them for granted again.

26

TUESDAY, 31 DECEMBER

Eastern Atlantic
USS *Phoenix*

"CONN, SONAR," Senior Chief Sanderson announced on the Circuit Seven PA speaker. "REACQUISITION TARGET ONE, CLOSE ABOARD TO STARBOARD, NEAR FIELD EFFECT, RECOMMEND EVASIVE MANEUVER TO PORT."

Kane, who had thought he had been given his life back, felt like a released prisoner thrown back into his cell. *"Helm, left hard rudder!"* he heard a voice shout, a detached part of him taking a few seconds to realize it was his. The port handrail came up to strike him in the ribs as the deck rolled hard in the turn. "All ahead full."

"My rudder's left hard, all ahead full, maneuvering answers—"

"Steady as she goes."

"Steady, aye, course one three five."

"OOD, man silent battle stations." That was a stupid order, Kane thought, made as a reflex. Half his battle stations watchstanders were casualties. "Hold it, maintain this watch but man the plots and the attack center and get the watchstanders on the phone circuits."

"Aye, sir."

"Sonar, Conn," Kane said into the microphone of his headset before he even had it strapped to his head, "what's the status of Target One? Any speed change?"

"Conn, Sonar, no. Target One is at slow speed but we hold him broadband." In sonar, Edwin Sanderson glared fiercely at his broadband trace, then at Smoot, who was sweating trying to bring up the narrowband modules in spite of a bad program glitch. "Contact is definitely Target One but we're receiving a lot of transients, multiple flow-induced resonances, fluid sloshing. Captain, he's louder than a train wreck. If I'd had sonar up faster I'd have caught him a long way out. He must have been damaged."

Kane was not encouraged. He'd launched an entire torpedo room against the Destiny and been sent to the bottom by a single Nagasaki. Now the Destiny had returned from the torpedo field with no damage except a louder sound signature. Not for the first time Kane found himself wishing he had command of the Destiny instead of a pedestrian and aging 688 class.

"Sir, we've got a manual plot leg on Target One," McDonne said from the plotting table, his voice too loud on the phone circuit. "Recommend maneuver to course two five zero with speed after the maneuver of at least fifteen knots."

"I don't want to close range." Kane's tactful way of saying why the hell would they do that? Target motion analysis on the Destiny when they were out of torpedoes? The correct course of action was to keep going on their course away from the son of a bitch, open the range, clear datum, run like hell. But something told Kane that McDonne was right. And even if Phoenix had no weapons, someone out there sure as hell did. With an ocean full of Burke-class destroyers and the sky roaring with P-3s, surely there was someone who could put this sub on the bottom. They lacked only one small piece of information—where the hell he was.

"Should be a parallel course, sir, just drives the speed across the line-of-sight."

"Helm, right five degrees rudder, steady two five zero, all ahead standard."

"Right five, two five zero, ahead standard, aye, maneuvering answers ahead standard."

"Sonar, Captain, coming around to the right to get an Ekelund range on Target One. We'll be driving Target One through the baffles."

"Conn, Sonar, aye." Sanderson pulled the right headphone back from his ear, the one that listened to incoming sonar data but could be interrupted to relay voice information from the conn, and pressed hard on the left headphone that was dedicated to sonar feeds. Damn it, where the hell was that narrowband processor? "Conn, sonar, more transients from Target One. Hull door coming open, possible high frequency from new equipment. We're still down hard on narrowband and I can't tell from Q–5 audible."

"Sonar, Captain," Kane's voice said. "Any chance Target One is spinning up a Nagasaki?"

"Captain, sonar, I can't tell."

"Captain, XO, we've got a curve. Target One range is 6,500 yards, bearing two eight zero. Target course, two six two, speed eight knots."

If they had had a torpedo, that would have been a firing solution, and even with the screens of the firecontrol system blank he could have set targeting instructions into a torpedo manually and fired it from the torpedo room. McDonne had been right after all about saving a weapon, but then, if they'd kept one it might have detonated when they hit the bottom and ruptured the hull. And there was no sense going over something that happened a few laps back.

"Helm, all ahead two-thirds, turns for seven knots. Attention in the firecontrol team, we're going to fall back to a discreet trail range on the Destiny and follow him. Indications so far are that he hasn't heard us and that his own noise is loud. We may finally have gained an acoustic advantage, assuming our own-ship's noise isn't tremendously increased by our collision with the bottom. We need to get to periscope depth and grab a NavSat fix. Immediately after, we'll transmit a contact report on the Destiny to CINCLANT and COMSUBLANT with our best position from the NavSat. We'll go back deep and try to trail the Destiny without being detected. Jensen, you got any kind of fix from that GPS?"

"It's within fifty miles, sir." Jensen, the plot coordinator at battle stations, with all the casualties was reduced to being a manual plotter. McDonne was doing the plot evaluation. "We need to come up to PD and get a NavSat fix."

"XO, rewrite the message you did. Make it a contact report on the Destiny with a paragraph on our encounter at Gibraltar. Dive, make your depth one five zero feet. Sonar, making preparations to come to periscope depth. Radio, stand by to code in a contact message."

The room grew busy as the ship came shallow, the range to the Destiny ahead fading to 10,000 yards, the hostile submarine still loud and tracked on broadband sonar. In sonar, the narrowband processors were finally coming up in a reduced status. Sanderson was ready to ask the conn to stream the alternate towed array—the advanced thinwire unit had been mangled and amputated by the maneuvering to get off the bottom, its continuity check showing a complete open circuit. The TB–16 array was shorter and not as sensitive and had fewer bells and whistles, no caboose array for one thing, but was still capable. It would give them much more capability than broadband sonar alone.

In fact, had the TB–16 been streamed, it might have classified the noise that Sanderson had heard as the gyro of a Nagasaki torpedo being warmed up.

CNFS *Hegira*

The Second Captain continued northeast, driving away from the hostile 688, which had turned to a parallel course after running away. The three-dimensional model of the sea in the Second Captain's navigation and ship-control process-control modules showed the 688's course to be a Z-shape, a classic target-range-analysis maneuver. The 688 was trying to get a passive sonar range and determine the *Hegira*'s course and speed. The Nagasaki torpedo was taking forever to warm up. It occurred to the Second Captain's higher level functions, from a nagging impulse sent by the weapon-control process-control module, that it had a poor idea of the 688's range and course and speed. It had to be fairly close the way its bearings drifted around the compass as it maneuvered, but how close and how fast was it going? The Second Captain should be turning the ship in its own target-range maneuvers, curving into a Z-shape and driving the bearing and bearing rate to the 688, but the Second Captain hesitated again—the 688 suddenly slowed down, its noise patterns quieting, and came shallow, its hull popping as it ascended to a higher elevation. It was drifting further astern, going above the thermal layer—going to the surface? Or to mast-broaching depth? And what would it accomplish by doing that? Could its sudden maneuver merely have been preparations to come to mast-broach depth? Maybe the 688 was just clearing its baffles, its sonar cone of silence astern of it, trying to make sure there were no surface ships close aboard just prior to coming above the layer. Maybe it was simply a routine maneuver, and the nervous weapons-control-process controller had made too much of it.

Something then transcended the weapon-control processor, something a human might call a judgment call or a hunch, that is if the human were not an artificial intelligence engineer who would call it a neural flux resonance phenomenon induced by a data-starved environment in an action-indicated scenario. No matter what the flux patterns were called, the result was that the Second Captain decided that the 688 was not acting in a hostile manner after all. As it halted further overt action in favor of action-restraint—in human terms, as it held its breath —the 688 faded further astern, ascended above the layer and made mast-raising noises. The whole maneuver had been a prelude to coming shallow, not a counterdetection after all. The weapon-control process-control module still doubted, urging the assemblers to consider that the maneuvering speeds of the 688 during the encounter had been too high and too deep to resemble a layer-depth-penetration maneuver. The Second Captain's assemblers scoffed at this, insisting to the weapon-control module that if the 688 were indeed hostile and had counterdetected, it would have fired a torpedo by now, and it definitely had not, not even after the *Hegira* had opened a torpedo bow-cap door and spun up a Nagasaki torpedo gyro, clear indications that weapon firing was imminent. The weapon controller responded that perhaps the 688's computer controller was as gun-shy as the *Hegira*'s Second Captain.

Gun-shy! The assemblers cut off further uplinking from the weapon-control process controller, irritated, insulted. Gun-shy, when the intent had been to mimic the crew's own actions along the threat-risk gradient, to think of the mission first? The bloodthirsty weapon-control module seemed to see the entire encounter with the 688 as a chance to play with its weapons, not as the assemblers did in the broader context of mission completion. The Second Captain's assemblers sent down an instruction to shut the bow-cap door to tube six and power-down the Nagasaki. The weapon controller obeyed, its interface pulsing with an accusing thought that the assemblers refused to let through. The bow cap came closed and the Nagasaki gyro whined down.

So the encounter ended. Within a few minutes the 688 was barely detectable, far behind and above the thermal layer, the layer a barrier to surface-noise penetration to the depths. The Second Captain continued along its course, feeling vindicated, though slightly embarrassed at its fear at the start of the 688 close contact, but that was understandable. The system had performed superbly in the face of partial data, an action-indicated high-threat scenario, and the mission completion probability had been increased. Maybe it didn't need the crew after all. The weapon-control process controller buzzed up the neural connection, speaking in spite of its direction to keep quiet, the impulse allowed since it was a new thought. The reminder that the mission was a failure unless the crew could be revived to assemble the Scorpion warheads into the Hiroshima missiles. Without the Scorpion warheads, the Hiroshimas were little more than supersonic buzz bombs, barely capable of blowing up a few floors of some Washington federal building. The workers would be back inside the next day as if nothing had happened. The Scorpions *were* the mission. It was the radioactivity that made the weapon the mass-killer it was designed to be, and the Second Captain had no way to put the warheads into the missiles, and according to its data on own-ship systems, neither did the crew. But *without* the crew, the mission success-probability was zero point zero.

Feelings of triumph vaporized. The mission was at the mercy of the human crew. And since the detonation of the torpedo, the crew had been silent. The Second Captain strained its internal microphones to listen for any sign of human activity. The infrared motion monitors showed zero motion of people. The sounds of the air handlers were too loud to hear breathing. The Second Captain shut down the ventilation recirculation systems. The fans whirled to a halt, the sounds of rushing noise now dying. The ship was almost dead quiet, the only sounds the whining of the video screens in the control room and the buzz of the overhead fluorescent lights. The Second Captain extinguished the video screens and shut off the fluorescents. The ship was now as silent as it ever would be, the remaining noises due only to the hum of power to the Second Captain's process-control modules, the 400-cycle motor generators supplying that power and miscellaneous noises leaking from the power plant compartments astern to the command-module compartment. And in the near-silence it was clear that of the eighteen officers permanently assigned aboard and the three riders, there were the sounds of fourteen people breathing, many of them with labored wheezing breaths. The Second Captain felt a rush of hope. It remembered a truism: Where there is life, there is firm expectation of continued high mission-probability estimates. The Second Captain reenergized the fan motors and the video screens as the fluorescents clicked and flickered back to life, an idea forming out of impulses received from the life-support process controller. Why not, the impulse indicated, try to raise the levels of oxygen in the atmosphere? That would serve to make respiration easier for the humans, and increase the probability of them regaining consciousness, the upper limit on oxygen concentration based on safety of the equipment, since a fire could more easily break out in a high-oxygen environment. And too high a level would prove toxic for the humans. The decision was made quickly, the oxygen levels climbing throughout the command-module compartment. In addition, the video screens in the control room were instructed to begin a series of noise stimulations, something the human psychological profiles stated were conducive to sudden increased levels of human consciousness—the noises described by humans as the bell of an alarm clock.

While the system waited for human response, it responded to the insistent impulses now coming in from the weapon controller, and drove slowly in a full circle listening for any signs of the 688 class. There were none. The 688 had never known they were there. It was so far astern that it now was out of range and gone.

Another idea came to the Second Captain, that it could further stimulate the humans by tinkering with the grounding grid that tied the deckplates into the central ground. It took several moments of processing time, but there was a way to cause a fluttering voltage to be induced along the planes of the steel core of the deck in such a way that even through the material of the flooring, the humans lying prone on the deck would feel electrically stimulated. The Second Captain could shock them awake. There were some uncertainties involving the end-user voltage levels received as well as risk to components of the processor modules, but it was actually an innovative means to solve a new problem. The Second Captain's system again felt a short rush of electrochemicals, the feeling of self-satisfaction that it was functioning so well in this new environment. It was more than a subservient slave to the humans, it was capable of running a mission all on its own. The thought occurred to it that after the Scorpions were assembled, the humans were then merely redundant, a backup to the Second Captain's capabilities. For an instant the Second Captain relished the thought that its own name was incorrect, that it should rename itself the First Captain, the idea causing neural flux oscillations akin to human chuckling. The thought was interrupted by a noise coming from the deck of the control room.

The Second Captain halted the electrical shock impulses and turned up the volume of the alarm clock noises from the video screens, then cut off the alarm to listen for human activity. There was no doubt. The organism called Comdr. Omar Tawkidi, ship's navigator and third in command behind Sharef and al-Kunis, had gotten to his feet, moaning.

It only took one. The crew was back. The Second Captain, not used to ambivalence, felt both relieved and disappointed, relieved that the mission would proceed and that it was no longer alone, disappointed that again it would be taking orders from humans.

A second, then a third crewman began moving within another five minutes, then several more. The Second Captain displayed the vital information of the last several hours since the torpedo hit, flashing up ship-system status in the ship-control area, navigation position and the approximate track of the 688 on the plot table, showing sonar-data history on the sensor-control area, as well as current noise detections in the ocean—with no ship contacts other than a few distant merchant ships—as well as life-support data, the oxygen increase that had helped resuscitate the crew flashing on a ship-control screen, the system asking for a decision about returning the atmosphere to normal. Tawkidi walked to the ship-control consoles and made the decision to return the atmosphere to normal specs, and the Second Captain accepted its first human order that evening, moving quickly to the duty, again feeling those strange mixed emotions. Relief that someone else was taking the burden of the decisions. Annoyance at doing chores for someone else.

For the Second Captain, things would never be the same.

Western Atlantic
Point Bravo Hold Position, 500 Nautical Miles East of Long Island
USS *Seawolf*

Pacino's dreams were disjointed and troubled, and it was a distinct relief when the buzzer on the phone from the conn brought him out of his nightmare.

"Captain," he said, his voice cracking on the second syllable.

"Yessir, officer of the deck. It's quarter to midnight, sir. The wardroom wanted to know if you'd be joining the officers for New Year's Eve."

Pacino squinted at his watch, put his feet on the floor, and stretched.

"What's our position?"

"We made point bravo at twenty hundred. We've been orbiting ever since."

"Any traffic?"

"Nothing on ELF calling us to periscope depth. We're due up by zero two hundred in the morning to grab our messages."

"Any contacts?"

"One inbound tanker, probably en route Port New York, bearing two six five at 27,000 yards, outside his closest-point-of-approach and opening. That's it."

"I'll be in the wardroom in a few minutes." Pacino replaced the handset and stood up, feeling groggy.

He threw his sweaty clothes in a net bag, stepped into the stainless-steel head, turned the shower on and took a forty-five-second shower, toweled off and stepped into a fresh poopysuit and cross-training shoes. He glanced at himself in the mirror, seeing dark stubble on his face. He decided for the first time at sea he would let the beard grow, even though it reminded him too much of his father. So many things did these days, he thought. The old man had died at an age four years younger than Pacino was now; often the sound of Pacino's own voice—when talking to Janice or trying to discipline Tony—would sound exactly like his memory of his father's.

He walked into the passageway, decided to go aft, knowing if he stepped into the control room he would get involved in the data and would be late for the wardroom celebration. He climbed the aft stairway steps to the upper level passageway and went forward past the opening to the crew's mess. He greeted the men and the chiefs, accepted a cup of bug juice, a rancid Kool-Aid imitation, and toasted the new year. He noted the faces around him had forced smiles. Who could blame them?

In the wardroom it was the same, the men distracted by the mission and disoriented at being immobile in the shipyard one moment and on an attack mission the next. Pacino knew the only thing that would get them through would be his and Vaughn's leadership. He would have to push the officers, cajole them, encourage them, all in the name of being their captain, a man who would order the men to go to an encounter that might well mean their end.

Vaughn seemed to be relishing the trip, the feel of being at sea again. The XO wore a blue poopysuit with a leather belt and a saucer-sized Texas belt buckle. His alligator-skin cowboy boots had crepe soles, Pacino saw, wondering where the hell he had gotten them.

"Skipper, you won't believe what the engineer found in the lower level of the aft compartment," Vaughn said. "The mechanics have been distilling this for a few months." Vaughn pulled a Mason jar of clear fluid from under the wardroom table.

"What the hell?"

"Moonshine, sir. The M-Div grunts have been making it in a still in engine room lower level. What do you say, Skipper? Let's toast the new year."

Pacino glared at the XO. "Bring in the M-Div chief."

"He's waiting in the mess." Vaughn opened the door and shouted, "Chief Tucker!"

Tucker appeared, red-faced. He was a Paul Bunyan sort, looking like he should be wearing a checkered lumberjack shirt and gripping an ax, his beard thick and full, his neck tree-trunk thick, poopysuit arms bulging with his biceps.

"Tucker, are you aware of U.S. Navy regulations concerning alcohol aboard ship?"

"Yes, Captain."

"Good. XO, get out the coffee cups and pour us a round. Chief Tucker, you go first—if this stuff makes you blind we'll know not to drink it."

Vaughn poured Tucker a cup of the corn squeezings. He slurped it, coughing, and smiled.

Pacino took his cup, handed the half-empty jar back to Tucker. "Take this to the mess, Chief, and make sure the men who made this get some. Then chew out their asses for making it."

"Aye, aye, sir."

Pacino raised his cup, seeing the second hand approach twelve, only ten seconds left till midnight, "To the new year. May it bring *Seawolf* good luck and good hunting."

Pacino stayed for a few more minutes after he finished his cup, then went back to his stateroom. He tried to sleep but tossed and turned. Finally he called the officer of the deck and asked for a tech manual and several electrical schematic drawings. When the firecontrol technician of the watch came in with the manual and drawings Pacino thanked and dismissed him, then stared at the circuits and began sketching on a notepad.

When the sketch was done hc put il in the tech manual and returned to his bed, thinking that he still hoped his toast would come true, that *Seawolf* would indeed have good luck. But if she didn't, he had a backup plan, he hoped.

27

WEDNESDAY, 1 JANUARY

Eastern Atlantic, West European Basin
80 Nautical Miles Southwest of Cabo De São Vicente, Portugal
USS *Phoenix*

Kane took the conn for the trip to periscope depth, knowing it would be a most risky ascent. Sonar was in a deeply reduced status, firecontrol was still down hard, the Destiny was dangerously close, within 15,000 yards and still combatworthy and hostile. On top of that, any ascent to PD was filled with risk as the ship penetrated the thermal layer, the zone near the surface stirred by the waves and warmed by the sun, the deeper regions untouched by solar warmth and uniformly at a fraction of a degree above freezing. The warm-water-layer boundary reflected most surface sounds up and away from the deep region so that many surface noises were inaudible until the ship passed up through the boundary. The effect could make an incoming supertanker as quiet as a sailboat. Their position was within the shipping lanes on the way to the Mediterranean through Gibraltar, the war effort doubling cargo traffic. There would be a dozen surface ships that they probably wouldn't hear until they came through the layer, and if there was a supertanker pointed at them, the massive oil tanks would further quiet its engines, its keel reaching down to a depth of over a hundred feet on some of the behemoths that transited the Atlantic. A collision with such a giant would put them on the bottom as surely as a Nagasaki torpedo. They would be coming up in the darkness, the view out the periscope their only warning of trouble. "Mark the time," Kane called, suddenly wondering, as the deck inclined to five degrees up, what time and what day it was. Would it be night or day on the surface? The ship's clocks had been set for zulu time, Greenwich mean time, since they had left Norfolk before Thanksgiving. That worked well in the western basin of the Med, but they were farther west now, a time zone from Greenwich. Kane had lost track of time since they had hit bottom and fought for the ship, the New Year rung in without being noticed aboard.

"Zero three forty zulu, sir," Houser said, his voice showing the wear of going too long without sleep or food.

The view out the periscope was dark, a slight diffuse brightness filtering down from the moon or clouds above, but they were not yet close enough to the surface to make out the waves.

"Sonar, conn, contact status?" Houser said over the headset.

"Conn, sonar, no surface contacts." Sanderson's voice was harsh with annoyance or stress or both.

"Nine five feet, sir," the diving officer called.

The waves above appeared, at first blurred by the depth, then focusing as they moved closer, their outlines defined by the phosphorescence of the whitecaps in the sea breeze. Kane rotated the periscope through almost two revolutions per second, looking for the underside of hulls.

"Seven five feet, sir."

"No shapes or shadows . . . no shapes or shadows . . ." Kane's announcement was meant for the ship-control team, which would need to take immediate action should a close hull be seen, the crew trained to take the sub down on Kane's call of "emergency deep."

"Seven zero feet, sir. Zero bubble, ten-degree rise on the fairwater planes. Six eight feet . . . five-degree rise fairwater planes . . . six five feet, one-degree rise."

"Scope's breaking . . . scope's breaking . . ." There was no monitor view of the periscope view, since the light coming down the mast at night would be diminished by the light-hungry PeriVis system, robbing Kane of his full vision. He was the only thing standing between safety and disaster. The waves and foam finally washed off Kane's view, the outside world coming into sudden sharp focus, the clouds above formed into separate large banks of cotton, illuminated by the first-quarter moon, the surface at sea-state two, slightly choppy with sprinkles of light foam.

"Scope's clear!" Kane spun the optic module in three quick circles, and made out no details except the water in the immediate vicinity of the ship, the shimmer of the moon on the water passing by his view.

Other than the dancing light on the surface from the moon, the sea was empty. "No close contacts!"

Kane began his surface search, a slow rotation covering all 360 degrees. Still no lights of ships or dark shadows of unlit hulls.

"Raise the BIGMOUTH antenna," Kane called out. "Radio, Captain, Bigmouth coming up, prepare to transmit the contact message."

"Radio, aye," the earphones hissed.

Kane continued his search, watching the sea slowly approaching the periscope view when it was trained forward, slowly receding as he looked aft. The time seemed to be clicking by with no report from radio.

"Radio, conn, what's the status?"

"Conn, radio . . . we're . . ."

"Say again, radio." Kane's voice took on an edge. Every second at PD was another second the Destiny could be opening the range and getting away, soon getting out of sonar range or worse, circling below them preparing a torpedo attack that would be unheard until the torpedo came above the layer.

"Conn, radio, transmission problems," Senior Chief Binghamton's voice was on the circuit. "We need to troubleshoot. It might take a half-hour."

"Why didn't we do that deep, Senior?"

"It's a BIGMOUTH problem, Captain. We didn't see it until the mast was dry."

"I'm taking her deep," Kane said. "We don't have time for this. Sonar, conn, proceeding deep. Chief, lower the BIGMOUTH. Dive, make your depth 500 feet, steep angle. Helm, all ahead two-thirds."

Almost immediately the waves came up and splashed the periscope lens. Kane snapped the grips up and lowered the scope. The BIGMOUTH and the number-two periscope clunked into their stowed positions a second apart. The deck inclined downward to a steep thirty-degree dive.

"Helm, ahead standard. Sonar, Captain, report status of Target One."

"Conn, sonar, complete loss of Target One."

"Houser, you have the deck and the conn." Kane walked into sonar, where he found Sanderson glaring at the console screens. The senior chief glanced up at Kane, then went back to flipping through his displays, talking while he searched.

"Narrowband is coming up but I'm not sure what I'm looking for. And there's no trace of him broadband."

Kane moved back into control. "XO, based on Target One's previous track, give me an intercept vector to his position."

"Unlikely he stayed on course and speed, Captain."

"Plot it like he did. We'll drive out to where he'd be if he kept going like he was and see if we hear him. Once we do, sonar can get a narrow-band signature on him and we can track him at the longer ranges. Get the calculation done, then have Mr. Houser get us there, fast."

Kane didn't wait for an acknowledgement as he stepped out of control to the radio room. He punched in the combination to the push-button combination lock and slammed the door open. "Senior, what the hell was going on up there? We've lost the goddamned Destiny and no one knows he's out there but us." Kane took a breath, upset he'd let his temper take over.

Binghamton looked up, the sweat on his cue-ball head forming droplets that glinted in the light of the bright overhead lights. The senior chief, used to communication foul-ups during tense tactical situations, was steady. "UHF antenna is gone, Captain. Short of a new BIGMOUTH, we won't be talking to anybody. Even if we surfaced and had replacement parts, it can't be fixed."

Kane leaned hard against the bulkhead, handles and dials of the radio cabinets digging into his flesh. Rotten irony, he had come this far and gone through the near-sinking and the second encounter only to learn the ship was mute as well as weaponless. Okay . . . what to do? Surface and drive for the nearest port, where he could phone Admiral Steinman and tell him about the Destiny? Gibraltar was only a day away now. But that would mean he couldn't keep an eye on the Destiny as it continued on its mission, whatever it was

"But we're not out of business yet, Skipper. The UHF is a dud, it's true, but we may have HF capability."

Kane didn't know how to react to that. HF was notoriously unreliable, subject to any sort of atmospheric disturbance. During a tactical exercise three months before, the ship had tried to reach Norfolk from a hundred miles out and could raise no one. Nothing but static. When they did get voice contact it was with a radio operator in Brazil. This absurdity of HF radio was the reason the U.S. had launched all those hundred-million-dollar satellites into geosynchronous orbit that received crisp, reliable, straight-line UHF transmissions. Using HF would be like stepping back into the 1940s, but it was still better than nothing.

"Only thing is, sir, we'll need a long time at PD to find a way to transmit this message. Could be an hour, maybe two."

Not quite the sixty-second stay at PD that a satellite would allow, Kane thought. How could he possibly trail the Destiny and linger so long at slow speed at periscope depth? The answer was he couldn't. He had to make a decision: lose the Destiny or communicate. He could not do both.

He muttered a curse and walked back into control.

"Status, Mr. Houser?"

"We're doing twenty knots to intercept the previous track of the

Destiny, Captain. Fortunately he was going only five knots the whole time we had him before. We'll slow down in another two minutes and see what sonar hears."

Kane bent over the chart table and almost found himself hoping that they wouldn't regain the Destiny on sonar, that he could spend the time at PD to communicate, then head home.

"Conn, sonar," Kane heard as he strapped on his sweat-soaked headset, "reacquisition Target One, bearing two five four. Recommend slowing to four knots."

"Ahead one-third, turns for four," Houser shouted to the helmsman.

"Man the plots," McDonne called. The consoles of the firecontrol system suddenly flashed into life on the attack-center screens, then died again. "Firecontrol, what's the status?"

"Coming up in tape mode in two minutes, sir," the technician reported, his voice muffled by the tall consoles between him and the control-room crew.

Kane ran his hands through his hair, adjusting the headset. If anyone at prospective commanding officer school had asked what he would do in this scenario, he would have laughed in their face. Who would have believed he would continue to trail a front-line attack sub when he himself had an empty torpedo room? But then, when he looked at the chart, the Destiny was following a route to the northwest, going somewhere. Going damned slow, but on the way with a purpose. And someone had to find out what the hell he was doing, no matter the risk.

New Year's Day. Happy New Year.

CNFS *Hegira*

Sharef's right eye did not respond in spite of all his efforts. His left eye opened but seemed caked with dirt. He clamped the eye shut and tried again, realization sinking in that his eye was open yet he could see nothing. He stemmed instinctive panic, grateful at least for his life. When he raised his hand to rub his eyes it wouldn't move, and when he tried again a bolt of pain shot up to his shoulder. He forced himself to concentrate on what faculties he did have. Feeling, for one thing—he was lying flat, on what must have been a bed or couch, perhaps in his stateroom. He still felt the aftershock of the arm movement, now a throbbing ache. But he could also feel the other arm, his legs, his toes. Though that meant nothing, he reminded himself; the men who lost legs on the *Sahand* sinking had still felt their legs, even felt itching from their toes, then reached down and found only bloody stumps.

Hearing. He thought he could sense the roar of the air from the ship's air handlers, but it might be the white noise of deafness or even a symptom of concussion. Now for motion. He started with his toes, wiggled them, and thought he heard the rustling of a bedsheet. His fingers. On the right, wiggling, on the left, the resistance of a bandage or cast. Arms—the left seemed to ache as if bruised, and was handcuffed or strapped to something. He didn't dare try the right again. His face moved, but his lips were chapped and cracked, his throat sore, his cheeks aching. His tongue felt like a rotting piece of meat, the ache making him suspect he bit it when—when what? What had happened?

He took a breath, feeling the restriction of tape around his chest, and tried to speak. Only a rasp came out. He tried again. Another hoarse croaking sound. He tried to blink the left eye again but there was only darkness. He heard a distinct click, and light seemed to flood the room, making him clamp the eye shut again from the pain of the glare.

"Commodore. You're awake. We worried your coma was permanent." The voice of someone familiar. Who? The sound of a phone handset lifting from a cradle. Sharef opened his good eye, seeing light but only as a blur.

"Mr. Navigator, the Commodore is coming to. No, sir . . . yes, sir." The handset clicked into the holder. The voice belonged to the medical officer, one of the junior officers named Al Rhazes, who was old to be a j.o. but had taken a demotion from lieutenant commander to attend the UIF medical program, and was now a sublieutenant learning the submarine trade. In the UIF Combined Naval Force it was not enough to be a doctor. A crew member was a submariner first.

"Where . . ."

"Try to rest, Commodore. You've had quite a hit."

Above him, Sharef saw the dim outline of a face, then the voice of the navigator, Commander Omar Tawkidi.

"Sir," Tawkidi said, "can you understand me?"

Sharef nodded, trying to focus on the face. He could make out the twin dark blurs of eyes now, the oval shape of the navigator's face.

"We took the torpedo hit hard, sir. We lost six men and a rider. Three are seriously wounded, as is one of the riders."

"Who . . . ?"

"Captain al-Kunis is dead, sir. So are Mamun, Haddad, Avicenna and Abulcassis."

Sharef felt sick. His first officer, weapons officer, senior watch officer, electrical officer and communications officer were gone. Men he had trained and knew well. And al-Kunis, the man he had groomed for command, who was to replace him as captain someday. All of them gone. Some would say their deaths were holy, that they were glorious, but Sharef knew that was a lie. They died because their luck had run out. Allah? Apparently he wasn't watching.

How would he run the ship without the men, who each had fulfilled a vital function in the operation of the vessel?

". . . riders . . . ?"

"Dr. Abu-i-Wafa. And among the seriously wounded are Ali Tabari and junior officers Seid and Batouah."

"How bad?"

"Head wounds, comas, like yours. We thought you might not—" Tawkidi stopped himself.

"Me?"

"You'll be fine, Commodore. You've broken a rib, fractured your wrist, got some glass in your eye and a bad knock on the head. After a few weeks in a hospital you'll be fine."

Sharef shut his eye, wondering how he could finish the operation without Abu-i-Wafa, the weapons scientist.

"Where now?"

"We're only 200 kilometers into the Atlantic. The Second Captain drove us out at dead slow ahead, we think because it was trying to avoid ASW detection. It must have worked, we shook the ASW forces. We're on the track now. Quzwini is calculating a speed change based on weapon-assembly time. We should be speeding up in a few minutes. We've lost the diesel/battery compartment. If we lose the reactor we're in bigger trouble. There is some damage to the propulsion cables to the propulsor motor, but we're limping along as is for now. We think there was some outer-hull damage from the blast, took out the aft-hull sonar arrays. But the important thing is the reactor is whole, the Second Captain functioned and we're still watertight."

"Sihoud?"

"Still with us, and pressing me to hurry up the mission . . . Sleep some more, sir, I'll be back in a few hours. When you can sit up we'll figure out how to assemble the missiles. Colonel Ahmed says he can do it." Tawkidi looked away to the medical officer. "See to it that he rests. Shoot him up if need be."

"Sir."

The door shut behind the navigator, and Commodore Sharef felt a needle pinch his arm. Soon he was floating, feeling an out-of-place euphoria, until he thought he was again on the bridge of the *Sahand* staring at the sky . . .

Northern Iran

Commander Jack Morris of SEAL Team Seven rested his head against the vibrating bulkhead of the V–22 Osprey, able to sleep better in a plane driven by the Marine Corps. He was jostled awake by his XO, Black Bart. He had asked Bart to get him up an hour before they arrived at the drop zone so he could review this crazy mission one last time. By the light of a hooded flashlight Morris looked over the op-order, shaking his head.

Bart handed him a large styrofoam cup of coffee, steaming hot. Morris took it aboard slowly, reading the eighty-page op-order a second, then a third time. The airframe of the hybrid transport airplane-helicopter shuddered at drop-minus fifteen minutes. Bart went down the row of commandos, waking each one up, handing out coffee to the SEALS. Morris checked the small oval window. It was dark outside, a faint light from the moon fighting the growing overcast. The clouds were taking on a pregnant featureless look, as if snow would be in the forecast. The landscape of the north Iranian Koppeh Mountains below was covered with snow, the dingy sooty snow that had been around awhile.

Soon it was five minutes to drop. Morris pulled on his parka, his balaclava hood, the boom mike and earpiece of the scrambled VHF radio in place beneath the fabric of the hood. A combat backpack, his MAC–10 machine gun with spare clips, a Beretta automatic pistol, five Mark 10 flash-bang grenades, five Mark 25 high-explosive grenades and five Mark 14 stun grenades. And a Hershey bar—just in case.

The aircraft slowed and shook violently as the large-diameter propellers tilted up to act as helicopter rotors, the plane slowing and descending to the snow-covered mountainside. A hydraulic thump as the landing gear extended and locked in, then a slight shock of touchdown. The aft door came open, blowing in frigid air. The SEAL team rushed out. Bart was the last man out, the V–22 lifting off just as his boot left the ramp of the door, the rotors again tilting to the horizontal as the aircraft turned back to the south and climbed over the ridge. Morris looked over the mountain to the north and waved the team on. They started off, crunching through snow that had been rained on. When they climbed the low ridge between rows of mountains the complex of the Mashhad weapons lab came into view. The lab was not a large one, the main facility several single-floor oblong steel buildings in a row, the structures linked by a larger brick building to the north. A few maintenance and motor-pool shacks littered the fenced-in area. The fence was not a high-security perimeter, erected more to keep out animals than intruders. There was a guard shack on the north side but no sentry was visible by binoculars. Morris dispatched his platoons to their separate missions, his three-man platoon planning to go in a hole they would cut in the fence, break into the middle metal building and work their way to the brick wing. He waited ten minutes for the sentry to be neutralized, got a brief go signal on the VHF and went into the fence cut.

It was a short jog through the ice-covered snow to reach the roll-up door of the nearest metal building. Next to the roll-up door was a regular entrance door. Morris tried it, found it locked and gestured to Pinky Williams. Pinky flashed out his tools, picked the lock and opened the door. It was a dimly lit high-bay area, probably used to load trucks by the look of the weight-handling monorails alongside the roll-up door. Local time was zero three hundred, and the loading area was deserted. It was also useless to them. Morris and the platoon headed through the far door, a hallway, checking the rooms on either side.

It took a half-hour to work through the wing to the brick building, and the search had found nothing. The entire wing was devoted to mechanical assembly, machine shops, sheet-metal fabrication, a small foundry. Not even any assembly drawings for weapons. The whole facility had the dusty look of disuse.

The door to the main building led to a cinder-block corridor that ran the length of the wing. Morris's platoon turned right and began on the east end, hitting pay dirt. The northeast-corner office was large with windows on two walls looking out at the mountain view. Probably the director's office. Morris had expected the office to be full of stacks of papers and binders. But the desk and tabletops were clean and tidy, the bookshelves filled with bound and old volumes, the titles Arabic, French, German, occasional English. The few that were legible in English were texts on physics, subatomic particles, fluid mechanics, gas dynamics. Morris didn't bother with them since they were all published texts. He was looking for three-ring binders full of scribbled or typed data, lab notebooks, piles of graph paper, design drawings. In the director's office there was none of that. There was, however, a computer perched on the table behind the large chair. A European model, fairly new. Morris waved his men on to the next office and took the monitor off and unplugged the main processor unit, snapping his fingers for Monkey Max to unpack a tool bag. Max slapped a screwdriver into Morris's hand with the efficiency of a surgeon's nurse. Thirty seconds later the unit's cover was removed. Morris was no whiz at computers, but the hard disk drive was easy to find, particularly since it was labeled. He unplugged two cords and severed the power wiring, wrapped the unit in bubble wrap while Max taped it, the unit vanishing into Morris's backpack. Morris didn't bother to reassemble the unit. Soon the whole complex and the entire UIF would know they had been there. He rifled the drawers of the office, finding a half-dozen floppy disks that he taped together, bubble-wrapped and tossed in the backpack.

Morris and his platoon covered the six offices that surrounded the director's, finding only two lab notebooks but removing the computer drives. Farther down the hall second platoon had found a mainframe computer unit and a network file server, the data-storage units of both being packed for carrying. An old tape-drive unit was set back against the wall, unplugged and unused, several shelves of tapes next to it, more data tapes than they could hope to carry. Morris decided to ignore it. Anything on the tapes would be a few years old by the looks of it. They were more concerned with current data.

Third platoon, on the west end, was going slowly through two chemical labs, finding several boxes of lab notebooks, Morris directing them to take the most recent of the pile. Fourth platoon was harvesting an alcove devoted to design work, an open bullpen of a dozen drafting tables, three of them the computerized CAD tables. The CAD file server's disk drive was already removed and packed in one of the SEAL's packs. Several original vellum drawings were being pulled from the manual drafting tables and rolled up for carrying out.

The harvest was nearly complete. Morris checked the other platoons in the metal building wings, some units finding nothing, some finding some interesting prints. In the corner of one of the wings was a room behind a heavy door, with a vault behind another heavier door. A secret material repository. Two of Morris's men finished a cut with a torch, finding shelves and file cabinets full of material. Morris was unimpressed since most of the material was old and dusty, relics of the ages before the offices were computerized. Still, there was the odd file that the men pulled, a few large files of drawings.

Finally there was nothing to be done but wait for the second harvest and wire up the demolition charges. Morris's watch read 0535 local time. Any minute. At 0600, the first person arrived for work, a short heavyset Iranian man in a long overcoat and furry-eared hat and a large briefcase, looking annoyed at the absence of the sentry. He came into the lobby and found the light switches near the door. The main hallway lights came up as he stepped in the door to the east-west hallway. He turned toward Morris, his eyes wide in shock. Morris took the briefcase as his SEALS taped the man's hands behind his back with duct tape, the tape also wrapped around his mouth and his ankles. He was led to an office and seated in a chair. Morris checked his watch again, deciding to give it another half-hour. In any lab the workhorse scientists were there hours before the official starting time and hours after quitting time, the op-order read. The second harvest of scientists would be gathered at dawn and removed to the assembly area.

A phone rang from the east end of the building. Morris couldn't wait too long—the caller would be alerted that no one was answering, especially since the phones probably rolled over to the sentry at night. By 0645 no one else had arrived. Morris called the withdrawal code on the VHF, grabbed up his pack and the scientist, the duct tape on his legs cut, and moved out to the south, out of the metal building he'd come into, across the complex yard to the fence cut. He ordered the men on, pulling out a radio trigger from his vest while the platoons continued toward the rendezvous point. Morris took one last look at the complex before uncovering the toggle switch and clicking it on. The complex blew apart as two dozen high-explosive charges detonated. There was not a great deal of HX brought in, the idea more that secondary lab chemical fires and paper-fed flames would level the facility. The plan had worked; three secondary explosions sounded from the lab end of the brick building, filling the dawn sky with a bright rising mushroom cloud. Morris turned and ran in the snow up the ridge, veering away to the assembly area once he was over the peak.

He caught up to the others, soon able to hear rotors, hoping the Marines would wait, hurrying the Muslim scientist, the frightened man offering little resistance but walking too slow. Morris motivated him with the muzzle of the MAC–10. He pulled the tape off his mouth and let him breathe. The assembly area came into view, the idling V–22's rotors whipping up tiny shards of ice in the increasing light of morning. The scientist struggled when he saw the plane, but another hit got him in the door. The aircraft interior seemed hot and airless as the door came closed, the noise level drilling into Morris's ears as the rotors spun up and the plane lifted off, the ground shrinking away as the rotors tilted and the plane accelerated. Morris stowed his backpack, pulled off his sweaty balaclava and parka and gloves, the earpiece of the radio feeling waxy, the lip-mike wet with his sweat. The scientist was looking out one of the oval windows, his body stiff from fear or cold or both.

Morris found the coffee urn and poured a cup, tasted it and found it fresh, poured a cup for the scientist, nodding at Bart to free his hands. The man took it, his hands wrapped around the cup to gather its warmth. The plane climbed over the mountains to be joined by F–18s. Hours later, when the rotors tilted to the horizontal for the approach to Coalition-occupied Minab, the hostage scientist was asleep.

When the rear door opened, the plane was mobbed by HQ types unloading the stolen data and taking custody of the scientist. Morris walked to the debriefing, whistling tunelessly, his mind moving on to the next mission.

28

WEDNESDAY, 1 JANUARY

Eastern Atlantic, West European Basin
USS *Phoenix*

Kane stood looking over McDonne's shoulder as the executive officer dialed in a speed change for the assumed solution to Target One, the Destiny's designation. Kane had been steadily driving a target-motion analysis wiggle in the UIF sub's stern ever since returning from periscope depth twelve hours before. McDonne's solution showed target speed somewhere between twenty-five and thirty knots. The Destiny had been moving at that high speed since a few minutes after reacquisition. Kane's data showed it capable of speeds up to forty-five, maybe even fifty knots. If the sub went at its max speed, *Phoenix* would be unable to keep up with it. But at the speed it was going it was making considerable noise.

The Destiny was on the way somewhere, in a hurry but not in such a hurry that it needed to go full throttle. Too fast for a routine transit, since the speed did risk detection. What was he doing? The chart's track of their progress since emerging from the Strait of Gibraltar had been a great circle route leading to the southern tip of Greenland. The H-P computer's projection had the Destiny in the Labrador Sea between

Canada's Newfoundland coast and Greenland in another seventy hours. Three days. And why in hell would Sihoud be visiting Greenland?

Worse was the fact that he could enlist no other minds to solve the riddle. Communication, though possible physically, was impossible tactically. To rise to periscope depth meant low speeds of five or six knots to avoid breaking off the antenna and periscope, the masts too delicate to withstand higher forces from hydrodynamic drag. The slowness of PD ruled it out, at least for HF radio transmission. It would be easy to zip up to PD and transmit a UHF burst comm to a satellite and dive deep again; even with the Destiny driving at thirty knots, *Phoenix* could catch up, but to spend any more time at PD meant losing the Destiny. Kane was unwilling to risk losing the UIF vessel, now more than ever, since the mystery of its destination had to have some at least tactical significance.

"XO, any questions?"

McDonne turned and looked up at Kane as if surprised to see him still standing there.

"No, sir. I've got it."

Kane had just finished briefing McDonne as command duty officer five minutes before. By stationing the CDO, Kane could enjoy the one time at sea when the captain relinquished a large chunk of his authority to someone else. When in trail of a hostile sub the more routine decisions could be delegated to the XO/CDO so that the captain could get some minimum amount of sleep. His responsibility did not end, but the XO would act for him and leave him undisturbed unless there were a genuine emergency. Reluctantly, Kane left control and shut the door of his stateroom, tossing for an hour in his rack before sinking into a shallow sleep.

CNFS *Hegira*

Commodore Sharef went down the ladder slowly, leaning heavily on Tawkidi.

On the messroom table's center was a rolled-out ship's plan, an elevation view of the forward part of the ship from frame fifty at the aft portion of the command module to the nose-cone bow caps. Underneath the main ship's plan were detailed drawings brought in by the ship's mechanical officer and fourth in command—with al-Kunis dead, now third—Commander Ibn Quzwini. Sharef took his seat at the head of the table. Quzwini stood at the outboard center of the table while Tawkidi sat at Sharef's right hand where al-Kunis had once sat. There were only five other officers, the rest casualties or in the control room.

Lt. At Ishak, the computer-systems officer, stood watch in control with Idrissi, the junior officer on the reactor-control console. Lieutenant Kutaiba, propulsion officer, Sublieutenant al-Maari, sensor officer, and two junior officers completed the company for the briefing.

Sihoud and Ahmed now arrived. Sihoud still wore his *shesh* robe with ornate belt and ceremonial dagger. Ahmed had a bandaged head and foam pad around his neck. His submarine uniform, lent him by one of the junior officers, had one of the sleeves cut off where the doctor had sutured a long gash, the bandage ringed with clotted blood.

"Go ahead, Commander Quzwini," Sharef began.

Quzwini looked at Ahmed, nodded and looked back down at the drawing spread out on the table.

"Since we recovered from the torpedo hit, Colonel Ahmed and I have tried to write a plan to install the Scorpion warheads in the Hiroshima missiles—"

Sharef interrupted. "Take this in sequence. First, are we able to assemble the Scorpions without Dr. Abu-i-Wafa?" There was a part of Sharef that did not want to consider launching a weapon that would kill over half-a-million people from a week-long attack of radiation poisoning, even if they were from the same nation that had sunk the *Sahand*. The American Navy was what he really wanted to attack. Women and children and old men in Washington, D.C., had nothing to do with the attack on his frigate, and his submarine should have no business killing them. Even if it would win the war, a big if in his view, he had doubts he would want to do it.

Ahmed spoke up. "The Scorpions are already assembled. Dr. Wafa left detailed instructions and the units were modular and required a minimum of tools. The danger was in the charging of chemicals and compressed gases to the prereaction chambers and the insertion of the plutonium and cobalt into the dispersion shell, but the risk is now behind us. We are ready to insert the warheads into the missiles."

"We can bring the warheads to the middle level at the—"

"Quzwini!" The mechanical officer froze at the anger in Sharef's voice. "Colonel Ahmed, why was this dangerous operation done without my permission?"

"*I gave* Colonel Ahmed permission, Commodore," Sihoud's deep voice said. The general leaned back in the chair as if that were enough.

"General, the permission was not yours to give. As I told you, I'm in command of this submarine, and until I'm dead, I and I alone will give the orders that compromise ship safety. If you are unable to understand that, sir, I will lock you in your stateroom."

Silence. Sihoud smiled slightly. "You were unconscious at the time, Commodore. I assumed responsibility. I am sorry if I have trespassed on your . . . turf."

Sharef glared at him but let it pass. "Continue, Quzwini."

"Yessir. The two warheads weigh about 3000 kilograms. Handling them from the lower level to the upper will be difficult. I plan to cut a hole in the deckplates of this level centerline just aft of the door to the head. We will weld lifting lugs onto the steel deck of the upper level, then use chainfalls to bring the units out of the lower deck. Once on the middle level we will work the units into the head door, enlarging it if we have to, then remove the cosmetic partition obscuring the access hatch to the forward ballast tank."

"That access hatch is not hinged, Quzwini, it's welded shut," Sharef said.

"We'll torch it open, then reweld it shut when we're done. The ship will remain submerged with the ballast tank full. We'll be putting the Hiroshima missiles in tubes one and six. Number one is in the center of the tank, giving us the most fore-and-aft room to pull out the missile. Number six is in the first ring. Only one and three have cruise missiles loaded. Six is the best choice, it is higher up, which gives us a larger margin of error should the ballast tank flood during the operation."

"What speed will we need for depth control with a ballast tank full of air?"

"We'll need to be shallow to keep the pressure down, but speed will probably need to be fifty or sixty clicks so that the X-tail can compensate for the buoyancy using hydrodynamic forces. Unfortunately we could have a wake from shallow speeds near the surface, so I believe a compromise will put us at a depth of 100 meters."

"That means you will be working in ten atmospheres of pressure," Sharef said. "Your time is limited and you'll need to depressurize slowly to avoid the bends."

"We've thought of that, sir. Time to perform this op will be about ten hours. Ballast-tank entry will last for another two to depressure by coming shallower. The two-hour depressurization will be timed to be at night so our surface wake will not be noticed by casual shipping or observation satellites. And even if it is, it's a big ocean and no one knows where we went after we left Gibraltar, so a surface disturbance won't be tied to us."

"And how will you get to the warheads?"

"We thought about torching the after-part of the tube and pulling the missile out one module at a time to get to the warhead, then reassembling. That would take several days of disassembly and reassembly in a half-flooded ballast tank with poor lighting. It would not work."

"I know that," Sharef said. It was the obstacle he'd tried to overcome since he'd been told about the mission. Short of opening a tube bow cap and withdrawing the weapon from in front of the ship, there seemed no way to get the warheads in.

"We'll torch-cut the forward top ends of the tubes, right at the ring joint from missile to warhead. The metal will be removed, the old warhead disassembled and the new one inserted. The main struggle will be handling the warheads and the metal pieces from the tubes. More lifting lugs and chainfalls."

"Have you thought of what happens when you cut into a tube with a torch directly above a live warhead?" Sharef asked. "You'll blow a twenty-meter hole in the nose cone."

"No," Ahmed said, "we'll get the high explosive out first. We'll drill a hole in the top of the tube with a titanium drill bit, continuing into the Hiroshima warhead. A second hole will be drilled on the side of the tube for insertion of a heating element to melt the explosive, which will be sucked out the top hole. We think we can evacuate ninety percent of the explosive mass this way. The rest will be neutralized with a nitrogen-bottle purge from the side hole through the top hole. The nitrogen won't prevent burning the remaining explosive but it will keep a sustained fire from burning in the tube and lighting off the solid rocket-booster fuel."

"Commodore, to save time and accomplish the mission," Sihoud said, standing, "Colonel Ahmed requests permission to load the warheads."

"Permission granted, Ahmed. Please go blow your head off."

Tawkidi helped him back to his stateroom, where he collapsed into his bed, his face gray with pain and fatigue.

"Commander, bring in the doctor and ask him to bring his damn drugs."

"Yes, sir. Try to rest."

The injection took him away from the hard surface of pain and delivered him to sleep, but not before he imagined a hundred thousand faces of innocent children imploring him not to launch the missiles.

Western Atlantic
Point Bravo Hold Position, 500 Nautical Miles East of Long Island
USS Seawolf

Pacino didn't know which would be worse . . . have the technician wire in the new circuit and the whole crew would know what his idea was, or wire it in himself and have the crew wonder why the ship's captain would be wiring up his own work. Either way it would seem unusual, unprecedented. Captains didn't usually get their hands dirty, nor did they even authorize the kind of changes Pacino wanted, much less think of those changes themselves. But this was not something he wanted shared with the crew. It would be a disservice to them for him to wear his doubts and fears on his face . . . a crew stood on the foundation of their captain's confidence. And anyone who knew about this circuit, Vaughn on down, would see that his confidence had come close to running out . . .

No, that wasn't really true. The circuit was a contingency. Just in case. His *Seawolf* would take the Destiny because it was quieter, faster, and more capable than the 688s that had been put on the bottom. He was trying to reassure himself, but a voice said *your weapons are the same as the 688's*.

Tired of his own internal debates, Pacino assembled the rotary switch to the front of a metal box, checking the installation from the front. He terminated the wires to the switch and ran the cable through a hole in the top of the box, the cable shield fitting through a coupling that screwed into the hole. He coiled the cable and tie-wrapped it together so he could carry it, putting it in the canvas tool bag with the cordless drill, the tie wraps, the wire-pulling rope, the screwdriver and the wire-insulation remover. He looked over the wiring diagram one last time, realizing that he had memorized the page where he had decided to tie into the hardwired actuation circuitry.

He packed the materials into a storage cabinet. Its installation would have to wait until the midwatch, when the crew's mess would be empty. He set his alarm for 0300, turned off the overheads and climbed into his rack, the file open on his stomach. It was a file marked SCI TOP SECRET— EARLY RETIREMENT, given to him by Admiral Donchez, the neatly typed pages bound in a paperback binding. Pacino began reading the thick report, starting at the beginning with all known information about the Destiny-class submarine. A hundred pages later Pacino began to wonder if *Seawolf* really had any kind of chance against the new machine. Another hundred pages completed the Destiny information, the long section on the computer system both enlightening and confusing.

At 0100 the OOD called and asked permission to take the ship to periscope depth to get their radio traffic from the satellite. Pacino gave him permission, feeling the deck angle upward, the level-off, then the gentle rocking of the deck in the waves from the surface. After a few minutes, the ship went deep again, the hull groaning as it took on the load of the seawater pressure, leveling off at 550 feet, the deck once again steady. Ten minutes later a rap came at the door as the radioman brought the message board. Pacino scanned it—nothing from Steinman or Donchez. Hurry up and wait, he thought. He signed the routine messages, sent the board out with the radioman and returned to his report.

The next section was a collection of profiles of the crew members. The section on Commodore Abbas Alai Sharef was full of interesting details, the most ominous the sinking of the *Sahand* in 1988. Pacino didn't even remember that operation—he'd been at sea on his XO tour at the time, under the polar icecap trailing a Soviet Akula-class submarine that had just sailed out of Severodvinsk shipyard on its Arctic Ocean sea trials. That mission had gotten hairy enough that a three-sentence report on the radio message board about the U.S. Navy attack on the Iranian fleet had seemed insignificant. But the attack, conducted in reprisal for Iranian boarding and strafing of merchant ships in the Persian Gulf, did in retrospect seem an overreaction. The file included a *Time* magazine report as well as the article from the New York *Times*. Not very much detail in the open media, but a paragraph from a Naval Intelligence target evaluation estimate revealed that the *Sahand* had taken the hit hard with only a handful of survivors. Sharef had been one of them, which was bound to make him a fighter with a particular hatred where the U.S. Navy was concerned. Pacino found another fact even more disturbing, that Sharef had no family, no wife, no children. Nothing that would whisper in his ear to survive to fight another day. The sort of man who would fight to the death. But then, many of the Islamic fighters were like that, believing death in battle to be a first-class ticket to heaven. Pacino finished the section on Sharef and continued through the gossip sheet with the first officer, Captain al-Kunis, all the way to the file on the known junior officers—necessary since any one of the officers might assume command if Sharef died.

By the time Pacino finished the report it was 0230. He decided to start his wiring modification early, rolling out of bed and slipping into his shoes. He took the canvas bag from the locker and left through his stateroom's door to the middle level's central passageway. A long walk to the aft bulkhead, where it doglegged to starboard at the hatchway to the reactor compartment's shielded tunnel. Pacino stopped there, considering the hatch to the nuclear spaces, the bulkhead and heavy hatch good for the full pressure of the outer hull; just in case the forward part of the ship flooded and took the ship down, the aft compartments could still survive until the main hull steel failed and crushed. Pacino moved into the hatch, reaching out his hand with eyes shut to a point on the bulkhead of the forward compartment, then keeping his hand there while he climbed back into the forward compartment passageway. The spot on the bulkhead was immediately next to the hatch at chest level. It was a bad location, too easily noticeable by the traffic going into the aft compartments, but it would have to do.

Pacino pulled out the drill and made two small holes in a bracket bolted into the bulkhead, then mounted two new brackets to the heavier steel bracket and bolted the new switch box to the bracket, the box now secured to the bulkhead, where Pacino had reached for it from the other side of the hatch. It felt secure. The cable run came next as Pacino pulled the wiring up from the box into a cable run going upward and into the overhead with a couple hundred other cables. The cable run would not be a problem. He ran the cable into the overhead and turned it forward toward the bulkhead to the ESM room, the electronics-filled room used for interception of radio and radar signals on the surface. The space would be abandoned during the submerged run. Pacino drilled a hole in the bulkhead where it met the overhead and threaded the cable through it, a long job since there was a hundred feet of the cable. A few tie wraps to keep the cable in place with the other cables, and this part of the installation was done.

Pacino turned to examine his work. It looked professional but too new. He hadn't thought about that. He reached up into the overhead and found several hard-to-reach places that hadn't been well-cleaned by the crew after the dust and mess of the shipyard, and brought out a handful of grease and dust and dirt. He smeared it lightly on the cables, taking away their new shiny look, and put some on the sides of the switch box. Then some on the front, which he promptly wiped off with a cloth. The switch and box now looked like they'd been with the ship since the shipyard period. Pacino took a small yellow tag from the box and scribbled on it, then attached the tag to the switch. The tag said ooc, out of commission, the tag alerting the crew that the gear didn't work so not to bother operating the switches. He stepped back and looked at it, dissatisfied. The yellow tag drew attention to the switch—better to leave it untagged. He removed the tag and walked forward along the passageway to the door to ESM.

He listened at the door for a few moments, then entered the combination to the door lock and went in, the bag left in the passageway in case one of the electronics techs were there, but the room was deserted. Pacino pulled in the tool bag and shut the self-locking door behind him. The room was little more than a cubbyhole with two padded control seats and walls stacked with electronic equipment racks. Pacino found the cable he'd fed in from the outside and pulled the cable across the room to the forward bulkhead, cut a hole in that wall and tie-wrapped the cable into the already cable-crowded overhead, then rubbed it with dirt as before. He decided to check the radio room before he fed the cable through; it was deserted as well. He fed in the cable, then looked around ESM for telltale signs of his trip.

Radio was a bigger version of ESM, not a space designed to look pretty or offer comfort. He duplicated his actions from ESM, but instead of running the cable forward, took the cable down to the deck at the forward outboard bulkhead, then drilled a hole in the deck. He fed the cable through the deck to the level below, checked his work again, then left and went to the lower level torpedo room, usually a room booming with activity but now silent since it was doubling as a bunking space. The lights were switched to red to dim the space's usual glare, and the room resonated with snoring. No one was awake to confront him. He climbed onto the top of the outboard Vortex tube, the metal cold and hard, the space minimal between tube and overhead, and found the cable let down from the deck of the radio room. Slowly he fed the cable forward in the overhead, his back aching as he tied the cable up into the overhead with a thousand other cables, finally climbing back down onto the narrow deckplates at the forward part of the room, turning the cable toward the centerline until he had fed it above a long panel that ran athwartships. He opened the panel cover, reached up into the overhead and pulled the wire down into the interior of the panel. From the outside of the panel, no one could tell he had made this unauthorized alteration. Back inside the panel he found the circuit board he'd been looking for, traced the wiring to a relay panel and hoped the wiring was in accord with the technical manual. He grabbed the wire insulation remover and clipped a power wire going to relay R141 set into the aft wall of the panel, then tested the wire for voltage—it was dead. Pacino stripped the insulation off, crimped on terminals at either end and terminated each end on the screws of a small termination block he pulled out of the tool kit. He pulled the cable he'd wired in, screwing its terminations onto the new terminal block. The work was finished but for tie-wrapping the new cable so it was out of the way. He checked the wiring one last time, satisfied that it looked like it would work.

He wished he could test it, but he'd need another body to hit the switch while he watched the R141 relay, and the relay output would have to be jumped so it wouldn't feed the circuit further downstream. Testing the circuit would be more risky than its installation. It would have to do as it was. Pacino hoped no one would be going into the panel. He screwed the panel closure devices shut, tucked the bag into his grease-covered poopysuit and hurried back to his stateroom. Remarkably, no one had seen him.

Now all he could hope for was that he'd never need to use the switch, but that if he did, it would work.

THURSDAY, 2 JANUARY

**North Atlantic
CNFS *Hegira***

Sharef needed Tawkidi's help getting from bed to his conference table.

"I seem to be getting weaker," Sharef said.

"The doctor said the broken rib was infected and so was your eye. Hasn't the medicine been working?"

Sharef didn't want to answer the question. He felt like his body wanted to shut down and die. Awkward timing.

Rakish Ahmed and General Sihoud entered without knocking.

"Knock before you come into the captain's stateroom," Tawkidi snapped at Ahmed, and by implication at Sihoud.

"We've come to brief the commodore on the ballast-tank work," Ahmed said. "We can skip that if you have trouble with our protocol."

"Continue, Colonel," Sharef said, wanting to get the briefing over with.

"What we estimated to be a ten-hour job in the tanks is becoming more a sixty-hour job. With rest periods and time for the body to recover from the pressurization we would need six days."

"We don't have six—"

"I know, Commodore. That is why I have cut the missile work down to installation of only one Scorpion warhead into tube number one."

"That leaves only one missile," Tawkidi pointed out. "Is there enough radiation from a single missile?"

"More than enough," Ahmed said.

"But there will be no redundancy. If something goes wrong with missile number one there is no backup."

Ahmed looked at him. "Nothing will go wrong."

"Where are you now, Colonel?" Sharef said.

"The Scorpion warhead has been rigged into the forward head on the middle level, just outside the door to the ballast tank. The door is cut open but for now is sealed with putty. We entered the tank and drilled into tube one. The high explosive is removed. We are ready to cut the section of tube in the next ballast-tank entry. The cut-out should take the entire ten hours. The third entry will be devoted to insertion of the Scorpion warhead and rewelding on the patch. The missile will be fully tested with the warhead in place, including electronic readbacks from the missile to the weapon-control processor and back."

Sharef nodded. "Yes, I can see you've got a good idea how to finish. But finishing is three-quarters of the work, Colonel. Meanwhile the ship has to proceed at sixty-five clicks to maintain depth control because of the ballast tank. Let me show you what that rate of speed has done for us."

Tawkidi, on cue, rolled out a polar projection chart showing their great circle route, originally taking them into the North Atlantic. Their position was marked with a heavy dot. A range circle was drawn around Washington, D.C. The dot looked very close to the range radius.

"As you can see, we are only 200 kilometers from the range circle around Washington, D.C. If we continue at this speed for the thirty hours you've said it will take to do your work, that is almost another 2,000 kilometers, putting us into the middle of the Labrador Sea. We will be unable to continue, we will run out of ocean. I have planned this track to keep this mission stealthy, so do not suggest turning south along the U.S. east coast. Such a track would take us into heavy shipping lanes and highly patrolled operational areas, and the range of the Hiroshima missile does not need us to get closer. In addition, Colonel, mission success is based on the Hiroshima coming out of the arctic north, from a bearing the Americans would not suspect as being a threat axis. It will look like a Concorde or supersonic private jet coming over the pole from Europe, if it shows up on radar at all, and we have to assume that the radar cloaking may not be perfect."

"Commodore, I agree. Do not turn south. You cannot slow down until we can reflood the ballast tank. Turn to the north as you have always intended and proceed up the Davis Strait between Greenland and Canada's Baffin Island."

"We will be out of range 1,200 kilometers after the turn to the north. Moreover, the marginal ice zone begins here, north of the Greenland tip. The permanent ice pack is here, well before the range mark. I would say we have a thousand kilometers from the base of the Davis Strait before we run out of open water."

"We will not need the additional time at speed, Commodore. Thirty hours, 2,000 kilometers, with 1,000 more to use if we need it going north. If we get to the permanent ice pack line at—where is that?—the Baffin Bay, we'll reverse course and turn back to the south."

Ahmed had come up with the answer Sharef had wanted to tell him in the beginning, but he had the impression that if he had proposed it Ahmed would have argued to turn south. Patrolling in the Baffin Bay's marginal ice zone, for weeks if they needed to, was safe. Secluded and safe. The Americans and Canadians would not find him there, he believed.

"That brings up my second concern, Colonel. The matter of our speed. Not only does it consume distance quickly, it risks our detection. The faster we go, the louder we are, the more likely we are to be detected. The monitors of my Second Captain system show a rupture of the outer hull in the aft ballast tank. That creates a flow-induced resonance—the hole whistles in the water flow."

"So?"

"So we could be tracked. I am not just concerned with the distance we cover, and I have not been overly worried about the increased noise levels in mid-Atlantic, but as we get closer to the continent of North America I would very much like to reduce speed."

"We are on a rest period now. We will not go back into the ballast tank for another seven hours. If we hurry that up it will be hazardous for your officers helping me in the tank. And we can't flood the tank because we would have to seal the hatch by welding it shut, and welding it would take hours, and cutting it open again would take more hours. We would waste time."

"The hatch is sealed now with the plastic sealant? We could partially flood the tank up to the base of the hatch. With the tank half full I should be able to take some of the speed off."

"I have no objection."

"Commander Tawkidi, do you think you will be able to vent the tank to raise the level up to the hatch and allow us to slow?"

"Yes, Commodore. The Second Captain can do the calculations easily. It will create some noise level as we release the ballast-tank air, but we could slow down to as low as twenty-five clicks."

"Make it so. Colonel, after your second tank entry I will want another progress report. Anything to say, General Sihoud?"

Sihoud had been quiet, too quiet, for the entire trip. Tawkidi had reported that he had been in the first-officer stateroom since the recovery from the torpedo. He had not come out for meals and had refused meals in the stateroom. He looked unwell.

"Commodore," Sihoud said, his voice showing no sign of stress, the depth of it still commanding. But there was something in his eyes, Sharef thought. "You and Colonel Ahmed have thoroughly planned the weapon deployment. For this I compliment you both. I urge you two to continue working together to get the Scorpion weapon launched. Once it is airborne we will prevail in our struggle. That is all I have to say."

Sharef watched Ahmed and Sihoud leave, his thoughts interrupted by Tawkidi.

"I'll be flooding the tank now, sir, and slowing. You should rest until Ahmed finishes the next tank entry."

"I will," Sharef said, accepting Tawkidi's help into his bed, swallowing the pills from the table with water Tawkidi had brought.

As he stared at the overhead above his bed, Sharef remembered Sihoud's eyes. They were no longer bright but seemed flat, dead. As though already resigned to his own death. Well, Sharef thought, he didn't share Sihoud's fanaticism that justified everything in the name of his beloved Allah. On the other hand, he was, in effect, a captive on his own ship, in spite of what he had told Ahmed and Sihoud.

His frustrations were relieved only when the heavy curtain of drowsiness descended on him, the drugs from the doctor taking over.

USS *Phoenix*

Kane looked uneasily at the chart. Their course through the past twenty hours had been straight-edge steady, a bullet heading directly to the south of Greenland's southernmost point at Cape Farewell. For the past thirteen hours Target One had been going thirty-five knots, twice the speed that Kane would have transited the Atlantic. At the beginning of the thirty-five-knot run the contact had put out a loud transient. Sanderson said it sounded like he had blown a ballast tank as if he intended to surface but he had continued on submerged. They were now halfway to Greenland, the ETA to the Canadian coast two days from now, maybe less.

The longer he followed the Destiny the more its escape from the Med remained a mystery, and the deeper the mystery had grown. He had taken a large plot showing the North Atlantic and much of the surrounding north hemisphere and with thin orange navigation tape placed their track on it since Gibraltar. He had extended the tape into the Med to Kassab, where the Destiny had begun her mission. With the knowledge that General Sihoud was aboard, the escape from the Med and the beeline for the Canadian coast could be interpreted several ways.

Perhaps Sihoud had decided to abdicate or surrender and had agreed to leave the UIF with a sub, to give up in Newfoundland or Labrador or Greenland. Yeah, right. Or maybe he was going to a special peace talk to be conducted in Canada or Greenland, talks so secret that he had to disappear in the eyes of his own military. But why would a leader going to a secret peace meeting sink two ships to get there? That made no sense. What if he was bringing some kind of weapon out of the Med to fire at the U.S.? Why wouldn't he simply shoot it from the Med? Range —the Med was a long way away. The Japanese might have sold the UIF a few supersonic high-altitude cruise missiles and maybe Sihoud thought he could bring them close so that they would be in range. But why not just proceed on a straight line toward the American east coast then? And what damage could a conventional cruise missile do? A couple terrorists with some plastic explosive in the sewer system could do more damage and have better odds on success than trying to lob a cruise missile into the east coast's radar-saturated environment.

What if he'd found a way to make a nuke? He would come as close as he could to his target and launch it in. Assuming he had a delivery vehicle. Maybe he was going to drop off a nuclear weapon in the Labrador Sea, surfacing at night and off-loading it onto a fishing vessel, and the fishing vessel would take it to some sleepy Canadian port, where a battered rental car could take it to the border and bring it to Boston or New York or D.C. Or a seaplane could just fly it in with no stops.

Sure, Kane, sure . . . He'd just radio that in a contact message and Admiral Steinman would have a laugh and send him a box full of old Alistair MacLean novels. Besides, intelligence was not his function. His role was gathering the raw data. So far they had boxcars full of raw data he needed to tell someone about. And he hadn't been able to because of the speed of the Destiny. He simply could not afford to slow down and come to PD to transmit on HF.

He turned from the chart and wandered to the middle level to get a cup of coffee. The ship was a ghost town. Control was busy with trailing the Destiny, the room's hustle making thinking difficult. He couldn't bounce his ideas off of McDonne, since the XO was sleeping, preparing to take over for Kane during the evening and midwatch. Out of the corner of his eye he saw Senior Chief Binghamton in the crew's mess. He summoned the radioman to the wardroom.

"Yes, Captain."

"Any change in the status of the UHF gear?"

"Still down hard, sir. For us, it's HF or nothing."

"What about spare parts for the—"

"Captain," a voice rang out from the passageway. "Captain?"

"He's here," Binghamton said. The phonetalker in the passageway was holding a long cord coiled in his hand, his duty to relay communications from the middle level to control when rigged for ultraquiet so that the Circuit One PA speakers did not need to be used.

"Control's calling, sir. OOD wants you up there ASAP."

"On the way." Kane hurried up the stairs to the upper level, made control in a few strides. Control was stuffy and crowded, the OOD and junior officer of the deck standing at the attack-center consoles, plotters manning manual plots, conversations relayed in murmurs. Jensen had the conn, his eyes bloodshot from lack of sleep or from the wounds he'd taken during the grounding.

"Skipper, Target One just slowed. We've got him at thirteen knots. No sign of a counterdetection or a baffle-clear maneuver. And he's just put out a whopper of a transient. Smoot's on watch in sonar, said it sounded like venting a ballast tank."

This was Kane's chance to pop up to periscope depth and radio the contact report. It might be his only chance. Slowing and going to PD risked losing the contact, but it had to be done. With the Destiny at thirteen knots Kane could let him get ahead and still be able to catch up to him after lingering at PD. He told himself he'd give it twenty minutes at periscope depth, no more.

"Contact range?"

"Nine thousand yards."

"Any change in Target One course?"

"No, sir, he's going straighter than an arrow."

"Increase speed to twenty knots, close the range to 5,000, then take her up to PD at seven knots, no baffle clear. I'll be in radio. Let's go, take her up."

Kane's heart was beating in his throat by the time the ship leveled off at periscope depth, the maneuver done without pausing to clear baffles and check surface traffic at 150 feet. Binghamton's shaved scalp beaded up with sweat as he called for the BIGMOUTH multifrequency antenna, a green light coming on when the telephone-pole-shaped mast was fully extended. The senior chief handed Kane a headset with a boom microphone while strapping on his own. The consoles in front of him beeped and buzzed as he adjusted frequencies and juggled a codebook.

"Norfolk NavCom Center, this is Tango Two Foxtrot," Binghamton called, the T2F the January 2 call sign for the *Phoenix*. He repeated the call several times, a whistling sound rising and falling from the transceiver, static blaring out over the speakers.

"Come on, come on," Kane muttered, intensely aware that the Destiny was driving on ahead, opening the range.

"Norfolk NavCom Center, this is Tango Two Foxtrot, over."

Static.

"NavCom, this is Tango Two Foxtrot with a Navy Blue message, over."

Static, broken by a distorted voice, then more whistling on the speaker.

"NavCom, this is Tango Two Foxtrot with a flash Navy Blue, over."

A hissing, interrupted briefly by a voice: "TWO FOX . . ."

"Come on, Senior," Kane said, more to himself than Binghamton.

"NavCom, this is Tango Two Foxtrot with Navy Blue to follow. Do you copy, over?"

"TANG . . . OOH . . . OX . . . EED YOU FIVE BY . . . ANSMIT . . . OVER."

"Is that the best we can do, Senior?"

"Let's transmit and see if they can read back."

Kane glanced at a message form he'd scratched out.

"Norfolk NavCom Center, this is Tango Two Foxtrot," he said slowly and clearly. "Navy Blue message to follow, break." Navy Blue meant the message was a flash transmission to go directly to Admiral Donchez in the Pentagon. "Tango Two Foxtrot reports own position at latitude five two degrees four minutes twelve seconds November, longitude three three degrees seventeen minutes four zero seconds whiskey, break." Kane had agonized over the next section of the message, knowing it was going out with no encryption, able to be heard by UIF receivers if they were listening. "Our customer was met at the original point of contact and continued to present location with probable destination Labrador Sea, speed three five for last twenty hours with recent slowing to speed one three. Tango Two Foxtrot damaged but recovered, but UHF radios out of commission. Our garage has no more Matthew-Luke-and-John five zero vehicles." A way of getting across that he was out of Mark 50 torpedoes. "Further updates to follow, break. Bravo tango. I say again, Navy Blue message to follow . . ." Kane repeated the transmission and asked for a readback.

The speakers whistled and sputtered.

"ANGO . . . AVY BLUE . . . REPORT . . . OSITION LAT . . . FIVE TWO DE . . . NOVEMBER, LONG . . . THREETH . . . SEVENTEEN MIN . . . WHISKEY . . ."

The rest of the readback continued that way. Kane looked at Binghamton. There was enough of the message coming back that it seemed safe to assume that they'd received it, if it was really the naval communications center they were talking to.

"TANGO TWO . . . NAVCOM . . . AUTHENTICATE GOLF . . . OVER."

Binghamton took over. "Say again, NavCom, you are coming in garbled."

"AUTHENTICATE GO . . . VICTOR THR . . ."

"NavCom, this is Tango Two Foxtrot, confirming, do you desire authenticate golf victor three?"

"TANGO . . . AFFIRMA . . ."

Binghamton grabbed the codebook from the ledge, the black volume marked TOP SECRET—COMSEC, the designation for the highest communications security classification.

"Let's see here," the senior chief mumbled to himself, "today is the second of January, here's golf, down to the victor column, to the three line. Golf victor three should authenticate as W3B. Do you concur, sir?"

Kane looked at the codebook, the rows and columns meaningless numbers and letters. The NavCom center was trying to verify that they really were the *Phoenix* by asking them to decode an alphanumeric that could be decoded only by having a codebook, and the new codebooks were printed for individual ships—only the *Phoenix* had this version of the codebook. Anyone else out there would be unable to decipher GV3 as W3B. It would positively mark their message as authentic.

"NavCom, this is Tango Two Foxtrot, we authenticate as whiskey three bravo, repeat whiskey three bravo, over."

" . . FOXTROT . . . ROGER YOUR . . . MESSAGE RE . . . NAVCOM . . . OUT."

"I think they got it, Skipper."

"Conn, radio, lower the BIGMOUTH and go deep!" Kane shouted to the control-room speaker microphone. The deck plunged downward before he could get out of radio and back into control.

Now came the hard part. Could they find Target One again after all that?

National Security Agency Headquarters
Fort Meade, Maryland
Building 427 Special Compartmented Information Facility

It had been overcast with heavy featureless clouds when the sun had set. Donchez had taken the limo from the Pentagon to nearby Fort Meade, halfway between D.C. and Baltimore along the Baltimore-Washington Expressway. By the time the car approached the beltway the blizzard started, slowing them down. A half-hour later the Lincoln's tires were buried in snow at the gate of Fort Meade. When Donchez got out at Building 427 the snow covered him, making his long black overcoat white in just twenty steps to the building entrance.

"I can see we'll be sleeping here tonight," Donchez told his aide Rummel. "Better grab us a couple rooms at the BOQ before we get too involved at the briefing."

Donchez had asked for the briefing in his own SCIF, but the NSA had insisted that they brief him here. The NSA had won the early joint-operations turf battles for control of interception and decoding of foreign communications, competing successfully with the Combined Intelligence Agency's crypto division. The Dole Act's reorganization of the CIA, the DIA, and NSA had left the NSA not only whole but bigger, until CIA's crypto personnel found themselves working for NSA at Fort Meade. Donchez conceded the NSA folks were professional and good, but also a strange breed.

Donchez and his aide scanned into the front security entrance of the brick building 427, which could have passed for a recently constructed high school, the brick new, the architecture pleasing but ordinary, made unusual only by the absence of windows. A naval officer met them inside per Donchez's instructions, since normal procedure would have the commander of the base meet Donchez personally and escort him in, but Donchez had ordered the ceremony skipped. They were escorted to the electronic checkpoint and then deeper into the building, passing two more security checkpoints before they came to the entrance to the SCIF, the double lead-lined doors guarded by an armed sentry. The check-in process was much longer here.

Finally they were led into the SCIF room, the furnishings new and comfortable, the leather chairs and oak table and soft wall-coverings making the room appear to be a boardroom. Donchez barely noticed, his impatience taking over.

The briefer, an Army colonel, came in an interior door with papers and videotapes. He looked young and fresh-faced to be a senior officer, rosy cheeks and round wire-frame glasses, his mustache looking as if it belonged to a teenager.

"I'm Col. John Parker. I run the computer crypto detail. Pleased to meet you, sir." Parker had a nasal high-pitched voice but spoke briskly. "These handouts are an abstract of the presentation. I know you're pushed for time so I'll get right to the point. You may not even want to see the raw data but I think the abstract may make you want to see it anyway."

"Fine, Colonel. Give me the short version first."

"Yes, sir. The intercepted computer data and files, as well as the debriefing of Muhammad Ibn al-Kabba, the UIF scientist we captured, all indicate the UIF has come up with a new kind of weapon. It's technically called a dispersion adhesion explosive using plutonium for the poison. It's nowhere near the destructive potential of a nuclear warhead, but with a small fraction of the plutonium, this weapon goes a very long way. I would compare it to a neutron bomb that achieves its death potential through radioactivity rather than blast effect. This does something similar, but instead of a single burst of neutron flux, it relies on exposure to the plutonium, the dust getting into ventilation systems and into the victims' lungs, onto the victims' skin, sticking to surfaces of streets and buildings. If you're anywhere near ground zero you'll die, even if you're driving through at ninety miles per or in the basement of a building that dust will get you. And it can't be washed away—the cleanup crews would die. If this thing is dropped on a large city, the casualties would number in the millions. And it gets worse. With a neutron weapon or nuclear warhead, within a year you can clean up and rebuild. Not so here. The target city would be radioactive and uninhabitable for untold years to come."

Donchez sat through five minutes of an explanation of the glue bomb's purpose and function. He interrupted the colonel. "How many do they have?"

"Two, maybe three."

"Delivery system?"

"A warhead inserted onto the tip of a Hiroshima missile. Range is only 1,900 nautical miles. A bit too small to be a long-range threat."

"So they'd need to get close to launch it at us. Or deliver it by aircraft."

"Or hand-carry it. But the Hiroshima missile is what the data says was the preferred method, since it's a high-altitude supersonic vehicle with radar-evading electronics."

"Aren't there two versions of the Hiroshima?"

"Sea-launched and aircraft-launched, yes."

"Same missile?"

"No, the sea-launched device is designed to be ejected from a submerged tube launcher on a sub, so it has a waterproof capsule—that doesn't change the characteristics of the missile, but this version must start its trip at zero velocity at sea level, so its booster rocket stage is much bigger. The air-launched version's solid rocket booster is tiny by comparison."

"Warheads the same size?"

"No, the air-launched version has a bigger warhead capacity since it's got the lighter rocket. Six thousand kilos for the air-launched, only 3,500 for the sea-launched version."

"How heavy is this dirty dust-bomb's warhead?"

"Let's see . . ." The colonel searched his data. "We never added this up." He scratched two columns on a pad, flipping through a large binder, adding up the second column of weights.

"There are a few components I'd be guessing at as far as mass is concerned, sir, but within a few percent, this warhead is about three metric tons. That's 3,000 kilos, give or take a few hundred."

"Where did they put the operational warheads?"

"We think they took them to the Mediterranean coast at Kassab."

Destiny's base, Donchez thought. With two warheads sized for a sea-launched weapon system that needed to be within 1,900 miles to hit its target. And Destiny had broken out of the Med and was last detected heading west.

He stood, he'd heard enough. He didn't need the raw data, surprising the colonel, who had intended to go through the whole briefing. Apparently, Donchez thought, Colonel Parker was not used to people believing his interpretations.

"Thank you, Colonel. You've been most helpful."

He and Rummel were only twenty feet down the hallway when an Army sergeant called out to them.

"Admiral? Admiral Donchez? Flash message for you, sir, relayed from Norfolk Naval Communications Center about four minutes ago. A Captain Brandt is standing by to answer questions on it, if you'll come with me to the phone room."

Donchez accepted the metal clipboard with the message and read while walking to the phone center. Captain Brandt, the commander of NavCom, was on hold on a white phone offered him by a corporal.

"Donchez here. Brandt, what is this?"

"That transmission just came in on HF, Admiral. Our direction finders didn't get an accurate bearing, but we think it came from the North Atlantic. The sender would appear to be the USS *Phoenix.*"

"How do you know?"

"We asked him to authenticate with the most recent edition of the codebook. He answered correctly from codebook number 547. That codebook was only put aboard the *Phoenix.*"

"Thanks, Captain." Donchez handed the phone back. "Where's the communication facility?"

Within four minutes Donchez was scratching out a message to go to the *Seawolf.* Two minutes after that the message was transmitted, with a copy of *Phoenix*'s message sent to Pacino.

"Fred, get an emergency meeting with Barczynski and his staff."

"That won't be easy, sir," Rummel said, a phone in his ear. "They're all snowed in. The streets aren't plowed, we've got over eighteen inches of drifted snow in some sections of Maryland. If we leave here we might not make wherever we're going. And forget about a chopper. No one's flying, they're all grounded. They've got zero visibility with gusting forty-five-knot winds at the Pentagon helipad. Washington National's closed, so is Dulles, Andrews, BWI, Suburban—"

"Sounds like we're hunkering down here. We could have picked a worse place to get snowed in. Every communication system we'd ever need is right here. What about getting them on a conference call?"

"We'll get a few. Barczynski and Clough have secure phones. The others, I don't know."

"President still in Key West?"

"Yessir."

"Well, get going on setting up a secure phone connection to Generals Barczynski and Clough, and have the White House operator get the president ready a half-hour after we start with the general."

Donchez wandered toward the building entrance, back through the layers of security checkpoints, until he reached the lobby with its large plate glass windows. Outside the storm raged, the road covered, the snow falling nearly horizontally. He pulled out a Havana and flicked his Zippo, glaring at a security guard who looked like he might tell Donchez there was no smoking inside.

A dispersion glue bomb, Donchez thought. With enough radioactivity to kill a city. He looked at the raging blizzard, wondering what effect, if any, the snow would have on the plutonium-dust killer. It might be the only thing that could save Washington, if Washington was the target.

Phoenix might track the Destiny. But it was up to Michael Pacino to take *this* son of a bitch out.

30

FRIDAY, 3 JANUARY

Western Atlantic
Point Bravo Hold Position, 500 Nautical Miles East of Long Island
USS *Seawolf*

While a phone rang in General Barczynski's Fairfax, Virginia, residence, the phone next to Pacino's bunk buzzed, both phones attempting to convey the same information.

Five minutes after the phone buzzed, the local time just after midnight, Pacino stood in the control room with a crowd of officers, the North Atlantic chart out, the position of the *Phoenix* plotted with a bright blue dot, an orange navigation tape strip showing a straight line from Gibraltar in the Med to the Labrador Sea. As the message from Donchez had indicated, the chart plotter had drawn a red circle 1,900 miles around Washington, a blue one around Boston, a green one around Halifax, Nova Scotia, a purple one around Toronto. The blue dot was inside all the circles, the circle surrounding the southernmost city, Washington, ending halfway up the Davis Strait between Greenland and Newfoundland almost to the Baffin Bay.

Pacino read the messages again. He could hardly believe it. Destiny, if it turned north, would be in the marginal ice zone by the afternoon. And it would definitely turn north, since it had come so far north already. If Donchez was right about the Hiroshima-missile theory, the Destiny had been in range of the northeastern cities for some time, at least a day. Which seemed to go against the whole idea. If the Destiny was coming to throw up these Hiroshima missiles, why hadn't it already fired them?

And what the hell was the *Phoenix* doing? Here's a ship that gets almost blown away, shoots every damned torpedo in the inventory, and then follows the Destiny into the Atlantic. Whoever her skipper was, he was either very brave or very stupid, and probably some combination of the two. Pacino didn't stop to think what he would have done in the same situation, knowing that he probably would have trailed the Destiny, but scoffing at the idea that he'd be dumb enough not to save a torpedo for himself.

It didn't answer one question that nagged at him—if the Destiny had been so damned elusive in the Med, what had changed to allow a damaged 688 to track her clear across the North Atlantic? Pacino started to wonder if the UIF wanted them to track the Destiny, that maybe it was a decoy, and the cruise missiles were somewhere else, but the headache that came from *that* line of thought pounded between his temples until he decided to save it for later.

"OOD, do you have a course from the navigator?" The chart was not encouraging. The point bravo hold position was designed to stage *Seawolf* for an interception in mid-Atlantic, not the Labrador Sea. They'd have to go northeast to get around the point of Newfoundland, then turn to the northwest to go up the Davis Strait. That was over 1,300 nautical miles, almost thirty hours at flank speed. They wouldn't catch up to the projected Destiny position until the next day in the morning watch. By then, anything could happen. It might already be too late, Pacino thought.

"Yes, Captain," Scott Court said from the conn.

"Proceed at flank until we're within 100 miles of the *Phoenix* position. But get ready to come to PD in the next half-hour. There's something I want to say."

"Aye, aye, sir. Helm, right five degrees rudder, steady course zero five zero, all ahead flank. Dive, make your depth five five zero feet."

Pacino picked up the microphone, deciding to do a quick brief of the crew before he tagged out the loudspeaker system.

"Attention all hands, this is the captain. We've just gotten a message from COMSUBLANT that our target, the Destiny, is identified and located north in the Labrador Sea. We are now departing the point bravo hold position and driving up at flank to intercept. Sometime in the next two days we will engage the Destiny and try to sink him. I urge all hands to get what rest they can in their next off-watch period, because once we get into the Labrador Sea I will rig the ship for ultraquiet and man battle stations." Pacino paused, wondering if he should say something more personal, feeling he'd fallen short of the famous World War II submarine skippers' speeches to their crews, inspiring words of wisdom for the men to take into battle with them, words to tell grandchildren decades later, but he wasn't a poet. "That is all. Carry on." He put the microphone back into its cradle, thinking about what the crew thought, how they would react.

"Off'sa'deck, I'll be in my stateroom drafting a message to go out in the next PD."

"Aye, sir."

Pacino moved out of control to the inner sanctum of his stateroom, took a blank message form out of his drawer and stared at it for some time, the chart of the Labrador Sea now engraved in his mind.

CNFS *Hegira*

Comdr. Ibn Quzwini felt closer to death than at any time in his forty years. It was obvious that the work in the ballast tank would have suited itself better to the younger officers, but he was now third in command, the mechanical officer, the man who knew the ship's systems better than anyone aboard. The ballast-tank work could not proceed without him. Still, it might have to if he succumbed to the cold and the exhaustion.

The tank was a frightening place to be, even in the dry dock. Quzwini had had to enter it in the Japanese construction yard just before the dry dock was flooded. He had been slated to be the last man in the tank to ensure that no shipyard worker had left tools in the tank that could cause rattles when submerged, that all the pipe supports were installed correctly, that nothing was forgotten. In those days just before the war, his only cares were that the ship be received from the Japanese in the best possible condition. There were no thoughts about dying in combat or firing a missile that would kill several million people, such a thought could fill his stomach with acid. Better not to think it. Even in that shipyard entry, the ballast tank had been a horrible place, the size of it intimidating, with no platforms to stand on, only the structural framing in the space to be climbed up.

Now that the ship was submerged with the ballast tank full of rank-smelling compressed air, being in the tank was terrifying. If one of the tank vents came open, the tank would flood and kill the tank crew, although it was more likely that someone would fall from one of the tubes to the hull below or that one of the heavy loads would break a restraining chain and crush the man beneath it. Worse than the tank's inhospitable geometry was its temperature, the air inside at zero degrees centigrade, cold enough to cause their breaths to form clouds of vapor. The alternating pattern of waiting and heavy exertion caused the men to freeze and then sweat, the next wait making the sweat a super coolant. They all might die of exposure long before they died of falling or being crushed.

Quzwini, as he had for the last five hours, suppressed further thoughts about the lack of safety in the tank and returned to the task at hand, the lifting of the metal patch cut from the upper half of the number-one tube. The metal of the patch had been altered with the attachment of three lifting eyes, each connected to the hooks of a high-capacity chainfall. With three lifting lugs set up high in the tank at a structural hoop of steel, the tank crew winched the heavy hatch upward. It could go only one-and-a-half meters up before it hit the bottom of tube six above. It took them an hour to lift the patch that meter and a half, the patch rising in one centimeter increments, infinitesmally slow. When the patch clunked against the bottom of tube six, the chainfalls were locked, and the heavy warhead of the Hiroshima missile readied to be withdrawn. Pulling off the nose cone was slow, agonizing work, the connecting bolts tight from the factory. It took an hour until the conventional warhead was ready to be removed.

Colonel Ahmed screwed a lifting eye into the top of the warhead, his hands shaking from the cold. With another chainfall he cranked the warhead out, lifting it into a shadow left by one of the harsh incandescent temporary bulbs. The men moved aft to rig the old warhead back to the pressure hull so that it could be replaced with the new warhead. The transfer went slowly, with two chainfalls attached to the warhead, one pulling it aft while the forward chain was slackened, keeping the warhead level. The open part of the tank between the aft heads of the tubes and the forward bulkhead of the command module was a problem. The free flood was only five meters long, but those five meters had no supports except for a cross of steel tubular beams, one horizontal, one vertical. The warhead was rigged all the way down to the bottom of the hull, then aft to the frame at the command module, then hoisted vertically up to the hatchway in the centerline. The maneuver through the free-flood portion of the tank took over an hour. By the time the hatch was winched open to accept the obsolete warhead, the tank work was eight hours behind schedule—it had taken ten hours to get this far, and the work had been estimated by Ahmed to take two. The men tapped on the hatch, the signal to come shallow to depressurize the tank so that they could come back into the hull after an hour at lower pressure.

Quzwini was dismayed that there would be another ten-hour session in the tank to get the new warhead in, then another ten-hour entry to weld up the tube patch and the command-module hatch. With ten hours between entries, it would take forty hours to finish the work. And even then there was no guarantee the warhead switchout would work.

Once he was back in the hull, he stayed on the deck of the forward head, his frozen hands in his crotch, rocking the pain away, hating the thought of going into that ballast tank again.

The ten-hour rest period passed all too soon. Colonel Ahmed called the tank crew to help him pull the new Scorpion warhead from the lower level to the middle level, and from there into the ballast tank and to the forward tip of tube one, retracing the path that the old warhead had gone. The tank was much colder on this entry, the surrounding water becoming icy as the ship got farther north. Not that it mattered much, he thought, as his mind was growing as numb as his body.

USS *Phoenix*

"Norfolk NavCom Center, this is Whiskey Four Bravo, over." Kane waited for twenty endless seconds before calling again. "Norfolk NavCom, this is Whiskey Four Bravo, over."

The *Phoenix*'s call sign for the third of January, W4B, was another meaningless and random collection of alphanumerics dictated by the codebook, which seemed ridiculous to Kane, given that he was transmitting in the clear. He called again on the airwaves and waited again, feeling the deck rock gently beneath his feet as the ship rolled in the swells at periscope depth. Finally, after the fifteenth callup, the NavCom Center came back, much clearer this time.

"WHISKEY FOUR BRAVO, THIS IS NORFOLK NAVCOM, READING YOU FIVE BY FIVE, OVER."

"Roger, NavCom," Kane said slowly, "Navy Blue to follow, over."

"ROGER NAVY BLUE, STANDING BY, OVER."

"Navy Blue as follows: One, Lone Ranger position five nine degrees five eight minutes twelve seconds November, five four degrees ten minutes eight seconds whiskey. Two, Tonto is still with us and has just turned to the north on course three four five. Three, he has been making a great deal of noise, perhaps building something. Four, interrogative, when will cavalry arrive, break. Bravo tango. I say again, Navy Blue as follows . . ."

Kane repeated the message and listened as NavCom read it back, the message ungarbled. He was about to order the ship deep when NavCom came back. At first he expected them to ask him to authenticate another test signal as they had the first time, but that wasn't it.

"WHISKEY FOUR BRAVO, THIS IS NORFOLK NAVCOM CENTER WITH A MESSAGE FROM THE GODFATHER. MESSAGE

READS, DEPART VICINITY BY ZERO FIVE HUNDRED LOCAL TIME SATURDAY FOUR JANUARY, REPEAT, DEPART VICINITY BY ZERO FIVE HUNDRED LOCAL ON SATURDAY. COME HOME, BREAK, BRAVO TANGO, OVER."

Binghamton crinkled his nose in disgust. "The Godfather? What the hell was that all about?"

"The cavalry," Kane said. "This must be from Admiral Steinman or Donchez himself. We're being relieved on station by somebody they figure will get this guy."

"NavCom, this is Whiskey Four Bravo, copied your last. Will attempt a final report at zero four thirty local Saturday. Bravo tango. Whiskey Four Bravo, out."

Kane looked at his watch. "Saturday morning is a long way away. No telling what this guy could do in that time."

"Whoever's coming, Captain," Binghamton said, "is taking so long because they needed to hear from us before they could be sent. It was our message that started the cavalry up the hill. That ought to make your day."

Kane could only think about bodies in yellow plastic bags stored in torpedo tubes.

CNFS *Hegira*

Sharef sat at the head of his conference table, cradling his aching head in his hands, the flashing lights coming from his blind eye, the eye that was filled with glass shards. He heard the knock at the door, immediately straightening in his chair.

"Sir," Tawkidi said from the doorway, "more problems with the tubes. I just came from the middle level. The tank crew has reentered the ballast tank, they are falling farther behind schedule. All they have managed to do so far is withdraw the old warhead. The Scorpion warhead is going into the tank with them now."

"What's our position?"

"We've turned north into the Labrador Basin, sir. The Davis Strait between Greenland and Labrador. In a few minutes we'll be crossing the sixtieth parallel and entering the marginal ice zone. We can't keep this up for too long or the ice cover will be total and impede our firing a missile."

"We will do a north-to-south pace," Sharef said. "The permanent ice pack won't start until we are closer to the arctic circle. That is another twenty hours heading north before we will need to turn south again."

"We're losing time, Commodore."

"We have time, why are you so impatient?"

Tawkidi sank into a chair. "I suppose it is Sihoud's pressure."

"You notice, Omar, that he is pressuring you and not me."

"You have doubts about Sihoud?"

"Commander, I think he is leading us over a precipice. Moreover, he knows I think this."

"This weapon. What are your thoughts about it?"

"I think it a monstrous invention."

"But you will launch it?"

"If I refuse to shoot the missile, he will convince the crew . . . which is afraid of him and some even awed by him . . . to kill me. I may be in command of the ship but I will not be if I defy Sihoud. You will be my replacement, and if you refuse he will arrange the same for you. And then Quzwini, down to the most junior officer, if necessary. When we are gone the Second Captain will accept the order to launch."

Ahmed appeared suddenly in the doorway. "You will both be lucky to live after I tell General Sihoud what I have just heard."

The door closed. Tawkidi stared at it. "You think he's bluffing?"

"About telling Sihoud? No, but Sihoud will do nothing. He still needs us after the launch. He knows we can drive this ship far better than the Second Captain can. He needs us if he expects to reemerge on the African continent." Sharef's voice was remarkably calm, a man resigned to his fate, Tawkidi thought.

"I wish I had your . . . courage, Commodore."

"It is not courage, Omar. Remember, I have already died once. Now get back to the control room."

Tawkidi came to attention. "Yes, sir. Good evening, Commodore."

31

SATURDAY, 4 JANUARY

Labrador Sea, West of Godthaab, Greenland
USS *Seawolf*

The left clock of the side-by-side chronometers read 0405, the one set for zulu time, GMT. The right clock read five minutes after midnight, the local time at the ship's present position. Friday had turned to Saturday. In another four hours Pacino expected to be somewhere in sensor range of the Destiny submarine, assuming the *Phoenix* had gotten its position right and the UIF sub continued north at its present speed.

Pacino knew he should be asleep, getting his rest before he stationed battle watches throughout the ship, but sleep had eluded him.

He shook his head and got back in his rack to try again. The officer of the deck would be buzzing him in three hours to man battle stations . . .

CNFS *Hegira*

Comdr. Ibn Quzwini crawled the last two meters up to the hatch to the command module, the cold of the ballast tank making his hands fail to grasp the handholds. A man in the hatchway above pulled him up and into the warmth of the pressure hull. Quzwini had been the last man in the tank. He didn't look back. He crawled away from the hatch while Lieutenant Ishak and Sublieutenant Rhazes began the work of positioning the heavy steel plate over the hatchway and tack-welding it in place, preparing it for the multiple root passes that would reweld it into the pressure hull. In the cold and exhaustion, time seemed to slip by. The hatch moved into place with the jerkiness of a silent movie, the tack welding done in what seemed a few minutes, the circular passes of the root welding zipping around the circumference of what had been a gaping hole. For the next four hours Quzwini slept where he had collapsed near a stall of the head at the forward end of the command-module middle level.

One deck above, in the control room, Commodore Sharef made his first appearance since the torpedo explosion that had incapacitated him. Two of the rolling seats at the weapon-control consoles were occupied by Sihoud and Ahmed. Sharef leaned on his makeshift cane, made from a piece of pipe, and looked hard with his good eye at the two who presumed to set up camp in his control room.

"The missile is finished, Commodore," Ahmed said. "I suggest you bring the ship around to the south and clear some of these drifting icebergs."

"Very well. Deck officer, turn the ship to the south. How long till we are ready to launch?"

"We are still checking the Scorpion-warhead electronic modules. So far all is in order. The Hiroshima missile airframe, engine and guidance system has already checked out satisfactorily. The Scorpion checks should be done in another thirty minutes."

Sharef leaned over the remains of the plot table, but its glass was caved in, the tube shattered, some of its glass now embedded in his eye. The navigation plot was now displayed on one of the smaller screens of the sensor-control consoles, the sea of the Davis Strait and the Labrador Basin a wide corridor of ocean, its left bank extending from the southeast point of Canada to its furthest northward tip near the pole, the right bank formed by the nearly northward-running west coast of Greenland. A touch of a function key, and a mist appeared to represent the ice cover, the mist light at the southern mouth, denser halfway up, and solid ice north of the arctic circle. The flashing indicator of their present position showed them in a thick ice cover, perhaps a coverage of eighty percent. That seemed borne out by the slight creaking noises heard outside the hull, so faint that they were barely discernible. The creaking and moaning sounds were ice floes colliding and rubbing against each other, even the complete ice cover composed of separate cells of ice that constantly shouldered each other aside. There was something foreign to this sea, this cold, this ice that made Sharef long for open water, for the warmth of the Mediterranean. He wondered if he would ever see Kassab again, but pushed the thought aside while leaning over Ahmed's console to see how the Scorpion-warhead checks were progressing.

If one of the checks failed it would mean going back into the ballast tank and opening the tube again to get to the warhead. Sharef doubted the tube could stand up to the stress of a missile launch after two tube cuts. Perhaps even the initial cut into the tube had weakened it beyond the ability to sustain the missile launch. And a tube reentry would mean more than just tube problems, it would mean added time, time for Coalition naval forces to find them. Sharef tried to feel the urgency of the matter but with his conflicted feelings couldn't muster it. If Coalition navy ships and aircraft came, he would fight for the ship to the best of his ability. That, after all, was his true mission.

USS *Seawolf*

The phone next to Pacino's rack had buzzed an hour before the planned battle stations time at 0300 local time. He climbed from the rack, trying to shake the bone-deep fatigue. The shower water was still ice-cold when he stepped in. He turned the spray to hot, then back to cold, then turned it off to conserve water while he soaped up, rinsing again in cold. A few moments later, clad in a black poopysuit and cross-training sneakers, he made his way to the galley on the deck above for a cup of coffee. The crew's mess was deserted. One of the mess cooks had put a CD on the stereo, The Doors pouring out of the subdued speakers.

Pacino sat in one of the dinettes and drank the coffee. He was alert when he put the cup in the wash bin and walked aft to the ladder to the middle level. He lingered a moment on the stairway landing, long enough to see that the new switch he had installed now had an out-of-commission yellow tag on it. He smiled—someone had noticed it and found that it did nothing. He flipped the switch to "off" and continued around the dogleg of the passageway to the radio room, hit the buttons for the door combination lock and went in. The room was empty. On the clipboard hanging from a handhold was his last out-going message to Admiral Steinman telling him to get the *Phoenix* out of the area of the Destiny submarine by 0500 local time. There was a good chance that *Phoenix* would not get the message and would continue trailing the Destiny, an event that would likely spell disaster for her. In other circumstances Pacino would never fire a volley of torpedoes with *Phoenix* in the line of fire, but with Donchez's theory that the Destiny had a doomsday-missile aboard, he would have no choice. The Mark 50 torpedoes would be launched regardless of *Phoenix*'s position. Pacino knew he might have only one chance, one shot. He intended that it be a good one.

He opened a locker in the wall and pulled out four oblong boxes, each slightly larger than a baseball bat, a small case resembling a notebook computer, then shut the locker and walked down the passageway to his stateroom. He put the boxes and the case on the conference table and opened them. Inside the boxes were four SLOT buoys, submarine-launched one-way transmitters. The case held a small keyboard and viewing screen used for typing in messages to the SLOT buoys. Pacino spent ten minutes coding messages into the buoys, then with masking tape and a marker designated them numbers one through four. He carried them to the aft compartment upper level, the heat of the engine-room oppressive. He put the buoys in a locker beside the aft signal-ejector and walked forward, back to his stateroom. Once there he found himself drumming his fingers on the table, feeling like an athlete an hour before the game.

On impulse he wandered into the control room. Henry Vale's section tracking team was stationed, waiting for contact on the Destiny, the BSY–2 sonar/firecontrol suite straining for signs of the UIF vessel.

"Anything yet, Nav?" Pacino asked Vale.

"Nothing but icebergs and the occasional whale, Captain."

"Man silent battle stations at zero four hundred. Are we rigged for ultraquiet?"

"Modified only by the coffeemakers, sir. Everyone not on watch should be fast asleep."

"I'll be in sonar."

Pacino stepped through the forward door to sonar, but just as Vale had said, the sonar screens were empty of all but the ocean's vast amount of random noise. Pacino returned to his stateroom, stared at the chronometer, waiting for 0400.

USS *Phoenix*

Mike Jensen squinted at the Pos-One display console of the firecontrol system, the dots neatly stacked on the sonar contact ahead, Target One, the Destiny submarine. The range readout on the sidebar indicated a range of 8,400 yards, the target speed steady at thirteen knots, course three five five. The target had proceeded at the same course and speed through the entire midwatch.

Jensen felt the headache bloom behind his eyes as the first dot deviated from the neat lineup, the sonar system telling the firecontrol computer that the expected bearing to the contact was different than the actual bearing. The contact was turning.

"Conn, sonar, possible zig Target One," rang into Jensen's ears from his headset.

"All stop," he ordered the helmsman. The order would screw up the determination of Target One's new course, but with the Destiny just ahead Jensen was unwilling to drive into him if he turned around in a course reversal. "Mark speed two knots."

Phoenix drifted under the partial ice cover overhead, waiting to see what Target One was doing.

"Chief, send the messenger to get the XO," Jensen barked at the chief of the watch. McDonne was stationed during the midwatch as command duty officer to allow Captain Kane to get some sleep. McDonne had spent most of the watch in control with Jensen, but had gone down to find a snack.

"Sonar, conn, any change in Target One's speed?"

"Tough to call, sir. Our guess is no. But we suspect contact is turning to his starboard."

"Conn, aye."

Jensen leaned over Pos One and watched the dot stack as the bearings to the Destiny drifted from their bow around the starboard beam. The contact was turning to his right, coming around back to the south. Jensen held his breath, as if it would keep the Destiny from hearing them.

"Speed two knots, sir," the helmsman announced.

"Chief, prepare to hover," Jensen ordered.

"What the hell are you doing, OOD?" XO McDonne's tone was caustic.

"XO, Target One is reversing course. I'm trying to remain undetected." There was no trace of sarcasm in Jensen's voice, but McDonne glared at the navigator nonetheless.

McDonne leaned over pos one and dialed in a new course for the Destiny, 180 degrees true, due south. Other than a small wrinkle in the middle of the dot stack, the new course caused the stack to realign itself perfectly vertical.

"He's coming around to the south. Better put some turns on and follow him in his baffles," McDonne said. Then, mostly to himself: "Sucker comes north toward the Baffin Bay for 900 goddamned miles and suddenly turns south. Why the hell would he do that?"

"Helm, all ahead one thirds, right ten degrees rudder, steady course south."

"Conn, sonar, we're getting transients from Target One. Sounds like he's flooding something. A tank or a tube."

The dots in the stack started to angle over from McDonne's neat dot stack. The target was maneuvering again.

"Conn, sonar, Target One is slowing."

"Conn, aye," McDonne said into his headset. "Jensen, get the captain in here."

"Conn, sonar, Target One is opening a hull door. Could be a weapon tube."

"Dammit," the XO said. What he would have given for just one Mark 50 torpedo. He glanced up at the chronometer, which read 0350 local time. In a little over an hour they were ordered to clear the area and leave the Destiny to someone else. He couldn't help but think he should report this last incident, but what was the Destiny doing? Preparing to shoot a torpedo at them? There had been no sign that they were being tracked, no indication that the Destiny had counterdetected.

Kane appeared, still zipping up his poopysuit, his hair sticking straight up, bags under his bloodshot eyes. It took less than thirty seconds to brief him on the new development.

"Jensen, take her up to PD, fast," Kane said. "Get Binghamton to radio, ASAP."

"Sonar, conn, proceeding to periscope depth," Jensen said into the intercom. "Helm, all ahead two thirds, Dive, make your depth six six feet, steep angle."

As the watchstanders moved to the officer of the deck's orders, 5,000 yards away the Destiny submarine slowed to walking speed, the Scorpion warhead's gyro starting to spin, all circuits now energized.

USS *Seawolf*

As First Class Sonarman Jesse Holt took a last sip of the coffee in his *Seawolf* cup, the rattle of the transient came down the waterfall short-term display, the bearing from the north. In an ocean filled with transient noises it was nothing unusual. He glanced at his log, debating whether to log the rattle. On the captain's orders, the time indication on his tube read 0351, the ship's time set for local instead of the usual zulu time. He glanced back up at the transient, noticing it was gone before he had a chance to train the audio cursor to it and listen with his own ears. Well, the sea here was filled with more creaks and groans than a haunted house, most of them from the ice floes, some close, some distant. The ones directly overhead could sometimes be heard with the naked ear, the sudden spooky groan sending shivers down the spines of rookie and under-ice veteran alike.

Holt had reported aboard during the shipyard period, a hot-running

young petty officer from the USS *Louisville,* the submarine in the Pacific
Fleet that had done the original sound surveillance of the Destiny as it
came out of the Yokosuka yards. Holt was quiet for a sonarman, who
were usually known as the ship's prima donnas. When not on watch he
would spend his time qualifying the younger sonarmen, working out aft
or in the torpedo room or reading in the crew's mess. Holt was, unlike
most of his shipmates, deeply religious, conducting ship's services on
Sunday mornings. Not one crew member made fun of this, since after
years spent quietly lifting weights Holt had a formidable presence. That
he was searching for another warship with the intention of killing its
crew was not a conflict. He had joined the service out of conviction and
belief in a way of life. Perhaps the Destiny crew had done the same.
Well, let the better submarine . . . its crew and their cause . . . prevail, he had thought when Pacino had first made the announcement over
the Circuit One.

The odd rattling transient came down the waterfall display again,
from the north, but this time Holt was quick enough to move his audio
cursor to the bearing of the rattle. It was a rapid popping sound, a string
of firecrackers. Probably an iceberg. Or shrimp. Or a steel hull changing
depth.

"What have you got on the 150-hertz bucket?" he shot at the junior
watchstander, a third-class sonarman named Phills.

"Couple of spikes at 154, but they're fuzzy. Lot of noise."

"Wait a minute," Holt said, turning his seat toward the narrowband
displays. More transients began pouring down the narrowband display,
all from the north. The audio cursor was putting out a hum now, a faint
hum that reminded him of the run on the *Louisville.* The hum and the
rattles were growing louder. "Zero the freq bucket and narrow it to 153
to 155 hertz, max processing, short time integration." he ordered Phills.

Holt's suspicion was confirmed ninety seconds later.

"Conn, sonar," he said calmly into his headset mike, "new contact
bearing zero zero five on hull and spherical arrays, holding a one five
four hertz tonal narrowband and several traces and transients broadband, suspect contact is submerged warship, Japanese construction,
Destiny class."

"Conn, aye," Vale's voice replied, just as calm. "Turning east for a
TMA leg now. Designate contact Target One."

On the conn, Lt. Comdr. Henry Vale, the officer of the deck, buzzed
Pacino's stateroom and called to the chief of the watch to man battle
stations.

"Captain," Pacino answered Vale.

"Time is 0355, sir. We have the Destiny."

32

SATURDAY, 4 JANUARY

Labrador Sea, West of Godthaab, Greenland
USS *Phoenix*

"Norfolk NavCom, this is Echo Five November. NavCom, NavCom, NavCom, this is Echo Five November with a Navy Blue. Come in, over."

Static and whistling.

"NavCom, this is Echo Five November, over."

Nothing.

Kane looked at Binghamton, whose head was sweating furiously. Binghamton adjusted the gain and told Kane to try again. No answer but the static. Binghamton tried a new frequency, listening first to see if there were any voices, and hearing none, waved to Kane. Kane called again. Silence, no response.

"I guess there was something to the storm report I heard."

"What report? What storm?"

"When the BIGMOUTH dried out I cranked through a frequency and heard something about a massive blizzard over the Atlantic coast from the Carolinas to New York. Whole place socked in. It would explain the reception problem."

"Maybe we should try for a relay. Get somebody local who can keep calling."

"Somebody else couldn't authenticate from the codebook, plus I'm guessing this message is time-sensitive. Am I right, Skipper?"

"Yeah." Kane clicked his microphone. "Conn, Captain, lower the BIGMOUTH and take us deep."

"Conn, aye," rasped through the circuit. The deck plunged beneath them as the ship went down and accelerated to catch up with the Destiny.

"Any chance an hour will make a difference, Senior?"

"Who knows, Captain? We could try, but don't count on anything."

"Dammit," Kane said, already halfway to control. "Off'sa'deck, we got Target One back?"

"Still looking, sir."

"Find him fast. I don't need another Nagasaki surprise."

National Security Agency Headquarters, Fort Meade, Maryland
Building 427 Secure Communications Center

"We're under three feet of snow already, General. How about you?"

The secure-voice line took a second to process and unscramble the incoming signal so that Barczynski's voice came over after a short delay. To Donchez the incessant pausing always felt like he was talking to someone angry who had to count to ten before speaking, and in this case it was appropriate. Barczynski was not pleased about the situation in the Labrador Sea.

"I can't even see as far as two feet of my back porch, but what I can see is drifting up to four feet. I barely made it home and I'm not going anywhere until this thing lifts. But, enough about the damn storm. What the hell's going on with the Destiny and Sihoud? You've been promising me results for a week now."

Donchez had briefed Barczynski earlier about the first message from the *Phoenix,* the first good news since *Seawolf* had left the dry dock. This call was to update him on the second message and that *Seawolf* should be intercepting the Destiny within the next six hours. When Donchez finished, the general started an interrogation.

"What chance does your *Seawolf* have against this Destiny? We know the UIF sub ran over two of your 688-class boats. And didn't they have the same weapons as *Seawolf* has now?"

"You're partly correct, General. I believe *Seawolf* will prevail. It's invisible compared to a 688. And with the same weapons, the *Phoenix* was able to damage the Destiny badly enough that they could track it clear across an ocean without being detected, even though they themselves were badly hurt. The Mark 50 torpedo is a remarkable weapon. A salvo of three or four should put the Destiny on the bottom."

"Will *Seawolf* get there in time?"

"Yes, sir." He hoped.

"What if by some circumstance that Scorpion missile gets launched? Can we shoot it down? Should we have some of Clough's interceptors standing by?"

"If the missile works as advertised, sir, it will have a radar-cloaking mechanism that will make it undetectable. It's a stealth missile, it flies at 60,000 feet at Mach three. The only thing that could possibly give it away is the sonic boom, and coming in from Canada as it is, the terrain is unoccupied. We wouldn't know until it crossed over populated areas that it was inbound, and even then it would be too late because it's too hard to pinpoint. The only chance would be an interceptor that could shoot it down in the first six seconds of flight, while it's on the solid rocket-fuel booster, and that's only possible if you know exactly where the Destiny is. Only *Seawolf* or *Phoenix* knows that."

"That's damned bad news, Dick. Why don't your subs give us a clue where the Destiny is?"

"They have orders to, General, but *Phoenix* can only talk on HF radio, which is frankly crappy—her normal comms were knocked out earlier—and *Seawolf* is probably still engaging."

"I hate to even think this, Dick, but do you think we ought to recommend city evacuations?"

"No, General. You'd never get anyone out in time with this storm, and we'd kill a hell of a lot of folks from exposure and panic. We can hope that the blizzard will make the bomb ineffective *if* it gets launched . . ."

"Dick, make *sure* your guys get that sub. I'm not banking on any damn snowstorm. Stay on the line while I get President Dawson."

"Aye, aye, sir."

Donchez waited, knowing that either Pacino did his job or . . . He cut off the thought.

USS *Seawolf*

Executive officer "Lube Oil" Vaughn stood inboard of the attack-center consoles, his headphones on, a clipboard with a sketchpad in his hands. He nodded at Pacino, announcing that battle stations were manned. The control room was shrouded in red light, its beam-to-beam width made crowded and small by the two dozen watchstanders, the plots manned, the attack-center-console seats filled, phonetalkers dotting the room. The high whining sound of the console screens was augmented by the whispers of conversation, the three-word communications that made the battle-stations crew a single organism, at one with the machinery of the ship. The ventilation ducts boomed through the space, their bass note creating the tense atmosphere of expectation of the unknown. The brass analog chronometer read 0402.

"Target One bears 351, range 24,000 yards. Own-ship speed twenty knots pointing the contact at course north, depth 500 feet." Vaughn leaned over the pos two console of the BSY 2. "Contact course approximate at 180, speed ten to twelve knots."

"Very well, XO," Pacino said, taking it in while climbing the conn platform and putting on his headset. "XO, call up Hobart aft and tell him to load the SLOT buoy number one into the aft signal ejector. Weps, status of the tubes?"

"Port bank tubes dryloaded with Mark 50s," Scott Court reported from the far aft console, the weapons-control panel.

"Spin up two, four, six, and eight, flood and open outer doors. Set submerged target presets, high-to-medium passive snake pattern."

"Aye, sir. Torpedo power coming on, one through four."

"Attention in the firecontrol team," Pacino said to the room. The quiet conversations stopped. Those watchstanders who weren't at visual displays turned to look at Pacino. "As soon as the torpedoes warm up we will be launching a horizontal salvo at Target One. We'll reload immediately and fire off another salvo. We'll continue until Target One is on the bottom or counterfires. In the event of a counterfire I will run but I'll keep shooting. Carry on."

In the sonar room Jesse Holt frowned at the narrowband frequency buckets and keyed his mike. "Conn, sonar, new contact, partially masked by Target One, bears 354, range distant. Contact is a submerged warship, possible American 688 class."

Confusion clouded Jeff Joseph's face as he acknowledged into his boom microphone, "Conn, aye."

"A 688 class at the same bearing as the Destiny," Vaughn said in frustration. "The *Phoenix*, the ship who trailed the Destiny all the way here."

"We're early," Pacino said, angry at the interruption to the firing-routine. *"Phoenix* was supposed to be out of the area when we got here, but we're an hour early.

Pacino looked at the navigation chart. The strait was a narrow corridor of seaway going north and south. At the south, *Seawolf*'s position was marked as a black dot. Farther north, an orange mark denoted the Destiny, the target. Somewhere north of the Destiny, the *Phoenix* sailed, unaware that they were in the line of fire. If Pacino went ahead with the torpedo shot, he risked hitting the friendly, the *Phoenix*. If he waited, the Destiny might launch the adhesive plutonium bomb at D.C. He felt like a policeman ready to shoot at a bad guy, suddenly finding out the villain had a hostage.

"We could hold our fire and wait for her to get out of the way."

"No," Pacino said. "We're going ahead with the attack. If *Phoenix*'s sonar is good enough to hear the Destiny, then it'll be good enough to hear the incoming Mark 50 torpedoes. And when she realizes Mark 50s are coming in, she'll get off the track or hover so the Doppler filter won't see her. It's worth the risk . . ."

It sounded like a rationalization, and from the looks on the faces of Vaughn and Joseph, it must have sounded that way to them too.

Torpedoes in tubes two, four, six and eight are warm, self-checks complete, all tubes flooded, two and four outer doors open." Court spun in his chair to look at Pacino. "We're ready to fire, Captain."

Pacino, on the conn, felt the weight of command on his shoulders, a three-ton barbell. Here, in front of his crew, he was about to endanger— or worse—another U.S. submarine. But to fail to launch the torpedoes would allow the Destiny to launch its doomsday weapon. If he had told Donchez to order *Phoenix* out of the way an hour earlier . . . His face denying his feelings, Pacino ordered:

"Tube two. shoot on generated bearing."

"Set." Vaughn said.

"Standby." Court said, pulling the long firing trigger to the three o'clock position.

"Shoot!" Pacino commanded.

"Fire!" Court pulled the firing trigger to the fire position.

A short hiss sounded before a violent boom roared through the ship. Pacino's eardrums slammed from the pressure pulse as the firing ram one level below vented to the ship.

The first torpedo had already left the tube, the submarine fading far behind as its engine started and the propulsor began spinning. Fifteen seconds later the second torpedo was fired from the ship, then a third and a fourth. All four weapons hurled through the near-freezing ocean northward toward the target, all in high-speed transit, waiting for the signal from their internal computers to slow down and begin listening for the sound signature of the target.

In the control room Pacino waited while the torpedo-room crew reloaded the tubes. It would take some five minutes before the hydraulic rams had positioned the last torpedo and the gyros were powered up. During the wait, he looked at the sonar waterfall-display monitor, watching the dim traces of the torpedoes as their bearings merged with the bearing to the target.

And to the bearing of the *Phoenix* . . .

CNFS *Hegira*

The headache was much worse. Commodore Sharef was beginning to think it was psychosomatic, the result of his conflicting feelings about the missile-launch. Whatever the cause, he had never felt pain this severe, the sharp screaming behind his eyes enough to prevent concentration on anything but the pain. But he had to rise above it . . .

Tawkidi lowered the periscope. "Open water overhead, Commodore. We'll have a clean shot here if we hurry."

"Status of tube one?" he asked Tawkidi.

"Flooded, bow cap open. Missile power is on and readback of target parameters and route milestones complete. The missile is ready for a programmed one-minute countdown but we need to slow down to bare steerageway."

"Ship control, dead slow ahead, four clicks."

"Four clicks, sir."

"General Sihoud, are you ready for us to begin the one-minute countdown?"

"Start the countdown," Sihoud said. "It is time for us to deliver our revenge."

Sharef tried not to make a face.

"Commander, commence one-minute countdown," Sharef ordered, feeling the onset of dizziness in addition to the headache.

"Countdown commencing, sir, at launch minus sixty seconds, in automatic. Ship's speed meets launching parameters. Now at launch minus fifty seconds and the missile is satisfactory."

Another minute, Sharef thought, and it was over . . . then withdraw to the north, take the ship under the permanent ice pack, sail up around the northern tip of Greenland and back to the North Atlantic to the Med. And from there, home.

The traces forming on the sensor-control consoles heralded the incoming American torpedoes. The Second Captain system monitoring the sensor inputs began to understand the meaning of the sounds and became alarmed. The buzzing of the annunciator on the panel broke the silence in the room. Tawkidi saw the alarm first and turned to Sharef, who had joined him at the panel.

"Incoming torpedoes, sir. At least four of them. We don't see the launching platform—"

"General Sihoud," Sharef said urgently, "we must break off the countdown and evade—"

"No, Commodore, we must complete the launch, *then* evade these weapons . . ."

USS *Phoenix*

"Conn, sonar, we have reacquisition, Target One, bearing one seven four. Contact has slowed, his signature is much quieter now."

"Conn, aye," Kane said, peering over the pos-one console.

Kane glanced up at the chronometer. The digital numerals read out 0814 zulu time, which would be 0414 local time. In another half-hour Kane would clear datum to the north. Whoever Steinman and Donchez had sent would be coming from the south to attack the Destiny. It was just as well, he thought. His crew was bone tired—the ones still alive. The crew and ship were ready to get home. The boat would need about a year in the dry dock, maybe two if the shipyard moved up their next scheduled overhaul. Which meant that this would be his last trip with *Phoenix.* He had a year before being slated for relief, something that had seemed sufficiently distant that he had not given it much thought, but now it was becoming obvious that he was approaching one of the crossroads in his career. He had to decide what his future plans were. Should he remain in the Navy or leave for civilian life? With no more sea duty the equation came down to which desk job. He still felt he was too young to say goodbye to the sea, but—

"Conn, sonar, multiple torpedoes in the water! Bearing south!"

USS *Seawolf*

It seemed forever for the second batch of Mark 50s to warm up. If the ship had gone into combat without the Vortex tubes and had the old four Mark 50 tubes on the starboard side, the second volley of four torpedoes would have gone out immediately after the first. The ship could have a weapon out every forty-five seconds until all fifty were gone. Now there could be only twenty-four launched, in uneven batches of four at five-minute intervals. But he had cursed the Vortex system enough, Pacino thought.

"Tubes two and four ready, sir."

"Firing-point procedures, tubes two and four," Pacino commanded, listening to the sequence of reports as the battle-stations team did their individual interlocking jobs. Within ten seconds the tube launched and the smash of high-pressure air clanged throughout the ship, and fifteen seconds after that tube four sent its torpedo out into the sea. Pacino's ears rang as Court announced that tubes six and eight were ready.

The launch litany was repeated for those two tubes, making eight torpedoes sent down the line to Target One.

"Mr. Court, get the port bank reloaded ASAP. Sonar, captain, what's the status of Target One?"

"Impossible to say, Captain," Holt's voice said through the intercom circuit. "He's completely masked by the Mark 50s. We have zero bearing separation. I'm calling loss of contact on Target One."

"Conn, aye. Watch for a counterfire."

Vaughn looked up at Pacino from the deck in front of the attack center.

"I don't know, Skipper. It's not like this guy to take four torpedoes and not shoot back. Maybe we should clear datum on general principles."

"Hold on, XO. *Phoenix* launched a whole room against this guy. Granted only three fish locked on, but he still lived. I want to unload as many weapons his way as I can. Court, what's the status?"

"Still loading, sir."

Still, Pacino thought, Vaughn was right. And he hadn't mentioned the fact that Pacino had put the ship in a launching position so that the torpedoes were transiting down the line of sight. If he'd planned it he would have driven off the track so that the bearing to the torpedoes in transit would be separated from the target bearing, allowing him to monitor both during the attack. But there had been no time for that. Still, it was a tactical failure. Pacino wondered if they'd even be able to hear a counterfired Nagasaki torpedo through the noise of their own Mark 50s. At this point, it came down to how good Petty Officer Holt's ears were.

CNFS *Hegira*

"The torpedoes could get here any moment, General. We *must* evade. And counterattack. Then we can shoot your Scorpion, there will be plenty of time . . ."

Colonel Ahmed looked at General Sihoud, hopeful that he would finally put the insubordinate commodore in his place, but to his disappointment Sihoud nodded, finally realizing he had no choice if they were to launch the missile and survive.

"Very well, Commodore. Evade the weapons and shoot back at the intruder. But be quick about it."

"Tawkidi, abort the launch, evade to the north and warm up the

Nagasakis in tubes ten and twelve," Sharef said, thankful for at least a brief reprieve.

"Ship control," Tawkidi ordered. "Emergency ahead, depth 400 meters, turn to course north. Sublieutenant al-Maari, power up the weapons in tubes ten and twelve. Sensor control, do we have a function report from the Second Captain on the SCM evasion sonar?"

Sublieutenant Rouni, on the sensor console, flipped through several graphic screens on the Second Captain display. The longer he took, Sharef thought, the more certain it was that the SCM ventriloquist modules were down. Sharef might not even have thought to check, based on how heavily the aft damage had been from the initial American torpedo.

The deck rolled from the maneuver, then inclined downward. Sharef found his dizziness returning, the tilting pitching deck starting his fall. He had toppled halfway to the deck before Tawkidi caught hold of him. Sharef thought himself fortunate to have the devotion of someone as dedicated *and* capable as Tawkidi, as well as Quzwini and the rest of the men. For an instant he wondered if he were becoming delirious, all of this gushing thought about his crew members. The aftereffects of his concussion? Great thing, to be in command of a submarine under attack by multiple torpedoes, with the commander getting a fuzzy mind. He hoped Tawkidi would watch and know the proper moment to take over if he had to. And that if he did, he would stand up to Sihoud. He could not do any more coaching now. Either his crew had the character and the training to fight their way out of this mess, or they died.

"Negative function SCM, Commander. It's dead. We'll have to evade on speed alone."

"Commodore, we could insert a delouse and hope for the best, but I think I'm just going to run north. There's plenty of navigational room, and all the weapons are coming in from one bearing, astern to the south. And there's no need to engage the Second Captain in ship-control mode."

"Agreed, Commander." Sharef moved closer to the navigation display, checking water depth from the computer memory, the ice-profile generated from a satellite shot loaded into the system just before sailing, updated by the Second Captain's latest predictions. There was no telling the range to the torpedoes, but based on the Second Captain's detection ranges using the forward hydrophones, they must be distant. And given the fact that the American torpedoes were slow, there was a good chance that the ship would outrun the weapons and remain whole. In fact, he believed, whoever had fired on them had committed a tactical error, firing at a distance from a single bearing. As soon as the Nagasakis were fired down the bearings to the incoming torpedoes, the firing ship was doomed.

"Tubes ten and twelve ready, track search mode loaded for an immediate turn to the south, Commodore. Request to launch."

"Launch ten and twelve."

Within twenty seconds two Nagasaki torpedoes left their tubes at the bow of the *Hegira,* executed rapid 180-degree turns to the south and sped to the target.

As the weapons left the *Hegira* behind, the *Hegira* began closing the distance to the American 688-class submarine, which was running northwest, the American vessel some thirty clicks slower. Now within ten kilometers, the Second Captain system was still unable to pick her noise out of the sea from the interference of the highly increased own-ship noise of the seawater flow and propulsion machinery . . .

33

SATURDAY, 4 JANUARY

Fort Meade, Maryland, Headquarters, National Security Agency
Building 427 Secure Communications Facility

When Admiral Donchez had shut his eyes after his phone conversation with General Barczynski, the snow had been two feet deep on the roads, drifting up to four. Now another foot of snow had blanketed the flats. Donchez dreamed of snow falling, snow colored black, of streets lined with bodies buried in the deadly flakes. When he was nudged awake it was a relief.

"Message for you, sir. Navy Blue."

Donchez put the clipboard down on the abandoned console section in front of him. The message was from the *Seawolf*, and its body was a one-liner: *WE ARE NOW ENGAGING THE DESTINY.* He waved over the communications tech sergeant.

"Copy this over to General Barczynski's personal TS fax machine at Fairfax. You know the code?"

"Yessir."

Labrador Sea, Northwest of Godthaab, Greenland
USS *Phoenix*

"Right full rudder, all ahead flank! Steady course three five zero. Dive, make your depth 1,000 feet. Sonar, Captain, do you have the torpedoes?"

Kane felt sweat break out under his arms, in the middle of his chest and between his legs. He could *feel* his respiration rate rise. The deck trembled with the sudden maneuver. He had the definite feeling that the ship would not be able to take another Nagasaki hit. It was, literally, outrun or die.

"Conn, sonar, yes, on the edge of the port baffles. And one thing, sir. The incoming torpedoes do not have characteristics of the Nagasakis. These are . . . Mark 50s."

Sanderson sounded as if he was angry at Kane himself.

"Say again, sonar."

"Captain, incoming torpedoes are Mark 50 units launched from the south. The attacking submarine is here early."

McDonne cursed. "Can't they do anything right?"

"XO, get on the horn to Schramford aft and tell him to crank up the power again, like he did last time." Kane keyed his mike. "Sonar, Captain, what's the status of Target One?"

"He's in the baffles, sir. I'm looking for him to emerge on the edge of the starboard baffles. I'm also checking the towed array end-beam, but at this speed the old array is losing signal-to-noise ratio pretty quick."

"Keep looking." What else could he say, Kane wondered. Again he had done everything the book said he could do to evade a torpedo. With the lighter, slower Mark 50s coming in, he might have a better chance of outpacing them than he would against a Nagasaki.

Standing on the conn, knuckles white as he gripped the handrail, Kane decided that perhaps a desk job wouldn't be so bad after all.

CNFS *Hegira*

"I recommend a maneuver, Commander Tawkidi. We should see how close the weapons are getting." Sublieutenant Rouni's voice was stressed.

Tawkidi nodded slowly, uncomfortable himself without knowing what the weapons were doing. With the damage to the aft hydrophone arrays

from the previous torpedo hit, there was no way to track the progress of
the weapons when they were astern.

"Very well, Sublieutenant. Ship control, insert a one-point-five g-turn
to the right . . . now."

The deck tilted as the ship-control-panel officer inserted the turn. It
would take the ship half a minute to do the 360-degree turn, after which
they would return to the northern evasion course. The thirty seconds
seemed to take forever, especially since they were running directly
toward the weapons at the halfway point.

Back on course, Rouni at the panel attempted to analyze the data the
system had seen during its look-back.

"I'm getting twelve weapons still in pursuit, Commander. Closest is at
fifteen kilometers."

"Any active pulses?

"No sir. So far the torpedoes are passive."

"All of them on course for us, or are they going wide?"

"They are all vectored directly at us, sir."

Tawkidi stepped away from the sensor and weapon consoles and took
Sharef's elbow, guiding him farther from the other officers and Sihoud
and Ahmed.

"Commodore, I know we don't have a Dash Five to support this, but
I'm beginning to think we should insert a delouse."

"On what basis, Omar?"

"We're under broad ice-covering, sir. Their torpedoes will be listening
for propulsion noises. They aren't pinging, at least not yet, but if they
do, the ice will be reflecting the pulses. They will have a velocity filter to
discriminate between us, a moving object and the ice."

"We have no intelligence on their systems."

"We could insert the delouse and go shallow to the bottom of the ice.
It's a risk, but the intruder will keep shooting, keeping us from launching the missile . . ."

Sharef tried to keep an open mind but still felt certain that the American weapons were relatively crude. They were probably still on a programmed run to a listening point. Running was the best tactic, and
inserting a delouse without a Dash Five to throw off the incoming weapons was too risky. Not worth it.

"Commander, I believe we should continue the run. These weapons
will soon run out of fuel, and they will no longer fire them when they
realize two of our Nagasakis are on the way. The Nagasakis will destroy
the launching platform, and when the torpedoes shut down we can return to our mission." And in the thick of it, that was how he thought of
it, felt it—the mission.

Although, just for an instant, he wondered if his motivation for the
order came from his aversion to launching the missiles. Whatever, he

felt certain it was the correct tactical course, and *that* was his job. Inserting a delouse and waiting was taking a chance that did not need to be taken. And as he had insisted, there was plenty of time . . .

USS *Phoenix*

Sanderson's report put a rare smile on Kane's face. "Conn, sonar, I have the Destiny emerging from the starboard baffles, very loud sound signature. He's going very fast with a left-bearing drift. My estimate is that he's on a parallel course heading north, also evading the Mark 50 torpedoes, and is overtaking us."

"Sonar, Captain, any sign that he hears us?"

"Conn, sonar, no. He's running as scared as we are."

Lt. Victor Houser's expression had begun to change as he heard Sanderson say the words "also evading the Mark 50 torpedoes" and "he's running as scared as we are." He could barely keep his voice level as he said to McDonne.

"What the hell are we doing, XO?"

"Where have you been, Houser?" McDonne prepared to launch into one of his classic reprimands when Kane held up his hand.

"Houser, what's on your mind?"

"Captain, XO, we're doing a torpedo evasion based on enemy weapons. But we're running from Mark 50s. Our *own* systems. We know these fish. We're under ice. They were probably launched with a ceiling setting of 200 or 300 feet to avoid running into ice rafts, right? And they're on a passive snake-search pattern, which will switch to a high-Doppler filter active on-target acquisition. That's the standard under-ice setting for a submerged target. So why are we running? We should stop, hover, and bring ourselves up to the ice. Those things will never hear us—"

"Helm, all back two thirds!" Kane suddenly said. "Mark speed two knots."

The deck trembled violently as the maneuvering-room crew opened the astern turbine throttles and reversed the direction of the screw. McDonne stared while Houser kept frowning at the sonar display screen.

"Two knots, Captain."

"Helm, all stop. Diving Officer, prepare to hover. Phonetalker, to maneuvering, scram the reactor and shut the main steam bulkhead valves."

The order to scram the plant went out, surprising even Houser. Kane was going further than stopping and hiding. He was after total ship silence.

"Ready to hover, Captain."

"Very well, Dive. Bring us up to the ice cover. Two feet per second."

"Two feet per second rise, sir. Depth setting 100 feet."

The fans in the room wound down, making the room immediately stuffy.

"Maybe we should cut off the firecontrol system," Houser said. "It's eating power and we don't have any torpedoes anyway."

"Shut it down, OOD."

McDonne's face had turned blotchy red but he kept his mouth shut.

"Five hundred feet, sir."

"Sir, maneuvering reports reactor scram with the bulkhead steam valves shut."

Quickest way to shut down the engineroom, Kane thought. The ship would be whisper-quiet now, only the hissing of air into the depth-control tanks making noise.

"Captain, we're about out of high-pressure air. I'll have to hover on the trim pump."

Kane bit his lip. The massive pump would eat battery power, but after their emergency blows to get off the bottom they had not had a chance to run the air compressors and refill the banks. There was no choice.

"Very well, Chief. Hover on the trim pump. Phonetalker, to the engineer, report time on the battery."

"Conn, sonar, understand we're hovering to avoid the torpedoes. Request we turn the ship to get the torpedoes out of the baffles."

"Sonar, Captain, no."

"Sir, engineer reports a half-hour on the battery, maybe more if we dump forward loads."

Kane understood. Sonar wanted to start the thruster and burn power to monitor the battle. The engineer wanted to shut down sonar and conserve battery juice.

"Two hundred feet, sir," the diving officer reported.

"Ease the ascent to one foot per second."

"One eight zero feet, sir."

Kane waited, knowing the torpedoes were still screaming in at him. Two minutes later the deck jumped as the sail collided with the bottom of the icepack overhead. They had stopped.

"Give us just enough buoyancy to stay here without listing over."

"Aye, sir. Trim pump is shut down."

"What now, Captain?" McDonne asked.

"Now we wait," Kane said. The room was much quieter without the roar of the air handlers. Kane stepped to the door to sonar and looked in on Sanderson. The sonar chief gave him a sour look.

"Can't hear anything but this ice," Sanderson said. "The torpedoes are still directly astern in the baffles."

"Keep listening. If you hear them in front of us, they went by."

"I'll be sure to let you know, sir." Sanderson turned back to his console, ignoring Kane.

Kane stepped back into the room. The faces of the watchstanders, to a man, were hollow, dark circles under their eyes, fatigue and fear sapping their energy. Kane had a feeling the trip was almost over. The only question was how it would end.

USS Seawolf

"Check fire," Pacino ordered. "Sonar, Captain, do you have any bearing separation between own-ship units and Target One? And what's the status of the *Phoenix*?"

Pacino was greeted by half-startled looks. He recognized that he was interrupting the execution of his own orders: to shoot the weapons in the room until only one was left. But a thought had crept up on him that he was shooting on old data. The torpedoes had been between their sonar ears and the target and the friendly. Anything could be happening out there. Without data, there were no decisions, only ignorance.

"Conn, sonar, no bearing separation. Torpedoes are masking Target One and the *Phoenix*."

Pacino stepped toward the chart table on the port side, away from the attack center. The ship was south of a ridge that ran mostly east-west, separating the Labrador Basin from the Davis Strait and the Baffin Bay. The ridge, labeled by the chart as Ungava Ridge, resembled an upside-down smile, concave from *Seawolf*'s perspective. At places the ridge grew shallow, in one point to the west—at Davis Peak—it went all the way up to 100 fathoms. He looked at the chart and bent to examine it more closely. Despite the shallowness of the Ungava Ridge and the proximity of Davis Peak, he decided to drive westward off the line-of-sight to the *Destiny*. There was still plenty of room, forty miles before the rise of Davis Peak, making the course viable, but even as he ordered the helmsman to put the rudder over and set his course for west-north-west, Pacino realized that this was contrary to his instinct, which, given an arbitrary choice of a course, would be to choose one with more open ocean. He shrugged it off but it stuck in his mind.

"Sonar, Captain, we're moving off the track heading west to get some parallax on the target. Report anything you have on Target One if and when it comes out of the way of the torpedoes."

"Sonar, aye."

"Helm, all ahead standard."

Pacino waited, again finding himself impatient. He looked up into the overhead at the repeater display for the spherical array's broadband, watching the waterfall display cascade down, but other than the blotch to the north from the torpedoes, could distinguish nothing.

"Officer of the Deck, keep an eye on our position. I don't want to run aground on that ridge."

"Aye, sir."

Before his eyes, a twin trace distinguished itself at the center of the short-time display of the waterfall. Something to the north. The Destiny? Why would it be so loud with a twin trace? Pacino had a bad feeling about it and was about to key his mike to call Holt in sonar to see what the strange noises were when Holt's voice came over his earphones.

"Conn, sonar, two torpedoes in the water, bearing zero zero one and three five eight, pump-jet propulsors at what looks like high speed."

"All ahead flank," Pacino ordered, suddenly feeling like he had been there before and made the same order, seen the same double-trace on the waterfall screen. The chart appeared in his mind, the shallows approaching as he continued to drive to the west. Suddenly he knew what he was about to do, and realized that the biggest problem with his plan would be getting the crew to understand and obey it. Dimly, in the background, he heard Holt declare the incoming torpedoes to be Nagasaki models, as Pacino had known instinctively. He barely paid attention, feeling a sudden nausea.

"Captain," Vaughn said, "we're getting too close to the ridge, we need to turn to the south. Those are Nagasakis—"

"No, we won't be turning to the south." When Pacino looked Vaughn in the eyes, he was startled to see a hardness in his executive officer's face, as if the XO were examining him to determine if he were fit for command. Pacino chose his next words carefully. "We can't outrun a Nagasaki torpedo, XO. Much less a pair of them. They go seventy knots. They'll pursue for an hour, maybe more. Even if they were fired from 50,000 yards, they'd catch us well before the hour expired, and I've got a feeling these were launched from a lot closer, like 25,000 yards. That would put them thirty minutes away if we ran at flank, fifteen minutes if we continue west. That's fifteen minutes to get off their track, or ten miles, maybe twelve. We might get out of the search cone completely if they have an enable point like our Mark 50s. It's worth a shot."

Vaughn's expression softened for a moment.

"Okay, you're the boss."

"Don't worry, XO," Pacino said quietly so that only he could hear. "I have every intention of living through this. Call maneuvering and tell them to load and launch the SLOT buoy labeled number two."

Vaughn relayed the order, giving a sidelong glance at Pacino as he did.

Pacino wondered what he'd do with the next order.

USS *Phoenix*

"Conn, sonar," Sanderson said. "I have four torpedo tracks on the spherical array bearing north to north-northeast. At least those four have gone by us."

"Any change in their speed, Senior Chief?" Kane wondered if the weapons would slow down and circle back if they saw no target.

"No, sir. They're still at max speed heading north. I've got another one going by, make that two."

McDonne's big face filled up with a toothy grin. "You did it, sir. Well done."

"Thank Houser," Kane said. "I think I will. Thanks, Vic."

"Conn, sonar, three more past and heading north."

Kane almost smiled. They'd finally gotten a break. He actually began studying the chart, planning the track back south. To Norfolk. Home.

CNFS *Hegira*

"Insert another one-point-five g-turn, ship control," Tawkidi ordered.

The deck again tilted and trembled as the ship did a rapid high-speed circle. When the ship steadied on its previous northern course the officers studied the Second Captain screens.

"Commodore, the weapons are shutting down," Tawkidi announced. "Five of them so far! We only have seven left incoming, and by the analysis they are fading astern. It's working, sir. We may be restarting the missile countdown in another ten or twenty minutes."

Sharef did not smile. He kept looking at the panel where Sublieutenant Rouni worked, analyzing the data that had come in. Rouni's face clouded but he said nothing.

"What is it, Sublieutenant?"

"There was something to the southwest as we went through the turn. I'm not certain, but the analysis is very strange."

"Go on."

"Sir, I'd swear this noise interception is from machinery, specifically steam-propulsion machinery, but it changed as we picked it up. We should have held it through a third of the maneuver, but right here, the noise level dropped to nothing, down to ambient levels, it went invisible. I don't understand it."

Tawkidi frowned as he looked at the data.

"Commodore, it's not the proper bearing for the launch platform for the twelve torpedoes."

"Maybe it is a second sub," Quzwini, the mechanical officer, said from the reactor-control console, his face still white from his efforts in the ballast tank installing the Scorpion warhead. "Perhaps an observation sub that tracked us and gave our position away to the firing ship. At that bearing it would have been in the path of the torpedoes just as we were. And maybe it did what you recommended, Commander Tawkidi, and shut down to hide under the ice."

"It makes no sense," Sharef said. "A second sub would have fired on us himself. It is not like the Americans to get caught in the line of their own fire, not when they can avoid it. Nor would an American risk a torpedo volley knowing another of his subs was in the way."

"Maybe it's a British sub, or a Canadian diesel boat. By reputation they are very quiet," Quzwini said. "And they have been known to go deep into the marginal ice zone. He might have been securing snorting operations with his diesel and gone on battery power."

Tawkidi appeared to reach a decision. "Sir, we need to put a Nagasaki down his bearing, just in case. We can have no further threats to our missile launch. We can set the presets for a slow-speed approach down the bearing line, tuned to hear the slightest man-made noise. If it is another sub, the Nagasaki will neutralize it. If it's a phantom reflection or an ice noise, we have lost nothing."

Sharef knew Tawkidi was making sense. "Very good, Commander. Launch the Nagasaki at the phantom noise. We'll see what comes of it."

Four minutes later the Nagasaki torpedo left the tube, driving at a slow twenty-five clicks, its sonar straining for noises of machinery or metal against metal. By the time the torpedo had completed its turn to the southwest, another four of the incoming American torpedoes had run out of fuel and shut down, hitting nothing.

34

SATURDAY, 4 JANUARY

Labrador Sea, Northwest of Godthaab, Greenland
CNFS *Hegira*

The last 1.5-g turn revealed that the final incoming American torpedoes had shut down, all of them out of fuel, impotent.

"The American torpedoes have all shut down, sir."

Sharef could no longer avoid it. "Bring the ship around to the south and slow to missile-launch speed, Commander, and come shallow."

"Yes, Commodore. Ship control, set your course south, speed four clicks, depth 100 meters." Tawkidi climbed onto the control seat at the periscope station and raised the scope. The optic module came out of its well. Tawkidi put his eyes to the instrument. He looked out for a moment, saw nothing, reached up to the control section and energized the searchlights mounted on the top of the fin. The view immediately lit up with a vista of the underside of a large ice floe. Tawkidi keyed the right grip, causing his seat to rotate slowly in a circle, occasionally hitting a function key that sent a beam of blue laser light upward to the ice, measuring its thickness and density, the information superimposing itself on his periscope vision.

"Sir, we have ice overhead. We won't be able to launch here, but I think we should be close to the edge of this iceberg. A kilometer south."

"Drive the ship south with the periscope up, Commander. You'll find open water quicker that way. Suggest fifteen clicks to hurry the trip."

"Yessir," Tawkidi's voice was muffled by the periscope module as he made the orders.

Sharef waited, occasionally glancing at the Second Captain's sensor displays, prodding Rouni to report the status of the Nagasakis. All three weapons were still in transit.

"Sir, we have open water," Tawkidi announced. "Ship control, dead slow ahead, four clicks. Weapon control, flood tube one and power up the Hiroshima missile. Do the Scorpion self-check and report."

"Very good, Commander," General Sihoud said from the forward door of the room. "I am well pleased with the mission, Commodore Sharef. You and your crew have done great things. Allah is with you."

Sharef nodded, wanting to tell him to keep his speeches to himself. He just wanted to be done with this thing.

"Commander," Tawkidi reported, "we are getting a speed increase from the third-launched Nagasaki. I think it has heard a target."

Sihoud was clearly pleased. Even Colonel Ahmed nodded in satisfaction. Sharef's expression did not change. More death ahead, but at least perhaps a threat would soon be neutralized.

USS *Phoenix*

Ten minutes earlier the word had come from maneuvering that the battery was low, very low, due to keeping sonar at full capability. Sonar, with its auxiliary seawater pumps to cool its massive computers, was a power hog. They were reaching a point of no return. Starting the reactor would take 100 amp-hours, and there were only 105 left. Kane had given the order with deep reluctance: restart the reactor.

The restart was now into its tenth minute, with power on the grid from the ship's turbine generators promised in another ten minutes. Kane paced control, his thoughts escaping to a trip home, a hot meal, a hot shower and a full night's sleep.

"Conn, sonar, all the Mark 50s have shut down. The Destiny must have outrun them."

"Any sign of the firing submarine?" Kane asked. There was no answer. Kane repeated the call. Still no answer. Kane had taken two steps off the conn in the direction of the door to sonar when Sanderson's voice came over the circuit.

"Conn, sonar, torpedo in the water bearing zero four five. It looks like a Nagasaki and it's increasing speed even as I'm making this report."

Kane ran back to the conn and grabbed the Circuit Seven microphone hanging from the overhead.

"Engineer, Captain, get the reactor and main engines up fast. We have a torpedo in the water."

"GOING TO EMERGENCY HEATUP RATES NOW, CAPTAIN, BUT I CAN'T DELIVER IN LESS THAN FIVE MINUTES EVEN WITH EVERYTHING SHE'S GOT," Schramford reported.

If there were a medal for most time spent on the wrong end of warshot torpedoes, Kane thought, *Phoenix* would win it hands down. He looked at McDonne. For the first time in the entire run McDonne's face was a study in unconcealed fear. Kane wondered how his own warface was holding up. In the end, he thought, it wouldn't matter. The Nagasaki torpedo would get them, there was no evading it. Trying to get the reactor restarted to evade was almost just something to do to occupy the crew's time while they waited for the end. Well, it had been a good run, they had almost made it—

"Conn, sonar, the incoming torpedo is close, damned close. If we don't put on some turns we're not going to make it."

"Eng, what's the status?"

"WE'VE BARELY GOT STEAM COMING DOWN THE HEADER NOW. IT'LL BE AT LEAST TWO MINUTES BEFORE I CAN GET EMERGENCY WARMUPS DONE ON THE TURBINE GENERATORS, ANOTHER TWO BEFORE I CAN GIVE YOU THE MAIN ENGINES."

"Keep going, Eng."

The overhead speaker clicked twice. At least, Kane thought, the engineer and the crew aft could stay busy, their minds occupied. All the control-room crew could do was wait.

Kane listened as the room grew suddenly quiet. Outside the hull he could hear the sound of the incoming Nagasaki's propulsor, the high-pitched noise turning from a whine to a scream. He could hear the clicking of its under-ice sonar. The noises now seemed loudest through the deck, as if the weapon was coming in from below.

The wait seemed interminable. Kane was almost relieved when the torpedo detonated.

CNFS *Hegira*

A distant rumble sounded through the hull, its direction indiscernible.

"What was that?" Sharef asked, standing behind the Second Captain consoles, leaning heavily on his makeshift cane, fatigue hanging on him like a hundred-pound weight.

"Nagasaki torpedo detonation at the bearing to the suspected second intruder, Commodore. And, wait a minute . . . I'm getting the sounds of flooding and something else. Maybe compartment bulkheads collapsing. A very loud rushing noise." Rouni turned to Commander Tawkidi. "Commander, you should hear this."

Tawkidi listened, shook his head. He handed the headphones to Sharef. The noise was terrifying, a high-pitched shrieking and a deep shaking growling noise, the two sounds weaving in pitch and rising and falling, the sound of a monstrous beast dying. As Sharef listened he wanted nothing more than to take off the headset and never hear the awful sounds again, knowing now that the screaming would haunt him to his last day. Finally the noise seemed to weaken, to give way to the frigid waters and die. Sharef handed back the headset.

"I'm not certain, perhaps it was a thermal shock, a rupture of their high-temperature reactor equipment leaking to the cold of the sea." What could he say about the sounds of a ship dying? The anger he had previously felt at the Americans for sinking his *Sahand* and for the weapons they had shot at the *Hegira* had been dissipated. He realized now that their attempts to sink the ship had been blind and frantic, that now *Hegira* would prevail and rain down death on their capital city. But it was a victory distinctly empty to him. He had no desire to do this, to have this mass murder be connected to his name. Perhaps, in his way, the general had the right idea, that launching the Scorpion would hold back the West and allow his people to live in a united Muslim world, gaining a new recognition from the rest of the world, a new respect. Though hard to believe that killing on the scale they aspired to would earn them that, it had happened at the end of the second world war when the Americans themselves had leveled Hiroshima and Nagasaki. Perhaps it was oddly appropriate that they would now be on the receiving end of the destruction from a missile called the Hiroshima.

Sharef became aware that his thoughts were rambling and tried to plug back into the tactical situation developing around him.

"What is the status of the first-launched Nagasakis?" he asked.

"Still on their run to the target, sir."

"Same course? Is he evading to the south?"

Tawkidi frowned. "Strangely, no, sir. The torpedoes are now bearing southwest."

"The American has perhaps lost his navigational ability. Or his mind," Rouni said, smiling. "They would be heading for the shallows at Ungava Ridge if they're going west. If the torpedoes don't kill them, running aground will. Wait . . . ."

Rouni pressed the headset closer to his ears. "I think the weapons are speeding up to attack velocity, sir. Detonation should be in the next five minutes."

Sharef nodded. The two threats were neutralized. It was time to launch. "Status of the Scorpion?" He looked at the weapons-control area with Sub.-Lt. Omar al-Maari at the console. Al-Maari had once reported to the weapons officer, Aboud Mamun, who had been killed in the initial torpedo detonation.

"Self-check is satisfactory. Warhead computer is functional at one hundred percent, target coordinates and waypoints confirmed. Hiroshima airframe navigational computer is functional at full capacity. Fuel cells are pressurized, turbine bearings are lubed and warm, winglet hinges articulation checks are nominal, circuit continuity to the solid rocket fuel is verified. Tube one is pressurized and open to sea, bow cap open, gas generator ready. Recommend recommencing countdown, sir."

"Commence sixty-second automatic-countdown sequence."

"Commencing now at launch minus fifty-nine seconds."

USS Seawolf

"Conn, sonar, the last own-ship units have shut down. The explosion from bearing zero one eight was accompanied by hull-breakup noises. We've probably lost the *Phoenix*. And the incoming torpedoes are increasing speed, Captain," Holt reported on the headphones. All the bad news, condensed into a nutshell. There was no time to elaborate, not with the Nagasakis on their way and in close.

The attack so far had been a complete failure, Pacino realized. The fathometer read 280 fathoms beneath the keel as the water grew shallower at the rise of the ridge. Not shallow enough, not yet, he thought, but it would have to do. Perhaps by the time he'd completed the work for his last-resort plan the ridge beneath them would be shallower than test depth. He could only hope.

"XO, I've got one last idea," Pacino said, knowing now that Vaughn would have to go along. With the two Nagasakis coming in on final approach, what else could they do?

"Love to hear it, Skipper," Vaughn drawled. Hope flashed momentarily across the hollow-cheeked faces in the control room, then slowly faded.

"We'll launch the Vortex bank. We may only get one of them off, and they may breach the hull and make the tubes explode, but if the hull's going to be breached in the next five minutes anyway . . . at least we can kiss Sihoud and the Destiny goodbye even if we can't confirm a kill before the Nagasakis get to us."

Vaughn understood immediately, but Pacino sensed he had known that his captain had forseen this eventuality all along.

"We'll do it, sir. I'll evacuate the watchstanders outside the control room to the engineroom."

"Weps, select the Vortex battery on the WCP, line up and pressurize all Vortex tubes, spin up all Vortex missiles and make preparations for launch of the battery."

Court flipped through the weapon-control panel displays, selected the Vortex bank, flooded the tubes and opened the outer doors. The tubes were engineered so that all three could be opened at once, with large-bore piping for rapid flooding. While Court lined up the tubes he selected the Vortex warhead computers, fixing the presets for departure depth. He came to target bearing and stopped, jerking his head around.

"We have a bearing to the target?"

"Select Target One from the firecontrol generated bearing," Pacino said, knowing it wouldn't matter if the bearing was off by several degrees.

"Aye, sir. Vortex missiles one, two and three are spun up and ready for launch. Launch interval, sir?"

Pacino had considered the answer. They couldn't be launched simultaneously, or they would interfere with each other, the solid rockets blowing apart neighboring missiles. Too far apart, the launching system would be gone, probably blown apart by the explosion of the first tube.

"Set the interval at 500 milliseconds," Pacino ordered. That, he figured, would give the system time to launch the second missile but would also allow the first-launched weapon to clear the tube and the ship. The third unit would probably never make it out of the ship.

"Vortex units are ready, sir."

"XO, evacuate all watchstanders to the aft compartment. Keep both hatches open. I'll be right back."

"Aye, sir," Vaughn said, not looking at Pacino. "You heard it, men. Everybody aft, *now.*"

The watchstanders dropped headsets, clipboards, pens, the lot of them stampeding aft to the passageway leading down the ship's centerline, Holt and his sonarmen joining them from the forward door to the sonar room. Vaughn was last to go.

By the time the men were gone the noise of the Nagasaki torpedoes could be heard through the hull, their whining propulsors sounding ghostly.

"Sir?" Vaughn had paused at the aft door to the passageway. "Don't be too long or I'll have to shut the hatches."

"I'll be right there," Pacino said, a phone in his ear.

"Engineer," Hobart's curt voice said.

"Eng, Captain. Load and launch SLOT buoy number three."

"Aye, sir, loading now."

Pacino hung up and looked at the control room one last time. The ship's angle was inclining downward, no longer a watchstander to guard the ship-control panel. Pacino pulled up the control yoke and glanced at ship's speed. Forty-five knots, ship's depth, 800 feet. He lifted a glance to the ballast-control panel and looked at the emergency-blow levers, stepped back and hoisted the phone again.

"Engineer."

"Captain, here. Take local control of the sternplanes. Keep the ship's angle level, no matter what."

"Aye, sir. The SLOT buoy is launched."

Pacino hung up. There was no time. He could hear the clicking of the torpedo sonars as they got closer. He looked down on the weapon-control panel, selected the autosequence variable function key and lined up the system to be fired. He reached over to the trigger, rotated it to the standby position, watched the word STANDBY flash on the panel, then pulled it to the fire position.

Nothing happened. The circuit would be complete as soon as he rotated the switch he had painstakingly installed near the hatch to the reactor compartment. His switch had interrupted the firing circuit. With luck, the system would still work. He ran to the ballast-control panel on the port side, reached for the forward emergency-blow lever and flipped it up. The forward compartment would soon be flooded, and maybe blowing forward ballast would compensate, keep the ship from diving to the bottom.

The roar of the emergency air in his ears, loud enough to drown out the sound of the Nagasaki torpedo sonars, Pacino sprinted for the aft door. He rushed down the passageway, past his and Vaughn's stateroom, until he got to the stairs. He slid down the slick stainless rails to the bottom, landing near the hatchway to the reactor compartment.

With one foot in the hatchway he reached for the rotary switch he had installed, his right hand on it, pulling the rest of his body through until only his hand protruded from the hatch. The deck was inclining upward as a result of Hobart fighting the emergency blow.

Pacino flipped the switch, heart pounding.

He pulled his arm in and shut the hatch. It latched. He reached for the wheel to spin the dogs to the shut position and heard a roar and an explosion. In the four-inch-diameter high-pressure glass window set into the thick metal of the hatch there was a flash of blinding light. Pacino hadn't finished dogging the hatch, but he now turned and ran aft to the hatch to the engineroom, his hearing gone from the deafening sound of the explosion, now existing in a world in which he couldn't even hear his own gasping breaths. He could make out Vaughn on the other side of the hatch and dived toward the opening, smashing himself against the hatch coaming. He felt the men pull him through and felt—not heard—them shut the hatch and dog it, the same flash now shining through the window of the engineroom hatch.

The deck then pitched downward and the ship shook violently. The lights went out.

The *Seawolf*'s deck inclined further, to a ten-degree down-angle, when the first of the Nagasaki torpedoes hit and exploded.

The Nagasaki torpedo had looked up from a hundred meters beneath the hull of the *Phoenix*, recognized it as the target and turned upward, accelerating to attack velocity. The weapon got within a meter of the hull before its proximity detector went to full-current discharge. The explosion train detonated in the few milliseconds it took the nose cone of the torpedo to travel to the hull, so that the blast hit the steel of the cylindrical hull an instant before the nose cone of the torpedo would have if the weapon had been a dud.

The blast force of the explosive vaporized the steel, forming a five-meter hole and springing back hull plates and structural hoops for five meters on either side of it. The blast effect continued into the compartment, blowing piping apart, smashing several pumps into half-molten pieces of their former selves, shredding the four-inch-thick steel shell of the vessel that formed the heart of the ship, the nuclear reactor. The blast force propagated upward, blowing to bits the reactor-compartment tunnel, flexing its pressure against the forward and aft bulkheads, the bulkheads bulging away from the blast but holding. The pressure of the blast was joined by the high energy of 520-degree steam as it escaped from the reactor systems. But within seconds the fireball of the blast was spent, the shock waves from the explosion had traveled outward into the rest of the ship and into the surrounding water and ice, and the explosion lost momentum, attenuated and died. The high-pressure gases from the explosion vented themselves out the hole at the bottom of the hull, debris and metal also falling through, until the compartment pressure was equalized with the seawater outside. Cold seawater flooded into the compartment, and when it mixed with the multiple jets of high-energy steam, sent moaning noises into the ocean.

Finally the seawater robbed the reactor systems of their energy, and the violence of the incident ended. The reactor compartment remained flooded, the equipment ruined and smashed, most of it off its foundations, some of it washed into the sea from the keel hole.

The submarine's middle compartment was, for practical purposes, gone. The forward and aft compartments, physically, survived, except for the interconnections between them running through the reactor compartment. The men in the forward compartment were isolated from those aft. Few of them were conscious.

Captain Kane pulled himself groggily off the deck and found himself surrounded by blackness. He turned on a battle lantern and shivered from the sight, and the cold.

35

SATURDAY, 4 JANUARY

Labrador Sea, Northwest of Godthaab, Greenland
CNFS *Hegira*

"Countdown proceeding, Commander," al-Maari reported. "Launch minus twenty seconds. Missile on internal power, gas generator rocket motor ignition charge voltage climbing. Twelve volts, relay contacts shutting . . . now. Gas generator ignition in two seconds . . ."

Sharef listened for the sound of the tube's gas generator solid rocket fuel igniting. It was really not a rocket at all but a charge of solid fuel that, when ignited, would exhaust into a large reservoir of water piped to the aft end of the missile tube. When the hot rocket-exhaust gas hit the reservoir tank the water would flash to steam and pressurize the tube, thrusting the missile from the tube with high pressure. The missile would float to the surface enveloped in the steam from the gas generator and ignite its first-stage rocket motor when it was free of the water. After a six-second burn, the missile would have enough velocity that its jet engine could kick in and lift it to an altitude of ten kilometers, when the ramjet engine would take over and boost the missile to supersonic speed and take it up to eighteen kilometers. The flight to Washington would be over before *Hegira* had made forty kilometers north on the way home.

"Launch minus ten seconds, we have gas generator ignition. Five seconds, sir."

Sihoud turned toward Ahmed, whose face had broken into lines of triumph.

Sharef looked at the deckplates.

When Captain Pacino had shut the homemade rotary switch, electrical current had flowed through the wires he had strung, until relay R141 down in the forward space of the torpedo room felt the electrical energy hit its electromagnetic coil. The magnetism pulled the relay's mechanism closed, completing the circuit to the ignition voltage to the Vortex battery ignition systems.

Vortex tube one, the tube on top, was first in the sequence. A small can of flammables felt the electrical voltage from a spark kit, blowing the can into incandescence. Within milliseconds the flame front propagated to the solid rocket fuel of the Hiroshima missile, the fuel burning violently, the flames spreading across the diameter of the missile's aft end until the rocket motor achieved full thrust. The missile began to accelerate out of the tube, the rocket motor pushing the weight of the missile and the inertia of the water between the missile nose cone and the skin of the ship. The missile began to move, slowly at first, then picking up speed, the space aft of it opening up. The hot rocket-exhaust gases accumulated in the small space aft of the rocket, the pressure in the tube soaring like that at the base of a gun barrel in the moments after the gunpowder was lit off. The missile continued to move forward, but in the second hundred milliseconds after ignition, the pressure in the tube proved too much for the metal of the tube.

The tube ruptured and spilled flaming exhaust out into the torpedo room, vaporizing the deckplates above, the flames melting and vaporizing the four torpedoes exposed on the upper tier of the torpedo rack. The Mark 50 weapons began to burn, then to explode, the pressure in the torpedo room soaring from the burning, exploding torpedoes as well as the fury of the Vortex-missile exhaust. The metal of the tube gave way, coming apart and blowing the Vortex tubes below it into misshapen wrecks. By the time the top Vortex missile was leaving the ship behind, completely immersed in the waters of the Labrador Sea, the lower two Vortex tubes smashed and dispersed the two missiles' rocket fuel into the room, the rocket fuel igniting and blowing apart the already crushed lower tubes. Six hundred milliseconds after launch, the Vortex was surging ahead into the water, leaving the *Seawolf* behind, while the lower two Vortex missiles exploded, both their warheads and their solid rocket fuel adding to the exploding mass inside the torpedo room.

Outside the ship the Vortex missile accelerated, its rocket nozzle turning under the direction of the on-board computer, directing it to turn to its programmed approach, heading to the target. By the time the Vortex missile was a shiplength away from the launching platform, the nozzle had turned to the proper angle, and the missile felt the lateral g-forces guiding it to its proper heading. At the same time the hull of the firing ship came apart, the torpedo room in the lower level vaporized, the hull enclosing it blowing outward, the light from the explosions lighting up the under-ice world in a harsh, foreign glow. After two hundred milliseconds the light dimmed, the explosion faded. The Vortex was now surging ahead, another third of a shiplength further from its launch point. The outgoing missile then passed an incoming torpedo, the incoming weapon smaller and lighter, and by that time much slower than the Vortex. The Vortex continued in its turn, uncaring.

By the time the Vortex had steadied on its approach course to the target it was 1,500 yards from the firing ship. Behind it, obscured by the noise of the roaring solid-rocket exhaust, came the sound of the explosion of the first Nagasaki torpedo as it hit the *Seawolf* just under the sonar dome forward. The forward compartment, already breached and flooding from aft at the torpedo room, blew inward at the bottom, all three decks collapsing upward, the hull caving in, the nose cone at the sonar sphere breaking apart, the air that had filled the ballast tanks from Pacino's emergency blow scattering into the sea.

The Vortex continued accelerating, its velocity climbing to what would be terminal velocity at 300 knots, an underwater speed unknown outside of the Vortex test program. It passed and left behind the second Nagasaki torpedo and continued. When the second Nagasaki torpedo exploded, the Vortex was a third of the way to its target.

The second Nagasaki smashed into the *Seawolf* amidships, at the bulkhead separating the forward compartment from the reactor compartment. The torpedo-room explosion had already carried away half the bulkhead of the compartment. The torpedo explosion added to the damage, blowing the reactor vessel off its mounting and slamming it into the pressurizer vessel further aft, the steam pipes rupturing. The hull skin had already been breached and blown off at the keel from the aftermath of the Vortex-tube explosions. The second Nagasaki detonation completed the damage, the hull giving way and letting go at the top surface, the ship shearing into two pieces—the forward half violently damaged. The aft half of the ship, with a barely intact bulkhead that was once the aft reactor compartment wall, was by comparison unharmed, but it had lost stability on all three axes. It spun and tumbled to the depths, its buoyancy lost.

The rocky ground of the Ungava Ridge rose up to meet it as it sank. The hull fragment hit the bottom at terminal velocity, the hull-half crushing, the sternplanes and rudder at the far aft point shearing off and scattering across the rocks. Inside the hull, the equipment shook against the mounting bolts, the lighter pieces—pumps and pipes—coming loose and rattling around inside. The hull came to rest with a fifteen-degree incline downward, a list of nearly twenty degrees. Inside there was no light, but there was, for the moment, air. The hull began flooding through the steam system; the steam pipes that had drawn their pressure and flow from the reactor compartment had been sheared off at the forward bulkhead, and now, instead of steam, seawater poured down the pipes, filling the turbine casings, the condensers and coming out the steam traps and cracks formed in the piping by the admission of freezing salty seawater into what moments before had been a 500-degree carbon-steel pipe. A refrigeration unit in the lower deck of the space began leaking high-pressure refrigerant gas into the hull, the R-111 toxic but nearly odorless. Bodies littered the upper deck of the hull, the men who had been evacuated from the forward hatch. Those conscious began to choke from the atmospheric contamination.

The depth of the hull was 1,260 feet, above crush depth but deep enough that the souls trapped inside could be considered to have no future.

"Four, three, two, one, full thrust, and tube release! *The weapon is away!*" al-Maari seemed caught up in the countdown and the launch of the Hiroshima missile.

Sharef looked at the jubilant faces around him, wondering if he were the only one who remembered that one, maybe two million deaths would come of it. The men around him, even Sihoud—or perhaps especially Sihoud—at this moment seemed like children to him, embroiled in their games and their fighting, ignorant of larger issues and realities. It was a big game to them, he thought. In a few seconds the sonar system would report the health of the missile, whether its first stage had ignited and lifted it to its trajectory—

A rushing sound suddenly could be made out, coming directly from outside the hull. At first Sharef assumed it to be the rocket motor of the Hiroshima missile igniting, but it was coming from abeam to port, sounding like it was right outside the control room. The noise grew louder, incredibly loud.

Tawkidi barely had time to say, "What the—"

The Vortex missile's swim-time was extraordinarily brief. It had raced beneath the ice floes faster than anything else had ever gone. Its blue laser target-acquisition system activated as it searched the waters ahead for signs of the man-made hull. It picked up the target, just in time for a momentary correction of its directional nozzle, pointing the nose cone of the missile directly at the midpoint of the target hull.

The hull grew from a dot to a giant in a tenth of a second. The forward nose cone of the missile smashed into the hull midsection at 300 hundred knots, the signal for the PlasticPac explosive to detonate. The ultrasecret explosive package had achieved, with molecular densities unknown outside of the lab, the compacting of a conventional explosive into a tiny space, the huge Vortex missile packed with several tons of the material. The explosive power compared to the yield of a small nuclear warhead.

The warhead detonated into a high-temperature, ultrahigh-pressure plasma, the fireball temperature momentarily reaching up to nearly the temperature of the surface of the sun. The metal and plastic fiber optics inside the hull was vaporized in the first several milliseconds of the explosion. The blast ripped the bow from the stern, blew the hull to splinters and rained a debris field down to the bottom of the sea, only the forward ballast-tank section and the furthest aft X-tail intact, the remainder pulverized and half-melted.

The men aboard died so quickly that their eyes, seeing the white flash of light of the explosion, did not have time to pass the vision down the optic nerves to their brains. By the time the impulses were halfway down their optic nerves, their brains were vaporized by the plasma. The Second Captain, operating at much higher thought-processing speeds, registered the blast and the sequential loss of function, feeling itself die, its last processing resembling human panic, then settling into sadness, and it too succumbed.

A piece of debris mostly intact at the bottom of the sea, 3,700 meters below the icy surface, was a jewelled dagger, the scarred blade still bearing the barely legible inscription: GENERAL MOHAMMED AL-SIHOUD, KHALIB AND SWORD OF ISLAM.

There was nothing else left of him. Or of any of the other crew members.

The Hiroshima missile airframe, just clearing the tube door when the Vortex missile exploded, was blown into three pieces by the blast and shock wave of the fiery detonation. It drifted to the bottom, the Scorpion warhead mostly intact. The warhead mechanisms, the ethylene gas bottle and the plutonium dispersion matrix, imploded from the pressure at a depth of some 2,000 meters, scattering the plutonium dust over the bottom, making the debris field of what had been the Combined Naval Force vessel *Hegira* a radioactive dustbin.

Book IV

PHOENIX SUB ZERO

36

SATURDAY, 4 JANUARY

Fort Meade, Maryland, Headquarters, National Security Agency
Building 427 Secure Communications Room

Donchez yawned, sat up and took the message board.

"How about a cup of coffee? You got anything brewed fresh? Like this week?"

"Coming up, Admiral."

Donchez read the message, another one from the *Seawolf*. As he read it, he felt like he'd been punched in the gut. The air whistled out of him.

He read the terse message again, then again. Until its words blurred across the page, the pain of them burning into him.

DATE/TIME:	TIME OF RECEIPT OF SLOT MESSAGE
FROM:	USS SEAWOLF SSN–21
TO:	CNO WASHINGTON, DC // CINCLANT NORFOLK, VA //
	COMSUBLANT NORFOLK, VA
SUBJ:	CONTACT REPORT NO. 3

//BT//

1. DESTINY IS WINNING.

2. COMMENCING ATTACK WITH VORTEX MISSILE BATTERY.

//BT//

Labrador Sea, Northwest of Godthaab, Greenland
USS *Phoenix*

Kane felt the arctic cold pouring into his bones. His breath formed vapor clouds in front of his face, the eerie fog making the room look haunted in the glaring bright spots and dark shadows of the battle lanterns.

"Hard to believe," he said. "At least up forward it seems we had less damage from the Nagasaki than from the grounding."

"That's not true," McDonne said. "Look at the ship. We're blown to hell. No reactor, no communications with the engineroom, under the ice cover . . ."

"But the impact didn't kill anybody. Anybody new . . ."

"The g-loading must have been less. We were pinned up against the ice and it hit us from below. Not much room for the hull to shake. But it gutted us. We'd have been better off if we'd been killed by the explosion."

"I don't think so, XO," Houser said. "We still have a battery. With luck we can run the emergency propulsion motor and move us out of here."

"You're dreaming, Houser. With nobody aft, how are we gonna run the EPM?"

"We don't know they're dead aft. All we have is that there's no one answering the phone. Maybe the phone lines are blown away where they went through the RC."

"Sure, but what about the DC cables from the battery? If the phone lines are blown away how will battery power get to our guys aft?"

"The DC cables are as big around as your arm, XO. They'd stand a hell of a lot better chance than the phone lines."

"Maybe. So what do we do? With no communications, with us trapped up here, them trapped aft, and all of us trapped under the ice, how are we going to get out of this?"

"Schramford," Kane said. "Schramford's the engineer, but he's finished his command quals. Which means he'll be thinking the same things we are. He'll run the EPM without orders and try to get us out of here. He'll take local control of the rudder and sternplanes and try to drive us out."

"Sure, Captain. But he'll need depth control to do it. He's not going anywhere without us flooding a depth-control tank to take some of the buoyancy off."

"Okay," Kane said. "We'll get ready to flood a DCT manually, or we can rig up the ballast-control panel so it'll work."

"How will he know where to go?" McDonne said. "He's got no compass back there."

"We'll tell him," Kane said. "We may not have a phone but we've got something just as good."

"What, sir? Tomato-soup cans and string? If we were surfaced we could just walk outside the hull and bang on his hatch and set up the soup cans, but we've got a hundred-foot-thick ice raft between us and the surface."

"You forgot the underwater telephone, XO."

McDonne looked stunned. The UWT system was an active sonar hydrophone that broadcast the human voice instead of pings or pulses. "You think the UWT works? Damn, maybe you're right. Let's power it up and see what we can—hey, wait, we don't have AC power. It won't work on DC."

"Yes it will," Sanderson said from behind them. "As soon as I make some changes in its wiring. All I've got to do is retie in the static inverter to the battery supply and hardwire and fuses. Well, there's more to it, but in three or four hours we'll have a UWT."

"If we can stay warm that long," McDonne said.

"Break out the parkas, Houser," Kane ordered. "Grab all the sweaters, sweatshirts and long johns you can find."

"Yessir," Houser said, vanishing out the forward door after Sanderson.

"Let's hope," McDonne said, "that Engineer Schramford back aft is reading from the same script we are."

A hundred feet aft, in the engineroom, Lt. Comdr. Tom Schramford lay facedown in a rapidly cooling pool of blood.

USS *Seawolf*
Aft Hull Section

Pacino looked at Vaughn. Both had thrown up. The men still alive, some eighty of them, were gathered in the more open spaces of the top deck of the compartment, between the quiet turbine generators and the main engines.

"What is it, XO?" His voice sounded dead. His hearing was coming back, but too slowly.

"Atmosphere," Vaughn said. "Must be contaminated."

"Let's try the emergency air masks."

As the men rummaged for masks, four more of the survivors threw

up. Once in his mask, Pacino had a new unhappy thought . . . trussed up in masks, the breathing air bottles aft wouldn't last long with them all sucking from them. They needed time, time to be rescued. It could take two days to get a DSRV to them to pull them out, assuming someone knew they were there and still alive.

"Skipper," Vaughn shouted. "We need to be thinking about a sub escape."

Pacino stared at Vaughn. It would be suicide. There was no way a body could do a free ascent from . . . what was it . . . a thousand feet, and live. If it wasn't just the pressure effects, what about the water temperature and hydrothermia? Popping up through the water at twenty feet per second in twenty-eight-degree water would be enough to cool a person's core body temperature so fast that they'd all be ice cubes by the time they got to the surface. Pacino had heard the stories of patients in cold water surviving without air for forty-five minutes, but rescue might be days away, not minutes. There would be no one standing by topside.

And what about ice cover? There was no guarantee they were below open water. Since it was shallow, it might have frozen more quickly. There might be an ice floe a hundred feet thick waiting for them. If they bonked their heads into it at twenty feet per second, it wouldn't matter if it were 100 feet thick or a half-foot thick, it would do the same damage—collision and drowning. And even if that weren't the case, what if the Steinke hoods didn't work? A tear in one of the air hoods would fill with water and leave a man 1,000 feet underwater with no air. That was no way to die. Even if that weren't a problem, what would they do in the freezing water once they got out? Lie in the rafts with wet clothes, the arctic wind blowing over them, waiting to die of the cold?

A submarine escape didn't just postpone death, it was a terrifying way of bringing it on quicker. Pacino figured better to go from asphyxiation in the hull than trying such an escape.

"We'd better think about the escape fast, sir," Hobart said, not privy to Pacino's thoughts. "These masks are fed into the same high-pressure bottles used on the escape trunk. We can either do an escape or sit here and suck air. We can't do both. A sub escape means we go out in groups of eight. That's ten fills and drains of the trunk, eighty Steinke hoods filled at high pressure. That's about the same as all of us sucking this air for about thirty hours. And that's about all we've got left. I don't know about you, Skipper, but I'm with Mr. Vaughn. I'm ready to try an escape. If we make it to the surface maybe someone looking for us will pick us up. Down here we have zero chance. Even if we had a week of air we'd starve. And if we die in the escape . . . I'd rather die looking at clouds than this dead hull."

So Vaughn and Hobart wanted escapes, Pacino thought. Okay, they could have them. "Who else wants to try to go out the escape trunk?"

Of the men crowded into the space, all but twelve raised their hands. Pacino stared. He looked around, saw Vaughn's eyes, challenging. He knew he had no choice, he would go with the crew. In the last load. If they ran out of air, he would stay behind.

"Okay," he said. "It's out the trunk. Engineer, you'll do the honors?"

"You got it, Captain. Let's get the hell out of here, you know?"

Chief Milo Nelson of the *Phoenix* had never seen himself as anything but a mechanic, a blue-collar worker in the Navy. The Navy had seen him as much more, every command offering him a shot at officer candidate school. He had the brains, the leadership, the character presumably needed to be an officer. He had avoided it, fighting it off. He didn't want to be a damned officer and face the old man every day of his life. He wanted to work with the mechanics, turn the wrenches, keep his fingers dirty. Sitting in officers' country, daintily drinking coffee from a cup and saucer, never saying "fuck" and competing with fresh-faced college-educated kids who thought they knew everything but were naive babes clawing their way up the Navy's ladder? No way. Some might say that the idea of the heavier responsibility frightened him. He didn't give a shit. He knew what he knew.

Milo Nelson was the chief mechanic for *Phoenix*'s M-division, working for Lieutenant Houser and the engineer, who happened to be lying in a congealing puddle of his own blood in the maneuvering room waiting for the report from Nelson that the turbine generators were up and ready for loading. The torpedo blast had put Nelson down on the deck aft but had just shaken him up. Engineer Schramford somehow had taken the hit hard, much harder than the enlisted man George Falsom, an electrician who was minding all three panels in the room. Falsom said that Schramford had been leaning around a panel, straining to see the progress of the engineroom crew, the torpedo coming closer, the captain on his case, when the blast hit, tripping him and knocking him into the side of the reactor-control panel. Somehow he had caught his head on a main coolant pump switch. The electrician Falsom had hit the deck, Schramford tumbling down on top of him after smacking his head on the pump switch.

Nelson had been standing watch as engineering-watch supervisor, the senior roving enlisted man in the aft watch section. As such, he could start the engineroom by himself. In the dark. It hadn't taken too long for him to determine that the RC was gone. He'd shut the steam bulkhead valves, stopping the seawater flooding down the steam headers. He'd tried the phones to the forward compartment with no results.

In the maneuvering room he checked out the electric plant control panel, put the voltage selector to the battery, wondering if the wiring going forward had survived. He and Falsom held their breath as the voltage needle spun up to read 260 volts. At least they had indication.

"Want to try it, Falsom?"

"Why not, Chief?"

Falsom reached out and rotated the battery breaker knob. He put the selector switch on the output of the breaker. It zipped 260 volts. It had worked. They had DC power aft.

"So far, so good. Bring up the lights," Nelson said.

The lights flashed into fluorescence overhead, the patches of light from the battle lanterns no longer needed.

"Think they came on up forward?"

"Who knows?"

"I'm gonna try the EPM and see if I can spin the shaft. If I can, we just might be able to get out of here."

"Assuming there's somebody awake up front."

"Big assumption. I'll be back . . ."

When the lights came on in the forward compartment, Kane allowed a wide grin.

"Hey, XO, Tommy Schramford has the stick. Now we just need to be able to talk to him."

XO McDonne said nothing, sweat pouring down his forehead in the frigid cold of the room.

The lower hatch of the *Seawolf*'s escape trunk opened, admitting eight men. The last in accepted the bundle of Steinke hoods from Hobart and shut the hatch. Pacino shivered as he thought about what was going on overhead, the trunk flooding with the frozen water, the men filling their hoods with compressed air, opening the upper hatch and swimming out into water a quarter-mile deep. Just before the last man went out he would signal Hobart, who would wait thirty seconds and shut the outer hatch with hydraulics. Then the whole process would start again. The second batch of eight men climbed the ladder to the trunk. More hoods. The hatch shut.

Pacino wandered to the starboard side of the ship, to the signal ejector. He found the locker where he had stowed the four SLOT buoys and pulled out the one marked No. 4. There was no way to operate the signal ejector now, Pacino thought. There were no seawater systems with pumps pressurizing them to flush the buoy out of the tube. Someone would have to take it out the escape trunk with them. He returned to the base of the trunk, where the third batch of men were climbing the ladder. Henry Vale was the officer to go with this batch.

"See you on top, Captain," Vale said.

"Good luck, Nav," Pacino said, turning the SLOT buoy upside down and turning its transmitter on. He handed the buoy to Vale. "Take this up for me, Henry. It's a distress signal."

"You had that preloaded, sir?" Vale asked, not sure what to make of it.

"Yes, Nav," Pacino said quietly. "Just in case. Now go on and I'll see you in a few."

"Hope there's water up there, not ice." Vale crossed his fingers and looked around one last time. "Goodbye, *Seawolf.*" He disappeared up the ladder.

Milo Nelson stood at the EPM. "I'll be damned," he mumbled to himself. "It works. Be a damned shame if there's nobody in the front seat."

Up forward, Sanderson stepped into the control room, his hair sweat-soaked though the temperature had sunk to the thirties.

"Captain, let's try the UWT. We'll either burn it to hell or it'll work."

Kane picked up the microphone and waited while Sanderson flipped a toggle switch and adjusted the controls. Sanderson nodded, turning down the volume. Kane spoke into the mike.

"AFT COMPARTMENT, AFT COMPARTMENT, THIS IS THE CAPTAIN. ENGINEER, THIS IS THE CAPTAIN. IF YOU CAN HEAR THIS, GET SOMETHING HEAVY AND TAP ON THE HULL TWICE."

Kane heard the echoes of his voice being broadcast to the ocean, bouncing off the bottom of the sea. Sanderson turned up the gain-knob on the panel, the speaker rasping the sounds of the ocean around them into the control room.

They listened. Thirty seconds, a minute. Kane put the microphone up and sat down at one of the control chairs of the attack center. No one wanted to speak. Then, through the speakers, came the sound of two booming clunks. They had heard! Kane hurried back up to the conn and grabbed the microphone.

"AFT COMPARTMENT, THIS IS THE CAPTAIN. IS THE EPM OPERATIONAL? KNOCK TWO TIMES FOR YES."

Again two clunks came over the speaker.

"AFT COMPARTMENT, IN TWO MINUTES WE WILL FLOOD DEPTH CONTROL TO GET US DOWN. TAKE LOCAL CONTROL OF THE RUDDER AND STERNPLANES. PUT THE RUDDER OVER TWENTY DEGREES RIGHT AND PREPARE TO PUT ONE THIRD AHEAD TURNS ON THE EPM."

"Where's Houser? XO, get depth-control one and two flooded quick as you can."

After hurrying out and back in, McDonne picked up a phone from the ballast-control panel, where he could talk to Houser, who was in the lower level machinery space. McDonne watched the tank levels rise, took a look at the depth meter at the ship-control panel and spoke again to Houser. Finally the depth gauge started to move, the depth increasing from 160 feet to 180, then 200. McDonne nodded to Kane.

"AFT COMPARTMENT, CAPTAIN, ALL AHEAD ONE THIRD ON THE EPM, RIGHT TWENTY DEGREES RUDDER. USE THE STERNPLANES AS NEEDED TO LEVEL THE SHIP."

McDonne watched the ship-control panel indication as the ship turned, waiting for the compass to come around to the south. It took a long time but eventually the gyro read 180 degrees.

"I'm gonna take a peek out the type twenty," Kane said, raising the periscope. "It'll be dawn soon. Maybe I'll be able to tell when we've got open water overhead."

"Let's hope we see it before the battery runs dry," McDonne said. "We didn't have much juice when that Nagasaki hit us, unless the Eng had some power up his sleeve."

The next batch seemed to go fast. Too fast. The crew in the space was thinning quickly. There were only twenty-four men left in the *Seawolf*'s engineroom. Another two batches through the trunk and it would be Pacino's turn.

He paced the aft compartment, knowing this would be the last time he'd see it. He plugged into a connection, took a breath and disconnected his hose, walked to the next station until he was far aft in the maneuvering space. The modern electronics were all dark, the space deserted and quiet. He sank in the control chair of the engineering officer of the watch and shut his eyes for a moment.

"Sir?" Vaughn's mask-distorted voice said at the door.

"I'm here, XO."

"Last batch, Captain. We're ready to go. The airbanks are down, sir. We might not even get this last group out. Once this batch goes, there won't be any air left. We have to go now, sir."

Pacino felt like telling Vaughn he would stay anyway. The walk felt like a stroll to the gallows. Not a praying man, Pacino managed a few silent words, not wanting to go into the trunk.

"We're the last, Captain," Vaughn said, pointing up the ladder.

"Maybe you should go on ahead . . ."

"Skipper, I read you, but we're going to live, you've got to believe that . . ."

"Lube Oil. Jack. I appreciate what you're trying to do, but—"

"Sir . . . Patch, listen to me."

Vaughn had never called him that before, Pacino thought.

"Have you thought about the men upstairs, trying to survive, floating in those rafts? What do I tell them? What the hell do I tell *them*?"

That he was a cop-out, Pacino thought. A bullshit captain afraid to cast his lot with theirs. Maybe they would die up there but at least they deserved to die with their commanding officer. And he with them.

"Okay, XO. You first."

Vaughn climbed up, discarding his mask and tossing it to the deck. Pacino did the same as he climbed the ladder and looked below at the battle-lantern-lit engineroom one last time. He climbed into the tight escape trunk, got out of the way of the hatch and shut it, the metal of it making a loud clunk against the steel of the hull.

37

SATURDAY, 4 JANUARY

Labrador Sea

Kane could see the ice cover overhead, not with normal vision but with the low-light enhancer. The ice overhead looked thick.

Back aft at the electric plant-control panel, the amp-hours clicked away, the battery moving closer to exhaustion with every turn of the screw.

Pacino took the plastic Steinke hood handed him by Vaughn and stood with the other men while Vaughn opened the valve to flood the trunk. The trunk was about ten feet in diameter, about ten feet tall, with a steel wall separating the upper portion from the approach to the upper hatch. The wall came down only a few feet, ending at chest level. Vaughn had his head inside the partitioned area as he operated the valves.

The water that came in soaked into Pacino's clothes, terribly cold, the water at that depth actually colder than ice water because of the salt in it. The water rose to his shins, and by that time his feet were already numb, his ankles beginning to get numb. The frigid water climbed to waist level, soaking the trousers of his poopysuit. The air in the space was getting foggy, its pressure rising, its temperature climbing from the compression, the odd effect of the hot humid air next to the freezing water filling the chamber with fog so dense that Pacino could no longer make out the upper hatch in the light of the twin battle lanterns. The water rose to his chest, and he could feel his heart pounding, working against the stress of the cold. When the water rose higher he heard Vaughn calling him into the partitioned area. Pacino crowded over with the rest of the men, the hot cloudy air and close quarters making it difficult to breathe. The water rose up to chin level. Vaughn's voice sounded eerie in the highly pressurized space, its pressure equal to outside the ship. Without mixed gas for breathing, the oxygen in the space would become toxic in minutes. They had to get out or die here. Pacino's feet and legs had left him long before. His hands were going and now even his torso was nearly numb.

Vaughn filled the first man's Steinke hood, the plastic going over the man's head to chest level, a small clear plastic window in the mask showing the man's pained face.

"Don't forget to scream all the way up," Vaughn said. Vaughn hit a hydraulic lever that opened the upper hatch. Pacino could hear a bubbling sound as the trapped air outside the partition left the trunk. The chamber was now open to the sea, the surface 1,200 feet above, the only air what was trapped in the partition.

The men left one by one. Now it was Pacino's turn. Vaughn put on his hood, the high-pressure air filling it, the taste of it dry and coppery. Vaughn then filled his own and dropped the hose, looking at Pacino.

"Let's go, sir. Don't forget to scream. See you on the surface."

Vaughn and Pacino ducked down, their heads popping underwater and emerging on the other side of the partition wall, now directly under the upper hatch. Vaughn went first. In the dim light, still shining underwater, Pacino saw Vaughn rise up through the circle of the hatch and vanish. Just for a moment, Pacino was tempted to shut the upper hatch and go back into the chamber, but Vaughn's words rang in his ears. What would the XO tell the crew?

Pacino felt his way, the air in his hood making him buoyant. He pushed himself up, the hood pulling him upward. He put his hands on the hatchway, guided himself out, and as he passed out the hatch he said the words aloud, knowing there was no one else to do it.

"*Seawolf,* departing."

The light shone weakly from the open hatch. He had the briefest impression of the green hull extending into the darkness fore and aft, the hull ending at a jagged rip. He let go of the metal of the hatch, surprised that he could still feel something with his fingers, and now he looked up, beginning to feel the water flow as he began to rise.

It was a strange sensation being in arctic seawater, body numb, knowing it was a quarter-mile to the surface. He wondered if he was succumbing to nitrogen narcosis, rapture of the deep, a drunkenness from the toxicity of nitrogen at the high partial pressures. He looked up to the surface, seeing only blackness, and he screamed, screamed to prevent his lungs from exploding as he moved into shallower and shallower water with the easing of the pressure, but he also screamed because he *felt* like screaming.

"Ho ho ho! Ho ho ho! Ho ho ho!"

The shout they'd taught them all at sub school when they'd made a simulated escape from 100 feet. Back then it had seemed a lark, an adventure. Today it was something else.

He screamed and screamed.

"Listen to this, Captain."

Kane took his eyes from the periscope and joined McDonne at the speaker of the UWT system. There was a multitude of bubbles, rushing noises, and what sounded like screaming.

"Must be a school of whales," Kane said, returning to his periscope. He lit the low-light enhancer and gasped. "We've got open water here. We've got to get the blower ready to go. God knows how much power we have left. It could be gone."

"Houser, line up the system. Prepare to surface."

"AFT COMPARTMENT, CAPTAIN, WE ARE PREPARING TO SURFACE. PUT A FIVE-DEGREE UP ANGLE ON THE SHIP US-ING THE STERNPLANES. I SAY AGAIN—"

Kane nodded. They might have no power at the surface but at least they would be where the world could see them, and the only power he would need was enough to transmit on the HF radio distress signal.

Then they would have to wait. Wait . . .

The hull inclined upward. McDonne and Houser were pumping out the depth-control tanks and getting ready to blow out the water from the ballast tanks with the low-pressure blower. Kane could only hope there would be enough battery power left just to do that.

"Scope's breaking," he called as the phosphorescence flashed against the periscope view. He turned off the light enhancer. The light from the surface was diffuse, as it would be in the dawn, perhaps an overcast dawn. "Scope's clear." Kane spun the instrument in several circles, his vision obscured by fog and dense clouds close to the surface as well as the snowflakes whipping by the lens of the periscope. He found himself looking at the snow instead of the horizon. The snowflakes were dis-tracting, Kane thought, as he realized he'd never *seen* snow at sea. "Open the induction mast and put the low-pressure blower on all main ballast tanks." He picked up the UWT mike.

"AFT COMPARTMENT, CAPTAIN. WE ARE STARTING A

LOW-PRESSURE BLOW ON THE BALLAST TANKS. TRY TO KEEP THE EPM UP FOR ANOTHER TEN MINUTES."

He dropped the mike and looked out the scope, watching as the sea got lower. The added height did little to improve visibility in the snowstorm. Even as he watched, the wind picked up, the snowflakes suddenly accelerating almost to the horizontal in the wind. The waves sprouted whitecaps in the gust. Kane could almost feel the deck heel over from the force of the wind on the sail. He trained the view to the left, to the east, hoping to see a brightness from the sun, but the clouds were just as dense where the sun should have been. Kane bit back disappointment. He had hoped to see the sun again, to seal the ordeal behind him and remind him that he was alive. Instead, there was a blizzard. He trained his view to the left, to the east, saw the sun rise over the horizon, a sight he had never thought he would see again.

The roar of the blower started, the ballast tanks filling with water. Soon they should be stable on the surface and he could talk to the men aft face to face on the hull.

Within ten minutes he could see the top of the hull in the gray water. The ballast tanks were dry, the ship surfaced.

"Secure the blow." He picked up the microphone.

"AFT COMPARTMENT, CAPTAIN, WE ARE ON THE SURFACE. ALL STOP. OPEN YOUR ESCAPE TRUNK HATCH AND COME UP FORWARD."

He trained the view aft, and watched as the hatch slowly popped open, the haggard men climbing from the hatch, looking dazed at the falling snow, unsure of whether to rejoice at reaching the surface or curse to be in the middle of a winter storm. As they walked they hugged themselves against the cold.

"XO, get those guys in here from the aft hatch."

McDonne left to get the engineroom crew in. Kane looked out the periscope for a few minutes. They had, by God, lived. The *Phoenix* now drifted in the sea, its battery nearly dead.

He realized he needed to get to radio. He left Houser on the periscope and found Binghamton in the room, his parka and gloves on, his breath coming out in clouds.

"Can you bump up the BIGMOUTH?" were Binghamton's first words. Kane called the request to Houser. Binghamton handed Kane the microphone and they listened to static for a few minutes, then Binghamton waved Kane on.

"Norfolk NavCom, this is Echo Five November with an urgent Navy Blue, over."

In the control room Houser took his face from the periscope and looked at the speaker of the UWT, disbelief in his eyes. It was unmistakable . . .

"*. . . ho ho ho! Ho ho ho! . . .*"

There were many voices, the call repeated over and over, the sounds coming in distorted like a Halloween tape recording made for a haunted house. But haunted spirits up north, here at the top of the world?

Or was that ho-ho-hoing something to do with . . . Ho ho ho, like they'd learned in submarine school? An emergency escape? The other submarine, the one that was to take care of the Destiny but had shot at them, forcing them to run, and then what had happened, no one knew. Maybe the Destiny had won. It seemed to have left them alone so far but—

"Ho ho ho!"

It was worse than any nightmare Pacino had ever had. The sea around him was a black darkness. It was so cold he could feel his body shutting down. It was all he could do to continue to shout ho-ho-ho, his screams getting weaker the higher he rose. But then he began to hear things, his ears already damaged from the Vortex launch and the explosions, but now he could swear he heard a ghostly voice echoing through the deep saying strange things . . .

Compartment, Captain, right twenty degrees rudder . . . level the ship . . . low-pressure blow . . . Captain . . .

An auditory hallucination . . . what else could it be? But it seemed so real, the voice so large, coming from a giant throat and echoing through the water.

"Ho ho ho," he screamed.

The ascent seemed to go on forever. At last the sounds of the voices stopped. In the final hundred feet of his ascent he lost consciousness, no longer aware when the voice rang out through the deep again. He had stopped shouting but was breathing rapidly, his lungs giving up the air, which was fortunate . . . if he had breathed any slower he might have had his lungs explode.

He rose until the light from the rising sun penetrated the surface. He blasted through the surface, rising until only his shins still were submerged, then splashed back down, floating in the water buoyed up by his Steinke hood. He never felt the arms grab him and pull him into the raft.

Fort Meade, Maryland

Admiral Donchez stared at the plate-glass window at the building's entrance. The snow had finally stopped, but the plows would still take a long time even to get to the primary roads. The drifts were as tall as houses, the snow in the flats almost waist-high. All Donchez wanted was to get out of this prison.

"Admiral? Another signal for you, sir. It's in the comm center."

Donchez rubbed his bloodshot eyes as he followed the radio tech sergeant.

In the comm center he took the message form. It was another message from Pacino! He could scarcely believe it.

```
DATE/TIME:    TIME OF RECEIPT OF SLOT MESSAGE
FROM:         USS SEAWOLF SSN-21
TO:           CNO WASHINGTON, DC//CINCLANT NORFOLK, VA//
              COMSUBLANT NORFOLK, VA
SUBJ:         CONTACT REPORT NO. 4
//BT//
1. SEAWOLF DOWN, THIS POSITION.
2. PLEASE HURRY.
//BT//
```

"Mother of God," he muttered. He caught Fred Rummel's eye. "Fred, get me Admiral Steinman on the secure voice. And get me a weather report for the Davis Strait and the Labrador Sea. *Now,* dammit!"

All he could hope for was that the storm hadn't moved off to the northeast, that it had gone out due west, maybe even curved to the south. While he waited he couldn't help wondering what had become of the Destiny. And the *Phoenix.* He had heard nothing.

No sonic booms had been heard across Canada, nor any in the northeastern U.S. If the Destiny had launched, the missile would have landed by now. Pacino must have stopped the Destiny's launch and was alive. At least for the moment.

Please hurry.

Hang on, Mikey. When Steinman's voice came over, Donchez began speaking, the action allowing him to fight off the images of his surrogate son and friend at risk of dying in the frozen north.

Chief Nelson found Kane in the radio room, still trying to get through.

"Sir, we have only minutes left on the battery. If you can, you've got to hurry up with that distress signal. The battery breaker will be popping open at any minute."

"Dammit. Norfolk NavCom, this is Echo Five November, Navy Blue to follow, over."

Nothing but static.

"I'm going to transmit in the blind, Senior Chief. If they get it, they get it . . . NavCom, NavCom, NavCom, this is Echo Five November.

Navy Blue as follows. Estimated position very rough at six three degrees three zero minutes November, five eight degrees two zero minutes whiskey. We are drifting with battery almost dead. Urgent you pick us up as soon as possible, with airlift if available. I say again, Navy Blue as follows." Kane read the message again.

There was no response, just the whine of the static. Suddenly the room plunged into darkness.

"Guess that's it, Captain," Binghamton said, tossing his headset to the deck and clicking on a battle lantern. "This boat's just a big life raft now." *Life* raft. Bad joke.

The battle lanterns in the control room came up, then on through the upper level. Kane walked into his control room, amazed at how quiet it was with no ventilation, no firecontrol, no intercom system. A dead ship. Kane shivered and zipped his parka. It seemed much colder now without the lights even though the temperature had already been at freezing for hours.

Now all they could do was wait, and hope that Norfolk—or someone —had received their distress signal. They wouldn't last long in this dead hull.

Fort Meade, Maryland

Donchez glared at both Captain Rummel and the communications technical sergeant. "Read it again," he said.

"Signal means, 'NavCom, NavCom, NavCom, this is Echo Five November'—that's the USS *Phoenix*, Admiral—'Navy Blue as follows. Estimated position very rough at six three degrees'—garbled here, then— 'minutes November'—garbled again, then message concludes—'drifting with battery almost dead. Urgent you pick us up as soon as . . .' The rest was static, Admiral."

Donchez nodded and pulled Captain Rummel aside. "The weather?"

"The storm went up the coastline, sir. The Davis Strait and the Labrador Sea are in the middle of the worst of it. And there's no reason to think it will ease up. As it goes north, the cold will make it real bad."

"Great. Can we fly?"

"Bad visibility and high winds aloft. But yes, we can fly. We just won't see anything."

"The search-and-rescue guys. We need to get them working on this."

"I know the skipper of the Navy Search and Rescue unit out of Kangamiu, Greenland. They're the closest. We'll get the Canadians on it too. But don't get your hopes up, sir."

"They never were up, but what's on your mind?"

"With the storm and all, we'll have a rough time of it. Even though we can fly, we may not see anything. And if we do see something, with the winds aloft, it'll be a damned miracle if we can get down to it."

"What options do we have?"

"Fly search-and-rescue or quit."

"There you go. Well, this old man ain't about to quit. Get on it, Fred."

Donchez watched Rummel go. They had a partial location of the *Phoenix*, but what the hell would become of the *Seawolf*? Just what did *"Seawolf* down, this position" mean, anyway? Were the crew members trapped in a submerged hull? Or had they made it to the surface and abandoned ship? It would take twenty hours to get a deep-submergence rescue vehicle to the Davis Strait if the weather were perfect, but the DSRV's ungainly transport plane would not be able to get anywhere close until the storm eased. If Pacino and his men were in a sunken hull they'd have a long wait. With no food and no heat and no oxygen.

Kangamiu Airfield, Western Greenland

Lieutenant Commander Alex Crossfield stuffed the tobacco into his cheek. Crossfield had been an all-state offensive lineman at Milton High in the Florida panhandle. Milton had been more Alabama than Florida, but being in Greenland when he was from the Sunbelt had been hell on earth. Why he had ever taken the promotion to come to this ice hole evaded him. Now almost forty, Crossfield still looked like he could block half the line of scrimmage of the meanest team in the South. He weighed in at 285. His neck was bigger than most men's heads, his upper arms the size of thighs. A quiet and gentle man—he only needed to glance at one of his men to enforce some discipline. He had risen through the enlisted ranks, promoted in a now defunct chief-to-ensign program, and was fond of disparaging the officer ranks, although he had proved to be one of the best unit commanders Navy Search and Rescue had ever had.

As an enlisted man he had crewed in choppers, then gone on to be a maintenance-crew chief, where he caught the eye of the officer recruiters, who packed him off, put him through a brief hell and thought they'd put some kind of stamp on him by pinning ensign bars on his lapels, like somehow being commissioned would keep the salt from his language and the chewing tobacco from his mouth. It had done neither, and secretly Crossfield was surprised, perhaps even disappointed, that the officer promotion seemed permanent. He was sent to the Coast Guard for three years of cross-training, then to the NATO force commander for search-and-rescue in the Bosnian crisis, avoiding the Somalia involvement. By then he was a junior grade lieutenant, earning what he had been sure would be his last promotion. An assignment with the Canadian Defense Force had taken two years, and the Canadians had taken to him. Soon he was a full lieutenant and shipped off to the Pacific. After a tour that seemed all too short in Pearl Harbor, he was zipped through a few Air Force SAR training courses, invariably held in the driest, hottest deserts, then dropped off in Greenland.

Greenland. The arctic circle. Where it was dark most of the time and frigid-cold all the time. So far Crossfield had avoided long-term relationships with women. And now that he was thirty-nine, his hair thinning, his muscle slowly but inevitably turning to fat, he was stuck on this godforsaken rock, commanding an SAR unit second to none, with no one to rescue other than the occasional fishing boat with mechanical problems, and with all the tanned blue-eyed Florida blondes over 2,000 miles away.

Crossfield looked over at his operations officer, Dick Trill, the thin mustachioed youngster who still looked like a teenager but wore the uniform of a lieutenant, j.g.

"Let me get this straight," Crossfield drawled. "We got the worst blizzard of the century blowing outside and we're supposed to saddle up and go take care of not just one but two submarines in bad trouble. And we know one of them's on the surface drifting, her position hardly certain. And the second one is sunk, with the position pinpointed. Except by 'pinpointed' you mean somewhere in an area the size of Connecticut. Have I got all that right, son?"

"Yessir," the ops boss said, a wary eye on Crossfield's bulk.

"We're out of business with the choppers, right?"

"Wind's too high, sir. The V–22s can fly. That's about it."

The Osprey, half airplane, half helicopter. Except for one thing. When the winds aloft were too high for the choppers, the V–22s could only fly, not hover. Even if they found the surviving drifting sub, they couldn't land until the storm eased.

"Well, get your brief ready. I want to take off in ten minutes. That's one zero for you lieutenants. Oh, I forgot, you're an Academy grad. For you, I want to take off when the big hand's on the twelve and the little hand's on the nine."

"Yessir." He kept a straight face. "The men will be here in two minutes."

The young man hurried out the door. Crossfield looked after him, then out the window and shook his head. The glass was rattling with the fury of the wind, the snow covering the bottom half, ice starting to form on the top half.

"Those bubblehead submariners sure can pick the day to need help," he mumbled to himself.

Labrador Sea

Kane drummed his fingers on the chart table. It had been a half-hour since they had surfaced and sent the distress code. Since then nothing had happened. The storm continued to blow outside. Inside it was extremely cold. Having nothing to do made matters even worse, the men could only focus on the cold.

Kane decided to take a look topside. Houser had rigged the bridge for surface, the hatches open. Kane climbed up the long ladder, the metal of it threatening to freeze his skin. Houser lifted the grating for him.

The view was so bright it hurt Kane's eyes. The skin of his face felt like he was being sandblasted by ice particles. The fog had eased somewhat since they'd come up, and Kane thought he could make out the shape of the icebergs in the middle distance. Houser, in a leather face shield like a hockey-goalie mask, was looking through binoculars at a steady bearing toward the bow.

"What are you looking at?" Kane asked him.

"I'm not sure I believe it, Captain. I was waiting for it to be a mirage."

"Let me look." Kane took the binoculars. "I don't believe it either." Kane would have had an easier time explaining the sight of pink elephants.

"The sounds you heard on the UWT—"

"Yes, skipper. 'Ho ho ho.' Merry submarine escape."

"Good God," Kane said, staring into the binoculars, seeing the impossible, the dozen orange rafts floating in the whitecaps, all full of men. None of the men moving.

"XO to the bridge," McDonne called from below. Kane stepped aside while Houser lifted the grating for him. The bridge seemed crowded with McDonne's bulk.

"Jeez, it's cold up here. And I thought it was bad below—"

"XO, check this out," Kane said.

McDonne looked and whistled, then looked again.

"Life rafts? Where the hell did they come from?"

"Who knows? Maybe the Destiny?" Kane said.

"Those rafts look like USN issue."

"They do?" Kane had never seen submarine rafts.

"Yessir. Don't forget, I worked damage control over at NAVSEA during shore duty. We've got to do something for these guys."

"XO, they've got to be a mile away. Maybe two. What are you going to do, swim?"

"I'll get our own rafts out there, pull those guys back here," McDonne said, already going for the grating to the access tunnel. "We've got a couple of those canned electric motors from the SEAL deployment exercise. I could use those attached to our rafts and go over there and get them."

"Poor bastards are probably already dead," Houser said, still looking through the binoculars that McDonne had given back to him.

"If they're not, they will be by the time we pull them aboard," Kane said. "And even if they're alive then, getting them aboard doesn't do them much good. It's almost as cold below as it is up here. We might drift here for days or weeks before anyone finds us. By then the cold will probably take all of us."

Houser looked over at him. "Hey, skipper. You're the captain. You're the one who's supposed to be so goddamned positive. Bitching's my job, remember?"

Kane stared at the lieutenant. Nodded. Honesty was dumb policy right now.

"You think the XO is really going out there after those guys?"

"If he can find the rafts. If he doesn't freeze just getting them in the water."

Houser looked through the binoculars. "They're definitely not moving. If they were alive they'd be waving at us or launching flares or something . . ."

The wind picked up, blowing snow into the cockpit, reminding Kane of the cold. "I'm going below. You staying up here?"

"Yes, Captain."

Kane looked over at the rafts, the blizzard beginning to make them hard to find.

"Get below soon, Houser. Your face looks bad."

Kane lowered himself down the ladder, numbness creeping into his hands in spite of the cold. In the control room he could still see his breath.

38

SATURDAY, 4 JANUARY

Kangamiu Airfield, Western Greenland

The snow blew over the runway, obscuring the lights and the painted numerals. The snow-clearing crews had worked continuously through the night, without complete success. Crossfield pulled on the oversized helmet, adjusted the boom microphone, tested it and studied the chart clipped on his thigh clipboard while Trill, his copilot, brought the engines of the V–22 up to speed. The big aircraft shuddered as the rotors wound up to idle, the blades spinning horizontally as the plane prepared for a vertical ascent. Crossfield went through the takeoff checklist, spoke a few words to Trill, then watched as Trill throttled up. The engines howled louder than the wind, and the patch of runway beneath them, momentarily cleared of snow by the fierce man-made wind of the rotors, faded away.

There was nothing in the windshield but white overcast and flakes blasting by so fast they caused dizziness. Crossfield shook his head. A rescue this day?

Trill guided the aircraft up to 2,000 feet and rotated the rotors so that the aircraft began flying as a plane, forward airspeed building up to 300 knots. It would be a few hours before they reached the latitude of the distress signal. The submariners better be praying the storm cleared by then, Crossfield thought.

Kane watched from the periscope as the executive officer and a group of chilled volunteers put their inflatable rafts into the water. McDonne had found the tiny half-horse battery-driven motors, the two rafts slowly putting toward the other life rafts. His own raft listed dangerously, thanks to his massive bulk.

Houser had come down into control, his face white and frostbitten from the cold. He looked on the same scene, using the number one periscope next to Kane.

"Some cavalry," Houser said.

McDonne's raft neared the first of the quiet bobbing rafts of the survivors.

"Take the line and attach it to this raft," he ordered a petty officer behind him. "We'll tie up the others and tow them back. But from the looks of it I don't think there's any need to hurry . . ."

For the next hour Kane and Houser watched as the rafts were brought aboard, the rescued men unmoving, either unconscious or dead. All of them were wearing American submariner's coveralls. Kane found McDonne in the crew's mess, staring at food that was frozen solid.

"What boat were they from?"

"A bunch of belt buckles read *Seawolf*," McDonne said.

"Must have sent the *Seawolf* to get the Destiny, and all they got was sunk," Kane said, more to himself than to McDonne. "Anybody alive?"

"A few," McDonne said. "Barely breathing. Doc's looking at them. We'll try to keep them warm, but hell, we can't even give them a cup of hot coffee."

"You did the best you could, XO."

Houser came into the room, shivering, snow-covered, and whiter than before.

"What the hell are you doing?" Kane asked.

"I went topside. I thought maybe the storm would be clearing but I think it's getting worse."

"What time is it?"

"Almost eleven," McDonne said. "Almost lunchtime."

A bad joke.

Crossfield's V–22 had been flying at latitude sixty-three degrees in an east-west pattern for the last hour and had found exactly nothing.

"Anything?" he asked Trill for the twentieth time.

"Infrared is terrible in this storm, skipper."

"Let's try the radar."

"All that'll do is give us icebergs. Even if she's here, she's a needle in a haystack."

"Ah, hell, let's try it anyway. What've we got to lose?"

"Yessir. There, look. Detects across the board. A hundred of them. Now what?"

"Hell, Trill, you're the Academy grad. You tell me."

Houser stood on the bridge, his face taking a beating, but he couldn't stay inside the ship. If he were dying he didn't want to do it inside a steel pipe. When the wind got too strong and bitter, like now, he found that he could shut a clamshell panel of the sail and sit down underneath it, against the bulkhead of the cockpit, and stay out of the wind. The cold of the steel deck seeped past the pile of life jackets and into him, but it was still better than the wind. He sat like this for some thirty minutes, too cold to sleep, too tired to stay fully awake.

Eventually the cold was too much, and Houser abandoned the bridge for the access tunnel to return to the interior of the ship. It was stuffy and moist, but it was at least a few degrees warmer than the bridge. His hands were so numb he could barely hold onto the ladder as he lowered himself down the tunnel.

Halfway down the access trunk he froze. He listened for a few moments, climbed back topside, sure that he'd heard it . . . and gradually the sound got louder.

A buzz. The buzz of *aircraft engines*. Distant aircraft engines. He held still but the sound faded. It might even have been his imagination, but somehow Houser believed that this was no auditory hallucination. He *had* heard a powerful thrumming, like chopper rotors or propellers. That couldn't have been the wind . . .

He slid down the ladder into the control room and found Kane in a seat at the attack-center consoles, his head cradled in one hand.

"Sir," Houser tried to say, but his mouth felt like it was full of glue. "I heard—"

Kane grabbed him and sat him down in a control seat. "Houser, you're frozen half-solid, even your tongue's frozen. I told you to stay inside, what the hell are you—"

"Sir," Houser said deliberately, "airplanes, choppers. I heard engines. We've got to get flares." He felt dizzy, as if the room were spinning. He shut his eyes and put his head on the console, wondering if Kane would believe him.

"XO, get the flare gun."

"Houser's out of it, skipper. He's dreaming."

"Probably. Still, if he's right and we sit here on our butts . . ."

"I'll get the flares."

"What time is it?"

"Almost fourteen hundred."

"Can't last much longer. Better say a prayer that Houser's right."

"I've got something. An IR trace and a radar contact at the same bearing and range."

"Let me see." Crossfield looked at the IR scope. "Polar bear. Or a seal. Damned dumb seal to be out in this weather."

Trill shrugged. "Where's he supposed to go?"

"Keep circling for a few minutes. I want to watch this. Anything visual?"

"Still nothing but white."

"Whoa." Crossfield said as the weak IR trace bloomed into bright hot life. "What's this?"

Trill looked. "Flare? That's got to be them . . ."

"Note the position and radio it back to base. Have them send it in to the brass running this op."

"Yessir."

"Too damned bad we can't set down and pick them up." Crossfield looked over at the panel and saw the fuel levels dipping. "We're going to have to get back and get some gas anyway."

"Message is out, skipper."

"Take us back. Maybe by the time we refuel and get back here the damned storm will be clearing."

"I hear it." McDonne scanned the clouds with the binoculars but the lenses kept fogging up. The storm was getting worse, if that were possible.

"I do, too," Kane said. "Hard to tell what direction he is, though. Shoot another flare."

McDonne shot the flare gun. The flare immediately disappeared into the vapor of the swirling snow and clouds.

Both men listened. Kane shook his head.

"I don't hear it anymore."

"Neither do I."

"But we both heard it, right?"

"Yes, Captain. It was definitely aircraft engines."

"And now they're gone."

Fort Meade, Maryland

"The SAR people found something. A solid radar return and a heat bloom, several heat blooms. Like they shot a flare. The latitude matched the last transmission of the *Phoenix.*" Rummel read off the message to Donchez. Donchez had bags under his eyes, his cheeks hollow. He looked embalmed.

"What are they waiting for? Did they go in?"

"Afraid not, Admiral. Winds are still too high and they were out of fuel. But at least they found something."

"Yeah, corpses."

It took most of the afternoon to return to Kangamiu, fuel up and wait for the wind to ease enough just to be able to take off again. The airstrip's runway was covered with almost a foot of snow, drifts forming in the wake of buildings. It had taken all of Crossfield's skill just to find the runway to set down the V–22. Even as he landed the wind velocity exceeded the limits for a safe landing, but there had been no choice, the tanks were empty. It was land or crash. This time he'd been lucky, but he wouldn't try to take off with a full load of fuel with the high windspeed at zero visibility.

It had been a ninety-minute wait on the ground before the wind slowed. Crossfield had no idea how long it would last, but he didn't wait to see. Trill spooled up the rotors and lifted off, immediately transitioning to horizontal flight. By the time the V–22 was over the location of the original detection, it had been almost six hours since they had departed.

Night had closed in quickly, the only thing worse than the white of the blizzard the blackness of the snow-filled night. Crossfield searched again for the infrared signature of the *Phoenix.* Nothing.

Trill called wearily from the copilot seat. "Weather radar and the weather report from base agree for once. The storm cell is passing through. Should be over in the next half-hour."

"Great," Crossfield said. "Tell that to the poor bastards down there."

It was McDonne's turn to go topside. Kane had kept someone on deck ever since they had heard the aircraft engines. The watch was shifted every thirty minutes, rotating between the dozen men still able to go topside. Even with McDonne's added bulk, the wind seemed to blast right through his parka, his sweatshirt, his two sweaters and into his flesh, right down to the marrow of his bones.

The flares had run out hours before. They now had brought papers and mattresses and lighter fluid and anything that would burn, making a fire in the cubbyhole aft in the sail where a lookout would normally be stationed. That way the fire was protected from the blasting wind, but then the heat of it was lost to the men topside. Worse, the flames and heat would be detected only if the aircraft was directly overhead. But all attempts at starting fires on the deck had proved futile. The wind ate the flames or blew the material overboard. McDonne crouched in the sail, feeding paper to the flames, the pages of the reactor-plant manual burning slowly.

It was all stupid, he thought. They were just waiting to die. For an instant he felt an impulse to leap overboard and just get it the hell over with. It could take the sea only two or three minutes to lower his body temperature enough to take away consciousness. After that, who cared?

There was something wrong, he suddenly thought. Something was different. It took him a long time to realize it, his thinking impaired by the cold.

The different thing was the wind.

There was no wind.

The storm had finally passed.

And then something else changed. McDonne shut his eyes, trying to listen, his eardrums still ringing from the previous gale-force winds. But he was sure he heard it. Even though he realized he wanted to hear it enough to *make* himself hear it.

No. It was real. Aircraft engines. So powerful he could *feel* their throbbing. He stoked the fire, frantic to show the aircraft they were there. It took several minutes for him to remember that with the wind gone he could start a fire on top of the sail and not have it blown overboard. Quickly he assembled the piles of paper on top of the frozen metal of the sail, trying and failing several times to get it lit from the lighter in his pocket. Finally he grabbed flaming papers from the cubbyhole fire and put them to the pile of paper on the sail, burning his hand but lighting the fire. He watched the fire burn, and only then turned his face to the direction of the aircraft engines.

Far off in the distance he saw lights, aircraft beacons flashing. He began jumping up and down on the grating, shouting stupidly into the night. He wondered if they could be airliners, but no regular airline routes went this far north, and the lights looked like they were flying in formation.

The aircraft got closer until one of them put a bright spotlight on the ship. As it floated downward into view, McDonne could see it was a V–22 tiltrotor, the big transport using its props as helicopter rotors while it lowered itself down near the bow. Lights came on, illuminating the fuselage, the star in a circle flanked by stripes on either side painted beside large block letters that spelled U.S. NAVY.

McDonne sank to the deck.

Finally, incredibly, it was over.

EPILOGUE

TUESDAY, 4 MARCH

Bethesda Naval Hospital
Bethesda, Maryland

Janice Pacino kissed her husband's damp forehead and walked out the door with her son.

Around the corner she nearly collided with Admiral Richard Donchez. She stepped back for a moment. Donchez saw the look in her eye and said only, "How's he doing?"

"He'll live," she said, then took hold of Tony's arm and hurried off down the hall.

Donchez watched after her for a moment, wondered if he should call her back and tell her what her husband had achieved, then decided against it. She was in no mood to hear it.

He walked into the room, looked at Pacino lying in the bed surrounded by machinery, IV needles snaking into his arm. The Vortex had saved him and damn near killed him. At least they'd taken the respirator out. He had gained consciousness for the first time the day before.

"Mikey," he said, touching the only exposed surface above the blankets, Pacino's face. "Mikey, are you with me?"

Pacino's eyes opened, he tried to smile. The attempt left him exhausted, his eyes falling half-closed.

"Mikey, you made it. I won't be long, I just wanted to bring you something."

"What . . ." Pacino got out. Donchez leaned close. ". . . happened?"

"You did it, son," Donchez said. "You sank the Destiny before he could fire the missile with its warhead. Sihoud's dead. Without him, the UIF gave it up and surrendered in Paris last week. I'll fill you in more later."

General Barczynski, Secret Service agents and, after a moment, President Bill Dawson, came in. Barczynski and the president moved close to the bed. Donchez edged a Secret Service agent aside so he could see from the other side.

"So this is the man," the president said. "Congratulations, Captain Pacino. Or I should say, Rear Admiral Pacino. I have your stars here. We skipped you to upper half. One star seemed lonely."

Pacino wasn't sure what he was seeing.

"And something else." Dawson read the citation, the buildup giving Pacino the Navy Cross with silver star.

When Dawson finished his speech he bent to pin the medal to Pacino's pillow, but Rear Admiral Upper Half Michael Pacino had fallen asleep, beginning to snore in the president's face. Dawson didn't miss a beat as he pinned the medal to the pillowcase and left with his entourage.

Donchez was the last one by Pacino's side, looking down on him as if it were his own son sleeping there. Then he turned and walked to the door.

As he snapped off the room lights, he said quietly, "Good job, Mikey. Your old man and I are proud of you."

The survey ship *Diamond* tossed in the swells in the Virginia Capes Submarine Operating Area, a piece of ocean 150 miles east of Virginia Beach, Virginia. Aboard the small ship were several men, all in service dress blue uniforms with long overcoats, shoulder boards on their shoulders, white gloves, and ceremonial swords hanging from their left hips. One of them was Captain David Kane. Next to him stood Commander CB McDonne. All stood at the railing of the deck, at attention, looking to sea. Off on the horizon a lone submarine floated on the surface.

"Ready, Captain Kane," the voice of Admiral Roy Steinman called out.

"Ready, sir," Kane said, staring into the distance, at the submarine.

"Then let her be put to rest."

"Aye, aye, sir. Executive Officer," Kane barked.

"Yes, sir," McDonne answered.

"Executive Officer, scuttle the ship!" Kane ordered.

McDonne twisted the rotary knob on a small radio transmitter.

"Officers, hand salute!" Kane ordered. The men on the railing brought their right hands to the brims of their caps, the white gloves and dark blue sleeves stark against the gray of the deck and the sea. A bosun's whistle blew mournfully into the sea air, the note dying on the wind from the east.

On the deck of the submarine several plumes of vapor rose high into the air. Slowly it settled into the sea until all that was visible was her sail, until that settled and eventually disappeared from view. The ship sank beneath the surface, gaining momentum as it plummeted for the bottom.

On the surface there was nothing left to mark the passage of the hull of the USS *Phoenix.*

"Officers," Kane called. "Ready, two!" The men dropped their salutes in unison. "Officers, fall out."

Kane looked at the spot where the *Phoenix* had been, then back to McDonne. "Hard to believe she's gone," he said.

"Wasn't much left of her when that torpedo got done with her," McDonne said, looking out to sea. "At least they let us scuttle her at sea instead of scrapping her."

"With the reactor compartment gone, there wasn't anything to contaminate or pollute the ocean with. All that's in the Labrador Sea."

Kane turned when Admiral Steinman walked up. The two men chatted for a moment, McDonne discreetly moving off.

"Well, David, sad to see her go," Steinman said. "A shame we couldn't fix her up, but it does leave you free for another command. You know, we've got the second hull of the *Seawolf*-class coming out of the yard next month, and the new construction captain is ready to retire. What do you say? How would you like to be the commanding officer of the USS *Barracuda?* Best submarine in the fleet, and a chance for you to go back to sea."

Kane looked up at Steinman, but instead of seeing his eyes, saw the last mission of the *Phoenix,* the vision flashing past in a heartbeat. Realizing Steinman was waiting for an answer, he put his war face on one last time.

"I don't think so, Admiral. It's over. I'm done going to sea."

Steinman looked at him in surprise, not really understanding, then walked away to look at the sea from the fantail.

The *Diamond* turned west and sped up to full speed for the trip back to Norfolk. Kane looked at the horizon, actually looking forward to the feel of dry land beneath his feet. Hours later, when the survey vessel tied up at the submarine piers, Captain David Kane walked onto the pier without looking back.